KU-590-304

The PILLOW BOOK *of the* FLOWER SAMURAI

BARBARA LAZAR

headline
review

Copyright © 2012 Barbara D. Lazar

The right of Barbara D. Lazar to be identified as the Author of
the Work has been asserted by her in accordance with the
Copyright, Designs and Patents Act 1988.

First published in Great Britain in 2012 by HEADLINE REVIEW
An imprint of HEADLINE PUBLISHING GROUP

1

Apart from any use permitted under UK copyright law, this publication
may only be reproduced, stored, or transmitted, in any form, or by
any means, with prior permission in writing of the publishers or,
in the case of reprographic production, in accordance with the terms
of licences issued by the Copyright Licensing Agency.

All characters in this publication are fictitious and any
resemblance to real persons, living or dead, is purely coincidental.

Cataloguing in Publication Data is available from the British Library

ISBN (Hardback) 978 0 7553 8925 4
ISBN (Trade paperback) 978 0 7553 8926 1

Typeset in Aldine 401BT by Avon DataSet Ltd,
Bidford-on-Avon, Warwickshire

Printed and bound in Great Britain by
Clays Ltd, St Ives plc

Headline's policy is to use papers that are natural, renewable and
recyclable products and made from wood grown in sustainable forests.
The logging and manufacturing processes are expected to conform
to the environmental regulations of the country of origin.

HEADLINE PUBLISHING GROUP
An Hachette UK Company
338 Euston Road
London NW1 3BH

www.headline.co.uk
www.hachette.co.uk

Keats Community Library

B16617

The PILLOW BOOK *of the* FLOWER SAMURAI

Acknowledgements

First, I wish to express my most profound gratitude to my superb agent, Alexandra Machinist, as well as to Dorothy Vincent and Kaitlin Nicholis at Janklow & Nesbit Associates. Second, my extraordinary indebtedness to Claire Baldwin, Emily Kitchin and Hazel Orme for their enthusiasm and their superb pruning, shaping and editing.

Gratitude to Fred Brandow who assisted initally, to Diane Capito, Ginny Ford, Barbara Gere and Leila Klemtner, a writing group who nursed the manuscript to its adolescence; to Jean Jackson, Butch McGhee, Diane LaCombe, Jacque Paramenter, and to the Penultimates – Tim Talbert, Beaty Spear, Steve Stewart and Marjorie Brody, who cherished and badgered it into adulthood. An extraordinary and heartfelt appreciation to Barbara J. Gere who is the artist who created the magnificent maps. I wish to thank the San Antonio Public Librarians, especially those at Tobin Oakwell Library and the Interlibrary Loan Department for obtaining the inaccessible, and the reference librarians at Trinity University for their never-ending assistance. A special appreciation to the Japan America Society of San Antonio, Peter Hoover and particularly Ikuko Groesbeck. Also my indebtedness to Curt Harrell and Dr Roger Spotswood for their lavish book loans and knowledge as well as Dr Fred Notehelfer, Dr Hank Glassman, Reiko Yoshimura at the Freer Gallery of Art, Sharon S. Takeda, Greg Pflugfelder, Ann Yonemura, and Michael Watson.

My love and wholehearted gratitude to Dr Diane B. Latona (nee Mirro) who gave me more wisdom and information than are in books, to my father who bequeathed a love of words, to my mother who bequeathed a love of reading and to my husband and life partner, Gregory Surfas, who endured my scribblings – mornings, evenings, middle of the nights and weekends – and whose love sustained me through each sentence.

Historical Note

The Gempei War, the cataclysmic clash between the Taira and Minamoto clans in late twelfth-century Japan, heralded the end of its Golden Age (794-1185). At this critical time in Japan's history, warriors continued their progression to power until they controlled the country several centuries later. Many Noh and Kabuki plays are set during this war because of the war's innumerable heroic exploits and battles. These plays are written from the Minamoto point of view, but *The Pillow Book of the Flower Samurai*'s point of view is the Taira's.

11 pm - 1 am

9 - 11 pm   1 - 3 am

7 - 9 pm   3 - 5 am

5 - 7 pm   5 - 7 am

3 - 5 pm   7 - 9 am

1 - 3 pm   9 - 11 am

11 am - 1 pm

Principal Characters

Kozaishō, writer of the *Pillow Book*, formerly Fifth Daughter

At a shōen *(estate)*

Daigoro no Goro, Buddhist priest (code name Three Eyes)
Chiba no Tashiyori, proprietor of the *shōen*
Akio, samurai (code name Oyster)
Tashiko, a girl
Emi, another girl (code name Lotus)
Master Isamu, samurai and master teacher
Uba, a boy and student of the martial arts

At the Village of Outcasts

Hitomi, owner and manager
Rin, *chojā* (head, lead) of the 'free' Women-for-Play
Aya, a girl
Misuki, a girl (code name Lumbering Badger)
Otfukure, elderly Woman-for-Play, teacher of the pleasing arts

At Rokuhara

Obāsan, Honourable-Aged-One-Who-Waits-On-Women in Michimori's
   household
Ryo, Obāsan's nephew (code name Snake)
Hoichi, Mokuhasa's cousin
Retired Emperor Go-Shirakawa (code name Fox)
Antoku, Emperor, son of Takakura and Kiyomori's daughter

The Taira Clan (Kozaishō's)

Michimori, a commander of the clan
Tokikazu, captain to Michimori (code name Genji)
Mokuhasa, samurai and special guard to Michimori
Sadakokai, samurai and special guard to Michimori
Kiyomori, uncle of Michimori, leader of the country
Koremori, cousin to Michimori (code name Wisteria)
Shigehira, cousin to Michimori (code name Oak)
Tsunemasa, cousin to Michimori (code name Drake)
Tomomori, cousin to Michimori (code name Large Cicada)
Munemori, cousin to Michimori (code name Purple Grass)
Norimori, father of Michimori

The Minamoto Clan

Yoshitsune, nephew of Yoshitomo (code name Tiger)
Yukiie, brother of Yoshitomo (code name Hare)
Yoshitomo, father of Yoritomo, Noriyori and Yoshitsune (code name Ox)
Kiso Yoshinaka, nephew of Yoshitomo and Yukiie (code name Rat)
Noriyori, son of Yoshitomo (code name Sheep)
Yoritomo, son of Yoshitomo (code name Horse)

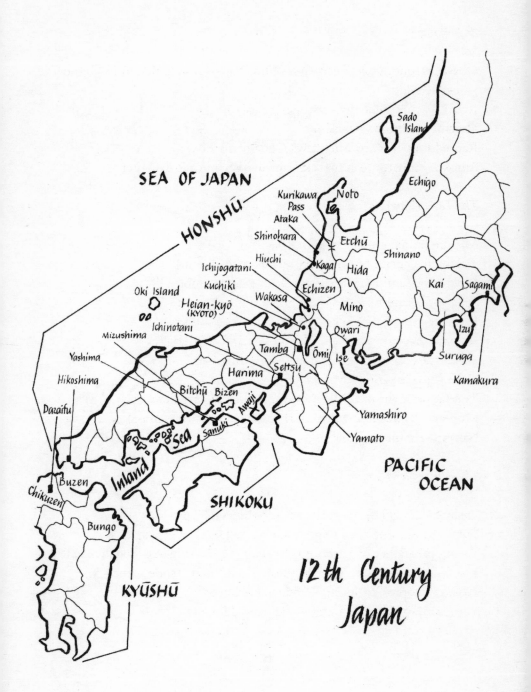

SEA OF JAPAN

HONSHŪ

Sado Island

Echigo

Kurikawa Pass

Noto

Ataka

Etchū

Shinano

Shinohara

Hiuchi

Kaga

Hida

Kai

Sagami

Ichijogatani

Echizen

Kuchiki

Mino

Wakasa

Oki Island

Heian-kyō (KYOTO)

Owari

Izu

Ichinotani

Suruga

Mizushima

Tamba

Ōmi

Ise

Kamakura

Yashima

Settsu

Harima

Yamashiro

Hikoshima

Bitchū

Bizen

Yamato

Dazaifu

Sanuki

Awaji

PACIFIC OCEAN

Chikuzen

Buzen

Inland Sea

SHIKOKU

Bungo

KYŪSHŪ

12th Century Japan

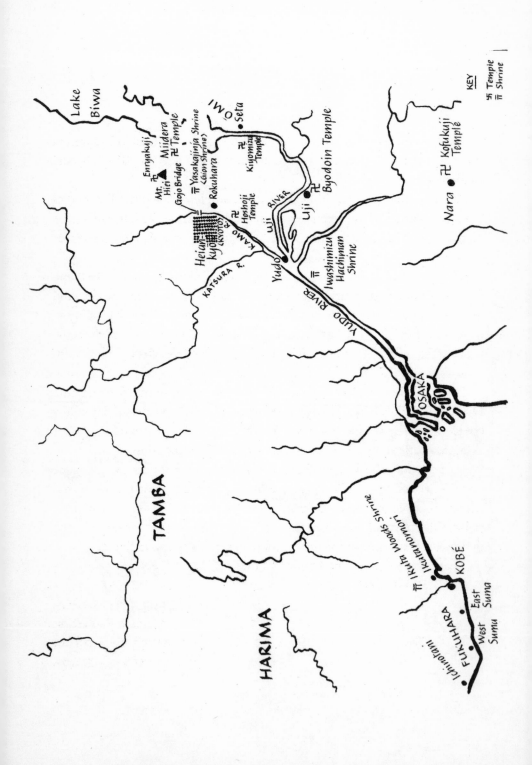

Lake Biwa

IWO

Seta

Enryakuji
Mt. Hiei
Miidera 卍 Temple
Gojo Bridge
卍 Yasakajinja Shrine (Gion Shrine)
Rokuhara

Kiyomizu Temple

Byodoin Temple

Hoshoji Temple

Byodoin Temple

Heian Kyoto (KYOTO)

KAMO R.

Uji River

Uji

Nara ● Kofukuji 卍 Temple

KATSURA R.

Yudo

Iwashimizu Hachiman Shrine
π

Yudo River

OSAKA

TAMBA

Ikuta Woods Shrine
π
Wataranori

HARIMA

Fukuhara
Kobé
West Suma
East Suma
Ichinotani

KEY
卍 Temple
π Shrine

For readers not familiar with the Kozaishō Diaries, Dr Sosiko Yatsumura and I worked Kobe, Japan's rugged terrain, from 2000 to 2010. The site yielded discoveries worth our blisters.

We unearthed a burial place with two complete skeletons. The bodies faced each other, in the extended position, the male on the left, the female on the right. The crowning glory was a document box sealed into a separate chamber.

The box was undamaged, wrapped in oiled cloths with a waxed seal. Gold and mother-of-pearl cranes fly across a heavily lacquered background of gold and silver dust on its lid. The seal was identified as that of Minamoto no Yoshitsune, the victor of the Ichinotani battle in 1184. The tests on the papers and other contents support the dating of mid-to-late twelfth century.

I save the best for last. Inside the box, intact, we found the Kozaishō Diaries or, as they were called in Heian Japan (the period 794–1185) pillow books i.e. diaries people stored where they slept. My deep thanks go to Dr Bernard Hoffenberg's hard work and superlative translation.

Readers may check the published papers about these documents. The diary was written from the Taira Clan's perspective, not the victorious Minamoto Clan of the civil war, the Genpei War (1180–85). There are a significant number of discrepancies with the *Heike Monogatari*, the fictionalized account of the war written about fifty years earlier.

I bet on the bones. The bones don't lie.

Dr Isabell 'Izzy' Jenkins
Associate Professor,
Archaeology Department
University of Arizona

I caress the dagger's dark curve against the breast of my white kimono. As I step outside the tent, the ocean wind batters my face, singeing my eyes with acrid smoke. Bile swells into my mouth at the stench of impromptu pyres. I swallow and compel my body to be quiet, to calm my mind and soothe my spirit. I do not wish others who may be watching to think I am afraid, although I sit secluded in the forest behind the Ikuta Shrine.

'My lady, time is short.' Misuki – my companion, my friend – brings the ties. Her hands quiver, but, together, we lash my legs. She and I listen to the remains of the battle, the rumblings of the sea, the screeching of the hawks.

Misuki's red-rimmed eyes splash her face with tears, but after protest, she swears to do all I ask of her. I trust Misuki with my life's work, my story. My death.

She practises the stroke. A soft swish brushes my neck. Its crisp sound is the last I will hear. I thirst – to be with husband, lover, perhaps parents and siblings, most of the people I love. Though not all. The blade catches the last of the sun. That I will not see the beautiful sunset eases me. I am ready.

In my left hand I hold a scrap of cloth, all that remains of the smock my elder sister embroidered, the smock I wore the day my life twisted on to this path. I smile as I place it in Misuki's hand. She knows where the scrap must go. Tranquillity pervades my bones – with Misuki's protection, with my life, and with that young girl I once was, the journal I maintained, and the last of my names, Kozaishō.

Book I

Like the pious man who planted an orchard so that
Others might enjoy the fruits, I trust these words
I offer may be of use to others.

I. Conspiracy

I shared the dream with my family at our morning meal. In this one, I sat in a polished-wood room. My many kimonos glittered while servants brought trays with artfully arranged food in lacquered bowls. I ate with glossy black chopsticks.

My parents listened and hugged me, but my mother clicked her tongue. My brothers ignored my dreams, and my sisters laughed. I frowned at my sisters and pulled their hair. I did not like their laughter, and they knew it.

Later that morning I tried to learn. 'Please let me try again,' I begged my next elder sister.

'Why do you bother? You never get it right.'

'I used the grinding stone.' I said. 'It took a long time, but I did it right. Please?'

'You have watched me many times.' Fourth Daughter continued her sewing.

'Perhaps if I sat next to you.'

Fourth Daughter spread her knees and lifted her cloth. 'Just this once. Keep away from the needles.'

My gaze followed her flashing fingers. Fourth Daughter was our best seamstress. I knelt on the straw-scattered earthen floor looking up through her hair. I leaned close.

'Her breathing ruins my stitches,' Fourth Daughter whined.

I bent closer and ignored her. I had to learn. Her needle pricked my forehead, and I wailed.

'I was afraid I would hurt her,' Fourth Daughter said to my mother, with the tearful tremors she had practised in her voice. 'I warned her!'

'Instead of helping, you hurt me.' I tugged her hair, hard.

Fourth Daughter screeched.

Mother scowled. Her eyebrows knotted together.

Second Daughter cocked her head and placed another finished embroidery on the mound atop a clean cloth. 'Could not Fifth Daughter do something else?'

'Nothing. She is useless.' Fourth Daughter rubbed her head. 'She scorches the barley. She could not carry the buckets to Father and the boys.'

'If Fourth Daughter can do it, so can I,' I said, hoping that this was true. I was excited at the notion of doing something else, although afraid I might fail.

'She is too small.' Mother tutted. 'Such an important task.'

'She is faster than a dragon, especially with farm tools.' Second Daughter defended me.

'She has not been to the fields since Winter Solstice,' Mother said, in a softer voice.

'Remember last harvest, when she begged to work the grinding stone?' Second Daughter reminded my mother.

Mother's shoulders drooped.

'That flat stone was almost as big as she was, yet she put the thick cords around her fingers and ground some barley.' Second Daughter had begun a new piece of sewing.

'I'm not sure she can carry the yoke and the buckets with the weight of the water.'

I widened my eyes and stared at her. 'I can do it. I can.'

'She cut grain as well as Third Son, and he is older by three years,' Fourth Daughter said. She had told me she hated carrying the buckets.

My place in the family would have been secure if I had been a boy. As if being the fifth girl was not enough of a burden, I had no skill in any feminine activity.

'Give me a chance, please.' I was thankful for Fourth Daughter's support, although the buckets were *her* task. Knees bent, I pretended I was already carrying that heavy weight. I clenched my hands, feet apart, solid in the straw. Hoping.

Finally Mother said, 'Practise first,'

I had ranked as less than useless. Perhaps I could do this important thing.

After putting the yoke around my neck, Mother attached the buckets. They were heavy, but I knew I was strong. Even so I would have lost half the water in two steps. The empty buckets swung too far out with every pace, but only at first. My sisters laughed, which made me want to pull their hair. I learned to walk with a rhythm – head up, shoulders straight and hands on the yoke.

'None of your older sisters could balance then so quickly, Fifth Daughter.'

Fourth Sister glared. I knew not to make a face at her or she would hit me later.

Mother demanded I wear my festival clothes, inside out as customary; she knew I loved them and would take extra care. 'You will not return with the usual filth.'

Years of wear had dulled the festival smock and trousers to pink. Mother had dyed them red for First Daughter, now married with two children. Second Daughter had burned a hole at the end of one sleeve. Third Daughter, just married, had torn a seam and repaired the trousers with white silk thread. Fourth Daughter had embroidered flowers on the front of the smock.

I dressed, and Mother made the directions to the fields into a song. She and I sang it until I had memorised it. She placed a kiss on my neck and folded a thick cloth under the wooden yoke and its heavy load.

'You will do well.' She kissed the top of my head.

Second Daughter wished me good fortune. Fourth Daughter crossed her eyes and wrinkled her nose. She was probably glad that I would do her task and not be underfoot all morning.

This was something I might be able to do.

I plodded along the paths around plots of land, careful to avoid loose soil, alert for stones, determined not to lose a drop of my father's water.

The crop grew short on the fields, not tall enough for late spring, perhaps because it had been cold, with little rain. The last time the barley had been short like this, the hot soup had tasted terrible, scratched my throat and had not satisfied my stomach for long.

O Earth and Harvest Gods, please let us not be hungry! Let me never again eat boiled earth.

I saw an animal on a far path, a huge demon, white eyes wild in its black face, hair flying like kite strings. A brown haze hid its feet, as if the animal trampled angry clouds. Its movement pulsed through the earth to my legs, like a drum, and I trembled. I checked my buckets; no water had splashed out.

I had heard of horses but never seen one. The black monster came directly for me, trampling the barley, ripping clods from the rows. I grasped the ropes to stop the buckets swaying and trotted fast, shoulders straight, desperate not to lose any precious water. The demon headed straight for me. A fist snatched at my chest. I wished Father was here.

Closer. The animal spun around me, swifter on four legs than I on two. If the horse wanted the water, he would not have it. My feet ran in another direction.

Earth Gods! Swallow me, with my buckets still full and my clothes clean.

Soil scattered around me. It dried my eyes and closed my throat and shortened my breath.

I blinked and coughed. I could not tell which way to flee in the heavy umber smoke. The yoke bit my shoulders. Mother's cloth padding as useless as a dried leaf. The buckets were still full, but my trousers were filthy. I saw Mother's frown. I needed to make my father proud.

The horse circled around me, nearer and nearer. I turned, feeling its hot snorts, smelling its musky odour. I looked for escape but could find none. I stopped. Whatever happened, I would defend my cargo.

The horse's hoofs stilled. Dust settled on the fields, like dark snow. I wiped my eyes, rubbed my palms against my cheeks.

The massive black animal panted loud and fast, smelling of sweet sweat. A strange man perched on it, dressed in thick brocade. White gauze swathed his head and face. He brushed the garments away from his face with the back of one hand. The other fingered his moustache.

Breathing hard, I watched the horse's chest, moving almost like mine. I licked my lips. They tasted of dirt soup, but I swallowed the spit – I did not know the man.

A deep bow would tip my buckets so I bowed only my head. Trouble? Perhaps I should offer him some water.

The man slid off the horse. I stepped away, still carefully, so he would not tread on me. He stood, like an egret, tall and lanky, his head almost too big for his body, the brocade, once white and purple, now lightly speckled brown.

My legs grew heavy. My hands stiffened around the yoke. I wanted to stare, but I forced myself to focus on the barley shoots he had ruined.

O Goddess of Mercy, let me be on my best behaviour. I must please my father and mother. I cannot fail with the buckets, too.

Head down, I studied the flowers on my smock, inside out, almost as pretty. I wriggled my toes in my sandals and made tiny puffs of dust escape through their worn straw. I hoped he would hurry. I could not be late to the fields.

'Girl. What is your name?'

Shrill as a buzzard-hawk, his voice prickled over my skin. I held the yoke firmly, ready to run. 'Honourable sir, I am Fifth Daughter.'

'You will do. Better than your sister.'

Better than my sister?

'Walk beside my horse,' he said. 'I will take you to your father's fields.'

My sister had met the priest. Which sister? Fourth Daughter? Or Second? Why had she not told us? Father might wonder why Fourth Daughter had not brought the water.

I imagined Father's praise for bringing a divine person to our field. Had Fourth Daughter already brought him? The priest could bless our crops this dry spring. Would that be better than my sister? Today I would make Father proud. I shifted and balanced the yoke between my fingers and palms, and gazed ahead at the priest's back.

What a fortunate day.

II. The Negotiation

As we reached our field, men and horses approached from behind a nearby hill, the one with the mulberry grove. Four sweaty men in loincloths held up a palanquin. Horses and samurai surrounded them as they strained to set it on the ground. Only one person in the world had such a transport.

The richly dressed man who stepped out had to be – could only be – Proprietor Chiba no Tashiyori, the Above-the-Clouds person who owned all the fields and was as rich as anyone in the world. Father said important people, the people Above-the-Clouds, had servants to carry them. They did not walk on the ground like us.

With care I trudged next to Father. My shoulders burned. My neck throbbed, despite the cloth and Mother's kiss. My eyes begged him for permission to take the yoke off.

He glanced down and the ends of his mouth lifted. His big crooked tooth laughed outside his lower lip. With one fingertip he tapped the end of my nose. Father gestured to my brothers. First Son came over and escorted me to the far corner of our plot. There, he relieved me of my heavy burden. We watched. No one spoke.

The priest left his black horse and strolled over to my father. His small eyes glistened in the near midday sun. When he opened his mouth, his black teeth made his face look like a skull. I trembled. First Son stepped closer to me, placed his big hand on top of my head, drumming his fingers in the gentle, playful way he always did.

Rubbing my stinging neck, I watched. This priest spoke to Father, but I could not hear their words. Proprietor Chiba motioned to the priest and next placed his forearms across his belly. The priest nodded, then laid his open hand on my father's back, pushing him towards the proprietor. When Father reached the proprietor, he bowed until his knees, hands and forehead touched the ground.

When he rose, he stood with his hands at his sides. Proprietor Chiba pointed to our fields and to each of my brothers. Father's shoulders slumped, and he stared at the ground. He and Proprietor Chiba spoke back and forth. I was still too far away to hear the words. This priest, his thin lips moulded into an odd smile, spoke to my father.

My father turned and waved for me to come. I did so and bowed. 'Stand. The honourable proprietor wishes to see you.'

Looking down, I rubbed the dirt off my smock and trousers and wiped my face.

I bowed like my father. Proprietor Chiba told me to rise. One of his fingers pressed under my chin, pushing my face up. With two fingers of his other hand he rubbed my cheek.

'Yes, Goro. Very good.' Proprietor Chiba nodded and spoke to the priest. 'In fact, perfect.' He released my face. 'Now, Fifth Daughter, off to your brothers.'

The priest and Proprietor Chiba thought I was perfect. I left, imagining what kind of reward my family would receive because of my good work.

My father, the priest and Proprietor Chiba continued to talk. The exchange took longer than the finishing touches to a meal when I was hungry. What were they doing? Perhaps they were going to reward me for carrying the buckets.

Father motioned to me again, and I hurried over.

I studied him, noticing his colourless face, his lowered eyes. There would be no reward.

'I can hardly believe I must say this to you, my child.' He gulped. 'Proprietor Chiba has offered me . . . us . . . our family . . . the extra land we have talked about so often. In good harvest years, we would not need to sell sewing for our winter food or charcoal.'

I heard such longing in his voice.

Father's throat bobbed. His fingers caressed my sore shoulders, and tears pooled in his eyes. 'But, Fifth Daughter, Proprietor Chiba wants you in exchange for the land.'

'The proprietor wants *me*? To do what?'

'I do not know, but in exchange for the land he wishes you to live with him on his *shōen*.'

'For how long?'

My father stood silent. He hung his head.

'Days? How many days?' My ears buzzed like a swarm of summer mosquitoes.

'A lifetime.'

A fist smashed deep into my core. He was talking about selling me. I would go away for ever. Never to return. Disgrace strangled me, like a rope around my neck.

No! Not me! Carrying the pails was Fourth Daughter's task. I could do other work, not the sewing but other things . . .

'No, Father! Not see you again?' The world spun. I seized his thigh to steady myself. Sweat dampened my pink smock.

'My little Fifth Daughter.'

'Not me!'

He placed both hands on my back.

'Do we really need the land?' Fourth Daughter should have been here. Why was this happening to me?

'You are my baby, my beloved daughter. How can I sell you?' he mumbled, as if he were speaking to someone far away, combing my hair with his fingers.

I gazed into his eyes. He had always resolved my troubles. 'Since it is spring, could I stay at the *shōen* until after the harvest, then come home? Would that pay for the new field?'

'There is no other way. For the family, I must sell you.' His voice embraced a final sorrow.

Tears hit my head. I touched them with my fingers. Father choked a little and placed a large hand on his throat. We stood in our field holding each other. A bush warbler flew over us, singing its beautiful '*ho-hoh hokekkyō*'.

'I love you, Fifth Daughter, but he . . . he is the proprietor.' He pulled away and ruffled my hair. 'The priest says this . . . change . . . will be easier for you because you are younger.' He laid one hand on mine and rested the other on my head. He swallowed. 'We have often talked about our family honour. You know how important it is.'

I tried to listen to what he said above the noise in my ears.

'This you must do so that we keep our honour.' He squatted. We were face to face, and he narrowed his eyes. 'You know that our souls belong to our family's spirit. That is our honour. You must go with Proprietor Chiba. Mantain the family honour.'

I nodded. My lips were too stiff to make words.

My father enclosed me in his arms, put his head against my middle and sobbed with no sounds. I held him. He smelt of dry soil and sweat. When he was calm, he placed a hand on each of my shoulders. 'Always remember,' his voice cracked, 'each day of my life I will love you. Your family loves you. Do your duty by going with Proprietor Chiba and following his orders.' His large hands encircled my face. 'I am sad to send you away, but I do so with great honour.'

I wrote his words into my spirit.

Father did not want me to go. I did not want to go. Yet I, Fifth Daughter, would provide my family with a complete new piece of land. I, Fifth Daughter, not Fourth Daughter, would permit my family to have food and charcoal – even in bad-harvest winters. They would never eat soil, as we did two winters ago.

'Father, I will do my duty. Please tell Mother and my sisters I will bring honour.' I, Fifth Daughter, had granted my family a gift none of the other daughters could: land. Precious land.

My eyes watered. With clenched hands, I turned and made a low bow to Father and smaller bows to each brother, even to Third Son. Looking up, I saw tears tumbling down Father's face.

He placed one hand on top of my head and the other on my back. Then he turned and led me to Proprietor Chiba.

I had never heard of a child, once sold, returning to their family. Perhaps I could. If I worked hard at Proprietor Chiba's, he would have to let me go because I had done my duty so well. I hoped to go home soon. With honour. My family's honour.

The proprietor grabbed my sore neck and twisted me in the direction of the palanquin, the samurai, the horses, his *shōen* and a new life.

A large samurai dismounted and strode to Proprietor Chiba and bowed low. 'Permission to speak? Permission to oversee this one on the walk, my lord?' He spoke with a quiet growl.

Proprietor Chiba replied in a voice as dark as a winter thundercloud: 'If you must, Akio. Yes, yes, as usual.'

Proprietor Chiba had spoken differently before. He had changed into another person. The samurai Akio boosted the grunting proprietor into his palanquin and mounted his own chestnut horse.

I surveyed the land to say goodbye and to remember. On my right was a small hill. A large mulberry thicket with little leaf buds grew on its west side. The priest had disappeared and a chill surged up my spine.

Later, I wrote this poem:

> Suddenly cold as
> The spring's Solstice Holy Day
> My family gone
> No one to scatter soybeans
> To cast out all my demons

III. New World

Ahead – an endless wall. The *shōen*. My new home. Without my family.

A man shouted, and five men pushed open the gate, bigger than my house. Was everything going to be so huge?

Inside the gate, the sweating men with sly grimaces and muffled grunts set down the palanquin. The priest dismounted and waited for Proprietor Chiba to stand.

After a small bow, the priest said, 'If she is satisfactory, I hope you will send word of my accomplishments to the Taira City or, dare I say it, to Governor Taira no Michimori, or his annoying emissaries.'

'Understood. Word of our actual arrangement to the commander would harm both of us. He would not favour either of us rising any higher.'

'Chiba, this one is so much more beautiful than the older sister.' The priest raised one eyebrow and smiled, showing his blackened teeth. 'The local temple here is, as I have said, becoming quite boring, except for our . . . business.'

More beautiful? Older sister? Fourth Daughter and me?

'Yes.' Proprietor Chiba smiled a toothy smile.

'Proprietor, this is the sixth girl I have directed to you.'

'Goro . . .' Proprietor Chiba lifted his palm to the priest.

'All the girls have been satisfactory. For both of us.'

'Yes – yes, Tashiko dances well.' Proprietor Chiba nodded, and his chins jiggled.

Tashiko? Another girl?

'She is a pretty child, is she not?' The priest tilted his face down to Proprietor Chiba's.

'Not as handsome as this one.' Proprietor Chiba pointed a pudgy finger at me.

I was handsome? Was I beautiful, too?

'It is an honour to perform at your temple here on your *shōen*, but as one is pulled up the ladder . . . so will another. And I must be invited to the Third Day Third Month Doll Festival.'

'Or what? I have the girl now.' Proprietor Chiba stuffed his fists on top of his hips.

Did he mean me? I looked about for other girls, yet saw none.

'Or what? There are so many possibilities, Chiba no Tashiyori. Revoke your tax-exempt status. Remove your samurai or . . .' The priest counted, one finger, two fingers, three. 'You may run this *shōen* but I control some Taira temples. I have influence over the commander, and he owns you. All I desire is a coloured hat.'

'I know. You shall have what you want, your tedious rank and a hat,' Proprietor Chiba growled, like a trapped animal.

'And do not damage the girls – do not injure them in any way.' The priest's body changed from egret to hawk, and he dropped his face closer to Proprietor Chiba's.

'Have I ever?' Chiba raised his shoulders and stepped away. 'But I must discipline them.'

Discipline? Damage? Hard words. Frightening words.

'You know what I mean. Otherwise—' The priest leaned towards the proprietor again.

'Goro, there is no need for threats. No need at all.'

'An invitation this year and every year, until we both move up. I believe we are truly destined to help this clan in a higher capacity. Do you not agree?'

'Naturally you shall be invited to the Third Day Third Month Doll Festival.'

'I believe now we will be going in the same direction . . .'

Proprietor Chiba walked away.

'. . . soon,' the priest finished, to Proprietor Chiba's back. The priest turned to me. 'You will see, Fifth Daughter. I was sold to a monastery when I was younger than you. What do you see now?' He opened his arms wide and pivoted from side to side.

He sounded pleased with himself. I had no idea what he meant. I merely bowed.

'Fine clothes, a horse, a house and enough to eat.' He fondled a lengthy piece of leather that hung at his waist. 'Authority and power. More importantly, soon, Fifth Daughter, soon I will wear a hat of colour, as well as these priest's robes.' He peered down at me. 'Then no one will dominate or control me.' He straightened in the saddle. 'I will visit you again, beautiful girl.' He mounted his black beast and rode away.

Proprietor Chiba glided towards me, tapped my head with his fleshy fingers and motioned me to follow. Standing straight, hands at my sides, I marched behind him. We crossed a wooden bridge to a large building I had seen from outside.

Thinking about what the priest said and resolving to follow Proprietor Chiba, I studied the wobbling expanse of his robes and fell. My head hit the small stones covering the hard earthen path. Hundreds of stone needles struck my face. I heard my mother shout, 'You have spoiled your festival smock.' In my shame and pain I lay still. I wanted to hide.

Strong hands, my samurai's, hoisted me. He rescued me. He came for me. 'Are you hurt?' He held me upright with both hands and looked me in the face.

My legs flexed like wet straw. 'I do not think so.'

'Can you stand by yourself?'

I said yes, but my legs dipped when he let go. He caught me. His eyebrows puckered like Second Daughter's did when I fell out of a tree or cut myself.

With several long breaths, my legs steadied. My eyes refocused.

Ahead, Proprietor Chiba motioned again to me with his chubby fingers. Standing straight, hands at my side, I caught up with him and marched behind him, as was correct.

Proprietor Chiba stopped, hands on hips. 'Let the servants of Big House assemble.' His voice resonated – needing to be obeyed.

'Bring Tashiko,' he barked. 'Ready Lesser House. We will need a kimono. This size.' He swivelled and pointed a fat finger at me. 'For my new acquisition, Fifth Daughter, whom I bought on my prescribed walk.'

I was an acquisition? If this had not reflected on my family's honour, the next time he pointed at me I would have bitten his fingers. I hated being pointed or laughed at.

Proprietor Chiba pushed me along the row of collected people. A beautiful array of cloth and colours flickered on each: deep leaf green with gold thread, sea blue with red flowers, earth black with dazzling sunset pink. I tried to concentrate.

I smelt sweat and food or soap when I passed each person. I also saw their hands and feet. The hands were reddened and rough, calloused like Father's and my brothers'. Would I ever see my father and brothers again? Others were coarse, chapped like Mother's and my sisters'. I would probably never see my family again. These feet – huge, small, or gnarled. One pair even turned inwards. Each person wore shoes of heavy cloth, not like my straw ones.

My toes already poked through my sandals, and my face grew warm trying to hide them. Father would not make me a new pair until the straw came in. No, he would not. He was not here.

I wanted to cry. My tears would not fall. I had eaten a little barley before dawn, nothing since. My throat and belly clawed at me. Night was approaching and darkness was breaking over me.

Yet on this day I had discovered that not only was I worth the price of land, I was handsome and beautiful.

BOOK 2

I. A Rival

A girl scuttled up and stood next to me, taller than I, perhaps one or two years older. A pale blue kimono encased her. With long fingers she grasped my arm above the elbow. Thick lashes made her black eyes large in her round face. She chewed her bottom lip. She bowed to Proprietor Chiba and murmured to me, 'Tashiko.'

'Tashiko will attend to Kozaishō,' Proprietor Chiba ordered to the people. 'If any observe Kozaishō in need, assist her. Do not speak to either girl directly, unless you have my consent.'

Tashiko pushed on my shoulder to guide me. Her sweet smell reminded me of bush clover and pinewood, not at all like the spicy sweat of my sisters.

When we were away from the others, I bowed. 'Permission to ask a question, Honourable Tashiko?' She seemed only a little older. Still, I wanted to make a good first impression.

'Just Tashiko. No permission needed.'

'Tashiko, what is a "prescribed walk"?'

'The ride Proprietor Chiba takes when he has been told to walk.'

This made no sense to me. Therefore I asked no more questions.

Tashiko steered me to a miniature house a short distance from the *shō*. 'Lesser House,' she whispered.

We climbed what Tashiko called 'steps' to a roofed floor around the house, which Tashiko called the *watadono*. 'For rain or shade,' she said. Yellow cloth covered Lesser House's window. I touched it when Tashiko's back was turned. My fingers remembered what Mother had taught me: it was a heavy silk. This type of cloth allowed the light in and also gave privacy. Mother's lessons. What if I failed here?

Inside, coloured woods, pieced together, covered the ground and shone like a full moon with no clouds. Heaviness pressed on my chest from breathing in its odd odour. Such a floor would be easier to keep dirt away. What other new things waited for me?

A thick *futon* lay bundled in one corner. Dolls sat on it, several dolls, all dressed in colourful fabrics, not straw. Their real eyes stared at me from smooth white faces, with real red mouths and real black hair and no expression. They were so beautiful, yet they did not seem happy.

I looked at Tashiko and around the rest of the house. A large brazier and screen crowded along one wall for the two of us. Winter nights might be warmer here. In another corner a round object of carved wood spread its legs like upside-down flower petals, as if it were bowing. A bowl of water perched on top of it.

'What is that?' I pointed.

'Table. For dishes.'

Tashiko taught me other words for things. Some I accepted meekly, some I came to love, and some I learned to hate.

Tashiko seized my hand and pulled me. 'Come. I must bathe you.'

We went beyond Lesser House and into the bathhouse, where she combed and fingered my hair. 'Your great beauty, so thick and heavy. Does it take long to dry?'

'At home . . .' pressing my lips together so I did not to cry at this word '. . . it takes m-most of a w-warm day to dry it.'

'Here, let me take these old things off,' she said, and removed my smock and trousers.

'They are not old! I want them! They are mine!' I snatched them and held them to my chest. Today I had lost my family; I would not lose my festival clothes.

'I shall keep them.'

'Promise?'

She tossed my trousers and smock into a corner. She pointed to a small wooden stool. 'Sit.' I ran and grabbed them back. 'Not till you promise.'

'I promise.'

I stared at her and then handed my clothes to her with great ceremony.

She rolled her eyes. 'Now sit. I will scrub you.'

'I did not play in the mud today.' I hoped this would save me from whatever she would do. Then I remembered my fall at the gate. 'Oh . . . I did.' I gave myself to my fate, but not my best costume. 'I still want to keep my clothes.'

She nodded. 'Proprietor Chiba wants you washed.' With a brush and a bowl of prepared water she began. Long strokes from my head to my bottom, up and down my legs to my feet, over and over again. She worked until my skin reddened. I glared at her. She did not stop.

Was she annoyed because I wanted to keep my smock and trousers? I had not done anything to her yet. What if I yanked her hair? But she was a stranger. I did nothing, except keep my eyes on my clothes, even though Tashiko had promised.

After the pouring of clear water, Tashiko pointed to a large deep round bowl raised above the floor. 'Now soak.'

She took my festival clothes from the corner, folded them and put them on another stool. Smoothing them, she murmured, 'Look at this.'

'Fourth Daughter embroidered those flowers.'

'An unusual colour.'

'Mother dyed it red for First Daughter. They will be too small for you,' I added, afraid she might take them.

She nodded. 'Put as much of yourself as you can under the water.'

The warm water made me feel as if I was flying, in a cloud, in a dream. I closed my eyes and my ears filled with the sounds of horses galloping far away, then trampling near the bathhouse and, next, children's giggles and laughter, a baby's wail.

My chest squeezed. The children's giggles reminded me of my sisters' laughter. I missed my mother's quiet scoldings. 'Who are the other children?'

'We are not allowed to play with any children here.' Tashiko's eyes went blank. She studied her toes.

Tears dripped down my cheeks and plopped into the bath.

Tashiko did not rub my head like Second Daughter did when I cried. My skin still hurt.

'Will you stop crying if I tell you a story?'

I nodded, thankful she had noticed.

25

Tashiko spoke magic words: 'Long ago, the great God Izanagi first cleaned his body by soaking it. He had gone to the underworld . . .'

'The nether world?' I asked, sniffling.

'Yes. Afterwards, Izanagi cleansed his body in the sea.' Tashiko stood up and rubbed her back. 'To what *inago* do I owe my suffering?' she muttered to herself. Her eyes shone with tears.

'What is *inago*?' I asked, encouraged by the story.

'The cause and the effect, *karma*. We pay with our suffering for bad things we did before.'

'Before what?'

'In other lives.'

'Other lives?'

'The Buddha speaks,' Tashiko said. 'Each has many lives. Goes to wondrous places. Has no one taught you this?'

I nodded. I did not remember any of it, although I had heard of the Buddha. What would happen? What wondrous places would I see?

The bathhouse door swung open behind me. Cool air floated over my warm skin. A shuffling, and the door swung shut. Tashiko motioned for me to come out of the bath. She scraped me with a thick cloth, hurting me again. She used a corner to wipe her own eyes.

I asked nothing.

She went to the door and returned with two pieces of clothing. One she called *kosode*, or under-kimono. The other was a kimono of pale moss green with embroidered trees and a bridge on the side. Tashiko dressed me.

The *kosode* and kimono hung off me as if they belonged to Mother. I recognised the kimono's design. The needlework belonged to my mother and sisters. Grief smothered me like a heavy quilt. I shivered as if I was cold, yet my skin felt hot. I wanted to go home.

Remembering my dignity, I wiped my tears, tracing the designs on the kimono where my dry fingers could reach, where my family had touched.

This cloth.

The willow trees.

The bridge.

All I had left of my family.

II. Rules

I put my head into my hands, muffling my screeching-crying sounds. Fourth Daughter hated me crying like that. What if I displeased Proprietor Chiba? My family would be disgraced. I did not know how, but I had already upset Tashiko. If not, why would she be unkind?

On my knees in Lesser House, I wiped my face with the backs of my hands. I did not wish to spoil my new clothes. I heard my father's voice; 'Keep our honour. Do your duty by going with Proprietor Chiba.'

I rubbed my neck where Mother had placed a kiss that morning and saw the face of Second Daughter as she sang me to sleep. Who would sing to me tonight?

I heard someone slide the door and come inside. I put my face to the ground – no, the floor. I caught the smells of fish, rice, spices and sharp body odour. Would I be allowed to eat that food? No one spoke. Who was it? Honour included doing as you were told. Therefore I waited, burying my nose in my new clothes to avoid the floor's uncomfortable scent. My head filled with my family's faces when my fingers brushed the cloth on which they had worked. I breathed in sorrow.

'Kozaishō.'

My name . . . I heard my name.

'Kozaishō, your parents have taught you your manners well. Stand in front of me.' Proprietor Chiba sat high on the doubled *futon*, smiling so widely that his cheeks made his eyes almost disappear. 'Today is the beginning of your new life. You will have many tasks, and you may also have pleasures. Do you understand?'

27

I nodded, facing down.

'When I ask a question, answer with your voice. Say "yes" or "no" or whatever the answer is, always ending with "Honourable Proprietor Chiba".'

'Yes, honourable Proprietor Chiba.'

'In this place it is correct for you to look me in the face. At all other times and all other places, I do not permit it. But here, Kozaishō,' a chubby hand floated up and out towards each wall, 'when you and I are together, just the two of us, you will look upon my face. It is my wish—'

'Yes, honourable Proprietor Chiba.'

'I had not finished speaking, Kozaishō. You must always wait for me.' He hit my head with his hand.

I fell to the side. Half of my face smacked against the wooden floor. I was stunned, then furious. Yet I heard my father's voice, 'Do your duty,' and did nothing. No jumping on him as I would my brothers.

My stomach growled in spite of the pain and surprise. Would I eat tonight or would there be more punishment? I did not know. I breathed, but stayed still.

'Always wait for me to finish speaking.'

I pushed myself on to my knees and waited. He said no more. From my throbbing head, my throat scratched out, 'Yes, honourable Proprietor Chiba.'

'It is my wish when we are in this place for you to look upon my face. It is my wish . . . and it is my command.'

I waited a bit. 'Yes, honourable Proprietor Chiba.'

'Tomorrow Tashiko will teach you your tasks – and see what I have brought you.' He smiled and pointed to the table on which lay a tray with many small covered dishes.

The food – those delicious aromas, so close, so far. All the bowls shining, most with covers, mostly black. Some had little flowers on them.

'Are you hungry?'

Despite my aching head and shoulders, my belly gurgled and I replied. All that food could feed my entire family.

'Shall I feed you, or can you feed yourself?'

'I can feed myself,' I said. How old did he think I was? 'Whatever the honourable proprietor wishes, honourable Proprietor Chiba,' I added, to be sure I included the right words. I did not wish to be struck again.

'Eat, and I will tell you about each dish as you do so.'

'I did my best to appreciate what he said. We had had no rice for years. I ate the whole bowl. I glanced at him every now and then. Would he hit me?

When I stopped eating, he said, 'Would you like a story before you sleep?'

'Oh, yes, honourable Proprietor Chiba.'

A story before sleep. Something familiar in this strange place.

He called Tashiko into Lesser House. She sat down closer to Proprietor Chiba than I and finished my leftover food.

She was older, yet I had eaten first. I did not understand. No wonder she had been unkind.

Proprietor Chiba told this story:

'Long ago Chōkichi, a charcoal-burner who lived near Sawaage, dreamed that if he travelled to Misokai Bridge at Takayama something marvellous would happen. He went immediately. Sitting on the bridge, a tōfu-maker came and asked what he was doing. The tōfu-maker laughed at Chōkichi's dream, saying, "Anyone who takes dreams seriously is a fool." The tōfu-maker continued, "I keep dreaming that gold is buried beneath a cryptomeria tree by the house of a charcoal-burner at Sawaage. It is only a dream. I need take no notice." When Chōkichi heard that, he went home and dug around the tree. He became quite wealthy.

'Girls, I am like that charcoal-burner.' He took a pudgy finger and poked himself in the chest several times. 'I have a dream. My dream is to entertain Taira courtiers here by the next festival. Two months away.'

He turned to Tashiko, leaned close to her face and smiled. 'Tomorrow show Kozaishō the *shōen*, especially the temple, but make sure you teach her the Butterfly Dance.'

He stroked Tashiko's face. She almost purred, like a cat. 'Fortunately for you, the Gods of Direction are unkind. I must to stay at the house of my brother-in-law overnight. An extra day for you to practise. Use it well. You will both perform all of the dances for my guests, in full costume.'

Tashiko waited two short breaths and acknowledged him.

I learned to take those two breaths before I spoke to him. He not only hit me but Tashiko too.

Tashiko moved closer to him. He smiled at her and rubbed her head. She glared at me, and her lips curved in a faint smile. Tashiko was to teach me what I needed to know, and we were already rivals.

III. Risk

No mother's song awakened me next morning, no sisters' punches. There was no crackle of a fire and no smell of barley cooking. Jaundiced light flowed through the window silk on to the *futon*. When I noticed the pale green kimono with those trees, I remembered where I was, with sadness and determination. No Tashiko either.

When Tashiko arrived, she carried shiny bowls, and we ate our morning meal, rice, just as delicious as the previous night. On my bowl I saw the same white flowers, too. Tashiko's had autumn grasses.

'What makes the bowls shine?'

'Lacquer.'

'Lacquer?' I had never heard of it.

'Potters put lacquer on the bowls.' She smirked.

I thought of the plain, chipped bowls my family used. 'Do we always eat from such beautiful bowls?'

'Yes.'

She gave me a jacket for the morning chill. Green, not blue like hers, with little embroidered rabbits huddled near trees. She turned the cuffs up three times. It was almost like wearing my older sisters' clothes. Tashiko did not make a game of dressing me. Second Daughter and I practised dance steps to help me dress. Not Tashiko.

'Come.'

'Yes, Tashiko.' I bowed. Perhaps if I showed her more respect, she would not be so angry with me. She would realise that I was not an enemy.

'No bowing.' Tashiko frowned and chewed her bottom lip. 'Walk.'

31

If I followed her and learned the Butterfly Dance, perhaps I could go home soon, or at least after the festival. Last night Proprietor Chiba had complimented my manners. I would do whatever I needed to do to bring honour to my family, as Father wished. Then I could go home. In my deepest, most secret place, I feared that might never happen.

I pushed the thought away.

As we walked, Tashiko spoke. 'Proprietor Chiba made places here where the high-born, the courtiers, like to enjoy themselves. Call them fancies. They wear fancy clothes.'

'What do they do?' She was talking to me. She did not seem angry today.

'Walk. Some ride. Sit and write. Watch the dances.'

'Where?'

'See?' She pointed to a nearby pond. 'Those islands in that small lake. When they come, we are not allowed to go outside Lesser House, except to dance.' She grabbed me. 'Today there is no one. No one.' She lifted her arms high and almost yelled, 'I can be free!' Her eyes filled, like dew on sunlit leaves. I glanced at her wide-eyed face and smiled to her. One day distant and disagreeable, today glad.

'Let's look. So many birds here this spring.'

I wanted to know how long she had been here – had she been sold, like me? I kept quiet now, not wanting to anger her.

We rambled to the lake. Skylarks, cranes, copper pheasants and ibis gathered. I loved the ibises' red beaks and black-tipped wings. Their white feathers shimmered against the water making clouds float across it. *Koi* and other fish swarmed among the pink and yellow water-lilies. They all had families.

A pair of cranes performed their courting dance. I did not stir until the male jumped high, spreading his black-tipped white wings wide to finish his courtship. Perhaps, after our work, I could play here, listen to the frogs and watch the butterflies and birds. If Tashiko forgave me or remained pleasant.

I thought I had seen the whole *shōen*, but Tashiko placed her hands on my shoulders. 'There is a Buddhist temple. Come.' I saw happiness in her eyes for a second time.

It was taller than any shrine to which my family had ever taken me. A high fountain thundered before its door, a typhoon of water. The wooden railings formed a delicate pattern. Only Fourth Daughter had the skill to copy it with her sewing.

As I moved closer, the fountain painted rainbows in the midday air. When Tashiko stopped in front of them, she put her hands over her stomach. Her eyes glowed and went far away at the same time. She muttered words I did not understand. I waited, silent.

I looked inside the temple. Many lighted candles stood on tables. I heard timeworn voices muttering my name and saw ancient eyes staring.

'Now to the samurai's game field.' Tashiko raced off.

Perhaps my large samurai would be there. I ran fast to follow her.

Far beyond the bathhouse lay a green field with no crop, only grass. Men played with a leather ball, running and kicking to keep it in the air. I searched, yet could not see my samurai. Tashiko followed the ball back and forth, her mouth and eyes stretching wider and wider.

This was something that made her happy. I liked the game too.

We returned to Lesser House in the late midday.

'Do you know the Butterfly Dance?'

'Yes, Tashiko.'

Tashiko sighed, seeming content. 'Good.'

Tashiko and I rehearsed the Butterfly Dance as I had with my older sister. Tashiko shimmered like a real butterfly in the twilight. A spring haze, with its fresh smell, cooled us. The cicadas trilled, and the bush warblers called their endearing good night, '*ho-hoh hokekkyō*'. The birds' song reminded me of saying goodbye to my father. I resolved not to cry, but instead to think of my duty and embrace it.

Dancing and singing, I pretended I was at home with Second Daughter. Outside, behind the lines of drying clothes, she and I had practised a difficult new dance for last autumn's Feast of Harvest. First she had shown me the whole dance. Next we had learned the steps separately, then the hand and finally the head movements. Last, I had put them all together.

We had sung and swirled. I had spun into the drying garments hanging under the cloudy sky. Mother ran out to see the muddy wreckage. Her lips turned down to her chin.

I thought, Besides a beating, no evening meal, but Mother's face softened and she said, 'Both of you stop and wash those clothes again.'

At the mild punishment Second Daughter raised her eyebrows – her look of surprise. She grabbed my hand. 'Come. Two of us can do this and have time to practise those steps again.' We learned that dance, Second Daughter and I, Fifth Daughter.

Now – Tashiko and I.

IV. Ambush

Tashiko and I practised the Butterfly Dance for the remainder of that second day and all of the third on Lesser House's *watadono*. The *biwa* player's music drifted around us, as welcome as the sparrows' chirps. Dancing was harder work than turning the grinding stone at harvest. It had the same movements over and over, in varied patterns: point the toes, uncurl the fingers, head tilted left and head tilted right; two beats, four beats, curl, uncurl and bend the fingers, over and over. Remembered or repeated. Later we did everything together again. Perfect for Proprietor Chiba. Flawless for my family and our honour.

Tashiko seemed impressed by how fast I learned everything, but the hand gestures troubled me.

I floated like two clouds following the sun. From time to time the musician brought water and snacks for us. He often smiled at me, a smile that relaxed my stomach. Yet I would have given all, the morning rice, the beautiful bowls, the dolls, the clothes, all of this to hear Second Daughter's hum as I danced at home.

My bath on the third evening was as the first. Tashiko scrubbed my skin raw, like new hemp cloth. This time, though, she sat on the same stool and used the same water to bathe herself. With a spongy brush her strokes were slower and gentler. She took her time drying, and when she had finished her skin shone like silk. Tashiko was older and in charge. I had to be cautious. How could I protect myself?

Back inside Lesser House, Tashiko dressed us in the dance costumes. How soft the cloth felt on my skin, pale green silk brocade, delicate.

Fourth Daughter did not have such beautiful clothes. I felt like a princess in the stories my mother and sisters had told me. Tashiko combed my hair with a care that reminded me of my sisters, bringing together lonely and happy feelings. If I was careful to listen and obey, Proprietor Chiba would not hit me, and perhaps this place would be magical, like living in a tale. Fourth Daughter would not believe I ate white rice twice a day.

Tashiko's breathy voice quavered, 'My mother's hair, like yours, thick, charcoal black. I combed it for her.' Her voice hardened like her fist against my head. She jerked back and pulled my hair hard. 'Hers had no tangles or knots.'

The pain forced me to recall I was not at home. I was with Tashiko in the *shōen*. Although I wanted to, I did not yank her hair because she was older and teaching me. I took deep breaths and checked that I could move easily in my new costume. I smoothed my hair to ensure Tashiko had not made me untidy.

When Proprietor Chiba came inside Lesser House that evening, he placed the dishes on the table. He dropped on to the doubled *futon*, while Tashiko and I made obeisance to him.

'Are you ready?' He directed the question to Tashiko.

Tashiko answered in what sounded like a rehearsed speech. 'Yes, honourable Proprietor Chiba. I . . . we are ready to present to you.'

'Go outside.' He waved his hand. 'Tell the musician to play and get your fans.'

Fans? What was a fan?

As Tashiko unfolded her body to go outside, I looked to her for answers. Her lips turned up, like an early crescent moon on the horizon. My breathing came faster.

The *biwa* music played from the veranda. Tashiko came back into Lesser House. She had two odd sticks in her hand. She handed one to me, pretending she had done this as many times as there were barley kernels in a field. I had never seen fans. From the way Tashiko posed, the way she handled them, I knew she had. My muscles tightened, yet I relaxed my mouth from its frown. My face heated with fury. She wanted me to look bad. I would not give her the satisfaction.

I positioned myself to see what she did with the fans. I remembered the foot and body gestures. Now the hand and finger movements made more sense – curled and uncurled, bent and not bent.

We posed in the beginning posture. Tashiko stuck her fan inside her belt. I did the same. The music played. On the third turn she flicked her wrist and transformed the fan into a butterfly's wing in the wind. I flicked and showed – the stick.

Proprietor Chiba grunted.

My cheeks burned, my chest tightened. We turned in a small circle, and Tashiko flipped her fan, one side, the other side, and repeated. I did the turn, but could not do all, and missed the next step.

Proprietor Chiba growled.

Tashiko and I stepped together, fluttering like butterflies. Behind her, Tashiko rotated her fan upside down and back in one quick movement. My fan went upside down behind my back and came to the front – only half open. The fan fell to the floor and I scrambled to retrieve it.

Proprietor Chiba roared, 'Stop!' Outside Lesser House the music ceased. Grunting like a boar, he rolled to his feet and pointed a fat finger to the floor. I copied Tashiko's example, pressed the fan into my belt and made obeisance.

'Tashiko, you said you were ready. You were not. You did not teach the fans. A beating for both of you. If this happens again, Kozaishō will be the one who beats you. Is that clear?'

'Yes, honourable Proprietor Chiba.' Tashiko's lips stretched tight like a drum.

'Fetch the switch.' Proprietor Chiba's voice boomed against the walls of Lesser House.

Tashiko returned holding a thin bamboo cane and gave it to him.

'Permission to speak, Proprietor Chiba?' If I took the blame for Tashiko's wrong-doing, she would owe me a favour. She would see I was not a rival. I needed at least one friend against this demon.

He waved his hand.

'It is only I who should be punished. I am the one who did not learn.'

'That does not matter.' Proprietor Chiba's lips turned upwards, demonstrating the sound of the bamboo rod. Swoop! Swoop! 'My order was for you to learn. Therefore you both disobeyed me. Strip to the waist and bend. Both of you.'

We made obeisance on his command. My fingers touched the floor, and shivers travelled all over my body.

'Kozaishō, sit up and watch what happens when I am not obeyed.'

Whack! Whack! Whack! He thrashed Tashiko. She yelped at each blow. Her eyes filled with tears. She cried for her mother, her father, her sisters. Proprietor Chiba's grin grew wider with each blow. I wanted to run away from those sounds but could not dishonour my family. Blood dotted her skin.

Proprietor Chiba made an all-teeth smile and turned to me.

Vomit scorched my throat. I swallowed it.

I prayed to the Goddess of Mercy that I would be brave.

Thwack!

I gasped with the blow.

Thwack!

Tears leaked. I bit my tongue to be silent.

He sucked in a breath. Thwack!

The floor shone with my tears. I did not let out a sound.

He wheezed when he hit me.

I bit my tongue each time. No cries like Tashiko.

He brought the switch down harder. I prayed to the Goddess of Mercy again that I would be brave and remain quiet.

I heard him panting and waited, unsure what would happen, hoping he would stop.

'You will remember this,' he croaked, breathing with a whistle. 'You will obey me completely.' He took our dinner and left Lesser House.

Tashiko rose, reached behind the brazier and took out a small jar. She applied the salve to my injuries with gentle touches. I had to bite my tongue again to stop myself crying out.

She handed me the jar and a cloth and turned around. Large blood-red welts and old scars streaked her back. I wondered if my skin would scar like that.

'Bite your lip or tongue.' I applied the salve. 'It will help against the pain.' She pivoted to stare at me, surprised. I thought I saw an apology through her tears.

I dabbed ointment on each bloody dot.

38

Two days before I had had someone to comfort me, at least rub my head or feet. Now, there was no one. Tashiko slept far away on the other side of the *futon*.

I stayed awake, lying on my stomach, rubbing my head but was not soothed.

V. Story of Samurai

The next day Tashiko wound heavy cloth around us to stop the blood seeping through our clothes. Movement made the pain worse. Still, I practised the dance. I learned the fans in a single day.

We were quiet, except when Tashiko paused, walked over to me, eyes down, and muttered, 'Thank you for taking the blame. I am sorry.'

I tried to smile. I was not sure I believed her, although I wanted a companion in this big and lonely place. I hoped to see my samurai again.

That evening we presented again. Proprietor Chiba applauded. 'Much better. You make a beautiful pair of butterflies!'

I gave all the praise to Tashiko.

'Look what I have brought you.' He presented us with new kimonos, wrapped in paper: mine was brilliant red with cherry trees in full pink and white bloom, and hers deep blue with clouds, mountains and trees. We admired them, put them on and then away.

'And . . .' Proprietor Chiba pointed to the table, which was filled with delicacies.

If Tashiko wanted to be close to a man who hit and rewarded us with the same hand, I would not fight her. I disobeyed Proprietor Chiba's pointing finger for me to eat and allowed Tashiko to eat first, willing to undergo another punishment. Proprietor Chiba did not interfere.

'I have a story,' he said, when we had finished.

I glanced up at his black ant eyes in the bloated face and did not answer until Tashiko had responded.

'Good.' He hugged me, squeezing my raw back. I bit my tongue so that I did not scream.

Tashiko scowled. I moved away.

Proprietor Chiba seemed not to notice. 'This story is in honour of our new girl.' He leaned over and pinched my cheek. 'I call it "Pink Flower" after you, Kozaishō.'

I watched Tashiko, who glared at me. After she had spoken, I repeated what she said. 'Yes, please, honourable Proprietor Chiba.' I stared at the gold-thread clasps across his large stomach. Maybe he would tell me how I had honoured my family. Then I could go home. I wanted to go home.

Once upon a time, a poor woodcutter heard a cry at the forest's edge and found it came from inside a pink flower stalk. He carefully cut it and found inside a girl, no bigger than his little finger. He carried her in his hand to his home. The woodcutter named her Pink Flower, because she ate only pink flowers and grain. In that first month she grew into a beautiful woman and worked hard. A wealthy man saw her and purchased her, leaving her adopted father prosperous. The wealthy man bought Pink Flower numerous presents and fed her wonderful food in beautiful dishes. They lived happily together for many years.

That night, I slept with my festival clothes under me because I did not trust Tashiko, but I dreamed of becoming Pink Flower and also of marrying a samurai. This samurai took me to his *shōen* where my family joined me. My parents, sisters and brothers never had to work or go hungry again. All of us lived with wealth, happiness and, most of all, honour.

Besides learning the dances, each morning Tashiko told me my other tasks. I made these into a song, just as my mother had done for me. Usually the tasks included deliveries of packages, or messages written on folded papers, which looked like flowers. These I took to the artisans who lived a far distance behind the *shō* – Big House, as Tashiko called it. I handed people the package or note and stole peeps at them. I did not have permission to talk to them, or they to me. The silence could be lonely.

After my back had healed, Tashiko gave me the wrong tasks. Once.

Proprietor Chiba fulfilled his promise and gave me the bamboo switch.

'It was my mistake,' I told him, in front of Tashiko, and refused to beat her. He beat me, and I bit the inside of my mouth or my tongue to smother my every sound. After Tashiko had smoothed on the ointment, with gentler fingers this time, I grabbed her hair, pulled, and spoke through clenched teeth. 'I will not do that again. If you try to hurt me one more time, I will not take the blame. I will beat you. Hard. Do you understand?'

To my relief, her eyes filled. 'Oh, Kozaishō. You were so brave.' She wrapped her arms around herself. 'Let there be a truce between us.' Her big dark eyes showed her misery. 'I'm sorry. He never told me stories. Let us truly be friends. Will you?'

I counted our beginning from that moment.

My tasks let me go throughout the *shōen*, which measured many *chō* from end to end. I wanted my home. Often I went further, to the outside walls, almost to the gate. Samurai guarded the gate. I remembered and returned to my tasks. Leaving would dishonour my parents. My entire family would be disgraced. If I were shamed, I could not go home. I stayed – I had nowhere to go. Yet I thought of home all the time.

I carried food or water to the samurai practising in the large fields. The few times I found my samurai, I watched him, hidden in the grasses at the edge of the field. I wished I could talk to him.

I studied the samurai's armour, their bows and arrows, their swords. The armour looked solid, but moved like grass in the wind. I learned each samurai by his armour's pattern. My samurai had deep blue and bright red in rectangular shapes, easy to find.

He launched an arrow, hissing above the field. It struck the target with a crack. I gasped with the sheer joy of watching. On horses, samurai were transformed into fierce beasts, shooting arrows from armoured bulges on their backs, arms wide, bow and arrow fully spread.

'Are there no other children to play with?' I asked, over the morning rice and pickled vegetables.

'No.' Her eyes aimed for her toes. I knew better than to ask any more questions. I hoped she had told me the truth.

When Tashiko's tasks in Big House were complete, Proprietor Chiba ordered her to teach me more dances. We practised, and she talked about the Buddha. 'After we master the steps, we will wear costumes. One costume has a mask to cover your head.'

She seemed pleased at this, so I was happy.

Almost every night I dreamed of practising with my samurai or riding a horse – bundled within a strong warm arm.

In my mind I decided to become a samurai. In my spirit, I was one already.

BOOK 3

I. Omens

After the first month my tasks were fewer, because I had to learn and practise the dances and to sing songs. Otherwise I studied the samurai, regardless of the weather, but always concealed myself from them.

When the samurai gestured, I imitated them. Sometimes I pretended to be the Great Protector wielding power. More often I became the magnificent Pink Flower, who in my mind had also become a samurai, although sometimes I played at being the Sun Goddess, about whom Tashiko told stories when she bathed me:

> As Izanagi purified himself in the stream, a God or Goddess was born from each part of him. The Sun Goddess was born from his left eye. Susanowo, the Storm God, was born from Izanagi's nose. When He decided to travel to heaven, the Sun Goddess gathered her weapons, put on her masculine fearlessness, and uttered a forceful roar of resistance.

At a distance from the samurai, I gathered my weapon-sticks and roared like the Sun Goddess. I studied the samurai's daily rituals beyond the bathhouse and vegetable gardens – there, I would often eat a sweet daikon radish or whatever I could find – always hoping to see my samurai, hoping to spend a moment with someone I imagined I could trust.

The samurai held each object up to the Sun Goddess. They bowed to each other before and after each fight, and, just as I had imitated my father and brothers, I imitated them: I grunted when they grunted; I thrust my arms out as they practised with their swords; when they moved, I moved. I sent imaginary arrows. Best of all, when I was alone, no one could trick me.

They rode, and I mounted my tree-branch horse to ride too. Once I fell and scraped my leg with the sharp end of a branch. I bit my tongue, covering my mouth with my sleeve as Tashiko had showed me. When I stood up my large samurai was beside me. I bowed, hoping he would speak to me. He did not and returned to his practice.

I hungered for more contact and continued hiding behind trees or bushes, following the samurai's actions, ever seeking my samurai. I moved closer, thinking I could not be seen – I must have been: one cold morning I saw my samurai motioning for me to come nearer. I stepped away from the bush and was warmed by his friendly eyes. My lips would not stop smiling. At that moment a white pheasant flew from behind the bush across the practice field.

He saw the bird and walked over to me. My heart beat as if it were threshing grain before early rain. Would he say something? Standing up, I brushed off my new smock – bright green with black, and embroidered autumn trees – bowed low, waited and hoped. His armour was laced with silk knots, all deep blue and red.

'Hello, little one.' He bent over, his hands on his knees.

He was speaking to me.

'Did you see that bird?' He pointed towards at the pheasant. 'A lucky omen.'

I had not known this.

'You have come to observe the great raging spirit of Susanowo, the Storm God?' He tilted his face down to mine. 'We follow the Great Impetuous Deity.' He smiled and held his long sword flat in front of his thick body, with tanned, wide-fingered hands. His dark brown topknot stired in the breeze, bringing smells to me of men's sweat and grass.

'I will tell you the story I tell my children.'

'Susanowo, the great Storm God saved a couple's eighth daughter, who was to be sacrificed to an eight-headed dragon the next day. The great Storm God placed a large *sake* barrel in front of each of the dragon's sleeping heads. When the dragon awoke, each head drank the *sake* until the creature was quite drunk.'

All this he showed me, walking lopsided, wagging his head, crossing his eyes. I covered my mouth with my sleeve to laugh.

He became serious.

'Susanowo slew the dragon, cutting off each of its eight heads. When Susanowo cut open the dragon, he found the Sacred Sword in its tail.'

He lifted his beautiful sword for me to see, and grinned.

For a few moments. I thought about his story. 'If that is how the sword was discovered, what did the Storm God use to cut off the dragon's heads?' I had thought the Sacred Sword the first sword ever.

The samurai chuckled. Then he barked, his head hung over his body and his chest heaving. With every yelp of laughter I grew smaller, my temper bigger.

His head was so low I could see only his hair and the sparse brown of his eyebrows, I thought those eyebrows ugly. I wanted to shave them off. I was sorry I'd spoken with him. How could he betray me like this?

He chortled until the other samurai stopped their practise. I breathed heavily. He was not a brother I could fight. He was not a sister whose hair I could wrench.

They all listened to him laughing and, when he did not stop, they walked up to us. I looked up at my samurai, hoping he would stop. There had been nothing funny in my question. By the time all the samurai were around him, he was still chuckling, unable to talk. I wanted to run away or hit something. I wanted to hit him, yet I dared not.

The tallest samurai wore green silk sewn through his armour, which was of white silk decorated with dark and light blue chevrons. He grabbed my samurai's arm. There was a grinding noise as their shoulders scraped. I jumped. I searched their armour, wondering how it could make that sound.

'Akio, what disturbs your meditative practice?' the tallest one asked.

'She asked what the Storm God used to kill the dragon, if not a sword.'

The tall one nodded and grinned, his long black beard, with white threads, bobbing up and down.

The rest of the samurai were cackling now. It was worse than it had been at home. All these strangers were making fun of me. Akio chortled again. I stood there, helpless, tight fists and lips. I thought about jerking their topknots, pulling out their hair, kicking them in the stomach – after they had taken off their armour. I knew of nothing that could kill a dragon but a sword.

When the laughter stopped, the tall one patted my head. I wanted to bite his hand. Not a good idea. That would not make Father proud.

'What is your name?'

'Kozaishō, Master.' I bowed, rigid and small – resentments had stiffened my entire body.

'There is no need for ill temper, Kozaishō,' he whispered to me. 'We do not laugh at you. We laugh at our own assumptions.'

I did not know what that meant, and remained silent. At least he had said that they were not laughing at me. At what were they laughing?

'What do you do here, Kozaishō?' the tall one asked.

'I live in Lesser House.' I pointed.

Akio glanced at the tall one with eyes I did not understand. I bowed, and the wind blew across the field. Large clouds formed in the clear sky, taking the shape of a huge dragon.

'Akio,' Master Isamu, the tall one, shouted. All the samurai turned. 'Kozaishō has brought an omen of good fortune.'

'Master Isamu, if I may be permitted to speak?'

The older man's eyes turned to Akio.

'When I first spoke to Kozaishō today, a white pheasant came out of those trees and flew on to this field.'

If they were omens of good fortune, would I be sent home? Would Proprietor Chiba stop hitting me?

'So, Kozaishō brings two different omens of good luck.' Master Isamu announced again. He raised his voice to the gathered samurai: 'Kozaishō must be welcomed here at any time.'

After that, he spoke quietly to me: 'Come. Akio will take you to a safe place to watch us. I will ask permission for you to join us, but until then, you may observe as your . . . duties allow.'

'You can visit us, little one,' whispered Akio. I could not help but smile when I bowed to him. 'You are special, Kozaishō. As special to me as my own girls.'

Later I learned about the many swords in the world. The Sacred Sword, encrusted with jewels, was special and different from any practice sword. He told me more about Cloud Cluster – the name of the Sacred Sword found in the dragon's tail. I never understood, though, why they had laughed so much.

II. The Practice of Omens

My family had measured time by harvests and seasons. People counted time differently at Proprietor Chiba's *shōen*. There, the day was divided into animals' names. Tashiko told me the story of the hours:

Once upon a time, the Emperor of Jade declared to all of the animals that he would name only twelve for the names of the years and the hours of each day. The twelve animals who arrived before him first would protect the people for one year. All of the animals wanted to be chosen. Alas, the cat was too excited and forgot what day it was. He asked his friend the rat, but the rat saw a chance to be rid of a rival and gave the wrong day. The day before, the robust ox decided to leave early, knowing he walked slowly. The rat hopped on to the ox to take advantage of the ride. The ox thought he would be first, but before he entered the Heavenly Palace, the rat jumped off his head and arrived first, with the ox behind him. The energetic tiger, king of the animals, reached the Heavenly Palace next. Then the serene hare, the mighty dragon, the wily snake, the forceful horse, the passive sheep, the clever monkey, the orderly cockerel, the trustworthy and loyal dog and, finally the persistent pig. The next morning, the cat came to the Heavenly Palace, delighted to be first. The guard told him to go home, wake up earlier next time and wash his face. Ever since, the cat and the rat have been enemies.

Next day, I leaped out of bed at the Hour of the Snake before the new summer sun had peeped above the ground.

'Are you in a hurry?' Tashiko asked, half asleep. We now slept together on the *futon*.

'Today,' I hugged her, 'I am invited to watch the samurai. I must finish my tasks before I can go.'

Tashiko laughed, ruffling my thick hair. 'I shall hurry to dress you and comb this bird's nest.'

The samurai were already at the fields. I had never been out so early. I saw some boys, too.

The samurai and the boys performed a slow dance in pairs. I did my best to follow their slow dance, the complex yet exciting movements, as I watched from a short distance away.

The next day, there was no visit from Proprietor Chiba.

Tashiko answered the question in my eyes: 'Konjin, God of Directions, forced him to stay inside Big House today.' She smiled. That meant she planned a visit to the temple after she had completed her tasks. Today she would be pleasant. My stomach relaxed.

'Who is Konjin? What is a God of Directions?' I could ask questions when she was in this mood.

'The nobles, the fancies, study how the Gods of Directions are going to be safe.'

'Safe?'

Tashiko sighed. 'Twenty-four gods, twenty-four directions. When a direction will be harmful, a fancy cannot go that way. Once Proprietor Chiba had to travel to another *shōen*. He stayed there for a month.'

She scowled, then looked down and her eyes filled. I placed my hand on her shoulder, and she shook it off, wiped her eyes and went to the temple.

Proprietor Chiba away for a whole month – that should make her happy, I thought. It would make *me* happy.

I helped Tashiko with her tasks whenever Proprietor Chiba did not want us to sing or dance, which was seldom, Because I helped, she had time to teach me games. We played Go. It was simple, though there were a great many black and white stones. She always won, but I liked the game and did not mind.

On most days Tashiko let me soak as long as I wanted after she had scrubbed me. She wiped her tears when she dried me. I thought she was tired or overworked. She had to look after all our new clothes.

In the evening Proprietor Chiba often ordered Tashiko to paint our faces white and dress us in elaborate kimonos. I loved her soft touches on my face. She taught me more dances, which I found easier to learn than sewing.

We learned more dances with masks. I liked the Lion Dance. I wore a bright purple robe and white slippers made of thick, knitted silk. They had deerskin soles, good for dancing. The masks were attached under our chins and behind our heads with strings. Tashiko used swords with the dance, and I liked to dance with the weapons. Proprietor Chiba encouraged me and told me I had talent and called me beautiful.

Proprietor Chiba recited the story of the Chinese General Ryōō. Because beauty distracted his soldiers, he wore a mask. 'You are such a lovely girl, Kozaishō.' Proprietor Chiba stroked my hair and face. 'I am happy to be distracted by your beauty.'

Tashiko received no such loving words, which troubled me.

Several days after my first welcome to the samurai fields, Master Isamu and Akio approached me. I bowed as they had taught me. Both men's eyes crinkled in return.

'We are called to Big House.' Master Isamu lowered his face to me. 'Kozaishō, you are also called to Big House. Follow us now.'

I had to walk fast to keep up with them. Perhaps they were sending me home. No. Tashiko had made clear that no one went home. What had I done? Was I dishonoured? What would happen to my family? To my family's land? They needed that land – which I had given them. My thoughts turned dark.

Proprietor Chiba stood at the edge of Big House's *watadono*. His jaw muscles jumped out and in. His thin lips disappeared into each other. The priest with the black horse sat next to him. Master Isamu and Akio greeted them and went up the stairs to sit behind Proprietor Chiba, one on each side.

I walked up to the steps and did the full five-point bow. Face to the ground, I waited. Was Proprietor Chiba going to beat me in front of them? Tell the samurai to use me as a target? Was I about to die?

'Kozaishō, it seems . . .' Proprietor Chiba's voice trailed off.

Master Isamu gave a little cough.

'It – it seems,' Proprietor Chiba blustered, 'those two omens together, the white pheasant and the dragon cloud, are . . . too powerful to be ignored.'

Master Isamu cleared his throat.

'I have agreed that you will . . . train with the boys.'

My mouth smiled; my whole body squealed. My dream had come true. I took a deep breath, but remembered not to move.

Akio cleared his throat.

'Eh . . . Akio shall be your tutor in these matters only,' Proprietor Chiba said, sounding strained.

I heard armour creak. I did not know who had made the noise. I dared not lift my head.

'And . . . and, ah, they shall be obeyed as I am obeyed. On the field. When you train. But only then.' He folded his arms across his belly. '*Only* then.'

'Kozaishō, it is good to see you again,' I heard the priest say. 'I love to see beautiful, talented girls.'

His voice rasped like an icicle on my bare skin. He stepped towards me and touched the hair at my nape. I shivered, but forced my attention to Proprietor Chiba's words.

'You must still practise your dancing. That is your first, your most important, duty.' Proprietor Chiba's words sounded loud, like thunder.

I took two breaths before speaking. 'May I please have permission to speak, honourable Proprietor Chiba no Tashiyori?' I used my politest voice, my nose in the dirt.

'Naturally, Kozaishō,' he said, his voice tight, like an out-of-tune *biwa* string.

When I lifted my head, Proprietor Chiba had twisted his fingers into pale fat worms. 'Thank you, honourable Proprietor Chiba, for the great honour you have bestowed upon me.'

'Tell Tashiko she is to see you are ready and on the training field at the Hour of the Snake,' Proprietor Chiba snapped. 'You may leave us.'

I raced to Lesser House, my hands over my mouth – otherwise my yelps of delight might have ruined the good luck. Later, safely alone,

Tashiko and I held each other, hopping up and down, singing our songs.

Besides befriending Tashiko, I hold that moment as one of the happiest in my years at Proprietor Chiba's *shōen*.

III. First Weapons

My stomach swirled, like a stream after heavy rains. I could not fail. Not at this. I would be sent home. My family would lose their land – the land for which they had sold me. They would not have enough food. I would bind myself to samurai work with all my strength.

Akio stood before me. I thanked the Goddess of Mercy. He was truly here. This was not a dream. His eyebrows danced like dragonflies above his eyes.

'Today, little one, I demonstrate. You must not talk. Tomorrow you will shoot the arrows and show me what you have learned.'

No talking? I could do that. Perhaps. Yes. I could.

Uba, one of the boys in my group, a thin boy with wilful hair, prodded me with his elbow. I grabbed his hair and heaved. I did not speak. He stopped, for a time. I had wanted to punch him, as I had Fourth Daughter, but the punishments here hurt much more than they had at home. Home. I remembered the *shōen* was now my home. No talking. No crying, either.

Uba and the younger boys tied quivers made of lacquered plant fibres around their chests. The older boys strapped on wooden or woven bamboo quivers. Tomorrow would be my day.

To be close to arrows flying through the air! The wind from them cooled my face. I held my breath until the heaven-splitting sound pierced me each time an arrow struck a target. The targets looked like men: painted faces and bodies on leather packed with straw. The older boys' arrows struck the targets more often than my group's. Their teacher scolded them more often than Akio did us younger children. I thought that rather odd.

Akio came to me. 'Hold these for me. Only hold them.' A bow, a *tsuru*, a bowstring, and an arrow, with the feathers of the fierce wild hawk, lay in my hands.

My hands shook from the force pouring out of them. Such power held in my small hands.

Rattan bindings reinforced the bow. I touched the loose bowstring. Hemp, coated with wax to make a hard, smooth surface.

Akio had told me to hold them. Perhaps I could string his bow for him. Surprise him with my strength. I had seen many people string bows. First I placed the bottom loop, bound with white silk ribbon, on the bow. I already knew the top loop from the bottom one: red on top, white at the bottom. Like Master Isamu, I stuck the top loop's silk flap between my teeth, then grabbed for the other end of the bow with both hands. I would not have to wait until tomorrow to show Akio my learning.

I reached – high – on my toes – stretched – jumped. Again.

My hands did not reach halfway to the other end. I could not string Akio's bow. I hated being short.

'Kozaishō, I did not say anything about placing the *tsuru* on my bow.' A shadow darkened my sky. Akio.

'I humbly beg your forgiveness.' I did not bow low because my hands were full.

'If you disobey again there will be consequences.' He grew closer, like spring thunder. 'If anyone disobeys a second time, they are no longer allowed to work with us.'

He took his weapons from me.

'Yes, Master Akio.' I made a five-point bow.

'No, no, little one. Master Isamu is Master Isamu, and Proprietor Chiba is Proprietor Chiba. I am merely Akio, your tutor.'

'Yes . . . honourable Akio.'

For all that, I promised myself that some day my arrows, with hawk feathers, would stand in my shining lacquered quiver next to my fully strung bow.

Remembering Akio's directions, I returned to study the boys' archery. Closer, each movement, the little mysteries I had watched from far away, resolved themselves. They did not just grab the arrow or the string. They positioned the arrow to the right of the bow. They hooked their thumbs under the arrows, placing the first two fingers on the thumb, which I copied, pressing my lips together. Left arm straight, right hand near the right ear. They relaxed the two fingers and at the same time turned the bow until the string went outside the arm.

Unsuccessful the first few times, I copied and watched, watched and copied, imagining how amazed Akio would be after he had given me my bow and I could shoot well.

Mid-morning, the Hour of the Dragon, servants came on to the field with water, rice and pickled vegetables. The boys stopped archery and took practice swords made of oak, *bokken*, from the selection laid out. They worked in pairs.

I was not allowed to string the smallest bow. I began with a rubber practice bow, a *gomuyumi*, and practised the eight movements of *hassetsu*: footing, correct posture, readying the bow, raising the bow, drawing the bow, completing the draw, release and continuation. Each movement had to be perfected, as with dancing. So, repetition and more drills.

In the time that followed, Akio could not find a *bokken* for me. A standard one was too long. When I held a child's *bokken* I could barely look down at the top. I hated being short. I lifted the weapon and needed both hands. The follow-through of every stroke threw me off balance, causing me to stumble and fall, usually on my partner. When I noticed this, I chose Uba. On my second attempt, he noticed it, too, and kicked me. I kicked him back, as I had fought my brothers. The only difference was that my sisters were not there to cheer me on.

'Kozaishō! Uba!' Akio bellowed. A big hand grabbed my shoulder. 'Stop!' He gave me a glance that reminded me of father, a testy, troubled look, which meant that if I kicked Uba again, I would be punished.

At least Akio had his other hand on Uba.

'Kozaishō, stand over there. Uba, stay here.' His eyebrows gathered together in the middle. 'Remember, Benevolence is part of the Way.'

The Way? What was that? It was not a good time to ask a question.

Akio went to the bushes and brought back a thick branch, nearly the length of my leg. I wanted to run. The branch appeared many times the thickness of Proprietor Chiba's switch, and his switch hurt enough. None of Tashiko's ointment would work on my wounds after Akio had hit me with the branch.

I moved a little away from him, a coil tightening inside me. Perhaps he would behave like Proprietor Chiba. He had seemed kind, but so had Proprietor Chiba at first. I might not be able to keep quiet, struck with that.

'Use this, Kozaishō, for sword work until we can find a properly sized *bokken* for you. Here!' Akio tossed the branch to me.

With the weight of the branch and the loosening of my insides, I slipped but, able to breathe again, I promised myself I would not fight Uba or anyone else. The branch Akio had found for me worked better anyway.

'Stick-girl! Stick-girl!' Uba shouted, almost every day that first month. He made sure he kept himself out of my reach. I ignored him. My brothers had called me names.

After the fight, Akio supervised us precisely, just as my father had the new green shoots after a long winter.

'Watch your right leg,' Akio warned.

'Straighten your arm.'

'Bend your leg.'

Over and over.

Uba whined, 'I am tired. How much more must we do? When can we have a break?'

'Well, I have the strength to go on. Will anyone challenge me?' I answered.

I was warmed by Uba's lack of grit and hid a smile. I enjoyed the samurai drills. I did not tire of them. I loved becoming the Pink Flower samurai.

To leave the practice fields meant working on the dances, dressed like a doll and ready to be beaten.

An older boy, who was tall like my oldest brother and had strung my bow, had heard me. 'I will. Begin.'

His group and mine made a circle around us.

I took my stick against his *bokken*.

Two strokes.

In two strokes he had me flat on the ground.

Uba cackled, and the other boys hooted. I promised myself I would work harder.

About a month after I had joined the lessons Akio called us younger ones into a circle. 'Kozaishō has been with us for a short time,' he explained, 'and she has learned well and fast.'

I raised my eyes to his for more praise. He made a familiar movement with one eyebrow, meaning 'no'.

'She has much to learn, but she will continue with this.' His eyebrows soared to his topknot as he displayed a bright blue square cloth, its four corners tied together, a *furoshiki*. He laid it on the ground on another cloth and untied it. Inside lay a *bokken*, made of oak like the other boys', yet thinner and shorter. He presented it to me. It was a perfect fit for my hands. The handle bore a carefully carved tree with full summer leaves.

'I am deeply honoured, Akio.' I bowed. The boys bowed with me. The *bokken*, my *bokken*, was spectacular.

I prayed to all the Gods, walking to Lesser House, that Tashiko would not be jealous again. I had allowed her to be Eldest Daughter. She had not given me the wrong tasks or dance instructions for a month or more – and I had no one else with whom to share my happiness. I decided to trust her.

I laid the *furoshiki* on the *futon* inside Lesser House. I loosened the corner knots, lifted the *bokken* and presented it on my palms to Tashiko. 'Akio had it made for me.'

'A tree in the handle.' Tashiko did not even turn her head.

'You knew? How?'

'Leave it here. I must bathe you.' Tashiko walked to the bathhouse. Her face was blank, but I noticed her eyes had crinkled at the corners.

When she undressed and scrubbed me, I persisted: 'How did you know?'

Her eyebrows and the corners of her mouth travelled upwards. 'Akio asked me what you might like, so I told him trees and rabbits.' Her voice held the rhythm of play.

'You did not tell me. You knew all the time.' My eyes lit up, at her thoughtfulness and that she had kept a secret from me. Then I wondered. I had thought Akio's friendship belonged to me. I did not wish to share him. Could he be friendly to both of us, like Second Daughter with me and Fourth Daughter?

'Akio could carve only the tree in such a short time. Perhaps,' Tashiko rubbed my shoulders and neck more gently, 'perhaps rabbits later.'

I stood up and hugged her. 'Thank you for not being angry about my present.'

'No jealousy. No wish to fight.'

'Thank you for sharing my happiness.' I hugged her.

She embraced me until she was drenched. 'Come!' she cried, undressing herself. I washed her and we sat together in the soaking tub. I chattered about my day and my new *bokken*. Afterwards Tashiko dried me, and I saw the tears I saw every evening when I bathed.

'Why do you cry? Are you not happy for me?' The *bokken* had never belonged to anyone else. It had been made for me, only me. It had given me the courage to ask the question.

'Some day you will know the reason for my tears. Not today. Today is . . . the day of the *bokken*!'

She flicked the drying cloth at me, and we pretended to fight until we were dry. We imitated *bokken* with our chopsticks during the evening meal. That night I whispered *'Bokken'*, to her before we slept in each other's arms.

I dreamed of the Sacred Sword in the dragon's tail.

> New wooden *bokken*
> Thick smooth oak-carved trees and leaves
> Skyward like mountains
> One friend and samurai's gift
> Which will prove more important?

IV. Third Month
Third Day Dancing

The musician huddled inside a quilt and strummed his *biwa* outside Lesser House. I practised dances on the *watadono* for the coming festival, regardless of the cold. Tashiko held Proprietor Chiba's switch and tapped my leg for each misstep.

'Perfect,' she told me again. 'Only two more days until the fancies arrive.'

I could not feel my feet while I was dancing unless I trod heavily on the wooden floor. A tap with the switch. Collapsing the fan too early: another tap. My fingers, numb and graceless, allowed my fan to slip on to the floor. A third tap.

What terrible punishment would befall me if I made a mistake? Would they both beat me, Proprietor Chiba and Tashiko? She spoke in quiet tones, especially when she was using the switch. Our friendship was new, and she knew my temper.

'Here.' She rubbed her palms together. 'Rub your hands together, fast, between each dance.' I copied her. She went into Lesser House and came out with some cloth. 'Take off your *tabi*. These pads go inside them so your feet will not touch cold floor.'

After this, Tashiko did not use the switch as much. Perhaps I could trust her.

The next two days disappeared with counting, clapping and fan gestures. The day before our performance, Proprietor Chiba sent a woman servant to rub our teeth with a thick black mixture. It tasted like dung to me and smelt like bad vinegar. Tashiko and I rinsed our mouths, over and over again. Our teeth turned dark.

On the actual day the woman covered our faces and necks with white rice paste, our brows and eyelids with charcoal, and applied a sticky red mash to our lips. I wore no expression and dared not talk for fear of smearing it.

Different kinds of flowers embellished the new red fans. I replayed the gestures with them to ensure they moved smoothly and comfortably in my hands, as the grinding stone had during last harvest. My mind flashed missteps, fans flying out of hands, thrashings. I asked Tashiko what would happen if I made mistakes with everyone watching.

'We will be perfect. Chanted *sutras*. Lit incense. The Goddess of Mercy and other gods will allow us to be perfect.' She clasped my shoulders and looked down at me. 'Remember to breathe. Remember to count.'

'Breathe and count. I can do that.' Breathe and count, I repeated to myself. 'We will be outstanding,' I said, to reassure myself.

Tashiko and I took great care to protect our silk costumes, which showed the spring colours: cherry and peach blossom, wisteria blue and violet, cucumber, pine needle and deep forest green. The woman servant had combed and oiled our hair, tying it at the nape of our necks with ribbons. I gazed at Tashiko, who looked like a doll.

She and I stepped with great care to the lake where the fancies waited. A puff of air cooled my neck, a treat, since our thick clothing was stifling and I usually wore my hair hanging loose. The music for our dances was playing. As I walked, I chanted to myself, 'Breathe and count. Breathe and count.'

I looked out for the gate, which shut me in with my new luxuries and shut me out from my sisters and brothers, my father, my mother. My legs tensed. I could walk out, go home. Yes – and walk to disgrace and shame, to the horror of my entire family, my grandparents and other ancestors. Not today. 'Breathe and count. Breathe and count,' I sang inside my head.

Crossing to the island, I saw a crowd of men, thirty or more, dressed in brocade like Proprietor Chiba's. Most wore the same curious round hat, made of lacquered and stiffened silk with two thin cloth strips flapping in the light wind.

Later Tashiko named the hats *kanmuri*. Although most were black, a few showed stronger colours – dark and pale violet, dark and pale green, dark and pale brownish-red, like azuki beans. The coloured hats sat in the front row. Dark Violet Hat sat higher than all the others, then Pale Violet, then the Greens and finally the Azuki Beans.

'The higher hats are the most important,' Tashiko whispered. She snatched my hand when she saw Goro. His mouth was set in a simpering smile. His eyes were directed only to those not-Black Hats. I hoped he would not stare at me, as he always did when he visited.

The musician's eyes nodded at us, the only friendly ones. I allowed mine to smile, just a little, in return. Two more unknown men stood next to our *biwa* player. They had to be drummers because they waited with long mallets behind covered cauldrons that were half the size of the one in the bathhouse. I looked at Tashiko, and she pressed my hand. Breathe and count. She and I would be perfect.

I assumed the beginning pose. Music started with the drums. My counting and breathing improved with the drum beats. I thought only of breathing, counting and the movements.

With each stamp my tied hair bumped my back. I focused – breathe and count. My fan slipped into my belt and opened in the right direction on the correct beat. Tashiko and I moved at the same time, on the same pulses. Her fan and mine opened and shut with their familiar *whish*. My opposing steps reversed Tashiko's on the same beats. After days and endless days of practice, the dance seemed over in a lightning flash. When I finished I heard a bush warbler cry overhead and remembered my father.

With my head tilted to the side, I glanced at Tashiko to see how I had performed. Her eyes met mine. I imitated Tashiko and bowed to the applause. I had given a near-perfect performance.

When Dark Violet Hat cheered, my chest lightened. My father and mother would have honour. All the other hats and Goro imitated Dark Violet Hat, shouting for us. I did not dare look at Tashiko.

Dark Violet Hat pulled a paper doll out of his sleeve, opened his arms and, with loud noises, breathed in and puffed on the doll. He threw it into the stream. A gentle wind brushed the water and the doll sank. I glanced at Tashiko. The corners of her mouth twitched. She had seen this before but had not told me about it.

Each Hat, in order of colour – dark and light violet, dark and pale green, dark and pale azuki bean, all the black hats – then Goro and last Proprietor Chiba did the same with their paper dolls. Some sank immediately, and some bobbed along in the rippling water, like ducklings after a phantom mother.

My mother. Two months since I had seen her. I pushed thoughts of my family far away. With no idea of what would happen next, I needed to keep my thoughts directed.

The Hats formed a line along the stream, starting with Dark Violet Hat, Goro and Chiba. Tashiko led me forward, between the stream and the Hats. With her arm wrapped around mine, I strolled by each Hat. Tashiko's body did not tremble. Perhaps they would not beat or hit us.

Tashiko stopped at Dark Violet Hat, who took a breath and exhaled – on her – and then on me. His breath reeked.

I waited.

Nothing else.

Tashiko squeezed my arm. Perhaps there would be no punishment. She pulled me on to the next Hat. Was this the culmination of the entire festival, being puffed with their breath?

I had to work to keep my expression neutral and not cough, despite the mouth-stench mixed with their heavy perfumes. The smells made my stomach clench. I imitated Tashiko and maintained my posture. I wanted to hold my nose.

When we arrived at Goro, Tashiko shuddered. His hand stroked her face, and he panted in and out on her. He did the same with me. His hand was cool and smooth, like snake skin. How fitting, since this was the First Day of the Snake in this Third Month.

Last . . . Chiba. I stood still and faced him. I glanced, but he did not have the switch. He made blustery sounds and wheezed. He put one hand on my chest and the other on Tashiko's. I turned my head to Tashiko.

He pushed me!

Tashiko and I plopped backwards into the shallow stream. The cool water shocked me. My costume was wet! Ruined?

All the men whooped again.

No one was upset.

Tashiko inspected me, opened her mouth and howled in glee. Her hair had changed to long wet grass, decorating her clothes and especially her face. Charcoal streaked black from her forehead and eyes through the dripping white rice paste. The red on her mouth smudged her chin and dribbled off. The more she hooted, the faster the streaking and dripping, smudging and dribbling.

She shrieked. I laughed. She and I sat in the stream, gazing at each other melting – giggling, chortling and chuckling. I had hardly ever seen her laugh.

That night after I had bathed, she and I each ate a big bowl of white rice with fish slices on top. The meal included special flattened square rice cakes, coloured red on top, white in the middle and green on the bottom.

'Once a year, *hishi-mochi*,' Tashiko explained. 'Red chases away evil spirits. White for purity and green for health.'

Tashiko ate the red first, next the white and last the green. I did the same. Delicious. I also munched *sakura-mochi*. When I asked, she showed me that the inside was filled with bean paste and wrapped with cherry leaves.

I feasted and chatted with Tashiko, listening to Proprietor Chiba and the Hats celebrating with their banquet by the stream.

When Proprietor Chiba came the following morning, he brought gifts: for me, a doll dressed in the beautiful colours of our kimonos, and for Tashiko, a section of the Lotus Sutra, her favourite, silver and gold squiggles on dark blue paper. Tashiko told me the squiggles were words. I asked her to teach me to read.

She began my reading lessons the next day, the beginning of that first spring. To my other questions she said, 'The dolls protect them from sorrows. By blowing on the dolls or on us, the fancies think they rid themselves of their their sins, their bad luck. When they throw the dolls or us,' she giggled, 'into running water, the water carries away their impurities.'

That night Tashiko and I cuddled and chuckled ourselves to sleep. She whispered to me, 'Chiba's *shōen* is the only one with living dolls.'

'I suppose Goro and Chiba have not yet earned their Hats.'

Tashiko giggled again. A beautiful sound.

V. Six More Weapons

For a long time my job was to maintain the equipment. Then Akio made me practise with the glove and the arrow. With them, I practised readying the bow, then the draw and the release. We beginners used a *makiwara*, a straw target, which I shot at from a distance that was just the length of my bow. I held my bow flat from my centre. I could always hit the target. Akio said this would help me concentrate on what I was doing, rather than hitting the *makiwara*.

I excelled with archery after Akio ordered that a special bow be made for me, shorter than the boys', which I could string for myself, when he said I was ready, with only a little help. The lacquered bow displayed my favourite trees and rabbits. I named it Rabbit-In-A-Tree. My fingers fitted around its grips. My arm's armour shone bright red and blue, like Akio's.

As I drilled, I heard Pink Flower challenge samurai to duel. My armour fitted close to my forearms with a two-fingered leather glove to protect my hand. The tanned leather had the distinct odour that pleased me. I did not tell Tashiko about the glove because she considered all death and leather sinful. She avoided the leather-processing areas in the village.

I challenged Uba and other boys in my group to best me in archery. I always lost before I was given Rabbit-In-A-Tree. Afterwards, I beat Uba, most of the boys in my group and many of the older ones. *If I did not mention Uba's name, Tashiko and I celebrated my victories and honour to my family.*

★ ★ ★

I began to beg for a horse, but months passed before Akio and Master Isamu finally gave in. My two samurai argued about how to teach me to ride. Finally, Akio tied me to an old mare. She bore no resemblance to the black demon the priest had ridden the day I had come to the *shōen*.

After only one season, I could stay on the horse for myself. What days they were – to ride high up and see the ground like a bird. From time to time, I wished I could fly to my real home.

Late in my second summer at the *shōen*, I sat on my own lacquered wooden saddle, with mother-of-pearl in the shapes of trees and rabbits, another gift from Akio and Master Isamu. I handled horses mostly without using my hands, guiding them with my legs.

I rode all over the *shōen*, not only around the fields but also around the lake and the ponds and through small streams – too fast for summer mosquitoes. I was careful to avoid the buckwheat fields. Proprietor Chiba loved buckwheat noodles so he would take the switch to anyone who spoiled the buckwheat. Now I thought seldom of escape.

Akio allowed us to hold a *tachi*, a real sword: grasping the handle, its brown bumpy ray-skin and braided leather strips. My finger traced the *tsuba*, the iron sword guard with its Taira Clan closed-butterfly design. I squinted at the shining steel blade, blinding me in the brilliant summer sky.

The *tachi* reminded me of farm tools I had used with Father and my brothers, familiar, comfortable. That brought on homesickness, which pierced me to my spine, like an arrow, grabbed at my throat and caused my chin to quiver. I turned away from the boys. One teasing word might have caused me to spill tears where I could be seen. I would not dishonour myself like that. Uba came after me, but I ran away.

Months after I had begun the *bokken* training a boy a bit heavier than me lay flat on the ground. I had my first victory! I clutched my weapon above my head, breathing hard, smiling, successful.

'Kozaishō! I am next.' I looked up at Uba, who was now taller than me: he had grown a quarter of a *shaku* in the last two months. The boy who had lost to me called everyone around us to watch. Uba took me in three strokes. Only three! On the ground, I heard laughing and whistling.

I stood up, my left hand clenched into a fist, jaw clamped, and scowled at Uba. I heard Akio ask if I wanted some water. I growled at him. He gathered the hair at the top of my head in one fist and led me off the field to the water jars. I drank and listened. 'I have something to teach you when the others have finished. You can use your size to an advantage.'

'How can *my* size be an advantage?' Akio had made himself absurd in my eyes. He knew I hated people to laugh at me. I wanted to return and destroy Uba.

'First you must control your emotions, if you are to be a samurai.'

I had become angry with someone else or myself – again. I took several deep breaths and let them out slowly, as he had taught me. 'Yes, honourable Teacher.'

'Use the energy of anger for your weapons.'

This interested me. 'Honourable Teacher, how can I do that?'

'I will show you after the others have left. For now, let me show you and the others the weaker places between the feet and the waist.'

We rejoined the group.

'Even if armoured, your opponent will still have weak areas.' Akio took his *bokken*, then pointed to and named the parts: ankles, wrists, back of knees, kneecaps, kidneys and, of course, phallus and testes. 'Remember, fingers are not good targets. I have fought and won with broken fingers.'

Fighting with broken fingers. I could not imagine it.

That evening he showed me how he used anger. First he smiled at me and lifted his hands and shoulders. 'See? I am relaxed and peaceful.' He threw a spear. It landed straight in the target.

Next he turned to me, gnashed his teeth, made an animal sound and brought his eyebrows between his eyes. 'I . . . am . . . angry.' He threw another spear. It landed in the target, ripping it and continuing through it. 'I was still angry, but I took that power and put that force into my arm.'

He made me do that.

I pretended that the target bore Uba's face.

My problem with anger was resolved. Almost.

Sword work frustrated me. Akio and I practised each of the weak body parts. He wore extra-heavy armour on all those places. 'Do not laugh at me. I know I look a little – odd.'

'You remind me of Proprietor Chiba.' I could barely say the words.

He looked down at his triple padded stomach, legs, feet and groin. 'Am I that big?'

'Almost.'

He guffawed.

He and I exchanged blows daily, month after month, until he saw I could at least hold my own within my group.

After that, I surprised a few of the older boys too.

My family – I could hardly remember their faces. I tried to find them in my mind. Often I could not. I awakened from dreams crying, throat tight, hands in fists pounding the *futon*. Tashiko held me until I stopped weeping. 'Yes.' She rubbed my head like Fourth Daughter had. 'Yes, I know. I know.'

Autumn came again, and a few samurai returned from a pilgrimage to the Takao temple, famous for its red maple trees. Each evening I listened to their poetry and clapped. The armoured men had taught me about poetry. I understood the verses and read many of them, yet I could not write the characters properly, no matter how I tried.

Master Isamu played the *biwa* while the samurai recited. In the brisk autumn breezes words fluttered like butterflies drifting across my eyes:

> Red carp in the pond
> Slowly hidden by red leaves
> Fish search the waters
> The maple tree sheds its leaves
> Bent branches over red pond

Master Isamu played and wept. Several others cried too. They held their long sleeves to their eyes and blotted them from time to time.

'Why are you crying?' I asked, because I had never seen these men cry.

'For the beauty,' Master Isamu answered. 'Yet there is another reason. While the Gods were being born, so long ago, She-Who-Invites, one of the first Goddesses, gave birth to the God of Fire. Unfortunately, She-Who-Invites was burned greatly. She receded slowly and became no more. He-Who-Invites mourned Her with outrage. He wailed, and his tears created the God who lives at the foot of Mount Fragrant's slopes. That is why it is good, especially for samurai, to shed tears in emulation of the Gods.'

I thought about this. It was good for samurai to cry at beauty, but not at pain.

The crying at beauty but not at pain confused me. However, Akio spoke to me often of the Eightfold Noble Path: right view, thinking, mindfulness, speech, action, diligence, concentration and livelihood. He emphasised Right Action to me. Master Isamu taught us more about the Way: loyalty, justice, courage, politeness, truthfulness, honour and benevolence. Loyalty was the most important. Benevolence meant I could not kick, hit or grab at any of the boys, no matter how much they teased me, especially Uba.

Tashiko did not like Uba. I could not talk about him without her sulking for the rest of the day. I found that confusing too.

Once Proprietor Chiba came to the fields himself, which was unusual, with a smile on his face, also unusual. He only smiled if he wanted something, was eating, or when he thrashed me and Tashiko. Master Isamu reminded me, in the middle of an archery lesson, 'The bow teaches the archer.' I remembered this, because Proprietor Chiba laughed and talked with Master Isamu.

'The Tax Collector has just left. I told him that because we are of the Taira Clan, we need not pay any tax at this time. But I encouraged him to watch my samurai practise.' Proprietor Chiba laughed loudly, his hands on his hips. 'With you we have no need to pay, have we? No need to travel to Heian-kyō, heh? No need to protest at the Grand Council?'

Master Isamu smiled at Proprietor Chiba.

'There are many advantages to having warriors around me.' Proprietor Chiba gave a wide smile, then laughed again. I did not recall ever seeing him so happy, except at Tashiko's shrieks.

I did not realise until years later that I had witnessed his downfall.

BOOK 4

I. Flaw

Tashiko hunched over me in Lesser House, as breathless as if she had just finished the Lion Dance, and arranged her irritated face into a neutral expression. 'Again. I show. You copy.'

This time would be successful. I studied and held my breath. I thought of needlecraft and that last day with my family. Fourth Daughter had demonstrated for me many times, but I could never make my stitches look like hers.

But I would not fail at this: I needed to write the poems I composed. The samurai expected it of me, and Proprietor Chiba had ordered me to learn, with threats of the usual punishments.

Tashiko leaned over my shoulder, making the character. 'See?' she said. 'Now you.'

I took the brush. Dipped it in ink. Wiped the brush and checked the moisture. Ready.

Silent prayer to the Goddess of Mercy, to the God of the Brush, if there was one. Akio had told me that samurai were skilful poets and musicians, as well as expert fighters.

Tashiko adjusted my fingers around the brush and pushed my wrist into position.

'Down, up and out,' she murmured, for the fifteenth or fiftieth time.
Down.
Up.
Out.

A mess. Almost a whole month on one character, and it looked as if a bird had written it with one claw.

Red in the face, Tashiko blew moist strands of hair from her eyes. 'I do not believe it!' She stood up and tramped away. 'I taught three other girls. You are the worst!'

'Three? Did they all do well?'

'Yes. All. Are you not even trying?'

'I am! I am!' I put my hands over my face. A diversion might help. 'How long have you been here with Proprietor Chiba?'

'Five years.'

'A long time. Were you alone?'

'No. Two others.'

This was not about writing, and her face was returning to its normal nut brown. 'You all danced?'

She nodded, with that sad shake of her shoulders. 'Sold, too. All were.'

'How old were you when you were sold?' I asked.

'Five.'

'I'm sure you know I was over six. My family has new land because of me.' I sat up straighter.

Tashiko's lips formed a weak smile. 'A new ox. My family can plough fields faster . . . and by now the ox has bred enough for my older sister's dowry.'

'How many older sisters?'

'Five. The two eldest are married. Two went to convent, but the convent would not take another without dowry.'

'Why not?'

'Too greedy?'

'How did you get here?'

'Prettiest one when the priest visited.'

That priest again. So, he finds girls. 'Daigoro no Goro?'

Nodding, Tashiko wrapped her arms around herself, although it was near midsummer and hot.

'Any brothers?' I asked.

'Five.'

'Only four, although since I have been here more than two years there may be another more. I think my mother was with child when I . . . left.

76

She said she did not show until her last month. My married sisters are, were, the same way when I last saw them.' I moved the brush in my hand. A mistake.

'Kozaishō, others have learned.' She sighed, looking at my hand. 'You do not seem to be able to write. You read well. Let us concentrate on the reading.'

I agreed, only too happy to give up the gruelling work.

From that day, Lesser House had name characters pasted on the table, the floor, the wall, the *futon*, the brazier and everything else. Akio and Master Isamu gave me words on pieces of paper. Tashiko attached them to the object they named, if possible.

Much later, I regretted that she had stopped teaching me.

II. Succession

Lesser House had been my home for more than two years. Proprietor Chiba still beat us, no longer for our performances but when his feet hurt or he had not slept well. The priest, Goro, visited often and followed me throughout the morning or during the Hours of the Sheep or Monkey. His visits brought reminders of my last day with my family. Were they doing well with my gift, the land? When I thought of them, my stomach churned and my voice cracked. The island in the pond supplied me with a shelter from others to mourn.

My riding improved. Even with my bow and the *naginata*, a spear with a curved blade at the end, I sometimes matched the boys in my age group. Uba and I competed in everything. I mastered move-in-towards-an-opponent and slide-out-of-range. I rehearsed the readiness stances with my *bokken* and worked on the introductory movements. Not perfection, but Akio gave me his 'satisfaction' grimace. An achievement.

One winter morning I woke up alone. There was no Tashiko, no fire, little water in my jug and no clothes laid out for me. I shivered in my *futon* and waited. She did not come. Looking around Lesser House, I saw her clothes were gone and so were her dolls. Tashiko had discarded me, I thought. I had been abandoned once more. I liked Tashiko so much – she was the nearest to my family I had had since my sale. Loneliness choked me. Tashiko said the Lotus Sutra could remove sadness and darkness. I sang some aloud, but still missed her. Allowing myself the luxury of tears, I hugged my favourite doll and curled into the quilt against the icy air.

Abandoned again
Inner winter icicles
Dripping through my eyes
Wild ducks call among the reeds
Their cry so sad I cannot move

After a time, I put down my doll and folded the *futon*. Saying more of the Lotus Sutra, I dressed myself in my warmest clothes and a quilted jacket. I did my and Tashiko's tasks, swept Lesser House's floor and brought in wood for the brazier. I carried buckets to the well.

Proprietor Chiba arrived, wearing his toothy grin. I wrestled with the water, which was difficult since it was frozen on top. 'Good.' He slapped the top of my head. 'You are already doing her tasks. Tashiko has gone.'

'Why?' I asked formally, my eyes lowered. 'She attended to me well. She lit the fire, arranged our clothes and cleaned Lesser House.'

Proprietor Chiba's eyes were distant. 'It is my business. I have sent her away. It has nothing to do with you. I order you never to speak of this, or her, again. To anyone.'

With Tashiko gone, my life at Proprietor Chiba's was transformed into emptiness. I did my utmost to manage. With all her tasks and mine, I hoped I would have less time to miss her. The extra household tasks did not help, but my work with the samurai distracted me a little.

Proprietor Chiba no longer brought me dolls or presents. Only after I had danced and sung for as long as he wanted could I beg for a story. I craved a tale to transport me to a fantasy world.

One evening he said, 'A new girl is coming. I want you to take care of her, as Tashiko did you.' She was to share Lesser House with me. I had to wash and groom her, teach her the dances and makeup.

Chills shook my body so hard I almost tumbled on to the floor. Suddenly I knew why Tashiko had had tears on her face as she had dried me at night. At that instant I wanted never to dance for Proprietor Chiba again. He had used Tashiko. He had used me. He was using me.

What had Tashiko done to displease him? Eventually I might be sent away – to wherever girls who offended him were sent. Later, however, on reflection, I realised I might see Tashiko again. That was the only spark in a large heap of damp firewood.

That evening, a bewildered little girl arrived. She was perhaps no more than five or six, younger than I was when I had come. She brought with her my same round face. A lifetime for me had been only a little more than two years.

I knew her fear, loneliness and loss, a budding flower plucked before the sun had warmed and opened it naturally. Yet I taught my replacement everything I had learned.

I did it for my family's honour. I remained hopeful that I might not be sent away, although Goro visited the *shōen* more often. His visits put a cold stone into my stomach, especially when he gazed at me dancing. The only word he said was 'Beautiful. Beautiful.'

A giggling girl, Emi must have been born during a famine because it took her days to learn a simple dance I had mastered in less than one. Songs required even more time, but she had a laugh that spread to others and a silvery singing voice.

I remembered how my skin had reddened in my first days and scrubbed Emi with care in the bathhouse. I wept while I was washing her, remembering Tashiko and her tears. Unlike Tashiko, I was always patient and gentle, as she had been after our truce. Emi relished dressing up and makeup, as I did, and we shared some happy moments.

With no possibility of her learning the Lotus Sutra, I taught Emi to say, '*Namu Amida Butsu*, honour to the Amida Buddha.' She would need it for her salvation. Eventually she would be alone and have to do everything for herself. She had a good heart, always tried her best and was aware of her slowness.

How sad.

III. The Gods of Directions' Directive

In my third autumn at the *shōen*, the Gods of Directions ordered Proprietor Chiba to stay away for two days. He left orders for me to teach Emi another dance for the Chrysanthemum Festival. Memories of Tashiko pressed on me, especially in Lesser House at night, and I often played the *biwa* out on our *watadono*.

In her free time Emi always bounded into the gardens, especially at harvest time when she could nibble all she wanted. I made a timetable for myself of our household tasks, dance rehearsals, the practice field – and then a visit to the lake. The geese, cranes and shrikes arrived with the dragonflies and charmed me.

After midday on the second day I heard steps behind me at the lake. The flowering bush clover's fragrance was so strong that it reminded me of Tashiko's scent. I almost thought it was she.

I turned, and found Goro, brushing at his garments. He was still dressed in the monastery robes and still as spare as ever. His black eyes contrasted with his pale skin and the colours of the clouded sky.

'Ah, I have found you.'

I bowed, my stomach clamped.

'How long has it been? Two years? Three?'

'Honourable Daigoro no Goro, it has been less than one month since we had the honour of your visit.' He stared at me on each of his visits, rubbing his fingertips, playing with that thin moustache, whether I was dancing or not. If he did not come for a hundred years, it would be another thousand before I wanted to see him.

'Little flower, I meant how long have you been here with Proprietor Chiba?'

He waved his hand, as Proprietor Chiba always did. I shuddered, as though a sharp winter wind had struck my face.

'I have had the privilege of being with Proprietor Chiba for more than three years.'

'Come closer, little flower. Let me see how you have bloomed.'

He chuckled at his wit. I moved only one step nearer.

'Ah, you have grown more beautiful.' He opened his arms wide, palms up. 'Since the day I first saw you, I have protected you. I have kept Chiba from you. He has not damaged you, has he?' Goro leaned forward, forcing his sour breath on me.

This was an opportunity, and I retreated a step. What was he talking about? I shook my head. 'Thank you, honourable Daigoro no Goro.' Another step back. 'Thank you for your kindness in asking.' One more step.

'Oh, no, little flower.' His fingers caught my chin. He held it and stroked my cheek with his other hand. His touch caused my skin to itch, as if ants were crawling over me. He brought his hand down my neck to my shoulder, where it stayed. 'It is my pleasure to see you, always.'

Agitation made it difficult for me to remain calm, but I did as I had learned. I tried to step back. 'Please excuse me. I have tasks to do.'

'Oh? What tasks? Dancing? With fans?' He pinched my shoulder, then loosened his grip and petted it, as if I were a cat.

I did not think it was the dances he wanted to see. My tongue said the first thing that came to it: 'I am required to clean Lesser House. It was Tashiko's task.'

The priest smirked and pulled aside, allowing me to pass. 'I shall accompany you.'

He had never praised me while Chiba was watching. I was alarmed. Looking at Lesser House, I kept my pace slow, praying to the Goddess of Mercy, hoping to see the musician or one of the samurai, especially Akio.

I parted the *shōji* of Lesser House. 'Thank you for accompanying me. How kind of you.'

With one hand he opened the rest of the *shōji*, and with the other he shoved me inside. I remained on my feet, frightened by the push.

He stood, his hands on his hips, feet apart. 'I am the priest for this *shōen*. Help me with one of my tasks.'

What could it be? How had I irritated him? From his tone, I seemed to be in serious trouble.

He rubbed his fingertips together and stroked his moustache faster. His eyes glinted as he licked his lips. 'The one with which Tashiko helped me, when the proprietor withdrew from the *shōen*. I want you to dance for me. With fans. With *two* fans.' He stared with that hungry look.

'Tashiko never told me she did tasks for you. Or dance.' His look made my tongue heavy in my mouth. I strode back from him to the *futon*. Akio spoke of the Eightfold Noble Path, but this did not feel like a Right Action. I wondered, though, if I was supposed to obey Daigoro no Goro.

'This task is more of a duty.' He pulled a whip from his belt. 'A duty, a privilege, that is now yours.'

'Honourable Daigoro no Goro, I must first finish my task here.' I worked to slow my breathing. Being beaten with that whip would be worse than the switch. Much.

I wished the *shoji* screens were all around so he could be seen. The priest closed the one screen and hung his kimono on the hanging tree where I placed my precious clothes. I was trapped. Could I tear open the silk window? No. I had no sword. Behind the priest's head was the calligraphy of the word 'love' and that was what he said to me but I didn't believe him. We were alone and no one could see us. Too far away for a scream to carry. A place of wealth and luxury would see my death – or worse, I thought, catching his wintry stare. No sword? But my *bokken* was behind the *futon*.

He laughed at me. I hated his laugh and I hated him. I paced backwards into the *futon*. Fixing my eyes on his, I reached behind me. My fingertips touched my *bokken*.

'Are your fans behind the *futon*?' He thrust himself towards me, fingers splayed. 'I have waited for this.'

'For what, honourable one?'

'For my diversion. With two fans. Dance for me. If you blunder, you will find that the proprietor is an amateur at . . . discipline, compared to me.' He grinned.

What was this priest saying? With that whip he could flay my back open.

'Have I offended you, honourable one?'

If he talked, perhaps someone would come. I had to run. I held both hands behind my back, one hand holding my *bokken*.

'When Proprietor Chiba is away, he allows me to pleasure myself with you dancing girls.'

'Pleasure?'

He cackled. 'Yes. Dance with the fans.'

Leaning against the table, he whistled a song from a dance, stroking the whip's handle with his long fingers as if he were stroking a baby's back.

He stood erect. 'I will wait no longer.'

'Honourable Daigoro no Goro, please allow me to retrieve my fans.' I reached behind the *futon*, left my *bokken* where I could easily grasp it and unwrapped the fans, keeping my eyes on him.

Taking only one fan, I began to dance and sing with great care.

He kept whistling. I glanced at him and saw him studying my feet.

I missed a step.

He straightened. His fingers twitched on the handle of the whip. 'I am a generous man. I will forgive you that one mistake.'

I bowed and thanked him, growing angry at his arrogance and wondering how to escape.

'I want the Butterfly Dance. Now. Use both fans.' He pounded the whip slowly on his thigh.

That sound trickled, like a melting icicle, over my skin.

I stepped backwards. Instead of reaching for another fan, I grasped the handle of my *bokken* and pulled it out.

'Ah. The proprietor mentioned you played with the samurai. Put that down and bring out the second fan. Use both. Start the dance.' He leaned back and whistled again.

I did not retrieve the other fan. I did not put down my *bokken*.

He stopped whistling. 'What is this? Disobey and the penalties will be . . . harsh.' His eyes glowed cruelly as he tapped the whip on the palm of his other hand.

Loyalty was the first quality of the Way. 'I belong to Proprietor Chiba, not to you.' I assumed a defensive stance, *bokken* ready.

'He is not here. I, the priest,' he said, spreading his shallow chest, 'the priest of this *shōen*, order you to submit to me.' He lifted the whip and came for me.

What should I do? Perhaps he was right. Perhaps I should yield. What would be honourable? Had I already dishonoured my family?

No! I could not let this man touch me. Danger oozed from him, like the stench of rotten incense. 'Keep your distance. I obey Proprietor Chiba, not you.'

'Your duty is to me.' He stepped back and lifted the whip to strike.

My one hand heaved and struck. A mild bump.

He rotated with my blow. His eyes spouted fire.

He grabbed my shoulder with his empty hand, and called me a name.

He raised his weapon hand.

I slipped beneath his arm and raced away.

He was still clutching my shoulder, his fingernails caught in my kimono.

I raced out of Lesser House, the priest clutching me.

'You will dance for me. I will have you,' he howled.

I ran along the *watadono*. I dared not go to Big House for help and there was no other safe place nearby.

'You belong to me now.' His face was a demon mask as he tracked me.

He stopped, panting hard, the whip held ready. 'Come closer. I will show you your duty.'

My heart was pounding loudly enough for the whole *shōen* to hear. 'I give you fair warning.' That was what samurai said to an enemy before engaging. I moved backwards, offensive stance.

He lunged with the whip. A savage sound.

I sidestepped, moved closer.

Our eyes held for an instant.

I rushed and struck his face.

Crack.

We heard the bone break.

His eyes widened. He shrieked. His hands went up to his face. The whip clattered to the floor.

His skin slipped to the colour of white rice, except where blood spurted out, defiling his precious clothes.

'What is this?' I heard Akio's voice from a side of Lesser House.

I did not speak, did not move, *bokken* in hand, defensive stance.

'She—' Goro pointed a skeletal finger. 'She attacked me!'

Akio positioned himself between us. He faced the priest. 'Why are you fighting?'

'Proprietor Chiba allows me the girls when he is not here,' the priest snarled, holding his face. 'Just look at this. I am disfigured. I will never be the same.'

Akio eyed the whip on the floor beside the priest. 'I know nothing of any arrangement. I do know that Proprietor Chiba would not permit you to hurt this child.' He put his hands by his sides, ready. His feet were placed in an attack position, his eyes almost laughing.

'I heard a scream.' Master Isamu sprang up to Lesser House. His eyes scanned the area, stopped at the scars on my bare back and made a passing nod to the priest. 'Honourable Daigoro no Goro, is there a problem?' His eye twitched.

'She attacked me! She will not do her duty,' the priest spluttered, one hand clutching his face, blood running through his fingers and down his arm.

Master Isamu and Akio caught each other's eye.

'Regrettably, Honourable Daigoro no Goro, Proprietor Chiba will not return today. I am most concerned for your discomfort. Allow me to take you for treatment.' Master Isamu stepped up to the *watadono* and led the priest down. 'I insist. We will address Kozaishō when Proprietor Chiba returns tomorrow. Akio,' he said, over his shoulder, 'escort her inside and see that she is properly dressed.'

Akio placed his hand on my neck, propelled me into Lesser House and closed the *shōji*. He knelt down and looked me in the face. 'You are unharmed?' His dragonfly eyebrows met in the centre of his forehead.

'Yes.'

He stood up and surveyed me.

'I was grateful to Daigoro no Goro. He arranged for me to give my family extra land. Yet his presence has always distressed me.'

Akio snorted. 'That is not surprising. Most people have more than one feeling about another person. Often those feelings conflict.'

I found another kimono and put it on.

'Our practice tomorrow will be interesting. I wish you to share today's experience with the others, to tell them of how you bested a full-grown man – and a priest.'

I hugged him, but he pushed me away. I felt like crying.

'Forget not, little one, little samurai, that you protected yourself today. But you also made an enemy. Think of that.'

After I had dressed, Akio opened the *shōji*, picked up the priest's whip and held it as if it were a dead snake.

I did not know what the priest told Proprietor Chiba, but the next day he sent me away.

IV. Honourable Hiroshi

My favourite green kimono and my favourite doll, with trees embroidered on her robe, and a new kimono, made of rich blue brocade with embroidered poppies were in my *furoshiki*. I did not think that Emi could have been so thoughtful. Perhaps the proprietor had packed them for me.

Akio's topknot shook with the billowing summer clouds. I thanked the Goddess of Mercy that he accompanied me on the ox-cart journey. While other samurai and many horses travelled, I trusted Akio. We rode for several days and stopped often at shrines along Takaido Road, the main route to the south-west. At each I washed my hands, rinsed my mouth and prayed to the God of the shrine.

Akio said we were going towards the capital of Heian-kyō and through the city of Uji, which was south of it. A city! I had never seen a city before! Towns were smaller than cities, yet the towns where we stopped had so many people. There were buildings big enough with rooms for all of us to sleep in. The sheds had enough room for the horses we rode and for all the others we brought. There were servants to care for the horses' needs and ours.

After we had left the first town and were halfway to the second, it rained. The rain came hard, but our capes kept us dry.

'These capes are better than the hemp ones my family used,' I said to another samurai.

He showed me the inside of his. 'See? It is made from string. Mulberry-bark paper is rolled into the string, then waterproofed with persimmon juice.'

The mulberry reminded me. I prayed to the Gods that I would see my family again. I searched the countryside, looking for the hill with the mulberry trees on its western side. I hoped to recognise the trees. The unfamiliar land, the large hills and rivers did not resemble my father's fields. The samurai might have let me go, if I had found my home.

I missed my family, Tashiko, even little Emi. I also missed Proprietor Chiba, although I did not miss the thrashings.

The food was different from what I had been accustomed to at Lesser House. The food bag, a big wicker basket with a cloth pouch inside, was in the ox cart. Usually we purchased grains and other foods we could not hunt or catch, but when the food bag emptied, we filled it in the towns. Sometimes the samurai allowed me to join the hunt, although they always caught our dinner. In the evening, after a long day following the ox cart and herding the horses, the samurai told stories. I had those Chiba had told me to tell them in return. These were what Akio called 'story duels'.

Akio and I rode together one hot day, lagging behind the others. I put my question to him anxiously, but tried to sound carefree. 'Have you ever seen a small hill with mulberry trees on its western side?'

'Yes, when you first came to the *shōen*. Finally, Kozaishō, it is my turn to ask why.' His eyebrows fluttered like tiger moths on his forehead.

'Because – because that is a hill near my family.' I gave him my most endearing look and raised my eyes.

'Kozaishō,' he turned to me in the saddle, 'even if I saw such a thing, I must do as my master bids. I am required to take you . . . where I am ordered to take you.' He motioned to me to ride on.

I did not spy that hill again but kept searching. With Akio ahead of me, and with the rain, he could not see my tears. I thought of my family, that last day with the buckets and the black horse. Would Fourth Daughter still carry buckets after all this time? I hoped she would marry rather than go to the *shōen*. Was Fourth Daughter married? I hoped her husband would be kind. Even to her.

'We are going near the city of Uji, south-west of the capital, Heian-kyō,' he began the next morning.

'The city? I have never seen a city.'

'No, to a village near it.'

'Is a village like Chiba's *shōen*?'

'No, it is a group of buildings, all different kinds. Together.'

'Please tell me where I am being sent,' I pleaded, again.

'We must all serve as our master directs.' Sadness darkened Akio's eyes, like storm clouds' shadows across a field. I knew not to ask. At least for a while.

That night Akio related the story of Honourable Hiroshi:

Long ago, a dying king charged his servant, Honourable Hiroshi, with the responsibility of his only son. The Prince was forbidden to see the Princess of the Golden Mansion's portrait. Despite Hiroshi's best efforts, the Prince saw it anyway, fell in love and begged Hiroshi to help him obtain her for his bride. Regrettably the king died. Because of Hiroshi's love for the new king, he helped him sail to the Princess's land, her court, and then to win her love.

Returning, Hiroshi saw three ravens fly over the ship, an evil omen.

First Raven said, 'A wedding gift of an ebony stallion will carry off the king.'

Second Raven said, 'Wedding kimonos will burn the couple's flesh.'

And Third Raven cursed, 'After the wedding the new queen will faint and die – unless someone nicks her breast with a knife and sucks three drops of blood.'

The ravens spotted Hiroshi listening and added, 'Anyone voicing these threats will immediately turn to stone.'

Hiroshi rode out and killed the horse. Next he threw the wedding kimonos into a cooking fire. Not knowing about the curses, the king defended his servant. But when Hiroshi saved the queen's life, he earned the king's rage. Hiroshi had barely explained when he turned to stone. With regret, the King ordered the stone Hiroshi to be placed in his bedroom.

As the pregnant queen neared the time of her confinement, the king wished aloud that his beloved Hiroshi could be alive. To his amazement, the statue spoke and told him how to retore Hiroshi's life. The royal placenta must be smeared on the statue rather than being buried. Honourable Hiroshi returned to life, and all lived happily.

Hearing this story, I found the courage to ask Akio about my exile from Proprietor Chiba's *shōen*.

'It is always necessary to obey?' I asked.

'Always, little one.'

'Even when there is a wrong?'

'Eh?'

'The Prince, he did not obey. He saw the picture of the Princess. He was not punished. Not sent away.'

'What has this to do with you?'

'I did nothing wrong. I tried hard to obey, even even . . . with painful things, but Daigoro no Goro was not my master.' I worked hard to hold back my tears. The thought of Goro made me shrivel inside.

'We know, little one.' Alio touched my shoulder.

'Why did Proprietor Chiba send me away?'

All the samurai were silent, gazing at me with strange expressions.

'Was I wrong? I was loyal to Proprietor Chiba. Why am I being punished?'

Eyes were lowered.

How bad had I been? 'Will my parents lose the land I gave them?'

'I do not know. I do not think so.' Akio squatted down to my height. 'Remember, Daigoro no Goro is a powerful priest and now he is your *enemy*. He is not another child you have kicked.' He sighed, shaking his topknot: a few hairs caught in his eyebrows. 'However, this may be your *karma*.'

'The priest is stronger than Proprietor Chiba?'

'Tashiko taught you the *sutra*s, Kozaishō. Life is *dukkha*, suffering caused by wanting. Act according to the Eight-fold Path and your longing and distress will be removed.

'There is a huge difference between the king, honourable Hiroshi and you. You are not a prince. You are not even the servant of a prince. Proprietor Chiba no Tashiyori owned you and has sold you to – ah – someone else.'

'Yes, Akio.' My lips trembled, yet I did not allow tears.

'I wish it were not so, my little one. Nothing must keep you from the Noble Eight-fold Path. The Right View, Thinking, Mindfulness, Speech, Action, Diligence and Concentration will lead you to your Right Livelihood.'

I sat beside the remains of the small fire. It crackled when a log slipped. A plume of sparks drifted into the sky. I might have been a spark from that fire. I had no idea to whom Proprietor Chiba had sold me. Would I be able to keep my family's honour in the new place? The paulownia trees whispered and moaned. Maybe their height allowed them to see my new home. I wished they could speak.

Not one of the samurai would tell me anything. Except Akio. All he repeated was we had to do as our masters bade. Who would be my new master? The paulownia trees exhaled like someone humming in a home I had known years ago. Perhaps the samurai did know and did not want to tell me either. At least Proprietor Chiba could not beat me now. There was no Emi for me to struggle to teach. Who would be a friend? These samurai watched out for me, helped me, taught me. Would I see Tashiko again? Or would I be alone?

Akio stroked the top of my head that night until I slept and dreamed of the Goddess of Mercy, who appeared in a circle of flaming light. She emptied a gift-filled *furoshiki* softly on to my *futon*: a bag with *tsuru*, bowstrings; a quiver filled with arrows; a knife; a whetstone; a straw hat; a rice pouch; a cup for water; salt; leggings and sandals. With each one, the Goddess said, 'Use this gift well, Kozaishō. You will become an extraordinary samurai.' She repeated this ten times, once for each of her ten gifts.

Extraordinary. Samurai. Me.

V. Madam Hitomi

Before we set off one morning, Akio announced, 'Today the Gods are against our direction. We need to go south.' He pointed to the way we had come.

'These Gods are extremely powerful,' a samurai said. 'Not so long ago there was a noble. He did not pay attention and travelled in a Forbidden Direction. By the time he realised his blunder, it was too late. Torrential rains, hail and floods arrived. Crops suffered. Many people died of starvation.'

'That is why,' a second looked at me sternly, 'we must pay attention . . . every day.'

'How are we to go quickly?'

Some of the samurai chuckled.

Akio quieted them with a motion of his hand, and I pressed my lips together to control my annoyance. 'It is better to go safely and slowly. There are many disturbances, as you know. Protection is of great concern.'

'There are no Minamoto here.' I clenched my hands, thinking of the enemies of the Taira. 'What other disturbances?' I blurted out, still upset by their mocking.

The second samurai turned to the others and murmured, 'She should know.' He returned his eyes to me, his fingers tapping his sword sheath. 'There are *sōhei*, monks from monasteries' armies, who roam near the capital, Heian-kyō . . . and where we are going. They cause . . . difficulties.'

'Disturbances,' the first samurai said.

'Daigoro no Goro may be one of these *sōhei*,' Akio whispered. 'Many years ago our emperor, Go-Shirakawa, said there were three things he could not control: dice when he gambled, the rapids of the Kamo river and the mountain *sōhei*.'

'They are brazen,' the second samurai said. 'They carry a shrine into Heiankyō to threaten the emperor. Years ago, on the Gion Festival, Chancellor Kiyomori, our clan chieftain, sent an arrow into the shrine that struck its gong, proclaiming the power of our clan and its arrows over the monks.' He lifted his bow into the air with one hand.

'Honourable one, what is the Gion Festival?' I asked.

'It is a summer festival in the capital to please the Gods and prevent the plague. During the day people parade on decorated platforms throughout the Gion shrines and temples. It is a large complex. Artists perform dances, songs and music. A famous festival,' the second samurai said.

'Nevertheless, Kozaishō, do not underestimate any *sōhei*.' Akio thumped my shoulder to help me remember.

No wonder Akio had been amazed that I had bested Goro. A *sōhei*. I revisited that last day at the *shōen* often in my mind.

Our country's capital city Heian-kyō was larger, with more people, than the city of Uji.

The Forbidden Directions made us change our path only a few more times.

On the last day of our journey, Akio rode up next to my horse, and said, 'We are now going to travel through the city of Uji. Go to the ox cart and cover yourself with a cloth so no one can see you. We can guard you there more easily from brigands who roam the streets. Remember the *sōhei*? They might steal you. There are disputes and spies. You must leave us, but we do not wish you to fall into evil hands before our duty is finished.'

I climbed under the bundles in the ox cart, remembering not to touch the blue *furoshiki*. Its tied corners flapped with each rattle and bounce, tempting me. How much evil was out there? Daigoro no Goro felt evil to me. What did I have that everyone wanted?

My chest hurt when I breathed. Through slits in the cart's woven sides I saw small groups of priests in hooded cowls, like Goro on the black horse, farmers with summer vegetables, barley and rice, people yelling their wares, many carts, animals, feral dogs and cats, birds and fish, dirt and mud, crowded huts, vibrant stalls – colours.

Everywhere there were delicious and dreadful smells, spices, incense, food cooking, oil burning, sweat and dung. Noises pounded my ears as powerfully as an earthquake. Whenever someone rode by, the dust burned my eyes and I took comfort from the cloth.

We rode through Uji without stopping. Gradually things grew quieter. I saw fewer people and more trees. I heard crickets and a few woodpeckers and smelt pine.

Several buildings clustered together on their own road near a grove of old pine trees. Over the short rock wall, with roses of Sharon growing near it I saw the roofs of many huts and a stable. Freshly harvested fields lay beyond the slight slopes. The cart stopped before a little gate in the wall.

A samurai stepped behind the ox cart and called to me, 'We are here. This is the Village of Outcasts. Madam Hitomi will be your new owner.'

Before I climbed out of the cart, I heard a punch and Akio's voice snarled, 'How could you tell her in that way?'

Outcasts? A band clutched my chest. Oh, Goddess of Mercy, protect me! My family honour still depended on me, no matter who owned me. What kind of honour would I find here? If any?

'Come out, little one, but stand behind the cart so no one can see you yet.' I heard Akio's voice and obeyed.

Fallen willow leaves littered the path. The pine and willow trees seemed to sigh with sadness in the autumn wind.

'I . . . we want to say farewell to you before you go on to your new abode.' He rapped my head lightly as he spoke. He twisted and opened the lumpy blue *furoshiki*.

'We have some gifts for you, little samurai,' he said. His eyes did not overflow.

The second pulled out my bow and my *bokken*, familiar with practice. As he unwrapped each package, he laid it next to the now untied and opened *furoshiki*.

They stood around me, as I opened each of the other gifts. The first was a bag embroidered with cranes flying over willow trees; it contained two strings for my child bow. As I touched them, I heard Akio's voice in my mind: 'Lower the point to sight. Smooth release between thumb and index finger. Keep your arm slightly bent. Breathe.'

Next a new quiver, filled with arrows, several with hawk feathers. Across this quiver, little rabbits and trees danced. Akio had remembered my favourites. He whispered to me that he had been saving it for when I won my next archery prize.

Other gifts included a knife, a whetstone, a straw hat – my size – for practice in the sun, a pouch for rice, a water cup, a container with salt for Purification, leggings for warmth and an extra pair of straw sandals. The gifts were the ones the Goddess of Mercy had shown me in my vivid dream before I left the *shōen*. I pretended to be surprised – I truly was – although I had believed in my dreams since Tashiko had told me her story.

'Proprietor Chiba and Master Isamu arranged them for you,' Akio said, but I knew the true provider of most of these magic gifts: Akio.

'You do me too much honour,' I said formally, and bowed, wiping my tears as fast as I could. Akio touched my head. I looked into his eyes. 'My gratitude has no bounds.' The words choked me with the pain of our parting and the thought that I would never see him again.

Akio put his arms around me while I cried. 'I will pray every day to the Goddess of Mercy that she will take care of you. We will all pray for you.

'Remember,' he added, 'commit no evil, do all that is good, and keep your thoughts pure. This is the teaching of the Buddha.'

> Friendship, the great gift
> Like a long growing summer
> Like the cuckoo's song
> Watered by distance's weeping
> Stands for ever, tallest Pine

At the gate a large woman dressed in harsh-coloured robes ploughed towards us like an ox. She pretended to smile, revealing blackened teeth. *Ohaguro* was a vile paste made from vinegar, gall-nut and powdered iron to darken the teeth. Everyone bowed. Her white scalp showed through her thin hair in the wind. Even through the heavy rice-powder paste she wore, I could see her wrinkles. They were like gullies eroded on a hill after a typhoon.

Beside me Akio whispered, 'Keep us in your thoughts, little one. Always – you will remain in ours. Soon, probably next month, you will receive a wonderful surprise.'

'Thank you,' I whispered, and brushed against his armour while bowing.

Unsure of what I should do, I resolved to do whatever was asked. If it was honourable. Why was this place called the Village of Outcasts? Could it be that everyone who lived here was unclean? Perhaps they butchered animals. Some people did eat meat. I wanted nothing to do with that. Oh, Kannon-sama, Goddess of Mercy, please do not let me be a part of killing anything or touching anything that has been killed!

'I bid welcome to the samurai of Proprietor Chiba no Tashiyori.' The woman's black teeth gaped in her whitened face. 'I am Madam Hitomi. May I offer you refreshments or . . . entertainment?'

'Thank you for your generous hospitality,' Akio said. 'Most of the horses are for sale. You are welcome to buy as many as you need. Proprietor Chiba no Tashiyori ordered us to sell what you do not take in Heian-kyō. We must return immediately. We ask only to transact our business and to water and feed our animals before we leave.'

'As you require.' She gestured to a young man nearby. 'I will take the girl. Hiroshi will show you to the horse master.' Her hand, with the longest fingernails I had ever seen, beckoned me closer.

Hiroshi! Like the story, 'Honourable Hiroshi'. I turned to Akio and our eyes met before Hiroshi came and showed them to the sheds.

Madam Hitomi seized my hand. I grabbed my *furoshiki* and did not dare look back. I bit my tongue and tried not to cry. She waddled in front of me all the way to my new home, beyond the gate, beyond the first building, which was almost as large as Big House. We hurried along a beautiful garden path to a row of small huts and, further, to another set of huts. A wide *watadono* encircled each one. A few women rested under the *watadonos*' roofs, fanning themselves with large leaves.

We stopped at a hut. Madam Hitomi opened the *shōji* and said, 'This is yours.' In a back corner a *futon* hugged itself. A rough wooden clothes-tree postured against the wall, where she directed me to hang my beloved kimonos. A water jug sat on the floor, as empty as my spirit.

Everything was going to be different. Would I find a way to train with the samurai? I had seen a few when I came in. If not, I had my bow, my *bokken* and my warrior tools and I would practise by myself. I would.

She ordered me to follow her to Main House, which seemed a walk of several *chō*. Inside, she slid open another *shōji* to a room of such luxury that my hands flew to my mouth. A heavily carved table squatted on the mat-covered floor. Lamps and more lamps of many shapes stood like blind samurai – with only one lamp lit, the whole room was transformed into a field under murky clouds. In the darkness I heard cats call and hiss.

Madam Hitomi sat on a wide cushion with high pillows behind it. Her voice sounded like a draughty hut in winter winds as she said, 'Let me look at you. This must be hard for you, but I know you will be obedient and do honour to me, your family and Proprietor Chiba no Tashiyori.' I thought of Akio and honourable Hiroshi. I remembered to breathe, and I bowed.

'Stand.'

I did.

Another woman, much smaller and younger, came in.

'Ah,' Madam Hitomi said. 'Here is Rin. She is the *chojā* of my Women-for-Play. She likes to meet all the new girls.'

Rin approached and unwound my kimono's ties. With one finger, she lifted my kimono off my shoulder. I stared at the green cloth and tie heaped on the floor. Next she pulled off my *kosode*.

Madam Hitomi opened my mouth, looked at my ears and eyes, then turned my head, arms and legs one way and another. She posed and asked if I could imitate her. I could. She made other postures, which I was to follow. She snorted after each one.

As I held each position, she ran her hands over my body as if she was petting one of the numerous cats that stalked the room. She scraped her knobbly fingers and long nails over my back, chest and legs.

'Tell her to pretend to be a frog,' Rin ordered.

When I squatted on the floor, Rin put her fingers inside me, in places for which I still had no name. She sniffed me at odd places, even between my legs. She yapped like a little dog, then smiled broadly.

'Yes,' Madam Hitomi said, sitting back on her pillows. 'Good, I see Chiba has kept his word and protected you.'

'From what?'

Rin goggled at me, then slapped my face. 'You will not speak of such things again.'

I apologised and bowed.

'From Daigoro no Goro,' Madam Hitomi whispered.

'Proprietor Chiba has moulded you well. You will do well for me here. Now dress yourself. Put away your grief. We are your new family.'

'I agree. Welcome to our family,' Rin said.

Her voice changed to a monotone and her eyes dulled. 'Here you will become a beautiful flower worthy of great admiration. You are entering a profession to which I have belonged all my life. Do me and our profession honour.'

Honour. I again thought of honourable Hiroshi. My family. How brave to do as I should! Madam Hitomi took her fan and tapped me sharply on top of my head. 'Tashiko will be your companion. Now go to your hut.'

Tashiko! After she had pointed, I went to my hut, singing Tashiko's name in my mind. My companion. What did she mean by that? Tashiko. So Chiba had sent me to the same place. Tashiko and I would be together – with no Chiba. We could play Go. Perhaps dance together without beatings. Did they beat us here? I wondered if this was the surprise Akio had promised. If it really was Tashiko, it would be a magnificent surprise.

So lost in thought, I was not aware of my surroundings until I reached my little room.

BOOK 5

I. Surprises

Madam Hitomi hauled me to a long, plain building, which, like Lesser House, stood with a roofed *watadono* around it, raised two steps from the ground. As she turned a corner, the scents of horses, heavy incense and a nauseating smell I would soon learn was the tannery attacked me. No gardens, no ponds, no walking paths were visible.

Certainly my life was going to be different. Would I find a way to train with the samurai?

'There.' Madam Hitomi pointed with a long finger, which looked as if it had been dipped in blood, to a small hut, third from the right. She raised her eyebrows, or the place where her eyebrows had been. She had shaved them off. She charged away without a farewell. So much for the manners Chiba had taught.

No *shōji* closed my new home, only a thin cloth curtain, flapping a heartbroken 'hello' with the hot breeze. I grabbed the knots of my *furoshiki* with both hands, comforted that its blue silk had touched Akio's hands, and pulled it closer to my chest, feeling each bulky gift inside. I was to live . . . here. So many houses. All tiny. I was not sure Akio's gifts would fit inside.

Outdoor shoes lined up along the bottom step to each *watadono*, whose wide roof showed many patches. I put my outdoor shoes with the others, remembering when I had received my older sister's shoes, which had been much too big. Loneliness speared my chest.

The curtain to my room slipped between my fingers. I recognised

Tashiko. She sat on a *futon*, her long hair draped past her knees, but her face was white.

What had happened to it? Had someone thrust her head into a barrel of rice flour? I could not believe she would allow them to change her like that.

'I can hardly recognise you, Tashiko. Are you the same person?' She had taught me about the *sutras*, yet she had allowed others to manipulate her into making herself different.

She shrugged, then smiled. I was relieved to see her teeth were the same, natural, white as honeysuckle flowers, not blackened.

My life could be worse. At least I was not with the butchering and leather, and Tashiko was here. I would be able to talk to people. I could talk to people during the day. I would not have to wait until I saw Chiba. I would not see Chiba!

'Kozaishō, little princess, I prayed we would be together.' She had grown taller, prettier than I remembered. 'My little house is only three west of yours.'

The sound of her breathy voice sang into my bones, my eyes splashed, the floor rolled beneath me as if in an earthquake. She swept me into her arms, bracing me before I fell. Her warm breasts crushed against me. I drew in the woody scent of her hair, swirled my fingers through its softness, soothed by her voice, calmed by her breathing.

A scream flew like an arrow through the walls and impaled its sharp point into me. I pulled back from Tashiko, trembling, quivering, gulping. The wailing continued, as if demons danced nearby. I dashed to the door and pulled back the curtain, but saw nothing.

Returning to the *futon*, Tashiko's eyes had turned downwards. 'As at the *shōen*, it is important to follow directions and orders.'

Another scream, this one higher, harsher, sending cold prickles down my legs, making my teeth sting. I held on to Tashiko, and she to me.

'What is this? I am thrown from one demon to a fiercer one? What is this place?'

'While Madam Hitomi does not leave marks like Proprietor Chiba, she is able to attain unthinkable pain and . . . more.'

'What hell am I in?'

She motioned for me to sit. We both did. 'This is a Village of Outcasts,

104

owned by Madam Hitomi. Rich. Owns the tannery. The untouchables, the *eta*, their shacks and the tannery are far from here. Also owns many Women-for-Play, including me. Rin is the *chōja* of the free Women-for-Play, but she advises Madam Hitomi.'

'Advises?'

'Meddles with . . . all.' Tashiko raised one hand above her shoulder and her lips lifted.

'How can you be content? Everything here is defiled!'

'Not all. Some Women-for-Play.'

I blinked at her, wary of this and the new her.

'The Women-for-Play sing and often dance. Some are skilled in other things, like musical instruments, or the *biwa* or pleasuring. That is what I aspire to.'

'Pleasuring?'

'Here, you learn about physical gratification.'

'What is that?'

'What men and women do together. Coupling.'

I wanted to pull her hair, but a breeze brought the smell of tanning animal skins. 'Tashiko, in this village of the unclean, there cannot be any honour.'

'No, Kozaishō. It is always honourable to serve as your master wishes.'

I sat up, 'Have you been talking to Akio?' That was what he had said to me on our travels from Chiba's *shōen* to this place.

'No. He serves Proprietor Chiba.'

'That is what he always says. How can that be true?'

'Obedience is honourable.'

'Here in this place? Never.'

'You do not understand, Kozaishō. Each level is honourable.'

'Level?'

'Four levels. First laundry, next cleaning, then attending to the Women-for-Play. That is what I do.'

'You are third level. The fourth is . . . ?'

'Being a Woman-for-Play.'

'Is that the most honourable?'

Her eyes said yes.

'I do not understand, but I am glad to be with you.' I stroked her hair, her downy chestnut hair. 'See.' I stroked my own thick mane. 'My hair has grown too.'

That first night passed, short and long at the same time, as if two ends of a candle burned together. Tashiko held me and talked to me.

Later she slept in my arms. I, unused to the pathetic howls, did not, picturing or dreaming cunning devils or evil spirits.

The next night Tashiko slept beside me on the *futon*. And the next. It was only a matter of days before Tashiko exchanged huts to be beside mine.

Was this the surprise Akio arranged for me? Here in this nether world, complete with another Proprietor Chiba, but one who did not leave scars, I needed a good surprise to help me sleep through the screams.

Madam Hitomi directed her girls as cautiously as my mother managed our winter food. New girls stayed away from the Special Houses, as distant as the earth from the sun. The distance worked to my advantage: I had thought about slipping away with Tashiko. Madam Hitomi assigned small duties on those first days, under close supervision, perhaps afraid that I would run.

I planned to escape, I wanted to, but my father had sold me to Chiba, and I had belonged to him. He could do with me whatever he wished. So that I did not think about leaving, I recalled my father's words, 'All our souls belong to our family's honour', and reminded myself of Akio's story, 'Honourable Hiroshi'.

My life needed to bring honour to my family. Running away would be dishonourable, unthinkable, even from this Village of Outcasts with its tannery and hovels of the untouchables, those disgusting *eta*. Each time the tainted odours of dead animals and excrement arrived on a breeze, I had to remind myself again about my family honour.

My only satisfaction lay in being with Tashiko, and the only honourable path lay in obeying a new master, no matter how much I came to detest her.

As a new girl I cared for the laundry. First level, the lowest. Going out to the sheds my first day at the Hour of the Dragon well after dawn, I saw him – strutting from the shed – Akio, my Akio, dressed for the hunt. I made a quick bow, not to show the disbelief on my face. What was he doing here?

106

He came towards me. 'Kozaishō.' His arms flew up to the sky, as did the corners of his eyes and mouth. 'I am your surprise.'

'I thought Tashiko was my surprise. How . . . When?' My head floated off my neck, and my eyes saw nothing but Akio's face, all else a thick mist. 'Does Proprietor Chiba know?'

'Naturally. I had his knowledge and the permission of Taira no Michimori, the Echizen governor.'

'Who is that? Why do you need a governor's permission?' I had heard that name before. I searched my memory.

'Proprietor Chiba was not my master. The Echizen governor was.'

'Was?'

'I belong to Madam Hitomi now. You and I were both sold.'

'Why you?' He was samurai. He could not be sold. Could he?

'I spoke rashly to Proprietor Chiba and taught you. He dismissed me so I came here.' One shoulder twitched. 'It was because of you,' he continued. 'Proprietor Chiba had brought yet another young girl to the *shōen*.'

'You had to move away from your family because of me?' Not only had I dishonoured myself, I had hurt Akio. My cheeks warmed. Tears came to my eyes at the disgrace.

'No. No shame,' he continued. 'I am glad to be here. My family is already here.'

'You are not? They are?' My stance changed, like a bush in a drought after the first rain.

'Especially my girls. They are quite young and I was afraid for them.' His eyebrows pinched together.

'I understand, Akio,' I said, but I did not understand.

'Proprietor Chiba brought yet another young girl to the *shōen*, to Lesser House. I could not stand silent any longer.'

'I regret your outspokenness has brought you to such a place.'

'I do not, Kozaishō. This Village is safer for my daughters.'

'How?'

'Daigoro no Goro does not visit here unsupervised. Here he cannot do . . . what he tried to do with you.' His face tightened, and he tapped the sheath of his sword.

My mouth opened.

Akio sighed. 'These low-caste people,' he gestured first to the little houses and next to where the untouchables lived, 'recognise my family's higher status and would never touch one of my children.'

'You are happy to be here?'

'Happiness is difficult to find. Remember, lack of want brings contentment. I am content to be here.'

'What will you do?'

'I offer security.' He touched his sword, and his eyes shone in the morning sun. 'I will not have to worry about my girls. Here, they will not have to endure what you and . . .' His face turned to stone, and his hands to fists. He placed a palm on each of my shoulders and tightened his fingers into my back. 'Your presence here brightens my day and my life.'

We stood in silence, thinking of the past. Finally I said, 'My only wish is to continue with the Way of the Bow.'

'I am delighted, little one.' He touched my cheek and stroked my hair. Studying my face, he chuckled.

I smiled.

His eyes sparkled. 'My wife and three girls are here. You will meet them soon, I expect.'

'What happiness, contentment, you give me in being here.' I looked around and saw no one. I moved to give him a quick hug.

He pulled back. 'No, little one. Not any more.'

'Why not? No one is looking.'

'Because it is not suitable.'

'Why?'

'This is a different place.' He sighed. 'I see you have retained your questioning tactics.' He pretended a grimace. 'We both belong to Madam Hitomi now. At the *shōen* Proprietor Chiba owned you, but the Echizen governor owned me and the *shōen*. We are changed because our stations have changed.'

I was no different. Was he?

He reached down to ruffle the hair on top of my head. '*This*, however, is allowed.'

At his touch, the stiffness that had grasped my chest loosened. A smile travelled from one side of his broad face to the other, a long distance. I breathed again, with comfort.

'Do you wish to continue your studies with me?' His eyebrows travelled up his forehead.

I thought for a moment and used formal language. 'First I must ask permission from Madam Hitomi. If she agrees, I will be with you whenever it suits her and you.'

He squatted so we were face to face. His horse, steel and sweat smells uplifted me, relaxing me with their familiarity.

'Spoken well.' His voice sounded sweeter than before, and he tousled my hair again. 'Loyalty is first. You carry the Way with you. I am proud of you, my beautiful Fifth Daughter. Allow me to ask. I will let you know what Madam Hitomi says.'

On the way to the laundry I remembered how, at first, I was not sure I could find any honour in this impure place. Now, with Akio, I might.

II. Work

Strengthened with possibilities, I met Aya, my work companion, in the shed by the stream. She looked and seemed younger than I, especially in her reasoning. She was like Emi, but slower.

'How long have you been here?' I asked, wondering if anyone ever left.
'Many months.'

Another eternity to me, but I smiled back because she looked so pleased with herself. She had lived near Wakasa, a large city; her father and brothers had fished.

'What was it like?'

To remember, she closed her eyes and spoke with difficulty. 'I liked the blue sea with white dots. I liked the crunchy sand.' She grinned. Her missing front teeth made her adorable, especially when she kept her crossed eyes closed. 'I did not like the sand fleas biting me.' She grimaced and slapped her legs, as if she had just been bitten.

Her face showed every emotion. When I said, 'Faster!' tears came to her eyes, and her work slowed, so I stopped saying that and worked at her pace.

Fortunately, there were several who took kimono panels apart, several who sewed them together, and a few who flattened them. Aya and I were to scrub, rinse and dry the panels. This task needed two people, and the only two people were she and I. I had to rely on her to teach me what to do so the first day's work was incomplete.

On the second morning Akio saw me as I went into the shed. He looked around, but I shook my head. Leading me to a dark corner, he squatted and said, 'Madam Hitomi did not give us permission.'

'What?' His words seemed to strangle me. Even with his hands on my shoulders, I felt as though I was falling.

'You have gone pale, Kozaishō.'

'The Gods are more important than Madam Hitomi.' They were, but the Gods' punishments usually did not make people scream in the night.

'This is risking much,' he said, 'but your white pheasant and dragon cloud are truly powerful. Are you willing to take such danger? Think carefully.'

'Yes,' I said, hearing screams, my heart drumming. 'Yes, I am.' I did not tell him about the Goddess of Mercy in my special dream.

Akio and I worked out the times and places where we would be hidden. Several nights for the bow, next the *naginata*, the horse, the *bokken*, a combination, and then repeat. Some nights he planned to bring his eldest daughter, a beginner, and much younger than I.

The second day was like the first in the laundry. On the third morning, while I was carrying water, Madam Hitomi came. 'Finish all the clothing and do it *well*. Today is your third day,' she snarled like one of her angry cats, but with her black teeth.

Why did she not warn Aya as well?

On the fourth evening she grabbed me and marched me to a little house behind Main House, the direction from which Tashiko and I had heard screams. Hitomi would look good with her whitened face hit, broken and bleeding. I saw my *bokken*, remembering the sting in my arm as it had crashed into Goro's nose. Where else could they send me? To the *eta*? At the thought my body throbbed and trembled.

Sweat ran down my spine and dripped off the back of my legs, despite the raw breeze through the camphor trees. My feet slipped on the slick mat of soggy, icy leaves. Hitomi pulled me into that little house. My family's honour. What could I do to uphold it?

Whips and metal objects hung on the wall, like a ferocious animal's fangs. The only other objects were a stool, a small brazier, with waves of heat showing in the cool air, and a plain table with many attached leather strips.

'Put all your clothes on this cloth.' She pointed to a corner. 'Lie on the table, on your back.'

The frigid evening gusts pushed through the walls. I thought about my *bokken* again, inside my *furoshiki*.

Lying on the cold table, which was too short even for me, my arms and legs swung down and the edges cut into my skin. I wondered if she was going to examine me as she had before. It would be difficult to pretend to be a frog in this position. She might have said this was a family, but I hated her more than I had ever hated Fourth Daughter.

'Tashiko has learned obedience.' She grinned with her red-rimmed black teeth.

I raised my eyes to the ceiling to calm myself, but the ropes and pulleys I saw slung above made me breathe faster. By the time I returned my eyes to Hitomi, she had tied an arm and one leg to the table legs with the strips. I had thought to admire her managing skills. That was my mistake.

'Oh, yes. I know about the priest, Daigoro no Goro.' She stood upright and stretched, then finished tying my other leg. She sucked in her breath, almost hissing as he had done. 'Proprietor Chiba sent me a letter.'

My limbs quivered at these names.

'Tonight is the consequence of not accomplishing your tasks. Do you understand? You may have fought before, but any rebellious actions here will mean severe punishments for you and *others*.'

'Yes, honourable Madam Hitomi,' I managed to stammer. My words made white smoke above me. My teeth clicked in the cold until I pressed them together, hard.

'Good. Today will help to remind you.'

She pulled down a metal prod from the wall and brought it close to my face. It had a wooden handle at one end and an arrow-like tip at the other. She turned to the brazier and shoved the tip into it.

'You must complete all the work each day.' She left the brazier to lean over me again. 'Yes,' she said, as she sniffed the air. 'My little reminder is ready.'

I smelt it, too. The scent of metal burning, smouldering. I shivered with dread and cold.

The prod's end glowed in the murky room. The bright point followed my features. The heat, with my eyes shut, was both pleasant and paralysing. I pretended I was in combat and she the enemy. She was. I breathed through my nose and willed my eyes open. I also willed myself not to flinch.

She moved the prod down from my face. Lifting one of my hands, she moved it closer until it almost touched the lower edge of my little finger's nail. Warmer, hot, scorching. Piercing pain raced through my hand, arm and up to my head until my eyeballs felt as if they would burst. I opened my mouth and closed it, biting my tongue, tasting hot iron, swallowing blood.

The prod went back to my face. Hitomi's eyes glinted in its red light. I prayed she would not require me to speak. I had almost bitten through my tongue, gulping and swallowing more blood. If she went again, I needed another target.

She did. Same hand. Same nail. I bit the inside of my cheek until a piece of it hung in my mouth. Raw, squeezing, stabbing pain boiled every part of my body.

But I made no sound.

'Dress. Finish all your work tomorrow.' She united my arms and left.

This fiend was worse than Chiba and Goro together. Not carry my *bokken*? Not be ready to hit back? Or run? Or all three? At that moment I was ready to kill.

That night I prayed to the Goddess of Mercy because the work seemed impossible. The next morning I did as the Goddess had shown me in a special dream.

I made sure that Aya and I carried the water to the big kettles before our morning meal, quite early. I made our rice into balls to carry with us throughout the day as we worked. While I was scrubbing, I told the story of the Greedy Hawk, but only a little at a time.

'Long ago and far away, the largest of the birds, the eagle, became caught in the fork of a tree.'

Aya's crossed eyes grew wider as her mouth opened in awe.

'He worked and worked, but could not free himself. Other birds came and pulled on him to help. They pulled on his feathers. One by one, all his feathers came out until he was completely bare.

113

Here I demonstrated. Aya and I played this out by pulling at the clothes faster to clean them. We finished in a shorter time. Concentrating on Aya, our speed and the story helped me to forget my pain from the night before.

'A large crow flew by. He saw the eagle. "That is no way to help." The crow told half of the birds to fly to the right branches of the fork and the other half to the left. With the weight of all the birds, the fork of the tree split and freed the eagle.'

I stood on one side and Aya on the other of each panel. Each 'bird' became cloth on a drying branch. She performed this task quicker than before. By the end of the day, all the washed clothing, spread on branches, looked like some odd quilt I might have sewn.

For Aya I invented tales in which women fled from make-believe terrors. We escaped or saved lives by beating our way out of pretend bushes and scrubbing clothes. When we dug ourselves out of make-believe tunnels, water buckets moved faster. Ghosts, especially the recently dead *yurei*, chasing the living, trees blowing in a storm created by a demon, mountains climbed step by step to escape some horrible fate, sometimes even the stately robes of princes and princesses: all became part of our daily work. Every day I remembered a new story, invented one or varied an old one.

The stories allowed me to escape over the walls of the Village of Outcasts to somewhere wonderful or, at least, somewhere else – where I might redeem my family's honour.

The stories served me better than her. I had discovered an honourable way to escape.

III. One Story

Tashiko and I went to Aya's hut with my good news.

Aya hummed and played with little dishes and her doll on the floor of her hut. Her freshly shortened hair shifted with the rhythm of her song.

'Aya.' I knew I had to have her attention before I spoke to her.

She turned her head, her sweet smile offsetting the crossed eyes.

Tashiko and I sat on the floor next to her. 'News.'

'Madam Hitomi promoted me to Cleaner-of-Houses in the Women-for-Play's working huts.'

She hugged me. 'Hooray,' she shouted, into my shoulder.

'But I will not be working with you any more.'

Tears dribbled down Aya's cheeks like slow rain. Tashiko lifted the rice cake, a gift from one of the Women-for-Play. Its scent floated up to me.

'Here,' Tashiko said. 'We brought this for you. Kozaishō says this is your favourite.'

Aya mewled like a cat with its tail caught.

'Is this not your favourite?' I said.

That was the wrong question. The mewing increased to a whine, and the tears continued to flow.

Tashiko scowled at me and began to sing a calming *sutra*. I joined in.

Another wrong approach. Now howling, Aya bent her head down to the floor.

Such noise caused trouble. Tashiko cradled Aya, and I rubbed her back, my roughened hands catching threads on her smock.

A torrent of tears accompanied her bawling.

I looked at Tashiko, shrugged my shoulders and kept a hand on Aya's back. 'Do you know the story of the mirror?'

I waited and murmured in her ear, 'Once . . . long ago . . .'

Aya's head rose. She was sniffing, her little chest heaving. The wailing stopped.

Once, long ago, a couple had a beautiful little girl. When the father's business called him away to a faraway city, he promised the little girl a special present. Returning, he opened a basket. He had brought cakes and a large doll for his daughter. He presented his wife with a metal mirror.

Soon the mother became ill and told her daughter, 'My darling, when I am gone, take care of your father. When you miss me, and you will, take this mirror and look into it. You will always see me.'

After she had died, the little girl looked into the mirror and saw her mother. For years it comforted her, even after her father remarried and she had a new stepmother who cared for her.

The tears were flowing again. 'I have no mirror to see you,' Aya said, wiping her nose on her sleeve.

'You remember how we saw ourselves in water buckets? When you look into the water buckets tomorrow, you will see yourself. Picture me next to you, as always.'

When Aya smiled again, Tashiko and I went to my new hut with the Women-for-Play. I would miss the stories but was relieved I would no longer have to push Aya.

'You amazed me,' Tashiko said, lifting her eyebrows, soft as a baby bird's down. 'Where did you learn how to tell such a story?'

A fist hit my stomach as I remembered the source. 'From Chiba . . . and Akio and the other samurai.'

'I heard stories too, but I do not recognise this one.'

'I make some of them up or change them.' I explained about Aya working faster and the story duels with Akio on the way to Madam Hitomi.

'Tell some to me.'

★ ★ ★

116

To make my work easier, I told stories to stop the Women-for-Play squirming while I dressed them and applied their makeup. They asked for me to arrange their hair and clothes because of my stories. This I enjoyed, and their attention pleased me, too. A well-timed story discouraged slaps for small mistakes or forgotten details or, worse, Hitomi's discipline.

Bigger mistakes brought Hitomi's punishments, so I learned as quickly as I could. Tashiko crept into my hut and held me and the dolls to ease her terror. While salves lessened pain, no one spoke of what occurred in Hitomi's hut, no matter how loud the shrieks.

At the beginning of each day Tashiko and I whispered together. The Women-for-Play served as subjects for conversation – prolonged discussions about the best way to rouge mouths that were as thin as chopsticks, to select complementary colours and arrange robes for a woman with a figure as bumpy as an aubergine or as thin as a burdock root.

After work, she and I continued to play the games we had played at Chiba's. Go was my favourite, and sometimes I won. Akio played go with me, and my skill improved. Hitomi allowed this activity, and Akio always called attention to us when we were taking the Right Action.

Tashiko persisted in the reading lessons, writing the names of objects on small papers. My writing still resembled bird scratches, but I could read more and more characters. Akio taught us new ones, those for weaponry, new poses and strokes.

From one grateful woman, I received a partial copy of the *Kokinshū*, a compilation of five-lined poems called *waka*. I copied them and later created my own. Tashiko did not appear jealous of my gifts for which I was thankful. I recalled her as a rival at the *shōen*.

The days ended with the evening meal and bathing. She and I murmured on into the night, until we were too tired to go on.

Months passed while I served the Women-for-Play, dressing, undressing, bathing, comforting, calming. I assisted with blackening their teeth, although the first few times I did not do it well. Those mistakes brought me to Hitomi's special hut, but I did not cry out. My tongue and cheeks, bitten through, meant I could not chew food. Tashiko gave me cooled rice broth until I could eat again, often many days later. My fury with Hitomi lasted longer.

Tashiko explained, 'If the work is not adequate, it is honourable to submit to whatever punishment Madam Hitomi decrees.'

I disagreed. Tashiko was trying to convince herself that our punishments were honourable. They were not, especially for honest mistakes or for someone like me who was learning. Whenever I was punished, I did whatever I had to stop myself crying out.

Only six months after my promotion to Cleaner-of-Houses, Tashiko shook my shoulder to awaken me. 'Madam Hitomi. For me.'

'Am I in trouble, too?' As a punishment, Hitomi always fetched the offender herself. She appreciated seeing the fearful faces.

'I do not know.'

I returned back to sleep, thinking of my twelfth birth anniversary and what the day might bring – gifts or abuse.

IV. Advancement

All the next day I did not see Tashiko. Before the evening meal she came into my hut with a smile.

I had been fearful for her all day, but it appeared her punishments had not been too terrible. However, the three Women-for-Play for whom I had worked after midday were especially irksome. They ordered me to redo all my tasks. I had to tell a different story to each one to soothe her temper.

The last thing I craved before the evening meal was a grinning religious zealot. 'What is it?' I asked Tashiko, in a sharper manner than usual.

'Wonderful news.'

'Not another revelation about some *sutra*.'

Tashiko said nothing.

A moment later, I said, 'Yes?' in a more neutral tone, but did not change the fatigue on my face. My practice with Akio had been poor. In the second movement, my three-cross relationship – shoulders, hips and feet – would not align properly. Akio had been disappointed.

'You are to become one of us.'

'One of whom?

Tashiko grinned like a happy monkey. 'Women-for-Play. Like me.'

'Women-for-Play? Truly?' I sat upright on the *futon*. She had played tricks before.

'Yes.' She opened her arms wide, in expectation of some excitement, perhaps.

Tashiko fetched my house shoes, putting them on my feet.

'Now what are you doing? Don't tease me.'

Her eyes dimmed like ponds under a dark moon.

I prodded her shoulder with a finger. 'Stop it. Not on my birth anniversary. You are treating me like one of those – those women.'

She lowered her eyes in the way she did when there was unpleasant news. 'I am doing what Madam Hitomi wishes.'

I rose from the *futon*, changed my mind and sat again. Cold dread moaned through the hut.

'I am totally unworthy.' I said the expected words. This was no game. Perspiration seeped around my neck and down my back. The walls whirled, and my stomach tossed bile into my throat. I grabbed the *futon* and sought Tashiko's eyes. Do not let this happen. My contented life was diving into a nether world.

Grabbing Tashiko's hands, I swallowed the bitterness and said, 'I am not ready to stop serving others, telling the stories and arranging the clothes.' I checked her eyes. They withdrew, turning dark chestnut.

She stood up and pulled away her hands. 'Kozaishō, there is nothing to be done.'

I had hurt her without meaning to. I wanted to be far away, although she was my friend and confidante. Apprehension raced through my limbs, like a strong stream after a sudden torrent in dry times.

I loved the stories and clothes, the songs and dances and makeup, but I despised the work. The work was the painful thing Goro had wanted to do to me. I had heard about it from the others, but Tashiko did not speak of it. I pushed at those shadows, but they would not go away. Everything was a dangerous wet snowstorm, a howling wind, no winter's end.

Tashiko plopped beside me and touched my cheek. 'It will hurt a little, at first, but you have never minded pain or hard work.' She grinned. 'Later you might enjoy it.'

'Enjoy?' What was she talking about?

'And we will have more time together.'

'Yes, well . . .'

'And you will have more time for Akio and your training.'

'Yes, well . . .'

'It is what Madam Hitomi has ordered.'

'The right action . . . and therefore honourable.' I said, defeated.

120

'Yes, Kozaishō.'

I guffawed with disdain and sighed loud and long. 'Oh, Tashiko.' Tears filled my eyes, and I turned away my face.

Her hand grasped my shoulder. 'In the fullness of time, Kozaishō, you will find serenity, even joy, in taking the right action.'

'Never. Not possible.'

She placed her arms around me, and her scent of brush clover and pinewood soothed me.

'I want to go and light incense,' I said to her, but kept holding her. Her eyes were hopeful – I believed she thought this to be a good thing – so I remained where I was. I would pray later to the Goddess of Mercy, I told myself, wondering if Tashiko could hear my mumblings.

Combing my hair with her fingers, she told me the story of Otsumae, how an emperor's prayers allowed her to be reborn in Paradise.

'We will say the Lotus Sutra,' Tashiko added. 'It will not be so bad. Remember honourable Hiroshi?' She hugged me. 'I will teach you. It will not hurt as much as you think. It did not for me.'

A cloud of sadness passed over her face. I ignored it, but remembered it.

We held each other, and I cried in the only way permitted: weeping without sounds.

'Madam Hitomi directed me to prepare you. I will take you. She said I could attend you. Soon Women-for-Play – together.'

'Thank you,' I whispered, and embraced her.

'The first one will be selected . . .' she pulled away so we were face to face '. . . with care.'

I nodded, not believing her.

'You are to tell each of them a story.'

'A story? Not sing or dance? One of *my* stories?'

'Yes. With the dances and your beautiful voice. Dressed as a character. It will not be so bad, with a musician outside and me as your serving girl – for now.'

'Truly?'

'Yes . . . We will learn the thirteen stringed *koto*. When you graduate from the six-string, we can play duets.'

Cleverness ruled Madam Hitomi's actions.

121

For a short time, Tashiko would no longer serve men. That delighted her. She helped with my bath, just as if we were at Chiba's, but with softness. She did not cry. I took this as a good sign. Like Akio, she directed me: 'Not like Lesser House. No eye contact. Bow frequently. First to the man and second to Madam Hitomi. Smile often. Do not cry. Keep your face blank.'

'Blank?' I asked.

'Go inside. Remain hidden.'

'Yes, I know. What else?'

'Keep to your stories or make compliments. Only pleasing words. Let your mouth be like your nose.' She pinched it and grinned.

This was like my mother saying, 'Show no emotion, say nothing and do even less,' but now I had to do things that were painful, repugnant – and impure.

I lit candles to ask my ancestors for help. Except for the blood defilements in practice, once touching Tashiko during her cycle, and being in the Village of Outcasts, I had been pure for a long time. Tashiko recited the *sutra* for longevity, to ward off any danger. The next day she dressed me as the emperor's daughter in the story. I wore three kimonos – a red under-kimono, a bright blue one with small designs of feathers and, last, a painted one with pink and orange peonies. Tashiko steered me to Madam Hitomi's greeting room in Main House. Harsh makeup stung my face. The stiffened cloth of my costume swaddled me as if I were encased to my neck in thick, scratchy mud.

Tashiko motioned for me to go into Main House. I wanted to squeeze her hand for luck, but it was too late. As I entered the room, I hid my trembling hands. I could not dishonour myself.

Peering into Madam Hitomi's room for the second time was like seeing into a large snake's hole – the darkened room, the glint of Hitomi's eyes among all her cats' faces, wondering if she would scratch me with her fingernails again. The man sat on pillows, as huge as Chiba, and was dressed in brocade – a dazzling green, red and yellow design. He lifted his face from one of the picture books. 'Spin around.'

As I did so, he spoke to Madam Hitomi: 'Much more beautiful than you told me. I am quite pleased.'

I worked to help my eyes blank, but I bowed at the compliment, remembering to keep my mouth empty, like my nose and my eyes.

The man did not acknowledge my bow, but stated formally, 'I understand this is a first time. I will do my best. Perhaps a serving girl should wait, as may be correct.'

'I appreciate your generosity and your thoughtfulness,' Hitomi replied. I had little idea of what they spoke. The words 'generosity' and 'thoughtfulness' had always related to pleasant things.

As I followed this man to one of the special houses behind Main House, Tashiko walked behind me. I was younger. I should have gone last.

Tashiko went inside and lit an oil lamp on its own table in a far corner; the doorway provided the only natural light. The man continued into the room and I trailed after him. Tashiko had not mentioned the house's luxury compared to my sleeping hut or even Lesser House.

The mats formed a floor, which looked like the blackened green of a *kemari* field below rainclouds. The *futon* and cushions matched in a slightly darker green. A jug and bowl, both trimmed in a deep sea-green, nestled near the lit brazier at the back. A bamboo stand on the other side stood with its arms held out like a starving person reaching for an embrace.

Tashiko turned to me and breathed, 'I will be outside afterwards.' She warned me again, 'No speaking unless asked, except for your story.' She bowed to the man, rubbed the back of my hand lightly, and left me alone.

I rehearsed in my mind what I had been told: remain mute; do whatever I was told; pretend enjoyment, no matter what happened; show respect, as if this man were Proprietor Chiba. My eyes could not meet his.

V. The Exceptions

The man sat on the *futon* and bade me stand in front of him. His lips formed a straight line. 'What is your name?'

'My name is Kozaishō,' I replied formally, and stared at the floor. Even with my head down, I could feel his eyes probing me.

He smoothed my garment, running his hands over the sleeves, the back and the front. He murmured, 'Kozaishō', and said, 'Little empress,' from the story again and again. He sounded like a hissing cat with its back arched. My stomach tightened into claws. Remembering Tashiko's instructions, I meekly showed gladness where none lived.

The man patted the *futon*, saying, 'Sit here so that I can hear your beautiful story more clearly.' He held me around my waist as I climbed beside the brocade covering his wide lap. 'We do not want to crush your beautiful kimono. Let me help you loosen it, my little empress.' Since he had not requested that I speak, I said nothing. He loosened and removed my outer kimono. Grasping each sleeve between the two fingers of each hand, he pulled it off me, sauntered to the other side of the hut and laid it on top of his robe. My kimono hovered, like a ghost, over the bamboo clothing stand.

He came back and motioned me to sit on his lap. He opened each of my other kimonos, carefully smoothing each garment. He stroked my chest and pulled my kimonos up over my thighs. His face changed from pale gold to red; his skin from dry to beaded and moist.

I shivered with my kimonos open, and he drew me towards him. He

124

made no effort to straighten or pull down my robes. However, he warmed my legs by rubbing them, which I appreciated.

I wanted to adjust my clothes, but I remembered Tashiko's warning about my mouth and nose. The man continued to rub my hips. 'Tell me your wonderful empress story,' he crooned.

I told each part. I left nothing out and worked my hands and face to emphasise the emotions, as I had practised. The man kept moving his hands, making it difficult to focus.

I came to a funny part. I laughed as the empress laughed, and he placed one hand on my lap and one on my chest. They stayed there after I had finished laughing. When his hands did not go to my sides, my stomach pinched. I took in a breath and let it out with a sigh.

'Ah, you like my touching you!' He cackled, with a wide smile. One of his hands scraped my nipples while the other grated my stomach, as if he were preparing vegetables.

Untying himself, the man strode across the hut, tossing garments over the bamboo stand until my kimono disappeared. He sauntered back to me. His hanging belly almost covered his Jade Stalk, which wavered back and forth, like the *bokken* of a novice boy.

He grabbed me with a hand on each side of my waist. He picked me up, rubbed his face across my chest and stomach. His eyebrows and moustache pricked my skin. Next he man pushed my legs apart, thrust a finger into me and pulled it out. He pushed me down on the *futon* and promptly pierced me with his Jade Stalk. I gasped in shock and surprise.

I had cried out! So quickly I had forgotten. Fortunately the man chortled. Perhaps he thought it was a gratification sound.

He grabbed my breast with one hand. Grunting, he shoved the other hand under my buttocks and repeatedly punctured me. The stabbing took a long time.

At my request Tashiko scrubbed me red to remove the man's assaults. Later in my hut I cried in Tashiko's arms, my stomach twisting hard.

'I am sorry I did not explain.' Tashiko put hand on each shoulder and looked into my eyes. 'I remember my first time with Goro, the ugliness . . . no gentleness.'

'Goro? Goro! What in the name of all the demons do you mean?'

'Well, I was the oldest. He waits. Until we are older.' Tashiko blinked several times.

Bile lurched into my mouth. 'Goro did that to you?'

'Every time Proprietor Chiba was gone.'

Her shoulders hunched, and I saw her as a small girl. 'How could he do that?'

'You were sent away. Remember? First I performed the dance with two fans for him. He liked that.'

'Yes. He asked me too.'

'Then . . . he took me.' Her body slumped. 'I truly regret not telling you about the first time. Goro said it was his right, his privilege. I thought he had done the same with you.'

I stood up. 'How could you not tell me?'

'Goro ordered me to say nothing to *anyone*. He said it was a special arrangement between him and Proprietor Chiba.'

Sore as I was, I stormed around the hut, ready to hit something, pull hair, or go to the practice field with my *naginata*, *bokken* or bow. 'Special arrangement!' I said, gritting my teeth and pounding my feet on the floor.

'Proprietor Chiba owned me. It is honourable to do whatever your master wishes. They may do with us as they will.'

'Not with me!'

Tashiko waited. Finally I sat down close to her and said, 'Chiba and Goro are in a conspiracy together.'

'Not truly a conspiracy, Kozaishō. I know Akio has taught you the Eight-fold Noble Path and the Four Noble Truths of Buddha, especially that "All life is suffering."'

'That's the one I hate.'

Her lips smiled, but her eyes were sorrowful. 'You may not always feel so. Chiba owned me, meaning he had the power of life and death over me. Whatever he allowed Goro to do, was, is, part of my *inago*.'

'What did he do?'

'You have experienced what Chiba likes, not only the hitting but the listening to pain. Goro has somehow come to love what was done to him in the monastery where he was raised.'

'You have not told me what it was!'

'Kozaishō, he loves to torture and rape. These bring him – fulfilment.'

126

She shook her head as if amazed by what she was telling me. 'It is the only way he is satisfied.'

I rose to my knees, my body stiff with disgust and horror. 'The only way? The only way!'

'Perhaps I injured him in a previous life,' Tashiko murmured, to the floor.

I put my arms around her, tears of outrage and love pouring, a heavy rain. 'Accepting evil as due to oneself from a prior life is against what the Goddess of Mercy upholds!'

'Not true. Let me tell you the story.' Tashiko began:

'Omaro came from the village of Kamo and was conscripted as a frontier soldier for three years. His mother accompanied him and lived with him, while his wife stayed behind to take care of the house. Omaro, for love of his wife, thought up the wicked idea of killing his mother and returning home, claiming the compassion due to mourning. However, his mother's mind, as usual, was set on doing good. He said, 'There will be a week's lecture on the scriptures in the eastern mountains. Shall we go?'

'His mother was eager to go. When alone together, he looked at her fiercely and demanded, "You, kneel on the ground!"

' "Why are you talking like that, my son? Are you possessed by a fiend?"

'The son drew a sword to kill her. She knelt and said, "We plant a tree to obtain its fruit, its shade and shelter. We bring up children to obtain their help and depend on them. The tree I nurtured has suddenly ceased to protect me from the rain."

'When the wicked son stepped closer to cut off his mother's head, the earth opened to swallow him. His mother grabbed her son's hair, appealed to Heaven, and wailed, "My child is possessed, driven to such evil!" Despite her efforts, he fell.

She brought his hair home and held funeral rites, putting the hair in a box in front of the Buddha's image and asking monks' prayers for her son.

'The mother's compassion and love were so great for her evil son, she practised good on his behalf,' Tashiko concluded. 'Indeed, we know that the unaffectionate wrongdoings of a child are punished at once, but evil deeds *never* go without penalty. Never.'

I shared with her what had happened to me with Goro. Telling my tale lessened the anger I had felt for Tashiko, but not that for Goro or Chiba.

'I cannot believe you broke his nose.' She shook her head, snorting with laughter.

'Yes.' I showed all my teeth, pleased with myself. 'You should have seen the blood spurting down his clothes.'

Tashiko's eyes widened. 'He loves his clothes. He must have hated that.'

'Oh, yes, and I think his nose will always be crooked.'

She placed her arms around me, stroking my hair. 'Easier after this.' She sighed. 'No more surprises.'

I looked up into her face. 'No more secrets.'

'The Women-for-Play *chōja*. The leader. A tenth of each gift goes to her. Any big changes, need to ask.'

'Which one is she?'

'Rin.'

'That other ugly old one? The one with not as many wrinkles?'

'Yes. Lie down. I will rub your back. "The Medicine King" from the Lotus Sutra.' I put my head in her lap. She leaned over, brushed away the tears around my eyes, and recited. ' "It is said that she who accepts and follows this will never again be born a woman." ' Our eyes smiled.

There were many other men. Several did not wait until I had finished the story. Yet because I became known as the teller of tales and the singer of modern songs, I slowly acquired an elevated class of customer. Tashiko often gave me knowing smiles when she saw the coin or two a wealthier man had left on the bamboo stand or on top of a kimono. Every time I received such a gift, I donated part to the Great-Heaven-Shining Deity, to secure good harvests for my family. Tashiko's ways differed, and she taught me to pray to the Buddha.

Many other things had to change as well.

VI. Metamorphosis

Despite Hitomi's ban, Akio and I worked with my bow and my *bokken*. Every day I went to the small practice areas within this Village of Outcasts. My three-cross relationship improved. Akio made me work more on the first part of the full draw. I pushed the bow to the left as my right elbow folded. I moved my arrow to half its length and my right hand was above and forward of my forehead. Tashiko also taught me more dances and music, especially the *koto*, the big one, thirteen strings. But the stories, dancing and music were not enough.

Rin said, 'You need education if you are going to be in my group.' She moved her large sleeve up to her large mouth and twittered, 'Both of you.' True, Tashiko and I kept each other's company except in the customers' houses.

Rin's laugh reminded me that she and Hitomi removed large amounts of the cloth and rice grateful customers gave me. Her big nostrils flared as she trumped up my supposed failure to sing new songs, use *sutra*s in my songs, or sing old ones. Their titters over wealth taken from me were the jarring cries of crows.

'First, you must look like courtly women,' Rin informed us. 'High society, the ranking Taira Clan members from Rokuhara and even from Heian-kyō, visits, not just men from nearby *shōen* and villages.'

Rin squinted. 'Oh, I forgot. You,' she scowled, leaning towards me, 'are from the country. Rokuhara is where the high-ranking Taira Clan *kuge* live. It is a huge city, with a great many mansions. Temples and shrines surround it. Many priests and monks come here from there, as you will see.

129

'*Ohaguro* – it is used in higher ranks,' Hitomi said, in a high, affected voice, through her blackened teeth. My spirit drooped to know I had to under go this process repeatedly to keep my teeth 'attractively' dark. A new tooth-darkening box, lacquered with a plum-tree design, consoled me only a little. The rest of the makeup was familiar, white rice powder for faces and rouge for cheeks and lips. The makeup the Women-for-Play used was better quality than the serving girls were given. We stored makeup in our toilet boxes. Tashiko called it her hand box, because our hands used the combs and applied the powder and rouge. She bolstered my spirits with her jests.

Next, Rin insisted we pull all the hairs from our eyebrows and paste dots of soot in the middle of our foreheads. In a moment of goodwill, or perhaps because we had been spitting black gall all day, Rin told us a story about 'The Girl Who Loved Insects'. Not only did this girl love insects, but she refused to pluck her eyebrows or blacken her teeth, and repelled her suitors with her gleaming, savage, coarse teeth. She never married, or so Rin said.

When she had finished the story, Rin put her hands on her ample hips and ordered, 'You are to do this also. This is what all the courtiers do in Heian-kyō.' Her eyes went sharp.

When we were alone Tashiko whispered to me, 'What a poor storyteller Rin is.'

Studying songs, especially the modern-style songs and dances, I practised the *koto* with the other Women-for-Play. Tashiko already played well.

For the rest of our 'education' Rin sent us to an ageing woman. Tashiko named her Otafukure. In her playful way Tashiko combined the words 'Otafuku', the God of Female Sexual Appetite, and '*fukure*', an old woman. She showed me the characters.

Otafukure's skin appeared as transparent as rice paper against sunlight. Her white hair hung in thin strands to the floor in her hut. She taught us reading and writing and we studied *The Handbook of Recipes*, a Chinese book. The pages had yellowed as teeth will without *ohaguro*.

Otafukure delighted in teaching us 'the art of joy', the Chinese recipes.

We learned names for parts of our bodies. She had us point, touch and name each part before we could continue the rest of the lessons. We studied all aspects of the Jade Stalk, the Positive Peak, the male part. The female parts included the Jewel Terrace, the Jade Veins, the Jade Gate and its Golden Gully. Otafukure emphasised the Cinnabar Cleft. This was in a woman's interior part, surrounded by the Koto Strings that grew outside.

Giggling, Tashiko played with my Koto Strings until Otafukure said, 'Stop this nonsense. Your life and your livelihood depend upon this knowledge . . . and its applications.'

We practised Propelling of the Peak in at least a dozen different ways. We used an artificial Jade Stalk, a *harigata*. Otafukure greased it, although it was so worn it did not need any preparation. With strips of cloth she tied it on to whoever was the man. The first time she tied it on to herself – she looked so funny that it was a while before she could stop us laughing.

The positions all had curious names: Bamboos at the Altar, Rat and Mouse in a Hole. Otafukure liked Double-headed Fish best and requested it most often. For this we lay facing up at each other with legs crossing over thighs. The *harigata* moved in and out, and our legs looked like fish fins. We truly appeared as a fish with two heads! This became my favourite.

When I saw Tashiko's face as Otafukure and I were practising the Double-headed Fish, her eyes flashed a strange look, the look I remembered from when I had first met her, when Chiba had first complimented me and not her. After that, I always insisted on practising Double-headed Fish with Tashiko, never Otafukure.

Tashiko and I learned to satisfy Otafukure with the *harigata*. She sang delightful wordless songs. Otafukure clearly indicated she was willing to barter more Chinese writing if either of us could make her sing these songs, but I think she preferred us together. I wanted to learn Chinese, but did not until Tashiko agreed to learn Chinese too.

I learned much Chinese.

VII. Backward Blessing

Tashiko and I went to the bathhouse after work to remove the men's stench. If the stable girls saw us arrive, they ignored us, much as we ignored them. I thought they were the lucky ones, despite their hard work and long hours.

On the way to the bathhouse we searched for the laundry people, for Aya. She grinned when we passed, but others averted their eyes. If no one else was about, Aya hugged me. Sometimes I told her a quick story. Tashiko and I went inside, scrubbed each other, talking about the work, men, songs, dances and especially clothes. How I loved the clothes!

Our conversation never included the marks and slashes. A few men enjoyed inflicting pain. She saw my bruises, and I certainly saw hers.

Some liked to hold us down. Some used ropes to tie us. Some cut us to see the blood, which Rin permitted, provided it was not noticeable for our next customers and did not scar. A few brought other men to join them. Some wanted two women.

With Tashiko's gentle tutoring, I found I could endure this, too. She spoke of the Four Noble Truths of the Buddha. She taught me that all life was suffering. Nothing in this world was real. All was transitory. The release from this suffering was the Eight-fold Noble Path, just as I had learned from Akio.

I made a song of the Eight-fold Noble Path so Aya and others could learn it too. Tashiko and I often sang this song scrubbing each other's backs. She loved to teach it to everyone around her.

Otafukure died after the season's solstice, *setsubun*. The evening before, the celebrations had roared through the village. Everywhere there were cries of 'Oni! Ogre! Go out!' and 'Happiness enter.' Some Women-for-Play chanted, 'Oni go out' and 'Happiness enter,' using the 'out' and 'enter' another way. I heard them as I walked with a client back to Main House. Later I laughed.

Everyone else was throwing the roasted soybeans that would keep the demons and *oni* away from the new spring season, or picking up the soybeans for luck. The superstitious girls' throws and shouts were the most enthusiastic.

The next morning at breakfast, Hitomi and Rin announced that Otafukure had died in her sleep. Everything stopped, and we all attended her funeral, because she had once been the *chōja*, as well as the teacher of Chinese and the pleasing arts. We built her a funeral house by the river. Representations of a goose, a heron, a kingfisher a sparrow and a pheasant brought the different required offerings. When I asked Tashiko why we gave these gifts, she simply shrugged. I presumed the reason was custom.

Daigoro no Goro conducted the burial ceremony. His voice was not unpleasing, although more nasal than it had been before I had broken his nose. The ceremony droned on, taking at least a full morning with all the prayers and salt scattering. Sometimes during his recitation, his gaze would find me. At those times, his voice thinned and his face tightened, especially around the eyes. Akio had been right: this priest was my enemy.

We sang and danced all day and night, but I, with a dagger strapped to my leg, and Akio watched him all the time until he left the Village.

After *setsubun*, icy winds penetrated my kimonos. We had enough food, but Rin measured our firewood, like worms for too many baby birds. A light snow had fallen, and the cold forced me to breathe through my nose. When I returned from archery or sword work and checked my mirror, my cheeks showed red even through my whitened face.

That evening, I looked for Tashiko in the meal room. She was not there, which was unusual. I checked her hut. No Tashiko. I found her in her work hut, lying on the floor, like a broken dish, not moving, bleeding all over. She could not talk. Her eyes and lips were swollen shut, cuts everywhere, but she was alive, thank the Gods.

I called for help and prayed to the Goddess of Mercy. Two samurai arrived. I ordered, 'Carry her to my hut.'

When Tashiko regained consciousness, I made sure she first heard my voice and felt my hands softly on her face. 'Relax,' I said. 'I am here. Breathe. I am going to Hitomi. I shall be back soon.'

Hitomi huffed and Rin jabbed Tashiko all over while she winced and groaned. Hitomi sniffed, and said, 'Unfit to work. Yakamashita will not see you again.'

Overnight Tashiko developed a fever. To ask for healing from the Gods, I placed a rice-straw rope around a tree where they connected with the earth. I used the tree near my hut, according to the traditions, to help her.

Rin gave me permission to attend my friend. That was good, because I would have anyway. She probably knew it. Hitomi furnished a salve to be applied several times each day so that Tashiko healed quickly without scars. Scarred, she would be worth little, and there were many gashes because of Yakamashita's long fingernails.

Her beautiful skin, under the ointment, looked like wet laundry. The ointment's sharp smell brought stinging tears.

'No,' she murmured, through her swollen lips.

'No what?'

'No ointment,' she said, although I could barely understand her.

'You need it. Without it, you will scar. You know what that means,' I said, as gently as I could.

'Let me scar.'

'What are you talking about? You have a fever. You are not rational. Do you know what will happen if you are scarred?'

Wincing, she said, 'Yes. I will no longer be a Woman-for-Play.'

'Is that what you want? To be away from me?' I could not believe what she said.

'Yes. No more men. No more Daigoro no Goro.'

I knew she had fevered thoughts. Yakamashita I could understand, but Goro? 'Hitomi said no more Yakamashita. What do you mean, Goro?'

She did not respond. A horrible idea came to me. 'Goro? Is this the kind of thing he did to you? This is what you meant by torture?' Perhaps the anger in my voice made her listen to me. When she had said Goro tortured her, I had thought – I did not know what I had thought.

'No – no – no more,' she mumbled.

'No? No more what?' I asked, more forcefully.

'Yakamashita goes with Goro. They like the same . . . things.'

'Goes with? Same things?'

Tears leaked from her eyes and ran into the slashes on her face, neck and chest. Each tear made her gasp. It hurt me to see her suffer. I grabbed a soft cloth and wiped each tear before it burned her. I asked again, 'Tashiko, how do you know?'

'Goro visited when Proprietor Chiba's Gods of Directions made him go away.'

'Yes, I remember. You told me.' I kept my voice calm and soft, while my hands itched for a weapon. My fingers dabbed away each tear.

'I told you . . . about the two fans?'

'Yes, Tashiko. You did.' That son of an *oni*, Goro, still lived, although not by my choice.

Tashiko laid a hand on mine. 'He – he forced himself on me after every dance.'

'I am truly sorry.' No wonder she had been sad whenever Chiba had Divergent Directions.

'He . . . For his pleasure, he likes to hurt.'

Wiping her tears, flowing fast now, I said, 'I know.'

'The hurting prepares him, his Jade Stalk . . . Otherwise . . .'

'So you danced, he beat you and – Yakamashita is like Goro?'

'Scarred, disfigured, they will not want me.'

'Let me help you. Let me help you heal. I can teach you to defend yourself. After all, I broke Goro's nose.' I leaned close to her mangled face, smiling as best I could, 'Imagine what we could do to Yakamashita.'

This brought a tiny glint to her eyes. It soon went out. 'I could not, Kozaishō. I must do as my master requests.'

'We have the same owner. She wishes you to heal. She ordered me to help you. Did you not tell me it is honourable to do as our master wishes?'

More tears, but she agreed.

I do not think I could have lived with her as an *eta*. That, or work as a lowly serving girl, would have been all that was left to her. I needed her with me.

135

She allowed me to attend to her. No cloth touched her skin because I had to apply salve to all her injuries. If covered, wounds festered, with greater danger of scarring.

Spring rains played drums on the ceiling. Hitomi gave us only a little charcoal, not enough to heat both of our huts. The meagre amount was enough to keep one hut warm. She rested with me, her *futon* next to mine. Too warm with clothes, I also slept without.

Nights were worse than days. Turning in her sleep awakened her, and her soft cries awakened me. Bodily functions were unbearable because of gashes to her Jade Gate. She did well, though, grimacing and making little noise. I fed her cooled rice water, as she had done for me. Tears formed in her eyes as she ate because her lips had been slashed.

To relax her, I combed her hair gently. I brushed her arms with my fingertips, rubbed her feet and stroked her face where there were no gashes.

Tashiko reminded me that the Buddha said all life was suffering. Then how could nothing be real? I saw her true suffering – yet she said all was transitory. I knew that eventually she would heal. Perhaps that was what she had meant.

I read 'The Bodhisattva Medicine King' to her and recited 'The Constellation King Flower', which said that if a woman heard that chapter and understood it, she would never be born in a woman's body again. At least, that was what Tashiko said.

Days later, Tashiko's fever gone, Hitomi and Rin came to check again. They scrutinised her body and the quality of my care.

Rin wanted to know when Tashiko could go back to work.

Hitomi said, mostly to herself, 'Yakamashita knew better than to scar you. But even if you do scar, we could probably sell you. With your clothes on, no one will know you are damaged.' She left, mumbling to herself, 'He has cost me much in the past . . .'

At this, Tashiko's salty tears on her injuries made her twitch in pain and opened the torrent of my anger. Sell her? They had better not. I would not lose her.

'I will be vigilant,' I promised her, and promised myself that I would keep my temper, holding her less badly cut hand.

'Perhaps my destiny is to be disfigured. If I am, I will accept it,' she said.

I would not accept it. To reassure her, I repeatedly read the part where the Medicine King burned his arms: 'He said, "I throw away both my arms, yet I am assured I will regain the golden body of the Buddha." His arms were restored instantly.'

This passage calmed Tashiko, so I read it every day.

After working so hard on the Noble Path, she was receiving all this pain! 'How could Hitomi allow such a low worm to do such wickedness? And to you!' I said. 'You have talent. You had earned a place with the higher-caste customers, as I have.'

Tashiko stared at me.

'How could Hitomi be so foolish, so wasteful as to throw you to Yakamashita?' I asked Tashiko.

'Greed. Jealousy. Of what others have.' Tashiko pushed her eyebrows up, blanching. After a few breaths she said, 'Every livelihood does not lead to the other seven of the Eight-fold Path. But the first seven of the Eight-fold Path lead to Right Livelihood.'

I looked at her. How odd. 'That is exactly what Akio told me before we came here.'

'Inflicting pain deliberately on others creates *karma*.' Tashiko took small sips of water so she could talk more. 'When Madam Hitomi values Yakamashita's wealth most, she creates her own *inago*.' She turned to a new position on the *futon* and grimaced with a deep grunt.

I patted her lightly where there were no wounds. 'What about Yakamashita's *inago*?'

'Life's suffering cannot be avoided. To impose it deliberately on others can be risky. Whatever a person created in this life, he will meet that *inago* in the next.'

'What really happened?' I had not dared to ask before.

Tashiko drank some water. She asked without words.

'No. He was never a client of mine. I have never met him.' I sighed with gratitude.

'Wiry but quite strong. Quite wealthy. Very long fingernails. Requested Tongue Cut Sparrow. Close to the end, but before miracle, I said, "The unkind wife cut the tongue of her husband's favourite sparrow because it ate her rice paste." His face flushed. Dark cinnabar. He breathed in. Hit me. Shouted. Called me an evil sparrow. "Evil! Evil!" He beat me. First hands. Fists. Nails. Those nails. Until I could not move. I do not remember when he finished.'

Sympathetic tears raced down my cheeks. I wished I had a spear to throw into Yakamashita's heart. I wondered if I would have fought back, even though it was strictly forbidden.

'Did you remember not to make a sound?' I recalled what some of the more experienced Women-for-Play had told us.

Tashiko nodded.

'Did you react to the blows? Any reaction causes more rage.'

'I tried not to.'

We sat quiet for a time.

'Recite "The Medicine King". It provides relief from pain to all the living.' Tashiko's eyes smiled, the only part of her that did not hurt when it moved.

Such foolishness, I thought, but I read, ' "Just as the thirsty are satisfied with a sweet, clear water, just as the freezing are warmed by fire . . ." ' I gave her water and stroked her forehead ' ". . . a boat at a river crossing, an emperor for a people, a light that replaces all darkness." '

'So,' Tashiko whispered, 'the Lotus Sutra removes all suffering, all illness. It releases us from the *karma* of mortal life.'

I tried to believe as she believed, but could not. This *sutra* did not truly remove her pain, although I certainly desired it for her.

There was no honour here with these defilements, the blood and afflictions. Had I failed my family? Where could I find honour?

BOOK 6

I. A Bright Time

When Tashiko's wounds no longer bled, I visited Main House and requested Purification rites. 'Because of the blood,' Tashiko had explained, when she asked for this.

I returned to tell her the bad news, my body tense with the fury of a cornered cat. 'Daigoro no Goro is now the priest from Uji. He will come.'

Tashiko shook her head. 'He performs the Purification rites here for women who give birth. Madam Hitomi boasted to us that she had obtained priests from both the Tendai Sect *and* the Taira Clan for her girls.'

'I cannot believe that, with all the priests around here, he is the one.' I wondered whether my *bokken* would be welcome at the ceremony.

We prepared for Purification with Abstention and Cleansing. We ate no food and drank only water for two days and two nights. Tashiko's stomach rumbled, and by the first evening her breath smelt sour. I had not eaten much while I took care of her, and my stomach was quieter with only the water.

The next morning we went to the Purification hut. Tashiko scattered a pinch of salt in each of the four directions of the bath. We scrubbed, rinsed and soaked.

'I wish to thank you, my dear friend, for all your hard work.'

'No need.' I prodded her with my toes. 'I am happy you are finally well. Besides, no men.' I relaxed in the water at the thought, but our eyes danced together.

We dressed in our best robes and went to a special place near the

141

birthing hut. My empty stomach knotted itself into a hard ball and battered inside me. I saw Goro.

The damaged nose lay askew in the middle of that bird face. His thin hair was combed flat against his skull, as courtiers wore it. His clothes were made of fine silk and carefully arranged. His eyes were hostile.

Hitomi walked back to Main House and nodded to Goro before he entered the hut. In one hand he carried a small *nusa*, with only three white cloth strips attached to its short handle. His empty hand motioned to us, and we made the five-point bow.

'May the Goddess Seori-tsu-hime, who lives in the white waters of swift-flowing rivers, purify you and grant you swift-flowing forgiveness.' He lifted the *nusa* and brought it down on each of our shoulders, making a slight whistle.

'May the Goddess Seori-tsu-hime, who lives in the white waters of swift-flowing rivers, send you white-water Cleansing with pure liquid forgiveness.' He repeated the movements with the *nusa*, then turned to leave.

'Honourable Daigoro no Goro, please, there is more,' Tashiko called.

What in the nether world was Tashiko doing?

He spun round on one foot. 'Do you not trust the Goddess Seori-tsu-hime?' His lips pressed and puckered together.

'Honourable Daigoro no Goro, we need to be purified. Completely. I trust the Goddess Seori-tsu-hime.'

'You have had adequate Purification.' His eyes gleamed like those of a rat in a night without a moon.

'I trust the Goddess Seori-tsu-hime,' Tashiko bit her lip 'but . . . not you, Daigoro no Goro.'

My shoulders arched up to my ears. I placed my feet in a defensive stance. What would Goro do? 'I, too, honourable Daigoro no Goro, wish to be fully cleansed and purified.'

'How dare you question me?' Goro inclined his head to mine, pushing his free hand towards us, palm down. Next he pointed to me. 'And how dare you talk of our Buddha?'

Tashiko sat back on her heels. She quoted 'The Medicine King' and other parts of the Lotus Sutra to Goro. Each statement reinforced the belief that Nirvana was accessible to all.

Goro's face flushed darker with each word she spoke, radiating fierceness like lightning strikes. His hands clamped on the *nusa*. It broke with a crack.

Tashiko assumed her five-point bow and sat back again. I imitated her.

'You will pay – you will both pay – for this insolence. And impropriety. I am no Pure Land prostitute priest. I am Tendai.' His face flashed evil. He turned and walked out of the hut. 'Madam Hitomi will know how you broke the *nusa*.'

Bitterness sprang to my lips: 'Do you know what you have done? What were you thinking?'

She shook her head. Her face had cooled to its usual pallor, despite the warm air in the hut. 'I needed Purification.' She forced her breaths, hard and noisy. 'Tomorrow is the Twenty-third day of the Fifth Month. Where I grew up, we always drank *sake*. Prayed to Kannon-sama, Goddess of Mercy. Prayed to Yakushi Butsu, Buddha of Healing, and especially to Jizō . . . patron of people in Hell . . .' Her voice trailed off. 'I just wanted – to be properly cleansed, to worship with you, you and me . . . in the temple. You and me – with the Buddha.' She bent over, tears gushing, and her chest heaved, like clothes flapping in the wind. I smoothed her head and back until she quieted.

I expected we would be among those who screamed that night, but neither of us received much punishment. I had acquired sufficient favour from Hitomi by soothing her important customers to avoid Hell Hut. She had lost money while I had not worked. Beating me or Tashiko would not be productive.

Tashiko brought out a tiny well-worn book from within her *futon*. 'This is the *sutra*.' She sang it in a chanting voice.

I sat on the floor. That Tashiko could treasure an object! Or that she had hidden such a beautiful thing from me, from everyone.

'This is the *sutra* that says even a woman can reach Buddhahood.'

'It cannot.'

'Everyone says that a woman cannot reach Nirvana.' She leaned over so our noses almost touched. 'But in here,' she tapped the book with the pad of her little finger, 'it says we can.'

Somehow Tashiko found *sake* for the next day. 'Since the priest did not complete our Purification, we are required to drink this. Because of all the wounds and the blood.'

I did what Tashiko asked, although I still believed as my parents did. We never had *sake* to cleanse blood, only water, rinsing mouths and hands. I promised myself I would do that also.

Tashiko returned to a full day's work. I took a few of her clients to lighten her burden. At the end of the day she was rubbing her back.

'May I practise on you to strengthen my fingers?' I mimed a massage.

She answered by lying face down on her *futon*. I sat beside her, found the knots in her lower back and worked them on them until they smoothed. After kneading her upper and lower back, my hands cupped her buttocks and lazily traced their perfect outline. The twilight, through the curtain of our hut, drew shadow patterns on Tashiko's slightly reddened skin. My breath stilled. Had Otafukure taught me enough? I sighed.

She turned over and, with both hands, lowered my face to hers. Footsteps crossed outside and stopped me, head up, for a moment. I realised my thick hair had fallen over her body and blocked my sight of her. I pulled it away.

My hands found her breasts, firmer than Otafukure's. A little breeze fluttered my door cloth. My fingertips kneaded her nipples, which contracted into small buds. My own nipples tightened. Tashiko showed crinkled skin over her shoulders and chest as if she were cold.

My hands advanced downwards to the places we had studied. Down to the sources of ecstasy. I noticed a small scar on her hip as I smoothed my hands over her glossy skin. Where had that come from? My fingers continued through her light brown hair. I pushed my face closer and inhaled her bush-clover woody fragrance. Tasted her salty sweetness. I lapped her substance. Tashiko did not sing, like Otafukure. She hummed the songs our mothers had sung. I heard the harbinger of spring, the brush warbler, its beautiful music. I thought of my father and how happy he would be to know I had found a new family.

Others chopped wood, gathered charcoal, cooked our food and even cleaned our costumes because of our status. Girls did all of that, as I had when I had first here come to at the Village of Outcasts. Tashiko and I enjoyed the bathhouse after the day's assignment of men, my lessons and lessons to others, and my practice with Akio, whenever we could find time. Tashiko and I ate the evening meal alone in our hut, unless Hitomi or Rin demanded we go to the communal dining room. The quiet brought comfort.

The true joy began. Tashiko and I rubbed each other's sore backs, feet, necks, hands and faces. Next came light licking and caresses until we both breathed short and heavy. The memories of the day's monotonous offensives faded into a forgotten dream and our tender fantasies flowered. We joked to ourselves, named ourselves royal clothiers who worked embroideries. Tashiko liked arm and shoulder designs, while I preferred neck and feet. We stroked lightly and petted, wove brocades of gentleness with fervour.

Some other Women-for-Play teased and called us 'stew-pots', a loathsome word for women who love each other, but we never referred to ourselves in that way. I did ask, after a particularly vigorous time, 'Are you the male or am I?' Tashiko lay on top of me, yet I had just pleased her. We laughed, and satisfied each other again.

One evening I whispered, 'Not since before I was sold from the fields of my father have I been so happy.'

Tashiko answered, with her smile of pure summer sun, 'You are my heart, just as the Buddha is my spirit. You are my reward for good deeds in a past life.'

It was a bright time, although work grew to be both heaven and hell. I loved my stories, their exotic places, gods and demons, which directed people into good behaviour, the costumes and dances that made my body content. Yet to follow wondrous tales with abuse created a deep, sorrow-filled well in which my spirit had to float or drown.

In the year I celebrated my thirteenth birth anniversary and Tashiko her sixteenth, we noticed changes in our bodies, the enlarging breasts, the sprouting of hair, the rounding of our hips and legs.

My cycle began two years after my arrival at the Village. Tashiko taught me to care for my 'usual defilement'. I was not happy about this for it meant I could not touch Tashiko until after my Purification. She and I had to sleep apart.

She also taught me to drink the steeped morning herbs each day to avoid a baby. Several Women-for-Play bore children. Infrequently a wealthy patron acquired one and took her away with him. I wanted no such hindrance to my martial-arts practice. I had no desire for a child of mine to be brought up as the child of a fourth or fifth wife or, worse, in this Village. This Village of the Unclean.

Our monthly defilements soon arrived together. Each month we relished a few days together – alone. We read *sutras* together, lit incense or a candle. She often read 'The Medicine King'. I do not think I ever tired of how the Lotus Sutra, like the sun, destroyed all that was not good – in Tashiko's voice, like the music of low drums.

When I complained about my work, Tashiko counted my blessings.

'To begin, Madam Hitomi,' Tashiko murmured, 'has not caught you and Akio on your daily jaunts.'

I shivered and thought of the last time I had eaten cooled rice water for three days because I had torn my mouth badly.

'You are blessed by the Goddess of Beauty. Even in misfortune you have risen to a place of honour.' Tashiko rubbed her lips along my neck, prompting in me tremors of exaltation.

'I feel no honour to be brought high in this place, this Village of Outcasts.' My fingers traced across her forehead. 'You, your kindness, the ultimate beauty.'

'Lie down beside me, and I will read to you.'

We journeyed together from there, every evening a pinnacle of tenderness and devotion, followed by the ruthless plunge into the dark cave of daily work, and next the return to our heaven.

My duty and my honour meant absolute obedience.

I performed my duty until I lost my most precious gift.

II. Additions

A servant called one day. 'Madam Hitomi orders you to Main House.'

A *bokken* hit me in the stomach. 'Me? Why?'

The servant refused to look at me, walked backwards, turned and ran. What trouble could this be?

I wanted to stay away from Hell Hut, but walking that route was the shortest from my hut to Main House. I did not wish to risk taking longer. Tashiko had named it Hell Hut, that demon's den I had visited when I had first arrived at the Village. Hitomi's assistant performed her services in there. Muffled cries and moans hovered in the air along with the snipes, autumn birds. My shoulders shook at the memory of hot pokers. Was I to be next? No. I was not going there again.

Hitomi sat in the big room of Main House, petting a grey and white cat big enough to be a dog and leaning against pillows as bright as my spirits were dark. Cat odours spread through the heady incense.

'Egret, Egret.' Hitomi rubbed behind big Egret's ears. Muffled screams brought a twist to the corner of her mouth.

Cats rubbed against my legs, mewing, as I made obeisance.

'You are late. What took you so long?'

'I came when I was called, honourable one.'

'Humph. The men say you tell them stories. Is this not so?'

'Yes, Madam Hitomi. Have I offended?'

'What type of stories do you tell them?'

I told her. 'Honourable Madam Hitomi, what have I done wrong?'

'Where did you learn these stories?'

'From the honourable Chiba no Tashiyori. Also from the samurai at the *shōen*. And the Lotus Sutra's stories.'

'Kozaishō, the men find your stories . . .' she looked at her cat, then turned her face to me '. . . alluring. You will have a tutor. You must learn more stories.'

Tutor? I worked to keep my eyebrows in the same place. Not only did I need to look like the aristocrats, the fancies, I was supposed to read and write like them. What did she expect of me?

'No, Madam Hitomi. You do me too much honour.' I made the token refusal.

'Why do you tell the stories?'

'Why, honourable one?' I explained about Aya and the clothes, and attending to the Women-for-Play. Perhaps she wanted to see if I would tell her the truth.

'It is settled.' The grey and white cat clawed, making holes in her dark kimono, then jumped off her lap. She picked up another cat and stroked it.

'No, Madam Hitomi. I am too stupid,' I said, firmness in my voice. 'Tashiko learns faster, and her brushwork outdoes mine.'

She held the cat under its jaw and scratched behind its ears. She lifted it off the ground by its jaw. The cat squirmed and tried to scratch her. 'When you study with a tutor, Kozaishō, you will gain in honour here.'

She knew my mission. She held me like the cat, but I did not give up. 'Honourable one, I humbly request Tashiko learn also.'

'It would cost too much. Just you.' Her lips remained straight, but were not pressed together. She was still scratching the cat, now back on her lap and held there.

'Madam Hitomi, you know Tashiko.' I used my submissive voice. 'She will be much better than this humble servant. She will teach the other Women-for-Play.'

Her hands stroked the cat along his back. It purred.

'Madam Hitomi, all your Women-for-Play could learn from just the two of us.'

'Yes, Kozaishō, all for only two. You and Tashiko do learn well.'

'Thank you, honourable one.'

'I have two servants who will help with your duties while you are learning and teaching . . .' She stood, and her eyes crinkled.

I waited. I used what Chiba had taught me.

She clapped three times.

Two girls stepped into the big room.

Each girl was dressed in a plain style, from the country, yet the clothes were well made, of excellent-quality silk and design. The black kimono of the smaller one showed pink streaks. Red flowers brightened the blue of the other's. I knew those fabrics from the *shōen*. My eyes widened as each girl bowed low to Hitomi without lifting their heads. A single clap from Hitomi, and they raised their faces. My lips went upwards – I was unable to stop them.

> Family again
> Surrounded three times again:
> Giggling sisterly
> Gossip, in sunlight – away
> From my dark forests' travail

There stood Emi, with her round face. From Chiba's. Warmth spread inside my chest. Someone I knew and could trust. So much taller! Still pretty, her teeth had grown in and her eyes crossed less.

The other girl was younger than Emi. I did not yet know her. Her look was different from that of the rest of us – oval face and golden brown eyes. Both were budding into womanhood, as I had been when I came to the village. One sister. Possibly two new sisters. Sisters. A family.

My own sisters.

At least for a while.

Unfamiliar footsteps stopped on the *watadono* outside our hut late that first night. I nodded to Tashiko and slipped my fingers around my *bokken*. I recognised the shadow cast through the thin cloth fluttering across our door. The new girl. Misuki.

'Come in, Misuki,' I said softly.

She bowed before and after entering.

Tashiko pointed to her chest. 'I am Tashiko. Speak.'

149

Misuki pulled her head out and down, like a turtle, and whispered, 'I bring a message from Master Isamu, at Proprietor Chiba's *shōen*. Master Isamu says he misses assisting Kozaishō at practice. He sends a message of greeting to Akio and his family also. He says prayers for you. He says you and Akio must be vigilant. You are in more . . .' she put her index finger in her mouth '. . . jeopardy, yes, more jeopardy . . . and danger.'

'Danger?' Tashiko's relaxed body shifted to arrow straight. 'What danger?'

'I do not know, honourable Tashiko.'

'What else did Master Isamu say?'

Misuki lowered her head and shook it.

'Tashiko, who have you told about Akio and me?' I asked, after Misuki left.

Her eyes stretched wider. 'No one. I would not risk your safety for my life.'

I touched her hand. 'I know. But someone has betrayed me.'

III. Emi Laughs

The next day I told Akio about Master Isamu's message.

Akio's one eyebrow pointed up in the middle. 'Little one, we must stop. Harm may come to you.'

'No, Akio. I must do this.'

'Must? Are you sure, Kozaishō?' I observed the squinting concern in his eyes. He grasped my shoulder with his thick fingers, as if he could lift me up with that one hand and cradle me in his arms.

'Not only because of the omens at Proprietor Chiba's. The Goddess of Mercy came in a dream. She said I am to be a samurai.'

'She did?'

I related the details of the dream to him.

'The Goddess of Mercy brought you all those samurai implements in your dream? Naturally we must go on.' Akio leaned over and put his hands on his knees. 'We will vary our meeting times. Do not come here by the same route every day.'

'Hitomi will not beat me because I bring in more profit than any other Woman-for-Play. Beating me loses her revenue.'

Akio straightened. 'Little one, if you trample on Madam Hitomi's pride, or Rin's, you may find Hitomi's pride is stronger than yours. And contempt is not part of the Way.'

My neck warmed with his rebuke. 'Yes, honourable Akio. I will take precautions.'

'The laws of *karma* are perfect.' He sighed with a morning-quail sound and adjusted the position of my wrist nearer the bow. 'I am eager for *karma* to visit Proprietor Chiba.'

I glanced up at Akio and saw his grin. I smiled too. With a thought of swift *inago*, an image of Chiba stood in front of my target, his big belly almost blocking it. My arrows struck him in the heart. Each time. By now I had graduated from the novice target, *makiwara*, to the smaller and much further away *mato*, which all samurai used.

Time passed like the snap of a fan. Summer again, and my two younger sisters had worked through the Village of Outcasts' hierarchy.

Over our dinner Tashiko mumbled, 'Misuki and Emi are going to be Women-for-Play. I am anxious for Emi.'

'We have to stop it. Emi is still a little girl in her mind.'

'Kozaishō, if the master orders me to do something, I do it. That is the only honourable way.'

I put down my bowl and chopsticks. 'Is it not honourable to save someone from the daily defilements of our life?'

'Not if that is their *karma*.'

'*Karma! Inago!*' I clenched my fists. 'You would allow harm to come to an innocent? That is honourable?' I pointed my finger at Tashiko. 'Are we not to use the strengths given us?'

'Yes – I suppose so.' She turned to me.

'Are we not to use these gifts with compassion and mercy?' I stood, fists to my sides.

'Yes, but . . .'

I crossed my arms and leaned my face lower. 'What is the "but"?'

'Well . . .' She lowered her eyes down.

'Is it honourable to allow someone to suffer if we can use our gifts to avoid that suffering?'

'Perhaps—'

'In the Lotus Sutra? The monk interfered.' I told the story:

'A man vowed to build a temple if he came home safely from combat. When he escaped harm, he went to the capital to exchange his belongings for gold and paints and reached the port of Naniwa. A seaman was selling four big turtles, and the man advised people to buy them and set them free. Then he rented a boat to cross the sea. Late at night the sailors, filled with greed, said, "Into the sea with you!" The man tried to reason with them, but they would not listen. Finally, after making a vow, he sank into the black waters. When the water came up to his waist, he felt stones under his feet. In the morning he found he was carried by the turtles. They left him on the beach after nodding to him three times. The turtles, which had been set free, came back to repay his kindness. Eventually the thieving sailors visited his temple to sell the gold and paints they had stolen from him. They were petrified with terror when they saw him. He did not punish them, but told them to make a Buddha image to be consecrated in the pagoda.

'Even an animal does not forget gratitude, and repays an act of kindness. How, then, could a righteous man fail to be grateful?'

Tashiko merely nodded.

'The monk interfered. We could interfere.' I sat beside her. 'We *should* interfere.' I stabbed my chopsticks into my rice, knowing it was not good luck.

Tashiko lifted her hand to me and took my chopsticks out of the rice. 'What can we do?'

'A story. A story might make Emi unsuitable to be a Woman-for-Play.'

'A story?' She pulled her hair away from her neck and twisted it with her fingers. 'Change Emi's *karma*? Go against Madam Hitomi? That is too great a risk.'

'Do you want Emi servicing men? What if Aya had to do it too?'

'No.' She grimaced. 'But a story? Something so simple could not change Emi's *karma*.'

'No. A story cannot change *karma*, but a story can change what people do and how they react.'

'True. Your stories have soothed arguments.' Tashiko rubbed my cheek with the back of her hand.

'I checked through my stories and consulted with our tutor. The *oni* is perfect. This story will do for Emi. First, let us share our plan with those we trust.'

'No, Kozaishō.' Her hand flattened against my arm. 'The fewer people who know the better,'

'What about Misuki?'

Tashiko nodded.

'Let you and me and Misuki be less productive. Slow down. Have more trouble with clothes and hair. Only a little. Not enough to arouse suspicion. When I tell Hitomi we need Emi for clothes and hair, our argument will be more convincing.'

'We can do that.' Tashiko's full lips twitched up.

'No. *I* can do it. This is too dangerous. *I* will tell the story. You should not be involved.'

'Emi is one of us. Chiba and Goro's cast-offs.' Tashiko gathered my hands in hers. 'We are in this together, Kozaishō.'

'Alright, but Hitomi's wrath will be immense. She will not appreciate losing someone she has purchased.'

Tashiko dipped her head to one side, committing to the plan.

Beyond the bathhouse, away from everyone else, I told the story to Emi with Tashiko and Misuki.

There once was an *oni* who captured a daughter, but her mother rescued her. The mother and daughter spotted a boat and escaped from the *oni* by travelling in the river. The *oni* came and drank all the water in the river in one gulp. The boat stuck in the mud and mire. As the *oni* approached, the horrified women prayed to the Goddess of Mercy.

The Goddess called on the mother and daughter to put their kimonos over their heads. At the sight of the women's nakedness, the *oni* roared with laughter. All the water spouted out of his mouth. The *oni* did not stop laughing until the boat had carried the women to safety. Since that moment on the river, every time they undressed, they remembered the *oni*'s roar and their miraculous escape, and laughed and laughed and laughed.

I hurled my kimonos over my head. Tashiko did the same. She laughed. I heard her fall down, and continue her hawk-like guffaws.

Emi did not laugh. Tashiko gave me an I-did-not-think-this would-work look, but I persisted.

I repeated the story, encouraging Emi to her pull her kimonos over her head. Tashiko and I pretended to laugh. The third time, Emi giggled. By the fifth time, she giggled more. I told her the story until Tashiko grew weary, and I was glad that it was short.

I needed to ensure that my plan worked. Tashiko and I located the adjoining room where Emi was going. It contained only the required watching-hole, a few pillows and a small basket for wiping cloths. I checked to see no clients hid already, as some desired, and posted myself.

Emi and her first customer walked in, a portly man. I eased my legs on to the pillows.

'So, Emi, this is your first time.' He patted her on the shoulder and smiled. 'Come here. We shall go slowly.'

Emi turned her pretty face and crossed eyes up to him and smiled back. My shoulder and arm stung, prickling all over. I adjusted my position on the pillows.

The man slipped off his outer robe, threw it on to the clothing-tree, and plopped on to the *futon*. His awkwardness reminded me of Chiba.

'Sit beside me, here.' He patted the spot next to him with one hand and, with the other, made beckoning gestures.

She did so. The man placed a wide wobbly arm around Emi's shoulders. 'Let us take off your kimono.'

With that, he loosened her sash.

I held my breath.

'Pull it off, Emi.'

Emi tugged at her sash. She looked up questioningly, the sash hanging across her hands like a dead snake.

'Good, Emi. Now remove your kimono.'

My fingernails almost cut through the pillow's fabric.

Emi drew aside the front of her kimono. The man licked his tongue across his upper lip.

Emi laughed. She didn't giggle. She roared, booming from her belly.

The man's face transformed to a big red chrysanthemum. His ears and scalp turned bright red too.

I waited, clamping my jaws, fearing the man's response.

Emi's laughter went on and on.

The man's skin remained reddened as he stared at Emi.

He put his head into his hands.

Turning his back to me, he stood up and pulled his robes off the clothing-tree.

When I could see his face, his mouth was trembling, hands clenched at his sides.

I would not let him hit her. The story had been to protect her against hurt. I stood up, bending over to look through the watching-hole but ready to rescue her.

The man chuckled.

I sighed.

'Perhaps another time.' He ruffled the hair on top of Emi's head and pinched her cheek. He left the room, sniggering.

I breathed again.

My story had worked, but now Emi would answer to Hitomi. I stole out of the room to tell Tashiko.

Later that day, Hitomi put Emi with a second customer and I hid again. This taller man was, muscular, with a long moustache and beard. He was no amicable uncle.

He entered, and she followed. 'Help me take off my robe.' His voice was flat as he turned his back to her. In my hand I clutched a small pillow, already shredded.

Emi tugged at his robe without removing his sash first. She found it and her fingers fumbled. The man bent his head. 'Here, let me show you.'

He flung the brown brocade outer robe on to the clothing-tree, like a shroud.

My fingers knotted to stop my stomach flying into my throat.

'Your name is Emi?' His voice was lower now, soft words and soft sounds like the hissing of an angry monkey.

'Yes, honourable sir.'

'Good.' He sounded harsh, irritated.

I prayed to all the Gods.

'Take off your robe.'

I bit my lip.

Emi lay back on the *futon* and melted into laughter, giggling and tittering. Her legs wriggled like those of the three-year-old she was inside. He waited. She persisted. He sat up, dressed. A brown mountain smouldering with the reds and oranges of a sunset, he glowered at Emi and stormed out of the hut.

I raced to Tashiko. We had to go to Main House.

Hitomi sent for Emi. Tashiko and I accompanied her. I prayed to the Goddess of Mercy to sway Hitomi. I could not allow Emi to suffer for something I had caused. I prepared myself to take the consequences, thinking of the cold rice broth.

Emi entered Main House first.

Everyone heard her cries.

Next it was our turn.

Hitomi rose from the pillows and pointed a finger at us, a cat leaping off her. 'You two again! She says *you* told her a story!'

I sat back on my heels. 'Yes, Madam Hitomi, I did. My idea. My story. Alone.'

Tashiko remained in five-point.

Hitomi harrumphed, returned to her pillows, sat high above us. Her nostrils flared open and shut. A cat curled next to her. She scratched behind its ears. It purred loudly, like the swell of rapid river water after a storm.

That sound gave me an idea. 'Honourable Madam Hitomi, may I speak?'

She said, 'Yes,' accentuated with silent daggers.

'I know of . . .

'. . . a farmer's cat that did not catch any mice. This farmer feared losing his grain. He was so worried, he could not sleep. His lack of sleep disrupted his concentration, and he cut his foot badly. The healer directed him to stay in bed for two days. Now the farmer worried more than ever and slept even less, until the cat curled up next to him and purred so loudly that the farmer fell into a deep sleep. The cat came back each night and helped the farmer sleep.'

All this time the cat purred. Hitomi's face calmed to the surface of a pond on a windless day.

'Honourable one, Emi can be like that cat. She *is* quite slow, yet everything has a useful purpose. She works well in the laundry and can assist Tashiko and me.'

Hitomi's hand stopped scratching, and the cat stopped purring. 'I do not believe she is *that* slow.'

'Oh, honourable Madam Hitomi, Emi needs months to learn a simple dance. I know, because I had the honour to teach her at the *shōen* of the honourable Chiba no Tashiyori.'

Hitomi's hand flapped at me, and the cat nipped her.

Tashiko sat on her heels and murmured, with her head down, 'Emi cannot play an instrument.'

'She has been here only a short time, not long enough to learn the *biwa*.' Hitomi rubbed her hand where the cat had left marks.

'She cannot rouge her lips – the sides are always crooked.' I worked to keep my face blank but was pleased that the cat had wounded Hitomi. I wished I could have clamped my teeth into her.

'She is adorable.' Hitomi reached for another cat.

'Her talents are with hair and flowers,' Tashiko muttered, with her head up.

'Honourable One, as unsuccessful as Emi can be, she would cheapen the reputation of Madam Hitomi's women. If she attended us, we could service more clients. We could work faster.' I raised my eyebrows, indicating an anticipated growth in her profits.

'Not much good at serving clients now . . .' Tashiko grunted, before I could stop her.

'Honourable Madam Hitomi, I will gladly share my food with Emi, if that is a consideration.'

Hitomi gathered another cat. It settled itself against her hip. 'Emi will receive a beating, naturally. Temporarily, she will work with Aya in the early mornings and with you in the Hours of the Sheep, the Monkey and the Cock.'

'You will each pay a visit to my . . . special room and see an extra customer *every* day. And, Kozaishō, you will come first. Tonight.' Hitomi smiled. Relief. Appeased.

Standing to leave, I brushed against Tashiko and breathed out a wind-in-mulberry-leaves sigh.

★ ★ ★

That night Tashiko applied ointment to my bruised back. I was too excited to feel the soreness.

'We are becoming Bodhisattvas. We acted with compassion.' Tashiko's divine soul shone in her eyes like a full moon over fresh snow.

'We saved Emi from this life. An accomplishment, eh?' I allowed Tashiko to believe that being a Bodhisattva was important to me. Now there would be more clients. More revenue. More power. Over Hitomi.

'Kozaishō, Emi and I will receive beatings, too.'

'Oh, Tashiko, no rice water tomorrow: yours and Emi's will be mild too.'

'Boasting is not part of the Way. Not honourable.'

'But we saved Emi. We saved her from this misery.'

'All life is suffering, Kozaishō. No one escapes.'

IV. A Contest

It began like this.

Summer's end, and the nights cooled. Cicadas shrilled against the noisy chattering of shrikes: '*key, key, kee-kee-kee, keey-keey-keey.*' Women-for-Play and servants collected outside my hut on the *watadono*, chatting of games, stories, dances and make-believe.

That night I told 'The Old Farmer and the Priests'.

Not so long ago, an old farmer could no longer service his wives, and they were growing restless. In desperation, he went to a nearby shrine. One priest suggested the artificial phallus-shaped *harigata*, but the farmer sighed and said, 'I love my wives and want to give them only of myself.' Another priest suggested using *higo zuiki*, which he could wrap around himself, but the farmer sighed and said, 'I love my wives and want to give them only of myself.' Finally a wise priest suggested peniform mushrooms. 'They will allow you to give only of yourself, but you will be stronger and more virile.' The farmer looked doubtful.

'We have ducks here,' the wise priest claimed. 'One evening we fed the drake a small peniform mushroom in some seeds. By next morning, we all observed the results.' He nodded at the other priests, already grinning. 'The drake mated the ducks for three days and, three long nights, from what all of us heard!'

So the sceptical farmer agreed to try peniform mushrooms. The

160

priests reported the farmer became a father three times three, and none of his wives, or his newer younger ones, ever left him.

Tashiko threw me a sly look. 'Only used *higo zuiki* three times in as many months.'

Several women's giggles echoed above the *watadono* at the thought of those plant fibres wrapped around some man's withered Stalk.

Tashiko's head rose. 'Never used mushrooms to stiffen a Stalk.' She wore a mask of smugness, quite rare for her. My face warmed.

Misuki stood and placed a wide hand on each hip. 'I have never used mushrooms or *higo zuiki*, although I am the newest Woman-for-Play.'

I countered in playfully, 'I have used *higo zuiki* for only one customer. I have *never* used the mushroom – because I can grow my own!'

More women cackled than had giggled before.

Tashiko and I stood face to face for an argument. With an audience Tashiko escalated our favourite squabble.

'You have!' Tashiko's voice lightened. 'The silk merchant from Uji and his . . . wandering eye?'

'Oh. Yes. That wandering eye. The old grandfather who had the long, long beard.'

The women hooted at the gesture I made with my hands. Tashiko laughed at my little joke. To see her laugh brightened me, like the noon sun over fresh snow.

She wagged her head from side to side and clicked her tongue, reminding me of my mother. 'Let us keep a daily record of who uses the *higo zuiki* and, may the Gods never allow, the mushroom!'

'Why not for a whole month?' A woman called out.

'Why not until O-Bon? We can celebrate our ancestors and learn who resurrects the most dead Stalks – without any extra help!'

I lifted my arms in anticipation of my success. I wanted to find out. I thought I was the best. Now I wanted to know for certain.

Tashiko created a tally with all of our names and two columns, marked '*higo zuiki*' and 'mushroom'. We named the tally 'Tsuneyo' after a huge *sumō* wrestler in another story.

The women gathered after work to check Tsuneyo, like sparrows after spilt grain. Tashiko made the little marks, and the women gossiped. The sleeping areas were transformed into nests of prattling. Many risked large wagers.

Rin's large shadow appeared on the *watadono* each night. The tally included her name, too, and she risked cloth and many *shō* of rice. She studied the tally and was never in a good mood when she lost.

Nights later Tashiko again tallied Tsuneyo in front of our hut. I had no marks beside my name. Tashiko had only one. I basked in my triumph and ignored what lay behind me.

A hand sped past my shoulder. Hitomi's pudgy fingers grabbed the tally and ripped it off the wall. Her robes swished, and her finger pointed. 'Kozaishō! Tashiko!'

Her thunderous voice brought the other Women-for-Play and their servants. Her accusations and the bad names she called us filled the air, like smoke from an unattended fire.

'Kozaishō! Tashiko! Come to Main House!' Hitomi gripped her robes, and I saw her hideous swollen ankles. A samurai stalked in front with her. Behind them, I plodded alongside Tashiko, who did not meet my sideways glances. Another samurai trailed with us.

The contest had improved the satisfaction of clients. Why was Hitomi so angry? Why the strange samurai? The contest was honourable. Tashiko and I had often discussed whether a specific action, in a specific situation, would be honourable or not.

Hitomi sprawled on her new silk pillows in her Big Room. I waited in the five-point obeisance. Tashiko came beside me, close, thighs touching, same position.

Silence extended, like fallen snow.

'Sit, Kozaishō, you ungrateful liar. You disobeyed me. And you, Tashiko, you are a conspirator too.'

This statement did not deserve rebuttal. What could be the cause of her wrath? The tally improved our services.

'You have used your time, which is *my* time, to play your games.'

'Honourable Madam Hitomi, I hoped the contest would increase the quality of our services.'

Her body straightened, and she pushed the pillows against the wall behind her. 'Increase the quality? How can what you do increase the quality of my Village?' Her voice was as shrill as that of a crow defending her nest.

'The competition encourages all the women to satisfy the men more fully.' I kept my voice low, but annoyance heated my neck.

'Your competition does nothing for my profit or my quality.'

'Honourable Madam Hitomi, the tally encourages the woman *not* to use the *higo zuiki* or the mushroom. Using them sometimes humiliates the men. Women-for-Play have had contests before.'

'You thought competition would help me? How can archery or swordplay improve my business?'

The exercises! Panic snatched at my throat, cutting off my air. How did she know? My secret! Akio? What had she done with Akio? His family?

'You do not own this Village.' Hitomi's voice sank a threat into my head, like a *naginata*'s blade.

No, I thought, I do not own the village, although I do draw the largest number of clients and bring *you* the most income.

'I am the owner. You belong to me. I do not tolerate disobedience. In any form.' She leaned over the cats and the voluminous skirts of her kimonos. 'Yet you have disobeyed my direct order. I forbade you to practise martial arts when you first came here.' Her arms crossed over her broad breasts, scattered the cats and creased her green robe, the colour being totally inappropriate for early autumn.

I rotated my eyes to the side and noticed an unfamiliar samurai stood by the door. She truly feared me.

'For how long have you deceived me?'

Should I lie? No. Lying did not belong to the Way. 'A long time.'

'From when you first belonged to me? When you first came?'

'Yes, honourable Madam Hitomi.' Hitomi's double question sealed my fate. I was doomed and condemned.

Could I save Akio? I looked up with my blank but sincere face, easy to do because I adored Akio, like a father. 'Honourable Madam Hitomi, Akio asked me, yet learning the exercises was *my* idea. I was the one who said yes. I insisted.'

'You will be locked into a room and let out during the day only to work – for me.'

Locked into a room. Like a criminal. No honour. A heavy quilt smothered my lungs. Sweat trickled down my back, between my legs. The top of my head disappeared. Humiliation. Away from Tashiko . . . I gasped. 'Honourable Madam Hitomi, may I be permitted to—'

'You shall be permitted nothing! You and Tashiko will be separated. Completely,' she bellowed.

How would I survive away from my Tashiko, Emi, Aya, Misuki, my family? Barred from my loved ones. Shut away from them. 'Honourable Madam Hitomi – my tutor?'

She grinned and snatched for a cat, and missed. I wanted to be one of those escaped cats.

'Nothing for a month.' Her eyes shot flaming arrows into Tashiko's face. Hitomi's lips quivered upwards.

Ice cold seared my belly. Not to study, not to talk to Tashiko about the *sutras*, not to . . .

'After the month, Misuki will study with you, not Tashiko.' The second cat broke free. 'And, Kozaishō, your work *will not suffer*. You will continue your stories and use them as usual or there will be worse.'

Hitomi's eyes glittered like Chiba's had when he listened to Tashiko scream.

A shiver stroked my spine.

My spirit ripped apart – a vast blackness in between. I did my best to staunch my tears.

Truly a Godless month and a Godless time had arrived, like a sudden typhoon.

Tashiko put her nose to the floor. 'Honourable Madam Hitomi, I implore you. No separation!' Her tears drizzled over her hands and dripped on to the floor. A cat rubbed itself around Tashiko's leg, mewing like an infant. 'If separate us. Take life from me. Not be able to work – with competence – for you.' Tashiko's back rippled with her words and heaved with her silent sobs.

My hands hurt not to touch her. She had never uttered the word 'love' to me, but now I knew she loved me. To watch her plead and cry in front of Hitomi was to taste mouthfuls of sand. Outrage tightened my muscles and despair hardened inside me, like old lacquer.

Tashiko sat and placed one soft hand across my thigh. Her fingers gripped tightly and quickly relaxed. She wanted me not to be involved. I had to let her fight alone. My interference might make Hitomi's decision more vicious. We were her property and, along with beating us, she could kill or sell us to anyone for anything, to the *eta*, to cruel men, to anyone in Heian-kyō – that huge city, bigger than Uji, where demons lurked in the corners.

Hitomi coughed, ruffling her silk pillows. Tashiko's body shuddered next to mine. I wanted to stare Hitomi down. I did so only in my mind.

'Humph. Sit up, Tashiko.'

She sat on her heels, close to me. My thigh pushed hers to express my regret in the only way I could. I had brought misery by disobedience. I had to obey the Goddess of Mercy. I had to disobey! Did following what the Gods directed lead to dishonour?

'No. You are not to sleep or eat with each other or even see each other for a month. You will learn this lesson. Well.'

Tashiko murmured thanks.

'I want to see your eyes. I want to see your gratitude, your indebtedness for my generosity. It is only for a month.'

Show her gratitude for a meagre crumb. I kept my eyes down. I wanted to crawl into the earth and die. I dived into a five-point again.

The dust and incense irritated my eyes. No more Tashiko with whom to sleep. No more Tashiko with whom to sing or dance. Tashiko only in my dreams. I blinked away the tears and spoke the only words that came: 'Thank you, honourable Madam Hitomi.'

'Kozaishō, I will see if you can still thank me after my . . . work in my special hut this evening.' She compressed her lips. That evening, my back would earn more scars.

I contrived plans to wreak revenge on my betrayer. Somehow I had to discover the fiend.

I managed to thank Hitomi after her work that day in Hell Hut, although I could hardly speak. I had nearly bitten through my tongue.

My life turned into a ceaseless blizzard. On the rare occasions I glimpsed Tashiko, she bowed her head and swung her nut-brown cascade of hair around herself, like an empress. My heart twisted at the sight of such elegance and the frustration of not being able to speak to or touch her.

I missed her voice at night because she had always sung the old songs our mothers sang. Her melodies had decorated our hut as bush warblers, with their honeyed notes, muted the thunder of a spring storm.

My degradation, locked into a room with a guard, meant I slept little and endured nightmares of Hitomi's hut, scars and funerals.

The storm persisted undiminished night after night, day after day, until it ended.

V. Treachery

It ended like this.

Early snow arrived in the Godless month, concealing colourful leaves and grasses with an icy brightness that hurt my eyes. It was even more bleak and bitter since I slept alone. I had none of Akio's exercises to distract me. In such a winter my family would have been sowing barley, perhaps on the extra land I had given them. That thought made me sad. I recalled a lullaby, the smell of barley cooking and a grinding stone, although I no longer remembered the faces of my parents or siblings. I wondered if they remembered me.

Had I forgotten Tashiko's face? No! I remembered her loam-brown eyes, her wispy hair and especially her voice, which soothed my anger and despair. How could I go on? She was the one with whom I awakened and with whom I slept. I shared my triumphs with the bow and failures with the *bokken*. She listened to my stories, then told me whether or not they would work with clients. She was often correct. I spoke with no one now, except clients, and all that was dissembling.

Twenty-three prolonged days and nights in a locked room, only allowed out, like an ox, to work. I counted the remaining days until I could be with Tashiko. I did not even have with me my pink festival smock, and I had never slept without it since my father had sold me. I searched for Tashiko's presence in my mind to ease my pain.

Rin usually brought my rice bowl each morning, her eyes gloating. That morning – it was not her footsteps that came towards my hut. The lock's heavy metallic *clunk* mixed with the buntings' early-morning prattling, '*tseewee-tseewee-tseewee-tseewee*'.

The door opened. Scents of rice and the last of the summer's vegetables floated into my prison. The back of a head on hands in five-point. I glanced for the samurai who guarded me and saw only the empty corridor to the big room is Main House. Where could he be?

'I bring you your morning meal, honourable Kozaishō.'

Misuki's voice. Why would she speak so formally? I tugged at her hair playfully. 'Thank you, Misuki.' Then I realised her voice had sounded flat and empty.

She stayed silent and on the floor. I pushed aside the bowl and placed my hands over hers. Our heads almost touched. 'What, Misuki?'

Motionless. Silent.

'Please sit. Misuki, tell me,' I whispered, my insides tightening to the breadth of a chopstick.

Misuki's tears fell to the floor. Thin cries bubbled from her lips.

I waited.

Something was wrong. What hideousness had a man perpetrated on one of the Women-for-Play now?

Misuki's cries slowed, and the words dribbled out: 'Kozaishō. Honourable Kozaishō.'

'Yes.' I stroked her thick, coarse hair.

'Kozaishō. I cannot believe I must tell you this.'

Those words sounded familiar – too familiar. I froze. 'Tell me.'

'Oh, Kozaishō.'

With one hand I continued to stroke her hair. With the other, I lifted her chin. 'Who, Misuki? Me? Aya? Emi? How bad is the harm?'

She shook her head with each name, her makeup dripping in her tears on to my hand.

I trembled, like an earthquake. 'No! Not—'

She nodded only with her eyes. 'Tashiko is dead. Do you want to see her before they prepare her?'

'Prepare her? Who is *they*?' Rage charged through me. I bolted from my prison. No one else must touch her!

This had to be an evil joke. Had Hitomi played a terrible trick for punishment? I rushed into Tashiko's work room. Disarrayed. Table, lamp, bamboo tree. All splayed out. No Tashiko.

I whirled back to Misuki. Outside the hut Emi and Aya wrapped their arms around each other. With tearful faces, my family stared at me. There was now a grinding stone on each of my feet.

With one hand I pointed to the chaos of her hut. I opened my mouth to scream— No words. No sounds. My legs did not touch the ground. I grew smaller. The room's commotion expanded and I dropped to the floor. No blood. Before, I argued with myself, there had been much blood. I saw no blood.

I pleaded with Kannon-sama, the Goddess of Mercy, for the health and safety of my precious one.

My three sisters came towards me. I heard Aya's bawls. I recognised Emi's gulping sobs. They circled me: hands stroked me, voices said my name. They pulled me to my feet.

'Do you want to see her before they prepare her?' Misuki could not look me in the face.

I ran to the unclean room set aside for such.

Tashiko lay on the floor, her lustrous hair swirled across her favourite pale blue costume. With the heavy makeup she wore, she appeared available for work, but it could not hide the line of raw flesh that twisted around her neck.

I ran out, vomited and retched over and over. On that day, the Goddess of Mercy – and all the Gods – abandoned me.

Wet leaves wiped my lips. 'Sip the water, Kozaishō,' Misuki murmured.

I did, although the sickly smell of vomit remained.

'Kozaishō, Madam Hitomi says you are not to touch her. You are not to defile yourself, she says.' Misuki's fingers squeezed my upper arm, as if that might stop me.

I flew into the Pollution Hut. My fingers traced Tashiko's face and neck. I placed my cheek against hers, her skin, soft, yet chilled. Her hair still smelt of brush clover. Her long neck, now torn, destroyed by a stranger's hands. By a stranger whose life I would hold in mine – soon.

Misuki touched me and joined me in the defilement. 'The human fire has already left her body, Kozaishō. Her spirit is gone. When this happened, the Lord Buddha came down to earth on a cloud. He has accompanied Tashiko to Heaven.'

A myth. My dear one, gone from my life. Misuki clung to my hands with both of hers. I did not know if this abomination had resulted from fun, a joke or part of a tale. I would find out.

My tears washed my beloved. Misuki anointed her body with pungent herbs, especially her neck. How could anyone have hurt Tashiko so? My desolation fought with my disgust. I shaved her head and took her favurite blue *takenaga* to bind her hair. Would I be allowed to have her *takenaga* and hair as a keepsake? Misuki and I wrapped her in white gauze. It roughened the pads of my fingers. Stronger, I rolled Tashiko back and forth. Together Misuki and I encased my loved one's body in the gauze until she appeared like the chrysalis of a caterpillar. If the Buddha accompanied anyone's soul to heaven, that soul would be Tashiko's.

I glanced around me. No one. I put my hands on Misuki's shoulders and whispered, 'Madam Hitomi has a samurai who lurks around me. Please, take the coins under my cleaned defilement cloths and pay someone, with a good brush, to write a *sutra* epitaph on a piece of wood or a stone. My brush is too poor or I would write myself. You can touch the coins now because you and I are already unclean.'

A few months before a customer had told me the courts had prohibited the use of coins. Perhaps officials would take me far away. Perhaps that would relieve the pain that continuously pierced my skin.

When Misuki left, I spoke to Tashiko: 'My beloved, I must undertake the honourable action. This I promise on my family and ancestors' honour. Know that I shall do everything I can to believe in your Buddha and your Bodhisattvas. Know I will avenge your murder.'

I wrote:

> Tashiko, my soul
> Press your essence into mine
> Only tears remain
> Until we can both return
> To love each other again

Out of the next morning's mists, the priest entered the Village, parading like a courtier in white and purple silk. Tall and thin, like late harvest straw.

BOOK 7

I. Knowledge

The one I hated, Goro.

He strolled to Main House. His purple and white silk robes swirled about him, like rapids around a rock. He hesitated, his thin hair slick against his skull. Our eyes met. His eyes, like water on a moonless night, the eyes of a man who feasted on others' pain.

He would not feast on mine.

'Tomorrow is the most propitious day for the funeral.' Goro's shrill voice scratched along the *watadono* in front of Main House.

Misuki and I, with Emi and Aya, stood far from the others because we were polluted by death. I searched the women, one by one, with my eyes. Who had killed Tashiko? Who looked guilty? Who did not return my gaze? Who kept their head turned away? Whose hands were not loosely at their sides?

Later that day I performed the purification rituals to clear myself of the death pollution. All night I remained with my cherished one, a noxious, cloying scent mixed with the aromatic herbs I had rubbed into her stiff skin. Shrikes landed in naked paulownia trees their eyes banded black for grief, like mine. These birds shrieked against the silence of my Abstention while I could not.

I attended to the world's silence without Tashiko's heartbeats.

The funeral seemed remote, like thunder before clouds are seen.

My three sisters dressed me in the chief mourner's black clothes. The coarse hemp irritated my neck, arms and nipples, reminding me to show no misery to this priest. Misuki placed the bamboo staff in my hand. She brought little flags with Tashiko's virtues written on them. Women-for-Play and servants also carried flags with virtues. They had loved her, too, but I had loved her with my entire soul. She had loved me in the same way.

The bamboo staff and the little flags were cold in my hands. My feet tripped on the smallest pebbles. Misuki supported me on one side and the staff on the other.

The gravesite altar was undressed, no flowers, now in the deep death of winter. The wooden tablet inscribed with Tashiko's name lay on the ground next to the shallow pit. Misuki had written the inscription, an exquisite brush. I recognised her writing. Four *eta* carried her body wrapped in the white cloth and lowered her into the ground. They carried my life wrapped in that white sheath to the grave.

Something shone in the shallow pit. Misuki nudged me and whispered, 'All the Women-for-Play donated to buy *gofu.*'

Seeing my confusion, she said, 'You know. The round jars. To protect from evil spirits.'

In the frosty air, Goro fussed with his robes and leered at the women huddled around Tashiko's body. His breath smoked in front of his face, like a dragon's.

He turned to the altar, placed his prayer book on it and nodded at Hitomi. Then his eyes flickered across my face. His hand signalled for the lighting of incense, and he chanted another prayer.

Each mourner was supposed to light incense at the altar. As chief mourner, I went first. Wretchedness stabbed my chest. All my coins had bought the tablet but there had been none for incense. How could I meet Goro's eyes without an incense stick? Such shame. Such dishonour to Tashiko and to me. As I rose, a thin stick was pushed into my hand. My hand pressed Misuki's in thanks. After me, each person went to the altar and lit incense in the burner.

A gust of wind ruffled pages. He put the book of prayers on the altar and, with both hands, patted the book open to its place again. He frowned, shifted his eyes to Hitomi and turned more pages.

He cleared his throat, read a short passage, turned pages. He repeated this again, and flipped to the last page.

Goro stepped away from the altar, his shoulders drooping.

Would he return to finish the prayers? I pressed my lips together and directed my gaze at him.

He turned the prayer book to the end. He moved his head. His eyes rammed on to me and held for a moment. The corners of his lips turned up. His hand went to his cheek and a finger touched the twist I had created in his nose. His eyes narrowed.

Tashiko's soul. His anger with me would cost Tashiko her place in Heaven. 'Please, honourable Daigoro no Goro, complete the ceremony.'

The muscles of my arms constricted. My feet itched to run. I ordered my face to remain smooth. I stepped closer to him. Misuki grabbed my arm. I jerked away. 'Let me be!'

Goro nodded to madam Hitomi and oriented himself towards the open grave.

He was going to stop. He would not finish the ceremony. Tashiko needed these prayers to go to Heaven. 'Wait!' I yelled, my arms as stiff as old bamboo, my hands ready, my feet in the attack position.

Goro lifted a hand into the air and looked down at me with disdain. He recited a short prayer.

He had lured me into an insolent and ill-mannered action. He trapped me.

'Please do not cut short her funeral prayers.' I bowed and made my best attempt to keep my voice low and respectful. My jaw clenched in fury at my outburst, my shame. My heart and breath rode at a gallop. Yet I could not risk my beloved's soul, regardless of the consequences to me.

'All that should be done has been done.' Goro's eyes went to madam Hitomi, who dipped her head, and then to me. With both his hands, Goro slammed the prayer book closed, stood erect and pivoted towards the grave, his lips in that odd half-smile.

He was not going to finish the funeral. My Tashiko might burn in Hell because of him. Because of me. I had to protect her spirit. How? Fierceness and despair melded in my core, like the steel of a sword. I desired to avenge my love, to shoot an arrow into the priest's gut.

Tears trickled. My limbs shook. I screamed at the fiend, 'Her soul will suffer. She must have the complete ceremony.'

'Madam Hitomi knows I am the only priest who will come . . . here.' He waved his manicured hand at the tannery where the *eta* lived.

175

A hellish fire soared in me. 'How can you omit prayers for my beloved's soul? How can you demonstrate such contempt for her? For me. I am the chief mourner!'

His eyes mocked me. 'You are the one with no respect for the priest-hood. You are the one showing disdain for your . . . loved one.' Goro pressed his hair with one hand and folded the other across his chest, where he did not have a heart. He straightened his posture and gazed down with a sneer.

He cackled.

Blades into my heart! My whole body tensed, heated, coiled and pulsed. I rushed up the *watadono* to him. My fists punched his chest. I grabbed his robes. 'You have no respect! You have no respect!' I screeched. Misuki tugged at my arm. I struck him with my other hand, 'Tashiko was murdered!' Misuki grabbed both my arms. 'Tashiko's soul will haunt you! Bring you disease! Her soul will come to you in your dreams! In your nightmares! She will give you no peace! She will bring you to an early, painful death!' I wrenched myself from Misuki's grasp and continued battering Goro.

He tottered with my blows. Yet he bent his head to my side and whispered, 'Tashiko begged me to take her, not you. She agreed to other games. The kind the monks taught me when I was a boy. The special kind I learned to find irresistible.'

Hitomi called, 'Guards! Hold her!'

My hands had opened. My arms fell to my sides. I let my breath out and tilted my head to the ground. Tashiko had sacrificed herself for me.

Goro's head lowered into my face, his tongue slowly tracing his lower lip. He murmured, 'Next time, you.'

Brawny hands each took an arm and lifted me off the ground.

'Never.' I spat, through clenched teeth, and saw my sword slice his throat. 'Goro!' I shouted, as if each word was a sword stroke. 'You are a devil who will never reach enlightenment – no matter how many lifetimes you spend as a monk, no matter how many *sutras* you write and chant. What you have done is so evil you can never erase it. Not through eternity!'

He scraped my cheek with his fingernails. I squirmed to escape him. My thumbs would be daggers puncturing his eyes.

'And now, Kozaishō, I leave soon for Heian-kyō to receive my Hat.'

I bit back tears at the injustice. 'They could not possibly give you one.'

'My revenge for this public disgrace will wait, but I will have retribution. Depend upon it.'

II. Proposal

A messenger from madam Hitomi requested my presence after I had seen my last customer. I trudged past the sleep huts, work huts and even Hell Hut, which I had visited many times in the almost three months since Tashiko, my love, had died. My slow pace testified to Hitomi's good efforts, since the wounds around my chest bled easily.

What new tortures did she plan?

Wisteria blossoms hung from the vines, and I envied their short lives. Overhead, cranes and wild geese flew in mated pairs. The constant rumble of melted snow racing along the stream soothed me, like Tashiko's voice. Alone I gazed at the rising Hazy Moon and remembered the first time I had watched that sky, dressed as a doll, drenched in a brook with my Tashiko.

In Hitomi's big room I made the five-point, like an old woman, bent down, creeping forward at a slug's pace so that I did not disturb my bindings or worsen the pain. Also, when the warm blood dribbled in this chill, my body shuddered. Hitomi mistook this for fear. I did not wish to contribute to her amusement.

'You may sit, Kozaishō.'

I raised myself carefully. She used courtesies now. For two months she had screamed and criticised my performance. She had listed all the complaints from customers, if they had continued to see me.

She reclined against her winter pillows. Why had she not changed to spring ones?

'Kozaishō, I wish to discuss your performance with clients. You are costing me revenue.'

Did she want me to sew her new spring pillows? I sighed silently to myself. If she dared put me to needlecraft, my poor skills would grant me permanent dwelling in Hell Hut. Had she just informed me her profits depended on me and my customers? No wonder she continued to harass me about my work, *her* livelihood. What power I owned, despite my desolation.

'You and I are aware that your performance is inadequate. My duties in special hut have not changed your behaviour. Customers leave and do not return. My profits dwindle.' She picked up a winter pillow and dangled it high in front of me. 'Yes. I know you noticed, Kozaishō. You notice everything. Well, your poor services are the reason I do not have enough to change pillows for the new season. Do you wish to spend more time in my special hut?'

I shrugged my shoulders. I did not care, without my beautiful Buddhist.

Hitomi used her screechy voice and gestured with her hands high in the air. 'Do you want to die?'

The inside of me was scooped out, like a melon, seeds and all, nothing left that the rind, unable to hold its shape.

She flopped against her pillows. Her nostrils flared and she grunted. She frowned and, from time to time, grumbled to herself.

Outside, sparrows called to each other in the new grass. Pheasants cooed, murmuring to each other about their clutches of eggs. The sounds of birds who had found their mates. Mine, lost for the rest of this lifetime.

'Kozaishō!'

Hitomi interrupted my rumination. I raised my head. She was not scowling.

'Kozaishō. But first—' She clapped three times.

The *shōji* opened and a servant scuttled in bringing the aroma of warm *mochi*. She bowed and set down a tray. More claps, and the servant left. No words spoken. This had been rehearsed.

'Let us eat these rice cakes while they are still warm.' She reached out and took one, at the same time maintaining her gaze on me.

'Whatever Madam Hitomi wishes.' I took one and waited for her to bite first.

She ate in silence. I did not eat *mochi*: the sweetness would turn bitter in my mouth.

'Eat it. You have lost too much weight.'

I nibbled at what I thought would taste like old straw. Warm. Delicious. My mouth watered. The old monkey! My appetite revived.

'Now, Kozaishō, you will meet your tutor on the Days of the Snake and the Pig. Correct?' Her voice melted into the air, as sweet as the *mochi* that dissolved in my mouth.

'Madam Hitomi, the Days of the Hare, Goat and Pig.'

'Because I know you enjoy your studies, he will come on the Day of the Rooster also.'

I responded with a small bow. I needed to be wary. She had bribed me. For what?

Hitomi squinted at me. 'Misuki will take lessons with you. Eat. Eat. You must fatten up if you are to concentrate on your studies.'

She pointed at my mostly eaten rice cake. I took another few bites and finished it. Disgusted with myself for the enjoyment. The *mochi* – a component of the bribe.

'I will also arrange for another tutor. For the *biwa*. On the Days of the Ox and the Goat.' She drifted deep into her pillows, her hands cross-fingered in her lap. 'For both you and Misuki. That will make it easier for Misuki to catch up with you.' She tapped her fingers together.

Misuki had learned fast. She had astounded me. Hitomi had surprised, no, unsettled me. Let her do what she wished with me. The tutors, more days. A *biwa* tutor. Now Misuki. Again, Hitomi wanted something from me. Was Misuki a spy for Hitomi? I smelt her fear. Perhaps she had spoken the truth. Perhaps she really did rely on me for her profits.

'Would you like another *mochi*? Here, Kozaishō . . .' She pushed the tray towards me. I took another, my appetite shamefully enticed into allience.

'Kozaishō, you and I know I hear grievances from your clients. My special hut has not motivated you to perform better. Therefore I have a proposal.'

My head snapped up. Here it came. Her voice smoothed over her anxiety, and her fingers danced. What else would she offer and for what? I had to find and kill Tashiko's murderer.

180

'Kozaishō, listen to me. You and I understand you have not managed your responsibilities. Here is my proposal.' She pressed her elbows on to her knees, her fists under her multiple chins. 'Each day I receive complaints you will be locked into the room here in Main House and not permitted to be with Akio.'

Akio! Akio – still here? To be with my great friend. To return to training. My bow? To strap on my quiver. To grasp my *bokken*. My back straightened, and the expected throbbing warmth seeped through my bindings. I steeled myself against the tremors, soon to come.

'You will go to Akio every day I receive no complaints from your clients.'

My face turned to the source of much pain these past two months. My eyes narrowed, as I envisaged a life again with someone who loved me.

She was manipulating me for her own comfort and profit, I knew that, yet tears of possibility leaked down my cheeks to my chin. What Hitomi's hatred and punishment had not achieved, this specious kindness had accomplished. I had not made a sound through any of her torments, but I allowed myself, that day, to utter a single sound of hope.

III. Framework for Vengeance

I hesitated outside the communal eating room, listened to the chatter, and relished the fragrance of rice and vegetables for the first time in months. Hitomi's sweet *mochi* remained on my teeth, reminding me of hunger.

I entered, and conversations melted like ice at the edge of a river on a hot day. Glances skittered across the room, away from me. Except Misuki's. She sat in a corner, far from the few women trekking to and from the rice and the pickled or fresh vegetable pots in the room's centre. I wanted to be alone, but she beamed when her eyes locked on mine, and she motioned me to join her, Emi and Aya.

I fixed a smile to my face. I had no wish to hurt Emi and Aya. Perhaps Misuki thought that now Tashiko was dead . . . but no. Never. No matter how many incense sticks she bought for me, I could not love her. I filled my evening-meal bowl and joined them in the corner.

Misuki halted her jabbering for a moment when I sat down with my bowl. The evening-meal talk remained hushed, but Misuki, like a priest announcing prayers to a large group, prattled on: the day, the full moon, this month, the season turning from Fire to Earth, moving towards harvest time, then Aya's birth year, Koshin, the Unlucky Monkey Year . . .

Stares prickled my skin as Misuki praised my fortunes, complimented my virtues – and stretched my patience to the thinness of a *biwa* string ready to snap. I finished my food quickly, nodded to Misuki and left, hearing the voices flood and flow now, up and down like rivers in their seasons.

Misuki followed me to our sleep huts. The frogs' loud songs shielded her whispers as we walked on the moonlit path. 'Madam Hitomi has you watched. They listen to what you say. No one should hear what my servant overheard, but you need to know.'

I had already spotted the same strange samurai who had lifted me at the funeral. 'What about Rin?'

'I do not know. She gossips and spends much of her time with Hitomi. Perhaps . . .'

Rin could not be trusted. Besides, she caused too many problems for a leader. Her size permitted her to grab or take whatever she wanted from anyone's hut. I had seen her. My beloved Tashiko had applied gentle ways to ask for the best for herself and others. I resolved to be more like Tashiko, serene, reserved – and cautious.

The silence of the frogs was interrupted. I heard steps behind us. I smelt incense. I squeezed Misuki's hand and placed a finger to her lips. The moon hid behind clouds. Darkness veiled us. The samurai?

I held my breath.

Rin marched past us. She slapped me directly across my welts in time with her heavy step.

That jolt and the shooting pains slowed me, but I made no sound. The wounds on my back opened, searing, then wet. I allowed myself a grimace in the darkness. Rin liked to help Hitomi in these ways. I strained beyond the pain to recognise the footfalls and scent of the samurai, and relaxed with the return of the frogs' and birds' songs.

In a clear voice I pretended to talk to Misuki: 'I believe Tashiko's spirit is in a clean and pure land, where people walk on lapis lazuli, and golden ropes mark the boundaries. Jewelled trees grow beside each road, and continuously flower and bear fruit. Heaven is what she wanted. Heaven is what she read to me. Heaven is what I pray for her.'

The sound of Rin's footsteps faded into the woods. The frogs' chorus rumbled to its full drumming.

Misuki stroked my shoulder and sighed. 'I will pray that for her also.'

If she kept agreeing with me, I might slap her. I doubted she could say what she had to quickly.

'My servant overheard that Madam Hitomi, Rin *and* the priest send money to the Tendai temple on Mount Hiei . . . the one near Heian-kyō . . . to buy Kuyō!'

I tapped Misuki's shoulder and leaned to her ear. 'Thank you for telling me.' Hitomi and Rin must be terrified if they had parted with money to the capital. I hoped the priest was mortified, too. Only the priests on Mount Hiei, that lucky north-east location reserved for the most potent threats, could say those particular protection prayers. *Kuyō*, to keep the living safe from the dead.

'Thirty-three years of prayers to keep Tashiko's soul from becoming a *yurei*. My cousin's wife died, and his priest said his wife's spirit had become a *yurei*.' Misuki placed her hand on my upper arm. 'Kozaishō, then he died, and then each of his children died. I have heard of wicked *yurei* who lure living spouses into fresh graves and cause innocent deaths.'

If Tashiko's *yurei* came for me, I would go – gladly. But I had fought for her complete funeral: she would attack Goro. Perhaps also Hitomi and Rin.

Misuki thrust her palm on to my hip.

I pulled away. Her touch angered me. I could not have feelings for her. I hissed, between my teeth, 'Men who are violent against women should be killed!'

'Ssssh!' She gripped my side with one hand.

My resolve to be like Tashiko had gone. I wanted to fight and to embrace Misuki. I practised breathing deeply to call in my reserved caution.

'Tashiko's Earth personality is quite strong and any sudden change would upset her spirit greatly. Naturally, being murdered . . . Oh, I am sorry, Kozaishō.' Misuki hung her head. Next she raised her eyes and softened her voice.

I had not considered Tashiko's Earth, although I was mindful of her power. I shared this story with Misuki, because it reminded me of Tashiko.

In a village of Nuribe, an extraordinary woman lived and married Maro, a useless man. She gave birth to seven children, but was too poor to feed them, since she had no one upon whom to depend. Because her children had no clothes, she wove vines into clothes.

She herself wore rags. She gathered edible herbs from the fields and devoted herself to staying at home and cleaning the house. When she cooked the herbs, she called her children, sat up straight and ate the food, smiling, talking cheerfully and being grateful. The continual self-restraint in mind and body made her spirit grow to be like that of a guest from heaven. In the fifth year of the old emperor's reign, Bodhisattvas communicated with her, and she ate special herbs gathered in the field in springtime and flew about in the heavens. From this we learn, 'One may achieve five kinds of merit by leading a lay life and sweeping the garden with an upright mind.'

Misuki pulled my hair away from my face. My vision clouded. I turned away.

'We cannot change *karma* but . . .' Misuki placed the tip of a finger in her mouth. 'But we need to do something?'

'Do something? What do you mean?' Her vagueness and use of 'we' irritated me. I could not trust her. Or anyone.

'I have no idea, Kozaishō.'

Change something – definitely. First, I would set a trap for Misuki to see if she was honest with me. In a low voice, I risked my main concerns: 'Men should not hurt us Women-for-Play. I must also find out who cannot be trusted.' Perhaps Misuki knew. I would know. Soon.

She stopped and placed her hands on my shoulders. 'Trusted? What are you saying?'

When her hands touched me icy twitches coated my skin, perhaps brought by the breeze, with its strong perfume of plum blossoms. What a mismatch; disloyalty was the ugliest trait.

The sandalwood incense of samurai drifted into the plum blossoms' aroma.

I laid a hand on her shoulder clucked, and murmured, 'Let us continue in private.'

Inside my hut, I whispered, 'Someone informed Hitomi about me and Akio. I need to find out who betrayed me.'

She placed a hand on each cheek, shook her head, and moaned, 'Aaaaaah!' like an old grandmother I saw once at a shrine with my parents.

When she spoke, she sounded like a hungry kitten. 'Perhaps it is not true what they say, that bad news runs one thousand *chō*. I thought you already knew.'

'Knew what? Tell me.' I placed my hand on her neck as she sobbed.

'I know.' She swayed with her moans.

'Tell me! Speak!' My hand tightened around the hair at her nape.

'An accident,' Misuki coughed out. 'She did not mean it.'

'Tell me who.' My hand itched with enough malice to shoot an arrow. Who could commit such a betrayal by accident? I pinched Misuki's neck. I had to know my enemies' identities. Could I trust Misuki's answer?

Misuki yowled, 'Be merciful. It was an accident. It was – it was – Emi.'

I threw Misuki to the floor. The thud smoothed a few thorns of my bitterness. Sweet Emi. 'No! Liar! Not my Emi. You must be the traitor.'

Misuki whispered, between sniffles, 'She was boasting about you. How well you dance. Your beautiful music. Your wonderful songs and stories. And your accurate archery – your archery.'

'Emi said all that? Where? When?'

Misuki hoisted her blotched face, dripping tears and strings of slime. How could Emi have gone against me? 'Emi is so proud of you. But she did not know what she was doing.'

'Who heard her?' I stared at the floor near her, as if it could talk.

Misuki wiped her eyes and nose, jerking with hiccups. 'Everyone. Before the evening meal. What will you do?' She sat, stiff with fear of my temper, to say nothing of my success in combat.

I pulled my face into a blank. Who could be trusted in this world, if not Emi? 'Nothing,' I announced, in as unwavering a voice as I could manage. 'Emi is the innocent. The one who informed Hitomi or Rin is my enemy. Tell me who overheard her.' I moved my eyes to meet Misuki's. 'Omit no one.'

Misuki flinched when my fingers gripped her arm. Next, each word I spoke was a sword stroke: 'Help me find my betrayer.'

'I will if I can,' she mewed. She listed almost all the people I knew, then said, 'How can we do this?'

I forced myself to show no emotion. Did Misuki know about Goro? Probably not. Hitomi's whippings, Goro's murder of Tashiko, Rin's and several unknown samurai's constant surveillance, and now perhaps another threat. My life required much vigilance. Yet it was my life, not Misuki's, unless she was the traitor.

'Too much is at risk. I cannot allow you to play a part. Misuki, I require, no, I *demand* you say no more to anyone, *especially* Emi.'

'Of course not. This is my choice, Kozaishō. Let us begin in the best places and on the best days. Let me frame the most advantageous places for our work huts. Perhaps I should also look at our sleep huts . . .' The fingertip entered her mouth again.

'Think over your participation in my – situation. Truly you, Emi and Aya will always be my family, my *sisters*.'

Two days later Misuki contrived, with our birth years and other information, the changes in the sleep and work huts required for my endeavours to be lucky. I located a new hiding spot for my coins and old festival clothes, since Misuki had known the previous one.

I had predicted that her sleep and work huts would be next to my new ones. No surprises. A few coins and one unit of summer silk managed the hut exchanges, the bartering completed, hopefully, without Hitomi or Rin's knowledge.

The next morning I met Emi alone. I explained how what she had said had hurt me. Her round eyes looked at me, eyebrows in a knot, tears spilling down her clothes. My stomach flipped and I wanted to stop my tongue, but I needed to protect both of us.

'You must not say *anything* about me to anyone else. You must not share *anything* I say to you with anyone else. Absolutely no one.'

'Sorry, sorry, Kozaishō.' Emi collapsed to her knees, her arms circled my legs.

'I know you would never hurt me on purpose.' I bent to hug her. When I knew she was listening to me, I continued slowly, 'Just remember, whenever anyone asks you what I said or did, or anything we said or did together, you must say, "We talked about the weather."'

'I promise, Kozaishō. Even today. We talked about the weather. Always. We talked about the weather.'

I stayed while she practised this sentence over and over and over, just like we had done at the *shōen* with dances and songs.

On the day after my first no-complaint day I rushed to the practice field to meet Akio. Awakening before the usual time posed no problem because

I had slept little since Tashiko's death. With Hitomi's official consent, I went to the stables, selected a horse and rode to the fields, without any hurry or secrecy. Pheasants and sparrows clucked and cheeped along the path. Wild geese in chevrons flew against the eastern horizon.

I searched for Akio's red and blue rectangular armour against the early light. No Akio. Was he punished? If so, I prayed to the Goddess of Mercy that he had not been banished, or worse. My mind travelled to many terrible places.

After I had asked several samurai, one answered my question: 'In his quarters. He is not permitted here until the end of the month. Did you not know?'

No one had told me. I galloped to the samurai quarters and asked the first one I saw, a young boy, who pointed out Akio's house. Dismounting, I sprinted and called.

A man ran to me, dressed in a red and white summer silk *hitatare* and a blue and white *hakama*. A stranger. Who was this? He kneaded the top of my hair before I had completed my bow. Akio.

'Little one, I have sorrowed for your unhappiness.' He pulled at my costume, which hung on me like a scarecrow before a storm in harvest time. 'You have become so thin.'

'Akio – oh, you are confined to your house.' What other punishments had Hitomi inflicted on him? He looked healthy, but so did I, because my back was wrapped and I stood well.

His hand gestured to his house. 'Internment. Nothing else. My wife and girls are healthy and safe. We are provided for.' He motioned to his *watadono*. 'Come. See them.'

I tied up the horse, and he led me into a main room the size of Lesser House. His wife, tall and calm at her sudden visitor, opened the *shōji* and greeted me, as I took off my shoes.

'I am delighted to meet you, the famous little one of whom my husband speaks often,' she said, in formal language, and nodded, eyes smiling.

Compliments batted back and forth between us. I inspected her hands to see if she also studied martial arts. I saw the marks of sewing, but not of the bow. No challenger here.

Akio left the room and came back escorting four girls. He introduced Fumiko, Naoko, Ikuko and Noriko, ages eight, six, four and three.

Beautiful, all of them. The eldest bore the telltale marks of the bow. A rival. Fumiko gaped at my fingers.

Akio's eyes met mine. Pride and protectiveness beamed from his face. He and his girls needed to be here rather than at the *shōen*. I understood. He nodded as my eyes moistened.

He carried a blue *furoshiki*, and we strolled behind his house to his makeshift practice area. 'See,' he opened the *furoshiki*, 'your bow, quiver and *bokken*. You have permission to keep them yourself.' He gave a small smile and pointed open-handed to the blue *furoshiki* he had given me when I had first come to the Village.

'May I practise the bow first?'

'The bow? I thought after all this time you would choose your favourite, your strength, the *bokken*.'

'First the bow, if you do not mind, honourable Akio.'

He nodded and I strapped on my quiver.

'It ties twice around you.'

'My suffering is deep,' I blurted. 'It was Emi, silly, slow Emi. She spoke of our sessions.'

After a silence, he said, 'No one can outrun their *karma*.' He touched my nose with one finger. His dark brown eyes glistened.

I wrapped my arms as far around his chest as they could go and placed my head against his *hitatare*, my cheek hot and wet against the cool spring silk, shielded and safe in the arms of the only person in the world I could trust.

I held on until I heard a bush warbler's song above us. Gulping, I related the story of the bush warbler and its song the day my father had sold me to Chiba.

He squatted down. 'Another powerful sign, little one.'

'Perhaps the bird is a sign of the Right Action. The honourable next Right Action . . .' I dared to finish although my heart battered like festival drumsticks '. . . would be not to see you any more and permit Hitomi to beat me until I die.'

His fingers gripped my shoulders. 'There is no honour in useless sacrifice. Not to perform what you can and are able for your master is also not honourable, Kozaishō. All life is pain. You know that is what the Buddha teaches us.'

He had said words like Tashiko's. My chest squeezed with loneliness. 'I do not think I can stay here in the Village without Tashiko.'

'Yes, you can. Kozaishō, the honourable action—'

'I need to escape. Now I have permission to work with you, I can sneak off and—'

'And what?' He looked down at me, his hands still on my shoulders. 'Where would you go? Where is the honour in that? Is that all I have taught you?' His eyebrows slid together between his eyes and he took away his hands.

Nowhere else to go. Nowhere else to find honour. I lifted my arms up and out to nowhere, then down, like my eyes, in shame. 'Nowhere, honourable Akio.'

'To leave, when you are owned and obligated to your master, is a deep breach of honour. Your family's honour and your own.'

'Would *seppuku* be the next right action?'

He pulled further away from me. 'No. Not at all. You are not the first person to endure a great loss. Even a great loss does not damage your honour, or your family's, enough to justify *seppuku*.' He put a thick palm on top of my head. 'You have only gained sorrow.'

He rubbed my head, which reminded me of Second Daughter, one of my lost sisters. I half closed my eyes with the ease of touching and memories.

I shared what I had found out. 'Goro murdered Tashiko. I saw her neck, Akio. I discovered purple and white silk threads in her wounds. Goro deliberately killed her.'

'Who?' His words cooled, like a breeze in summer heat.

'Daigoro no Goro. Goro, the priest. He admitted it to me at her funeral.'

Akio opened his mouth, then closed it, pressing his lips into a line. He made the noise he taught us to make with the perfect sword strike, the *tachi-kami*.

We gazed at each other, tears running out of my eyes and rage from his.

Carefully and evenly, as if giving me new rules, he said, 'There is no honour in running away, or in allowing someone else to kill you, or in killing yourself. You know what you must do. You must avenge her murder.'

'How can I? If I cannot leave here, I cannot find him. If I cannot find him, I cannot kill him. He went to Heian-kyō!' I screamed, my feet in attack mode, my hands clenched.

'Kozaishō, are you a samurai or not? You will find a way in this life, or perhaps the next, to exact retribution.'

'Until the *next* life? A man murdered Tashiko.' My finger flew against my chest with each word. 'In *this* place. In *this* life.'

'Find a way. An honourable way. A samurai way. Until you do, use that anger to relearn the skills you may have forgotten. You will need them, in any case.'

'I have loved Tashiko since I was sold from my family!' My tears leaped again.

'Such a disgrace. To murder her . . . like that.' He shook his head, but his topknot barely moved in the tranquil spring morning.

'Especially heinous, Akio, are those men who murder defenceless women. They should be reincarnated as worms in late spring when the birds migrate and are especially hungry. They should return to be ants in a flood and all drown, slowly. They should become krill in the middle of a whale pod and be the last to be eaten. I want their agony and terror to be stretched to the maximum.'

'So heinous, too, is your display of these emotions, shameful. Here, but especially at the funeral.'

'Yes.' I lowered my eyes. The morning sun had brightened and mocked me.

'Everyone has emotions. A samurai contains them. Emotions should not and cannot control you. A samurai stands by death at every moment. Your emotions, words and actions at the funeral were dishonourable.'

My chin touched my chest. My shame stiffened me. The silence between us thickened with my humiliation.

I touched his arm without his armour for the first time. 'Yes, Akio, you are right. What must I do? Please help me take the Right Action.' An early spring gust, heavy with dew, brushed my face; bush clover, the scent of Tashiko's hair. My throat closed.

He smiled grimly, the air warmed, and the *tsuba* on his sword flashed in the rising light. 'Master Isamu often shared this saying with me: "Submission is not surrender. Submission is action and has its own valour."'

191

I bowed at the wisdom.

'Kozaishō, I have learned to face the flying arrows. Never turn your back on them. Announce your name to the world. Embrace the inevitable. Face the bright sword.'

That was what I was about to do.

Vengeance must be taken.

By me.

IV. Decision

My exertions for the dances and on the practise field absorbed some of my rage. Practise also provided a quiet time to deliberate.

In the stillness I devised my plan. Escape was not an honourable option. I had to remain alive, in solitude and captivity. I must survive and find Goro. I must to put an arrow through his body and stick his head on a pike. I had to become the Women-for-Play *chōja*.

I would alter the only honourable freedom I had: my stories.

I would fashion my stories to gain more control over the men who came to me, thereby amending their attitudes and behaviour towards women. I had to become the *chōja* because then I would have connections that would help me find Goro, avenge Tashiko, and protect the women in this place.

Each night and each morning, I lit incense and candles, chanted prayers, and promised Tashiko, 'Submission is not surrender.'

'No. I do not think that will work.' Misuki tossed her head on another of our long walks after the evening meal, safe from other ears and eyes. She had spoken softly. If the birds were silent or took to flight, I would know someone approached.

'Even with what you accomplished for Emi. I am delighted they allowed it – she loves the laundry. She and Aya talked about you and your stories.'

'I see,' I agreed, despite her tactless reminder of Emi's loose tongue. 'Why will it not work?'

'Emi and Aya are . . . Well, they are too trusting, easily deceived. They would agree to almost . . . anything.' She straightened her shoulders and gestured with her hands. 'But your customers – are intelligent and educated. Some are of the nobility – others have ranks, even Coloured Hats. Some live in the capital and in what I have heard is the grand Rokuhara city with its estates, each as big as Chiba's *shōen*.'

'You seem to know my customers.' Did this prove she spied for Rin? 'With whom should I start?'

'Well, as they say, to become a Buddha one must first become a novice. But first – first let me calculate the next auspicious day. To begin correctly.'

I humoured her and waited. Especially since I desired to have the first story meticulously designed to the smallest detail. In all of them, brutality focused on the men's enemies, never their daughters or wives. Never, never again, to women.

> Each man will be touched
> By my loss of purest love
> Guileful, like the Fox
> To gather violent harvests
> And transmute into respect

My grief was as it had been in the endless days after Tashiko had disappeared from the *shōen*, like a poor harvest followed by a long winter. In another of my vivid dreams, Tashiko's spirit appeared in an immense circle of fire and flew through a murky forest.

'The way out approaches!' she called, her hands open to embrace me, her face in a Buddha-like smile.

The trees sparkled with sunlight on freshly sprinkled rain. Her hands held books written in gold and silver on dark blue paper. Her eyes flashed with the light. 'Hold on to the brightness! I will guide you!'

I awoke. Tashiko was gone from my life and I, all alone, was in a dark forest.

I prayed my plan would work. I prayed to a Luck God, the one of Justice, Bishaman. I held on to this small hope.

V. Systems

Misuki said, again, 'I do not think this will work.' Her eyes circled up to her pasted-on eyebrows. She and I walked to our work huts. Tashiko's voice echoed in my steps. Altered stories: the only honourable path, compared to any other. My changes had to change the men to whom I told them.

'It is a difficult thing to do.' Akio settled a paw on each of my shoulders. 'To maintain one's honour while one takes vengeance can be difficult.'

He did not mention the obvious: that I was Woman-for-Play, small, and in possession of barely passing warrior skills.

On the other hand, Misuki counselled, 'Fear is only as deep as the mind allows.' Unlike her other maxims, I appreciated this one.

She and I had discussed each detail of 'Last Chance':

There was a Buddhist priest known to transform huts into mansions, old shoes into farm animals, and more. A lazy and greedy man hounded the priest to teach him this magic. After much begging, the priest finally agreed, but on the condition that the man must carry no eating utensils or anything made of metal.

Thinking of his future wealth, the man agreed. Afraid of the priest's power, he hid a dagger in his loin cloth. When he arrived, the priest pointed a finger where the dagger was hidden and commanded, 'ALL DISAPPEAR.' Suddenly, the man was alone in the middle of the forest, a half-day's journey from his house, and his dreams of wealth gone. He never saw the priest again.

The man played the Buddhist priest, while I acted the greedy man who begged for favours and appeared despicably grasping. I arranged my robe to open as I begged. That did not work. The greedier I became, the angrier the customer grew.

I reversed the scenario for the next customers. It made them angrier and rougher with me. The exact opposite of what I wished.

I modified 'Last Chance' again by a few details. Not one of my clients wanted to beg for material things. None desired to be the greedy man, and none wanted to say, 'ALL DISAPPEAR,' except to be more aggressive with me. Again the reverse of what I had hoped and often painful.

'What did you expect? A bean-jam cake falling into an open mouth?' Misuki said later, and made an effort not to smirk, but her balled fists remained pressed into her sides. Then she added a stupid proverb. I did not speak to her for the rest of the day. Displeased with her, I was more upset with myself.

The next morning Akio did not help my spirits. 'Kozaishō, men truly believe they will reap what they sow, especially so quickly. That is why we must continually be aware of the laws of *karma*.'

My arrows scored the lowest in many days. My footing was faulty. I received more blows from Akio's *bokken* than ever before. My thoughts were not on my work. That evening, Misuki stayed away and she told most others to do the same.

'Last Chance' was a miserable first chance at adapting my tales. Misuki knew better than to give me a I-do-not-think-this-will-work look. I had to find stories the customers would accept Also, I wanted to prove Misuki wrong.

Next I used 'Flying Water Jars'.

A temple near Heian-kyō was by a river where the younger priests competed in skill and magic. An especially gifted young priest made a water jar gather water by itself. One day, while he was watching his jar do the work for him, he saw another fly through the air, gather water and fly away. Startled, the young priest followed the flying jar to an old priest's house close by.

The young priest peered inside. Angered by the sight of an old priest sleeping while making jars fly the arrogant young priest chanted 'Spell of Fire Evil'. He sprinkled water on the sleeping priest, but drops splashed on to the young priest's kimono, setting him on fire. His screams awakened the old priest who put out the fire and tended the young priest's burns.

Impressed by the old priest's kindness, the young priest begged for forgiveness for his conceit, and pleaded to be allowed to study as an apprentice. The old priest forgave him and allowed him to stay and learn.

Some of the men adored the water splashes, especially in the warmer weather. Other treasured my screams. None learned not to arrogant.

Mother used to say I was the most determined of all her children. I always considered this a compliment. I asked my tutor, with whom I studied every third day, and read whatever he gave me. I found 'Grave of the Chopstick'.

Once there was a beautiful princess. For three successive nights a strange young man entered her sleeping chamber. Each night he brought a flawless gift: the first night, a red peony, the second, incense, and the third, a kimono. From these superior gifts and the young man's evasion of the palace guards, the high priest determined he was a deity. The young man and the princess were married on the fourth night.

The two were inseparable and happy in the evenings but she never saw him during the day. She wanted to know why. Before the young man answered, he asked her to promise to react calmly. When she looked into her oil vial the next day, she saw a small white snake. The princess shrieked and screamed.

That night, a young man again, he accused her of breaking her word and left the palace. She called out, reminding him he had pledged his love and promised to be with her always. They had been so blissfully happy! He did not turn back. In her hopelessness she grasped a silver chopstick, plunged it into her heart and died. She was buried near Nara. A ring of white flowers grows there every spring, and each flower has one red petal in memory of the broken promise.

To add realism, Emi made white paper flowers and painted one red petal on each with leftover rouge.

My clients and I played new bride and immortal with great relish. In this way the man aligned himself with someone of superior skills and power. I gave him a white flower with one red petal.

Customers learned to keep their word – the start of respect. The first night I used 'Grave of the Chopstick' successfully, I dreamed of Tashiko in her forest and flames.

'Well,' Misuki said, when I told her of the day's favourable outcomes, 'fall down seven times, stand up eight. Perhaps you could find a story we could use to teach the men to be better husbands. Ants go to sweet things.'

I found the Empress Kōken who had lived and loved when Nara was the capital, hundreds of years ago.

The Empress Kōken became enamoured of Fujiwara no Nakamaro. Alas, his rank was too low, the match impossible. After only nine years she abdicated and retired to a convent, yet continued to administer the government from the temple.

Dōkyō, a handsome and ambitious monk, seduced Kōken in the cloister. The empress followed his political schemes, due to his sexual powers, and returned to the throne. She appointed him to high positions and sought to raise his rank enough to become her heir, but she died before this could happen.

The first session began like this: I impersonated Empress Kōken and wore a dozen rich 'silk' layered kimonos, which swished like those of a court woman. I sat up on pillows and allowed the 'subject' in for a 'viewing'. I dressed in an outer purple kimono with 'gold' peacocks, my painted violet house shoes (Emi's work again), and my hair arranged. My *ohaguro* complete, I smiled to show blackened teeth, face powdered white, eyebrows glued with fresh charcoal, lips and cheeks bright red. Dazzling.

My first customer with this story pretended to be Dōkyō, the power-hungry Buddhist monk who claimed vast healing and magic powers. He needed to seduce the empress for influence. As he approached, I spoke: 'Why use your powers, when your other abilities will make this woman a dutiful and devoted slave? Why not seduce the empress?'

'Thank you, Empress, for your advice. I could call on the Gods to entice you, but I am struck by your beauty.'

I leaned away from my mock-throne in mock-rapture. 'As I look on your handsome face, your virile and strong body, I imagine all the powers and pleasures therein. There is but one path to win my heart, and only you can walk it.'

Then I murmured, 'I shall tell you what to say and do to win my heart. Follow my directions.' He nodded. 'Touch my feet, admire them, take off my shoes, and kiss my entire foot – all over.'

'Ah, Empress! Such great power in such small, dainty, graceful feet.' He lifted one foot to admire it, rubbed it and removed my shoes. I beamed at his surprise.

'What a wonder the empire is ruled on such tiny and beautiful feet!' He moved his lips over my bathed and perfumed feet. 'What a marvel your toes are!'

He licked the top of each and started to suck the largest. I whispered, with my eyes almost closed, 'Start with the smallest and finish with the largest one for best results.'

He looked up. He had not expected correction, but I had decided to risk it with him, a familiar long-standing client who was eager to please. With success, perhaps a few of his wives and concubines would appreciate me. He took my smallest toe in and out of his mouth with little sucking noises. I responded with sighs of delight and deeper breaths, which he enjoyed.

This elderly customer withered easily, unfortunately. No matter. I became his empress slave – which he loved to repeat for many months – to Rin and Hitomi's profit.

Gradually this client visited less often. Hopefully, he found devoted slaves in his own household. The older customers loved to play the desirable young monk.

Every tender and respectful man was another victory for Tashiko and her memory.

VI. Information

The majority of my customers maintained contact despite or because of the gradual though radical modifications I made to my stories. The Gods approved my plans, or perhaps I found my Right Actions and Livelihood.

I created a system to keep track of the adjustments to each story, to eliminate violence towards women. I maintained a log by customer and by story, so no one, no servant, no man, and especially neither Hitomi nor Rin, could discover my plan. My rage at Tashiko's brutal murder was the dry wood for this, my revenge fire. Payment for her death was grass bending before the wind, meekly, quietly, in small ways, but always growing.

The log had a twofold purpose: for me to become *chōja*; to locate and kill Goro. Such a lengthy process. Some customers came so infrequently that the changes for them in my stories were not completed for some time. For others, who visited many times a month, it happened faster. I maintained my log with caution and painstaking diligence.

Every moment I worked to avoid detection. I hid my log of my customers and stories under my *futon*, a large floor covering and the floor. Those who cleaned my hut could suspect nothing.

Except for Misuki, whom I decided to trust, I told no one of my plans or records. No one else knew of them. The disastrous Tsuneyo contest burned in my nightmares.

Beside my stories and customers, my extensive records included the cost of my clothing and makeup. These increased progressively with planned irregularity: a little glitter, a new kimono, a story requiring a particular colour or cloth or style. Witch sand demons altered their forms to camouflage their intentions. They required elaborate costume changes within a single story. Significant props of lacquered toilet boxes or inlaid quivers that appeared in the stories *had* to be included. That happened infrequently, for special occasions and feast days or for customers who paid well. Critical strategies require the finest scheduling. Calculations, cunning details and circumspect timing. Since I had lost my love, I wanted to take from Hitomi what she loved most, her wealth, and from Rin, what *she* loved most, her power.

Time disappeared, and with the addition of more sisters, young and younger cast-offs from Chiba or girls from poor families, more sadness filled my spirit. Almost two years had gone by since Tashiko's death, but I continued to burn incense and candles in her memory each day. I maintained my log, and my costs expanded slowly despite the perils.

Several times a month my tutors continued to teach me and Misuki, who remained an apt pupil. I sought always to locate Daigoro no Goro. To do this, I read more of everything: history, commerce, accounting, shipbuilding, war strategies, poets, philosophers, teachers, scholars and healers. Everything I learned I tried to include in my stories, depending on clients' interests, business and desires. The primary purpose was always to track down the priest with the impenetrable eyes and the sadistic, murderous heart.

How did I come across all of this information, all of this writing? My tutors did not supply enough of what I wanted. Clients became the varied source of materials I read. Some customers asked, 'How can I thank you for your entertaining ways?' I asked them for anything written that was no longer needed from their business, obsolete ships' logs or accounting sheets.

'Any trifle you could spare for a silly girl.' Stroking them suggestively, I would add, 'It will warm my heart knowing it has touched your hands.' While I called it a trifle, I knew how rare paper was and how expensive scribe services were.

I received scraps of this and that. Sometimes, after clients were satiated physically, I probed for the meaning of something I had read earlier. My log aided me in displaying a seemingly total interest and devotion to their smallest gifts. Naturally, this pleased them – and it was my duty to give joy, however bitter my spirit. This was my revenge for Tashiko.

With drooping bellies, dripping sweat, they whispered to me, 'You know, the hero should never have bought silk in spring because . . .' or 'If that prince had married a daughter to this neighbour, just as Fujiwara did with . . . a terrible battle could have been avoided.' I wrote these entries by separate classification in my log. After each, I recorded new information to use the next time.

When they puffed themselves up on 'discovering' their recommendations in my stories, only my memory of Tashiko kept a satisfied but grim smile from my lips. I could blush at will by holding my breath. Often their discovery, accompanied by a low bow with such a blush, yielded a coin or a gift of writing.

Presents I received included small copied parts of the Records of Ancient Matters, the venerable Chronicles of Japan and more. These I read and read again. They proved priceless to me because at this time I reasoned all knowledge could be used to entrap and tempt the men into foolish games, which I controlled. The games plucked elements of their savagery and transformed their brutality without them knowing it. The process was extraordinarily slow, but so burned the coals of my hatred and revenge.

Akio encouraged me. I shared my systems and information with him. He shared fighting strategies, which I adopted for my retribution.

The moment came when I taught as much as I learned. After a time, I gave more advice than I received. As their heads lay on my lap, I whispered, 'Register your lands to a temple, or have your lands confiscated by a temple and then repurchase them.' Several new landowners learned this and were indebted to me. Some gave me weapons or new armour. A rack in Akio's armoury grew heavy with gifts to me. A quiver, arrows with the special black-banded hawk feathers, pieces of armour that a clients' children had worn, all found their way to my cache.

Two older women came to serve me. They became servants when their faces, voices or ageing bodies no longer attracted clients, and were glad to be with me. Their only other choice was abject slavery or the *eta*.

When my first servant came to me, I was too kind and forfeited my authority. She lost her respect for me. With the second, I did better. I was

202

strict, but not rigid. I acquired the skill to be compassionate but not empathetic. In this way, we maintained our separateness, and I my authority.

More than four years had passed since the death of my beloved Tashiko, years of reading, studying and learning. My plans were succeeding. Madam Hitomi increased my price often, like a perennial plant returning every year to flourish and grow larger. When Rin had died from the coughing illness, I orchestrated an elaborate funeral hoping to entice Goro to the Village. He did not take the bait.

Hitomi named me *chōja* before my eighteenth birth anniversary. I garnered a tenth of everyone's earnings, which swelled my resources. My stories and services intertwined business advice, military strategy, political advice and customers' needs as the threads of a heavily patterned brocade. My clients became wealthier, more powerful, higher-ranking, and able to help me learn even more.

I translated what they told me into tools to fool them into kindness and gentleness, the only means to honour my Tashiko's memory. Many men were transformed at Hitomi's Village.

> More learning: writing
> Politics, noble people
> Chinese poetry
> My dear one's memories still
> Fill my heart as moonlight, my eyes

BOOK 8

I. One In Particular

'My dear Kozaishō, why do you tell me this story?' A new client, a well-dressed Taira samurai captain, Kunda Takiguchi no Tokikazu, stopped me in the middle of 'The Flying Jars'.

His words shone like gold and silver lettering on indigo paper. It took me a few moments to absorb what he was saying. No one had ever asked me such a question. I lowered my head and knelt in front of him. Would he hurt me? Complain to Hitomi, so that I would lose my fee?

He took my hands in his. 'Men usually come to women, such as yourself, to play out their desire for power and control. I believe you know that much.'

I controlled my temper and concentrated on his melodic speech. Its smoothness quelled my panic. After all, Taira samurai from Rokuhara, familiar with the capital and all the high-ranking people, should know more than the customers from a local *shōen*.

'Most men would not wish to pretend to be an inexperienced, arrogant priest. They would not agree to play the role of a conceited priest humbled to learn from an older one. I would not.' His eyes gazed straight into mine, and I saw his spirit. 'So, I ask again, why do you tell this story?'

I thanked him for his honesty. I could not tell him the truth and remained silent. What would he do?

His warm brown eyes beamed kindly at me. 'Sing for me. I have heard rumours that your voice and songs are enchanting.'

I reached for the *biwa*, relieved, yet troubled by the rumours. Who had spread them?

He put his hand on my forearm before I could play and lowered his voice. 'I have also heard that you practise to be a samurai.'

With effort my face remained blank but it grew hot.

'After our transactions here, may I have permission to train with you?'

His courtesy and calm of his voice caused my body toquiver. He was a powerful man. I nodded. 'Yes, honourable Kunda Takiguchi no Tokikazu.' Where had he heard about me? From whom? And how?

Tokikazu and I marched on to the practice field. The rising summer moon was almost hidden by swollen clouds, foretelling of a coming storm.

On the practice field, Akio's pupils enlarged and his eyes grew black. He made a small bow. I made a large one to Tokikazu, wondering at Akio's agitation.

Akio and Tokikazu glared at each other, like two cocks ready to fight. Fireflies swirled about them. The cicadas rumbled, while the *hototogisu* sang to announce the summer.

Tokikazu asked Akio for a *bokken* session with me.

Permission was granted.

We began.

Every ploy Akio had taught me to take advantage of my height succeeded. I was confident because Tokikazu was lean and only a little taller than I. But my second time with each gambit failed – altogether.

'Here.' Tokikazu put up his hand to stop after I lay on the ground for the fourth or fifth time in succession. He pivoted his wiry body to Akio and nodded. 'Akio! Please, let us demonstrate for Kozaishō.'

Akio walked over, his shoulders hunched defensively, his fingers pale around his *bokken*.

They performed. Akio sliced at Tokikazu, who deflected. Next Tokikazu countered with his *bokken's* edge. He rolled backwards on to the ground, righted himself and thrust up into Akio. With another stroke Tokikazu 'sliced' from neck to belly.

Akio fell backwards, roaring with laughter. 'Well done, Tokikazu.' Akio stood up, brushed himself down, and made a little bow.

The rest of the evening we practised together, two at a time. Akio and I ran through the tactic later until we were comfortable and familiar with it.

I wondered, for several years, why Tokikazu never returned to visit me, and why his memory persisted in my thoughts.

Most clients relinquished their old ways as I worked my stories on them. For example, another direct subordinate of the Taira governor, a lieutenant, had developed a fondness for food and grew larger at each subsequent visit. Completion no longer satisfied him unless he was eating at the same time. He preferred feasting to almost any other activity, including my singing, which had earlier pleased him.

I found three stories that served. In the first, an *oni* decided to eat his wife, but instead was consumed by a lion and a tiger. In the second, 'The Woman Who Ate Nothing', a female *oni* covered her true mouth on top of her head with hair. She ate her husband's friend, but her husband saved himself by hiding in a forest. For the third, I altered 'The Handless Maiden', whose hands were chopped off while she ate. My alternative was that an evil brother cut off a prince's hands; and the prince wandered until he performed a kindness for a peasant woman and the Goddess of Mercy restored his hands.

These stories instilled changes in the Taira lieutenant. He shrank with each visit until he was of normal size. My log showed that the process continued for more than a year. When I had finished with him, he was gentler, kinder, slimmer and grateful.

II. Premonitions

In my eighth summer at the Village of Outcasts I awoke remembering a dream, inspiring me like a winter full moon. Tashiko came in an immense ring of fire, and through the smoke I heard the thrush's call. It announced, 'Someone's coming! Someone's coming!' Arising, I shared this with Misuki and my serving women.

Misuki closed one eye, and half smiled with the other. 'This morning spiders' webs decorated a corner of my hut . . . Remember the old poem – "Where spiders' webs show, a woman's lover will arrive"?' Lifting her eyes to mine, she lowered her voice: 'Two signs together . . . are auspicious.'

Rare as such dreams were, my serving women nodded because I had shared the signs with them.

'Perhaps it will be a new and wealthy client.' One woman tittered. 'He will give you many coins.'

'A baby. Yes, it is an omen of a baby for you.' The second grinned, putting up her sleeve to hide her glaring white teeth. I knew my morning tea prevented conception.

Uncomfortable, I dressed early and went to the practice field, thinking of the white pheasant and the dragon-like cloud, the signs for which Master Isamu had allowed me on to the practice field at Chiba's. While I was practising my archery on horseback, a visiting samurai arrived almost undetected because of my disquiet. Since he and I had done so before, we drilled with the sword.

'You have improved, in our short time together. Indeed, you display great aptitude for the sword.' He gave a small bow.

Afterwards, I walked back to my hut, gratified at the compliment but still discomfited by the dream and Misuki's premonition. Since it was not a day when a tutor visited, I collected my servants for the bathhouse. Emi prepared the scrubbing mixture while Misuki and I reviewed clients, songs, costumes, makeup and dances. Misuki tracked costumes in the order required. Since her brush was still far better than mine, she wrote the lists.

With Misuki's direction, Emi prepared the room with all my requirements. She oversaw my hair ornaments and was a meticulous hair arranger, whose attention to detail had carried over from her love of flowers. In the coldest winter I had painted flowers.

For 'Grave of the Chopstick' Emi painted the one red petal on each white flower for those who did not keep their promises. Her flowers matched the stories' seasons and complemented my face and costume. She also compounded the correct incense – under Misuki's guidance – so the scent was appropriate to the story. My clients delighted in what I did and how I looked, but especially in the fragrances of my hair and body. The flower must hold the passer-by not only with its shape and colour but with its scent.

In the middle of our morning discussions, Madam Hitomi, wearing a vast array of seasonally inappropriate kimonos, burst into the bathhouse. She had neglected to gather her skirts and her hems trailed in a muddy sweep. She stood at the door with the morning light behind her.

The corners of her mouth turned down. Strands of hair jutted out, and she chattered like a screeching bird. Startled, Emi bowed, covering her open mouth with her hands. Madam Hitomi had never arrived in such a manner. Indeed, she never visited the bathhouse when the Women-for-Play were there. Perspiration poured down her face in the steamy air, removing her painted eyebrows. It soaked her rouged and wrinkled cheeks. Drops rolled off her rounded chins, wetting her coat, which gave off a rancid smell. She had put on weight lately and now looked like one of my clients, especially the Taira governor's lieutenant before he had shrunk. Hitomi glistened and dissolved in the late-morning sun like a rotting vegetable.

'Kozaishō!' She cocked her head.

Misuki and Emi's mouths were agape, eyes large with anticipation. Madam Hitomi had never bowed to me, ever. I had received at most a heavy eyebrow movement when I performed so magnificently that someone overpaid her.

Through the steam, she strode directly to me. 'Do not make plans for your regular customers. An emissary has arrived. An honoured personage is coming and has reserved you for the day – all day. He wants no other to attend him.'

Gulping, I tried to pay attention to her words, rather than her hair, which was dripping around her creased neck. I succeeded in not smiling – for the honoured personage, surely a high-ranking man, was for me. Half scrubbed by Emi, I bowed quite low. 'Thank you for the honour, Madam Hitomi, and for your confidence in me.'

She snapped, 'You must do your best today. Ask for whatever you need. It will be given.'

'Thank you for your generosity,' I said, bowing low again. 'I have a small request. May I know something of the identity of this lord who is to honour the Village today?' I could barely keep my voice soft. Still bowing, I did all I could not to raise an eyebrow. I had rehearsed giving her the illusion that the control was hers.

'It is an emissary from the governor of Echizen province, Taira no Michimori, third rank junior grade. He arrived this morning. Word of my house and my well-trained women has spread to Echizen Governor Michimori himself. He is travelling with his troops, but because of an ominous Divergent Directions for him today, the commander must stay here. Naturally, this great lord would never invite evil from the Gods of Directions.

'You are to entertain him. Many of his lieutenants and other high-ranking officers will be with the others.'

'Madam Hitomi, I am overcome with the great honour you give me. I will attempt to bring honour to you and to your house.'

She beamed, grunted and left, mumbling to herself . . . sounding a bit like Tashiko. Remembering my dream that morning and the spiders, I sent a silent prayer to Kannon-sama, the magnificent Goddess of Mercy, for what I hoped would be a benevolent day. I bowed again deeply. Wet and naked in the late morning, I shivered in the bathhouse steam, although there was no chill.

III. Preparations

As Madam Hitomi left the bathhouse, my head swirled with ideas. Emi gave up trying to scrub me. I tried to picture the perfect tale for the governor – the third rank Taira Clan commander – about whose wondrous deeds we had heard. Misuki squeaked and squealed, pinching herself to make sure we were not under the spell of a demon spirit seeking to harm us with good news.

Allowing a few moments for cheer and elation, I regained my composure and demanded attention. 'Let us prepare for his arrival.' I attempted to be stern with the girls. Sitting down on the scrubbing stool, I motioned to Emi to continue cleansing me. After practise, especially with a sword, I required several washings before I was clean enough to soak.

While she scrubbed, I considered the situation. Misuki remembered the stories, but Emi required frequent reminding. She needed to display the proper respect for this great lord or she might forfeit her life.

I turned to Misuki. 'Let us tell Emi about the Echizen Governor Taira no Michimori so she can honour him.'

'Yes, my lady,' Misuki moved closer to us and sat on another stool. Our eyes touched, and I knew she understood.

I began, 'Taira no Michimori's uncle, Kiyomori, is now chancellor, junior first rank – the highest rank any subject can achieve, all because of Kiyomori's bravery in the Hōgan and Heiji rebellions.'

Misuki said, her forehead and cheeks high in colour from either the hear or the importance of our new customer, 'The Taira Clan built the seaport city near here, Fukuhara, and the glorious city of Rokuhara. Michimori's family is the most powerful in the empire.'

'Thank you, Misuki,' I said, and checked Emi's eyes to see if she had understood this. In my fervour. I was impatient: we had much to do. I added, 'Michimori's uncle is a great leader who saved the emperor's life many years ago.'

'How?' Brow creased, Misuki had asked the right question.

I simplified the famous story of Michimori's uncle and his uncle's ascendancy in government. When I had finished, Misuki asked Emi, 'Do you understand?'

Emi nodded and said, 'When did this happen?'

'Many years ago. Kiyomori was once a plain person, of low rank, but now his grandson is the emperor, Emperor Antoku. An uncle of the emperor is coming here.' Misuki spoke slowly, emphasising each word.

'Michimori is the nephew of Kiyomori,' I repeated, this time drawing the Taira Clan genealogy on the floor with my finger, showing how close Michimori was to the emperor. This was finally sufficient for Emi. At least, for the moment. She rocked her head at the odd angle she always did when she understood. I hugged her to make up for my brusqueness.

'We must make sure everything is perfect. He is the most important customer we have ever entertained – a relative of the emperor.' By now I had finished soaking and stood up. I hugged Emi again and smiled. The poor girl was trembling.

'Do not be afraid, my Emi. This is what we will do.' I climbed out of the bath, wrapping myself in a drying cloth Misuki held out. 'The governor has always the best, the finest of everything. Today we will do a story that is the opposite.'

I took a long breath and began to explain my plan. 'We will use only plain fabrics with no decoration. Strip the room bare, except for the *futon* and the table. Cover the floor lightly with clean straw. I want one instrument, playing a single melody, no harmony, and place the musician far outside. Lay my makeup on the table. I will put some on as an element of the story, so Michimori can be part of it.

'First, rags under my formal greeting robe. My hair tied loosely, like a peasant's. Emi, you will help me with my hair and flowers, but only plain flowers.' I smiled at Emi's bewildered face and explained, 'Make a wild flower for the first part.'

Elaborate directions followed for costume changes and the music. Misuki wrote everything down. Emi began to scurry out, but I called her back to explain how she should greet the great lord.

As I was teaching Emi, I felt my father's sweet presence because he had taught me the proper bow: 'The five parts: two knees, two elbows and head.' Now I taught Misuki and particularly Emi. We practised bowing with our knees, elbows and head on the ground. After such a bow, I taught the girls to walk backwards while bowing. To make mistakes with this was to lose a head.

We practised until I was sure Emi could do it perfectly and repeatedly. 'You will bow to the ground before the Echizen Governor Taira no Michimori each and every time you see him,' I instructed. 'When he dismisses you, leave backwards. Do you understand?' Misuki's face wore the little smile that said, 'Very well,' so I ordered Emi, 'Go outside to pick the flowers,' and she left.

'Fortunately, my lady,' Misuki confided, 'the story is familiar. No need for practise.'

'The client has always aided me with makeup. We do not wish to ask the Echizen governor to help me.'

Misuki grinned at the ridiculous thought of the great governor applying a woman's makeup. 'Perhaps when the needy hero returns, he can send a servant to prepare the one he loves. That will be myself. I can dress you. Help with the makeup.'

'Ask for other girls to help with the sewing. Next, send our serving girls to my house to help groom me. After you have overseen the others, come back. We will review and choreograph the timeline.'

While a serving girl oiled and combed my hair, another scented my clothes. As they fussed, I evaluated each detail of the story. I changed each element to fit the aspects of the military genius of the commander Michimori and his famous family. From what I had heard and read, I created what would please and surprise him.

IV. A Beginning

The hem for my first simple kimono was not sewn at all, and a few seams were not sewn twice. We did not have time – even though so many worked – my own serving girls and several borrowed from other Women-for-Play. Perhaps because of these omissions the effect of poverty startled me.

The next day I had to rap the third sewing girl's fingers gently with a stick, but I gave her an extra ration of food from the feast. It was always necessary to enforce discipline.

Before his arrival, Taira no Michimori had eaten elsewhere. Especially while waiting, I was nervous and shaking a little from the excitement, which went undetected by those serving me. Perhaps Misuki knew, but she did not betray my agitation. Besides, I argued with myself, I was a good judge of men, especially empowered, wealthy and self-assured men. He was, after all, merely another man.

Peeping out from my work hut, I saw his honourable lordship walking towards me with Madam Hitomi, who was as puffed up as a mating bird, bobbing her head. Governor Michimori had little of the ornamentation some of his officers wore. The two entered my work hut.

His honorable lordship lived up to his reputation. His thick glossy hair was in the topknot for samurai. It was clear from the deference his aides and servants showed him that he was in charge, the governor, Taira no Michimori. He dismissed all with a gesture, including Madam Hitomi, who was bowing backwards, mumbling spurious exaltations.

With an impressive brow, the stocky, muscular man strode forward, like a god on the earth. (I had once seen a play about such a god at Chiba's *shōen*.) When he saw the straw-covered *futon* and floor, he cried out in delight, like a small child with a new toy. Fists at his sides, he roared, his dark eyes spouting laughter that ricocheted against the little walls of my work hut until the entire Village of Outcasts reverberated.

The time passed in an eye blink and lasted my lifetime. His honourable lordship asked about my life and I answered him, albeit briefly. I was not there for my enjoyment, although it seemed to please him to learn about me. He shared some of his own story with me. After his next foray into battle, he would return to Rokuhara. I stifled a gasp when he mentioned the magical, mystical city, built by his uncle.

My lord Michimori conversed between my songs and dances, which reflected a natural quality I thought he would enjoy. Several were old ones I had learned from my family. After I had finished the story, songs, music and dances, we were together as rusticated peasants in an ox shelter. Laughing again, he managed to say, 'I travelled all this way to lie down in straw!'

At first Michimori allowed me to lead, but I knew with this man that there would be no teaching. I stroked his chest and back, softly brushed the powerful legs, as they lay relaxed, perhaps for the first time since he had been travelling. I rubbed his thick shoulders and neck. He allowed himself the luxury of a little humming. The incense he wore, combined with the scents of his body, earth and horse, was as delicious as that first meal with Chiba.

I found scars on his chest, back, legs and arms. I asked about each one. For some, like the scarred knuckles on one hand, he just shrugged and moved my fingertips to where he wanted. Others he explained. A short curved scar came from when he and his cousins, as boys, had practised swordplay. As a prank during childhood practise, the cousins had cut the shin guards from his calves. Later, unaware, and on horseback, another cousin had hurt him, practising with a *naginata*. The scythe-like blade had carved a thin curved scar on his left leg. The deep ones on his chest were from arrows that had worked their way through his breastplate. I traced and caressed each one, honouring the foolishness of his boyhood and the strength of his courage. He allowed me to touch all of his body.

For all his strength, when he took charge of our coupling, his nimbleness surprised me. He pinpointed the little places Tashiko and I had explored together: earlobes, neck and nape, inside the elbow, back of the knees, toes. He concentrated on each, until he had assured himself I was satisfied.

He played a sweet tune on my Lute Strings, claiming they were flower petals to bees. As each part palpated, his reassuring voice spoke praises. By this time I no longer feigned.

His voice softened. His words shortened. His touches heightened. Finally, he drank from me. Deeply. Eagerly, as a hungry baby suckles. He persisted.

He poised himself above me, outlined my mouth with a thick finger. Until then I had been oblivious to my sounds. I opened my eyes and saw the complexion of his Stalk, golden as a spring dawn. Astonishing myself, I ached for him. He entered me.

We held each other. We gazed into each other's faces and lay silent for a long time without words. This was the first time I had enjoyed myself with a man. Tashiko had said it was possible, but I had not believed her.

We coupled again that night. I must have slept because I stirred, feeling his hands on me. They were soft yet relentless. First stroking my back, then my shoulders. Next, firmly and gently, my breasts and neck.

Keeping his hands on me, he folded one leg against me and straightened the other. He moved his hands around and under me, lifting me slightly until I was sitting on his legs. He sat up, and pulled me closer to him. Leaning over, he sang soft notes and caressed.

I was drenched. He was ready for me. His Jade Stalk had been tapping an ardent rhythm on my stomach. He entered me, lying down on the *futon*, taking me with him. My knees bent, my hands above his shoulders, I crouched over him. His hands remained around me.

With the strength for which he was known, he lifted me up and down, thrusting me on to him. I began to move in rhythm with him. He took one hand and moved my face to gaze at his. His eyes filled. He manoeuvred my body to intensify my delight. My eyes wept, and we completed at the same moment.

I crumpled on to his breast, and we contemplated each other, content. I stirred to sit up, but he held me. At last, we slept.

When I awoke, his honourable lordship rubbed my face with the back of his fingers and whispered, 'Besides the need for Divergent Directions, my reason for coming here was to thank you.'

'Thank me, my lord?'

'The lieutenant, several of my lieutenants have . . . improved themselves.'

I knew of what he spoke, but said nothing.

'I asked them, and they each told me of your stories. Finally I realised where their new strengths, their new influence had come from.' He listed their names.

'Yes, honourable lord, they did each call upon me.'

'Many times, by their recollection.' He smiled, stroking my forehead.

Blushing, surprised at myself, I agreed. It was genuine blushing, not false flirting.

He continued, 'These men have become better husbands. One can now mount his horse easily. Their wives are now content, and there are no tales of betrayal, causing problems in the clan. Again I thank you.' He played with my hair, lifting it to the light, using his fingers like a comb.

'You do me much honour, Lord Echizen Governor Taira no Michimori.'

'I hope you will honour me as well. Would such a path, such a partnership, be favourable to you?'

I did not understand his statement, or what he meant by 'path', but I motioned in agreement. I was afraid a question would dart out like a flying insect if I dared open my mouth. He enfolded me briefly, then prepared to leave. However, before he and his soldiers departed, he sent a note, folded like a flower, with this poem:

> My complete spirit
> Has been stolen from me
> Snatched and soaked into
> Every stitch and thread
> Of the kimono you wear

Although I had difficulty in drawing words, I recognised beautiful writing when I saw it. Misuki and I admired the words and the way they were written. The paper itself was an elegant cyan and transferred his scent. Reading the poem again, I dared not dream what I thought I understood. Misuki and I discussed it for the rest of that night and early into the next morning, too exhilarated to sleep.

V. Purchases

That morning Hitomi sent a girl quite early. I was annoyed that she could disturb me so soon. I sighed, still tired, but dressed myself and went to her apartments. I shivered, thinking of her punishments, as I walked in the morning damp. Then I smiled inwardly, remembering the shivering when Hitomi had come into the bathhouse to tell me of the great Taira no Michimori. Perhaps my smile was more for Michimori than Hitomi.

I wondered what new petty thing had upset Hitomi. Reviewing the events of the night before, I could think of nothing I had done wrong except that one hem.

But Hitomi rarely, if ever, awakened so early. Something else had gone wrong. And, with Hitomi, it was never pleasant. I thought through the list of possible misdemeanours. My heart beat faster, and my tongue stuck to the roof of my mouth, yet I maintained my decorum. My steps did not falter. There was so much gossip among the Women-for-Play. I did my utmost to avoid anyone learning my business from my movements or face.

During my perfunctory obeisances to Hitomi in Main House, I saw that something was indeed amiss. She lay sprawled across the cushions, her face knotted into a snarl. She always pressed her lips tight when administering penalties. There were to be none. I breathed again. The throbbing in my chest slowed to a light thud.

Rubbing her eyes, Hitomi pretended to stifle a yawn. 'There has been a request.' Her voice was tense, but her body appeared not to be. I wondered why. This had to be bad.

Keeping my eyes blank, I gazed at the floor. She would speak when she was ready. Hitomi valued power and control. I waited. But I had seen her eyes.

'Echizen Governor Taira no Michimori is preparing to leave. He has decided to purchase you.' Here she scowled, lowering her face to her cat. 'He has ruined me, my sweet one, just ruined me.'

My face tingled. My fingers trembled. Gongs struck throughout my body to a rhythm I had never felt before. To go. To leave the Village of Outcasts. Purchased by someone of third rank. Giddy, like being lifted high above the clouds.

Hitomi elevated her eyes to my level with an unambiguous glower. 'You are leaving with his troops at the Hour of the Sheep.' From almost closed eyes she hurled her bitterness. 'Remember well what I have taught you. Remember whence you came.' Then she faced her cat and stroked it again.

Rage blasted through my stomach and up into my chest. It flashed in my face as I glared at her. I would remember what I had taught myself. What had she taught me but indignity and regret? Catching myself, I dropped my eyes and bowed low. Thankfully, Hitomi was staring at her cat, and I missed a farewell thrashing.

Evidently Governor Michimori had offered her a fair price, but not what she wanted. As governor, he could simply have taken me.

'Thank you, Madam Hitomi, for all your teaching and wisdom. This humble serving girl will try her best to do you honour,' I lied.

She smiled feebly for an instant, then stopped.

'Pack your things and be ready to leave.'

'Yes, Madam Hitomi.' I was leaving. I was going.

'Oh, yes, Kozaishō,' she added, making a poor attempt to sound nonchalant. 'You may take Misuki and Emi. The governor has bought them as well.'

I managed to stand on precarious legs. 'Thank you, Madam Hitomi. As you wish.' I bowed. My body felt like leaves dumped into boiling broth. I did not run to my hut. I dared not. My body shook inside, not to be depended upon, but my mind sprinted ahead, already there.

What could this mean? Why would he buy me . . . *and* my girls?

Misuki still slept. I tugged at her sleeve until she awoke. She had rested only a little longer than I. 'My dream has come true! Governor Michimori has acquired us – you, Emi and me! We are to pack and leave today! At the Hour of the Sheep!'

Misuki put a hand on each side of my face. Her eyes opened wide and spilled. Mine did also, and we hugged. We were leaving, escaping.

Michimori had appeared kind. Would he allow me my secret desire?

Misuki interrupted my reverie. 'Tell me! How angry was Hitomi?'

I told her all.

She kept saying, 'Are we leaving? Are we really going?'

At each question I nodded. We stared at each other, touching each other in disbelief. We hurried to Emi's hut to tell her.

'What will happen to all the violent men?' I whispered.

'I do not know.'

'I will continue to pray for Tashiko. Perhaps her spirit will intervene.'

Misuki did not respond. I wondered if I should tell her about my secret dream.

'Do you think we will travel near my family? Or yours?' she asked, her eyes bright.

My throat thickened. The one question I had wanted to ask. I moved my head to show I did not know. No words would come. Hearing my secret wish spoken aloud paralysed my tongue.

Our shoulders pressed together, we went to find Emi.

BOOK 9

I. Echizen Governor Taira No Michimori

I scarcely remember going to Lord Michimori's tent and waiting with one of his guards until I was escorted within. Papers lay everywhere inside the worn yet meticulously clean tent. The Echizen governor's face bore a glazed look. His armour awaited him on its stand, erect like a warrior ghost, battle-ready. Incense was burning, and I glanced at it.

'I use it to perfume my helmet.' Michimori grinned. 'If I lose my head, I do not wish to offend an honourable opponent.' His servant helped him with his armour, and he continued, 'I am so pleased the Gods spoke of the need of Divergent Directions for yesterday and today.'

He flashed a most appealing smile – a smile I remembered from our first day and night together. 'But now my spies . . . my *messengers*,' he emphasised the word with a shrug, 'tell me there is an emergency. I must journey towards the capital immediately.' He looked directly into my eyes and I, after his prompting the day before, returned his soft gaze.

'I have heard of your accomplishments on the horse as well as the practice field.' He clasped my hands in his. 'If I provide you with a suitable animal, will you accompany me?'

'Yes, my lord,' I said, thinking of nothing except what I had heard from Madam Hitomi: I belonged to Michimori and must do as he wished. I was to leave the Village of Outcasts.

'Will you take the Pledge of Loyalty to me?'

What was this? He owned me *and* he requested loyalty? It would be unnatural for me to be disloyal. Yet his eyes were so steady. As Tashiko had said would happen, a man had satisfied me. Tashiko. How I still missed her. How I would miss Akio. How could I leave him – my mentor, my teacher, my protector?

'Honourable lord . . .' I paused.

His eyes encouraged me.

'Please forgive my boldness. Aside from your generosity in purchasing my servants, there is one more who has protected and taught me since I was eight years old. His name is Akio.'

'Where is he?'

'Here, my honourable lord.'

'Here?'

'Here, at the Village of Outcasts. He had to move his family from Chiba no Tashiyori's *shōen* because of me.'

'Extraordinary.' He tapped his right foot slowly and gently.

I had no idea what this gesture meant, so I continued: 'You are known for your fairness and generosity. I dare to ask that he and his family go with you.' I prostrated myself on the ground, my nose in the dirt, wondering if I was about to lose my head. Akio had risked so much, his family and his life, to teach me. I prayed to the Amida Buddha and waited.

A hand patted the top of my head and lingered on my hair. Amida, Amida. I prayed to Tashiko's spirit as well.

'Yes, Kozaishō. Tokikazu will arrange it, if it is vital to you. You will have to meet with Akio at another time, however.'

At another time? When would that be? I dared not ask more. I took the Pledge of Loyalty:

> I pledge loyalty
> With my body and my life
> To honour you, your clan,
> Until sale or death separates
> Me from my duty to you.

He turned away, picked up an object with both hands, and returned with the pieces of an iron collar. 'This is for you, for the journey. You have only a face protector.'

I bowed and found myself quivering as our fingers touched across the cool metal.

He turned away again, and when he turned back his eyes beamed, like the sun after rain. Across his hands lay a magnificent helmet. The construction, impeccable; the shape, perfect in its roundness. Its seams were edged with gold.

'A master in Heian-Kyō made this.' He placed it in my hands. I could only bow. 'Let your serving girls arrange your belongings, and let them ride in one of the ox carts. They, and all but the weapons you need, will follow us with our supplies.'

He answered my unasked question by telling me that reliable guards would accompany my servants and possessions. His special samurai, Captain Kunda Takiguchi no Tokikazu, would lead my personal guards. I bowed.

I recollected the captain's name, but could not match it with a face.

After scurrying to my hut, I directed Misuki to arrange all our belongings in as many *furoshiki* as were required and ready them carefully. I told her what to take, what not to take, and what to sew into the hems of garments. I had learned to do this for safety's sake from a Lotus Sutra story. 'After they have sewn all the papers, documents and my coins into the seams or hems of our garments, place them carefully in each *furoshiki*. Do not fold or tie them until Madam Hitomi has seen and approved.'

Misuki's eyes questioned me.

'Do not fret.' I squeezed her shoulder briefly. 'Hitomi will assuredly come to inspect what we are taking out of her . . . realm. If she finds even one item amiss, she will ransack all of it. No lumps in any hem! Be excessively scrupulous!'

I thought again of the story from the Lotus Sutra about the man who had sewn a jewel into his friend's garment. I wondered, after all my years at Madam Hitomi's, what the real jewels from the Buddha would be.

Misuki arranged for those women we could trust or bribe successfully to do this work immediately.

Next I gave orders for my immediate needs: rice balls, a change of clothing, my swords, my dagger. After checking my quiver, which Akio – my beloved Akio – had given me, I placed my arrows in it and prepared my bow. I was leaving Akio. Would I be allowed to say farewell to him and his family?

With the usual assistance from Misuki, I dressed as a warrior, with all the armour I had and my gifts – the collar and helmet. Emi arranged my hair: she parted a circle around my head and pulled some through the hole at the top of the helmet. The rest she wound beneath it and set in knots.

After a hug and a slight moistening of our eyes, she sighed. 'I will miss you so much, dear lady.' She thought we were parting for ever, having forgotten, again, what she had been told just a short time ago. Too over-whelmed to speak, I looked at Misuki, asking her silently to explain to Emi. Suddenly I realised that I had been at Hitomi's longer than I had lived with my own family. With no time for melancholy, I stroked Emi's hand and went to mount my new horse, another gift.

Beyond a hill outside the Village of Outcasts, I joined Governor Michimori. His captains surrounded him, observing the ground while he marked lines with a stick. I waited, since it was clearly some type of strategy meeting, walking my new bark-brown horse up to the posted guards. How strange and serious this was. Another world.

Armour protected my horse from head to hocks. Its metal chamfron gave its head the silhouette of a dragon. Small padded pieces of lacquered leather covered its body, and flanchards hung from the saddle on both sides, made of the same fabric as body armour for its protection. This horse would not easily die under me in battle. Battle? What was I thinking?

After a while, Michimori dismissed his captains with a wave. He smiled at me – with his eyes – and gestured to a guard, allowing me to approach. I did so. His eyes scanned me slowly from shin guards to helmet, spending extra time on the *tachi* and dagger sheaths.

'My information about you is accurate.' He inspected me. 'You are more than adequately prepared for our journey. Let us go.' With that, he tapped the back of my hand once before he mounted his horse, Thunderbolt, of which I had heard tales of intelligence and courage. He turned his head briefly and ordered me to follow Tokikazu, the third division from the left. Then the Echizen Governor strode ahead, leaving me with strangers on a strange horse.

II. Messengers

With more than a hundred of us, it was more than a day's travel to Heian-kyō. Captain Tokikazu introduced the samurai who would accompany us. One was so large, he dwarfed his horse. However, none of us spoke while riding, so I surveyed the area, mostly watching the governor.

Michimori rode his horse as if he had never owned legs. Five or six captains rode up and spoke with him during the day. After a glance to see who was within earshot of the conversation, the governor shook his head, barked orders, or spoke softly into their ears. He was the steady hub of his army.

At night we stopped only for brief rest and nourishment because it was summer. Each shred of daylight propelled us to the target, which I thought was Heian-kyō, the magical capital city of the emperor. Instead of sleeping, Michimori talked to a captain in his tent.

At Captain Tokikazu's request before retiring, I told a short tale to him, Mokuhasa and Sadakokai, the two other samurai assigned to me. They especially liked the story of Kihachi. When I told of how Mikoto could not catch Kihachi because he passed gas and the odour was too strong, everyone laughed. When I told how Kihachi's body was cut into hundreds of pieces and his head flew into the sky, everyone cried.

That night, I prepared for the governor to send for me, but he did not.

In the morning, we trekked around the hills until we reached Seta at mid-morning. There, Michimori halted the soldiers without explanation. Many sentries scanned the hills, the captains too, appearing stiff and serious, more so than the soldiers. The atmosphere was quiet and still, like the moments before a thunderstorm.

The silence was broken with the sound of galloping hoofs. Horse and rider stopped near a captain, one of the Echizen governor's personal samurai. The weary messenger almost fell off his horse and stumbled on the ground, but bowed to this captain, who offered him some water. He drank it eagerly, spilling some, which trickled over his dusty armour.

The samurai and the messenger talked and pointed. Eventually, the samurai walked over and bowed to another. Tokikazu explained, 'No one approaches the commander without first seeking one of his personal samurai.' The governor agreed to receive the message and motioned for the samurai to approach.

While checking their weapons, Mokuhasa, Sadakokai and I spoke of this messenger.

Mokuhasa began, 'We have known Prince Mochihito has been gathering forces against we Taira.'

Raising his face from rearranging his daggers, Sadakokai stuttered, 'Is th-there not an Imperial D-Decree b-b-banishing the Prince?'

'Yes.' Tokikazu turned to me. 'Banished, a cloistered monk, our Taira ally tried to forestall the Minamoto attack on Rokuhara. The leaders of the Minamoto tracked him to his cloister and razed it. They injured and killed the innocent monks and disciples. It was then that the Imperial Decree was issued.'

Mokuhasa added, with sadness in his voice, 'Lady Kozaishō, this monk returned to Rokuhara, told his story and informed the Taira Clan leaders that Prince Mochihito was on his way to Uji, not even waiting for his reinforcements.'

'Our leaders tried to find help, but neither the *sōhei* at Mount Hiei nor the city of Nara sent any succour,' Tokikazu added, with an unripe persimmon expression.

Sadakokai's large hand motioned to Mokuhasa. 'B-b-but now the Miidera *sōhei* monks are agitated and en route to Uji.'

'There is going to be fighting, is there not?' I said, knowing it was not even a question, although I was unfamiliar with these recent machinations. Mokuhasa and Sadakokai answered with their silence.

The governor and his men drew maps in the soil. Then we moved out at a rapid pace and across to the Seta bridge. Following the Uji river, I heard a faint commotion coming from around a curve.

Michimori prodded his horse and his captains to the front of the divisions. I followed Tokikazu as I had been told, trying not to attract notice. The distinct sounds of yelling and shrieks, people and horses, stung my ears. My belly shackled itself around my throat. I heard the Hell of Incessant Misery, where swords constantly gnaw and slash people's bodies. I bit my lip to make sure I was alive. To what hell was I going?

With a swift hand gesture and the semaphore flags, Michimori slowed our entire horde to a quiet walk, so different from our previous unrelenting dash.

Another messenger came through the morning fog, covered with mud, his horse glazed a dull brown. The governor and his captains murmured in low tones to each other. The governor revolved them into what I thought of as his circle of power. With the heads of each division and himself, they planned strategies with their backs to all. We could see only the special guards, who stood facing out from the circle. If they had been petals, instead of soldiers, they would have created a wonderful flower, open to the sun, dark armour gleaming with glints of coloured silk laced through the black metal.

The circle of power closed. No one spoke to me, but I followed as closely as Tokikazu allowed. Next, all walked cautiously until we rounded the bend in the Uji river. Just beyond the white-crested and dangerous water, I noticed the famed Byōdōin and its Hō-ō-dō – Phoenix Hall, more imposing than I had heard, with wings and ornaments. It looked like a huge bird recently descended to earth.

The governor stood up in his saddle and gave a cry such as I had heard only in my worst nightmares. Singing-gourd arrows squealed across the sky: the voices of hell-demons. Pandemonium surged – I felt as if buckets of ice water had suddenly drenched me. The men urged their horses faster; mine followed.

I galloped into the morass of men. Most of the Taira forces were on the other side of the river. In its deep, strong flow so many bodies wore Taira colours – as if they were doing laundry with their clothes on . . . in red-tinged water. The horror of the bodies, the dead men, seared into my thoughts.

I can see all now. The governor stays back briefly behind his captains and soldiers. I can almost hear his mind drawing strategy lines in the mud as he surveys the panorama. Cries, grunts, howls surround me. I pull out my arrows and place my horse well behind the governor's men, looking . . . eyeing . . . watching . . . aware. Arrows hiss by with a sound that makes my blood pause. The Taira foot soldiers encourage the others to ford the river. More men stagger over bleeding bodies and arrow-struck corpses to go to the river's south side. The snarled orders of the governor and his captains overshadow the shrieks of battle. I move with the men. My arrows are gone; I drop my bow while searching, seeking an enemy target, ignoring the stridency that is swirling, squeezing my head. With my left thumb I push on my *tsuba* and release my sword.

III. Battle

The men are so close – our own and the Minamoto. For a time I am so hedged in I have to check before I tug my horse in any direction. I see a clearing to the Minamoto. I trot through our foot soldiers. With one hand I assure myself of my *tachi*. Soldiers yell. My mouth opens and I scream into the throng. My horse moves swiftly. A soldier on the ground – I cut into his upper chest, where his torso meets his shoulder guards. My blade crunches through either armour or bone. Not daring to look back, I urge my horse forward.

Another soldier and horse with the Minamoto colour white. I meet his eye. He comes to me. We exchange names. I strike my *tachi* before his sword can touch me. It slices across his neck. His sword drops. Eyes glare up, but his mouth is full of blood. He tumbles from his horse. Again, I do not look back.

Seeing an open space, I move to the temple front, the great Hō-ō-dō, Phoenix Hall, the large red bird with wings, hovering over the river.

The Minamoto huddle, surrounding someone, who staggers and clings to a stone lantern in front of Phoenix Hall, then falls. A broken arrow pierces his shoulder, which bleeds, spilling scarlet. He removes his armour and places it behind him. He opens his robes to expose his naked belly. Without a sound he holds his dagger in two hands and slits himself open.

Men around him stop fighting to watch. His bloody intestines seep over his lap and on to the ground. The gold from the temple roof reflects the sun. He crumples, his face in his own shining viscera.

I return to fighting, but now it is easier. The Minamoto are stunned and quickly killed. One man barely raises his sword before I split his neck. He collapses and falls close to his horse, blood spraying like a waterfall. Another warrior spies me, perhaps not expecting a woman. I slash him across the chest, deep under his torso sheath. He drops into the mud. I do not look back.

After what seems like months and a moment, the fighting slows. I see only Taira, no Minamoto, except those who are fleeing. Not knowing what to do now, I hunt for the captains or the governor. A captain is beside me. It is Tokikazu, and he motions. I follow him to a place near the Phoenix Hall of Byōdōin. His eyes are grim, but content. He and I are covered with blood.

The governor gathers the captains who have survived with another of his small gestures, and they obediently crouch around him. He motions and allows me into the circle.

'Today is a good day.' He lifts both hands, palms outwards, to his men. 'We have vanquished Minamoto no Yorimasa, once ally of the Taira Clan. He has committed *seppuku* in front of the temple.'

My stomach seizes as I realise who and what I witnessed.

'We have captured and killed Prince Mochihito, the traitor! Chancellor Taira no Kiyomori will be pleased. I believe our emissaries have enlightened us properly. With you men on this side, we led our troops across the river to victory! Yorimasa and the traitorous Mochihito are dead!'

With that, he motions to Tokikazu, speaks to him, and again calls his circle of power with their mysterious drawings on the ground.

Tokikazu accompanies me away from the circle. 'My lord Taira no Michimori bids me to take you and your serving girls to Heian-kyō. He is required elsewhere immediately.' Tokikazu faces me closely; his eyes smile. 'My lord desires me to tell you that you did well in your first battle.'

His eyes shine as if he is gratified.

He continues, 'As they say, we gathered like ants but must be dispersed like birds.'

Suddenly a great hungering to see the huge ruby-bird temple surges inside me. 'I humbly request a few moments to enter Phoenix Hall. I have not seen it before, worshipped there.'

'You have not begun your Purification so you cannot enter the temple, but you may stand at the entrance. As a boy I was often there. In this sunshine you can probably see the Amida Buddha. Jocho was the sculptor. He perfected *kiyoseho*, the joined wood technique. Examine it carefully, if you can.'

I nod my thanks and bow, saying I will return shortly – I know he is anxious for us to begin. I leave my horse and walk along the river to the temple. Unexpectedly he follows me. I wonder why.

IV. Byōdōin

Tokikazu said, 'More than a hundred years ago this palace was built to the west of Byōdōin.'

While he talked on, I examined the shining crimson bird, its roof ready for flight, golden sunlight gilding its wings against the stark azure sky. I wondered if he was trying to impress me.

'There is a stone lantern outside the Phoenix Hall, and the statues inside were commissioned from Jocho,' he added.

Without warning, pictures of bloody and dead bodies flashed in my mind's eye. As if knowing my attention had drifted, Tokikazu touched my shoulder. 'Jocho was raised to the rank of *hogen* because of his exemplary work here.'

He seemed attracted to me. I turned to him as he spoke, but kept my face neutral.

'When Emperor Goreizei visited here, a brocade canopy was laid over this pond so His Majesty might have shade while worshipping. A complete recitation of the Buddhist canon was made here.' He took his hand off my shoulder and pointed to indicate the place.

'See – on the roof there is a demon on its back.' He raised his fingers to the north-west corner of the hall, then led me towards Phoenix Hall's great door. The door handle was iron with copper, shaped like an enormous lotus flower. The raised petals seemed so real that I was almost afraid to touch them, for fear they might come off in my hand.

I saw Akio by the great door. My Akio. He had come! He trotted over to us, dismounted and paused in front of me.

'Who are you, and by whose authority do you approach?' Tokikazu said, hand at his sword.

'Akio. Sent by Commander Taira no Michimori.'

'What is your duty here, Akio?'

'The security and comfort of Lady Kozaishō.'

The wild boars squared off. Why was there animosity between the two men?

'I am Captain Kunda Takiguchi no Tokikazu. Address me as such. *I* am charged with Lady Kozaishō's security.' Tokikazu turned to me. 'Are you comfortable?'

'Yes, Captain.' I stared at Akio. I had never before seen him so overbearing.

Akio gazed down at me. After a time, he said, 'Good. I will stay here.' He mounted his horse and remained at the hall's door.

Tokikazu's eyes spat sparks at him. The two boars did not slash each other's shoulders, but this month was not the rutting season. I drifted towards Hō-ō-dō.

Standing outside the entrance, I beheld the Amida Buddha, golden and radiant, ethereal and vast, on a giant lotus. The Buddha's eyes followed me, His expression placid and serene. His halo and the encircling canopy danced for me in hectic beauty. Around Him were Bodhisattvas, winding, cantering on winds or clouds, heavenly manifestations. His light saturated my entire body, like warm *sake* on the coldest night. His presence passed into my being, and at last I comprehended Tashiko's peace.

> The Buddha! Below
> Protecting radiant dome
> Glowing, beaming forth!
> Bodhisattvas swirling by
> Golden Love soaks through my soul

The next morning, Tokikazu requested I wear my full armour in case we met the enemy again. He directed me to ride abreast of Misuki and Emi in the ox cart. Throughout the trip, he often rode alongside me.

V. Advice

With all that had happened in so short a time, I had not speculated as to my future with Michimori. Perhaps he wanted me for his samurai, which would mean some physical hardships – so many men. Certainly I would endure, and indeed I held happy memories of training with the samurai at Chiba's *shōen*. I waited eagerly to greet Akio again.

Yet I revisited the poem in my mind. Surely I could not have misread Michimori. Surely he had affection for me. Surely one of my dreams would have told me if evil awaited. Surely my body's responses to a man, this man, would not lie.

Misuki and Emi, the only other women, sat in their ox cart, and I near them, either on my horse or in Michimori's palanquin. The trip lasted two days because of the slow ox carts and the awkward palanquin that could not easily be taken up or down the steep slopes.

The samurai obtained for us all we women required, with one exception: they answered no direct questions. That night, after the evening meal, we enjoyed a story and a small fire, which was a luxury not afforded us on our way to Uji. Tokikazu, carefully casual, strolled over to where I sat. Emi and Misuki were already asleep in the tent.

'I have seen you in battle, little samurai,' he chuckled, 'so I know I can trust you not to reveal what I am about to say to you.'

A lump began to form in my throat or my stomach, perhaps both. Tokikazu, somehow becoming aware of my discomfort, bowed a little. 'Please, have no fear. I do not bring impure information.'

He motioned for us to sit in front of the palanquin, away from the

238

others. 'What I have to say concerns your future and is unrelated to your past.' I lifted my eyebrows in surprise. Since it was dark I thought he could not see my face clearly.

'There are two matters I wish you to know. One is that I was privileged to ride and accompany you during this battle. You have had little training,' I saw his eyes waver in the firelight as if to stay my protest, 'and have been occupied with other matters, but you are good for a beginner.' He nodded for emphasis, and I put aside my objections.

'There will be further conflicts, more fighting, and usually we have no knowledge of when or where. I have observed in you a curious mannerism that may not serve you. I wish to share this with you.' He paused and I preserved a neutral face which was as much as I could manage, despite the darkness. This was a mystery to me, but I gestured that he should continue.

'Each time you encountered an enemy, attacked and bested him, you proceeded on to another. May I ask the reason for this?'

'I did not wish to look at what I had done.' Thinking of the gruesome pictures in my mind, I lowered my eyes. 'The reason is, was, I did not want to see men hurt or dying, the ones I killed.'

Tokikazu leaned towards me. 'Thank you for sharing this with me, but it is, I must tell you, an inordinately dangerous thing to do. You must never do it again. It is important to discern what is around you, to check behind you, each side, especially after fighting with another samurai. Please inspect the entire area before you turn your back and ride off. It would be easy for another to wait his turn. You might be taken by surprise.'

I thanked him for his concern and promised to maintain caution in the future. What future had Michimori, the great governor, planned for me?

'There is more,' Tokikazu added. He glanced to see if any of the other samurai were listening. 'You must keep this within your heart, for Echizen Governor Michimori gave me direct orders, yet I feel strongly that I must honour your bravery.'

I lowered and raised my eyes, giving him leave to continue.

Tokikazu whispered, 'Commander Taira no Michimori ordered me, Sadakokai and Mokuhasa to remain with you in battle to protect you. He has never done this before. It is most remarkable. I felt you should know.' He stopped talking and placed his hand over his chest.

'You do me too much courtesy,' I said, understanding the tremendous honour both Michimori and Tokikazu had paid me. My eyes blurred. Wearing my full armour, I could only wipe the tears with my palms, and marvel at the love and loyalty Tokikazu gave Michimori.

'It is my privilege to be your guardian, because of the honour and love I have for the governor. He has been alone, and I believe he is alone no longer.'

I looked up from my tears in disbelief. Tokikazu was correct. The governor had acquired me, Emi and Misuki, taking us with him. It was a sign of great distinction for me to have Tokikazu and his samurai to protect me not only through the battle but all the way to Heian-kyō. I had much to think about throughout the remainder of our journey.

By the time we arrived at our destination, there was yet another river. We passed large hills and valleys and travelled around and through small villages. Their poverty closely resembled that of my own home village. I recognised the dirt floors in smoky huts, barefoot children, bare-bottomed babies. Their mothers' faces were drawn, tired, yet showed their delight in their children.

It was at these times that I wept silently in the dark for my dear lost Tashiko, my family, and what my life would have been with them. Some of my tears indicated my growing warmth for the care Michimori had shown me in purchasing my servants and arranging for Akio and his family to accompany us. Such sensitivity showed potency and power. I gave thanks though my tears to the Goddess of Mercy for such a man, not at all like the fearsome People-Above-the-Clouds my father had portrayed.

Again I ventured into the mysterious future, promising myself to do honour for someone else without knowing what or how. Once more my life was to be transformed.

BOOK 10

I. Homecoming

The samurai had one more *shōen* to collect from before travelling to the Taira Clan city near Heian-Kyō. These fields appeared much like the others but I felt uneasy. They seemed familiar. Perhaps I was mistaken. After all, the huts here were no different from any others. But I recognised that cluster of six over that small hill—

'We are close. Those are the outbuildings of the next *shōen*,' Tokikazu said, leaning over my horse.

My stomach tensed, a symptom I had come to trust. I scanned the horizon. To the left, a hill stirred a sharp memory. A mulberry thicket on its west side. My thoughts thrashed, like a wet cat. The trees had grown in ten years.

That last day. The odour of rich soil and sweat surrounded me now. Had we already passed my father's fields? Could I break away? No! Dishonour.

I had met him here. Heavy ropes tightened around my chest. My stomach seized into a hard fist.

The estate of Chiba no Tashiyori.

Led by Mokuhasa, our foot soldiers ran past us to secure the area. I closed ranks with the captain and Sadakokai, and saw the gate. The same gate. Akio had rescued me there from a fall. Now my horse balked, skittish suddenly.

By the time I had calmed him, we were inside. At the sight of Big House across the path, my thoughts blurred. My tongue was thick and dry. The sickening cruelties and deceit. My training returned. I breathed slowly. I cleared my mind, but my hands were taut. My horse became restless again, shook his head and stamped.

Tokikazu pulled his horse closer. 'Is this not where you were before you went to the Village of Outcasts?'

I forced myself to take a long breath and say, 'Honourable Captain, may I ask you to tell me the reason for your question?' My horse pawed the ground.

His sparse eyebrows rose in surprise. 'It seems that this proprietor, like the last one, has kept taxes that belong to my lord Michimori.'

I willed my thoughts to stay in the moment.

'Does that surprise you?' he asked.

'No.' At last, Chiba was found out, the lying, cheating, betraying thief. I thought my smile went entirely inward, but perhaps it reached my eyes. 'Not at all.' Who was this man? First he had taught me not to turn my back on an opponent. Now he had told me that Chiba, a demon in my life, had been found out.

A foot soldier dashed up to us, presented the captain with a note and sprinted away.

'I have just been told where the proprietor is hiding. I need to . . . speak with him. Would you please come with me?'

From his tone I believed he knew a great deal more than he had said. No! I thought. I did not want to see that creature, that *oni*, ever again. The Buddha taught tolerance. 'Thank you, Captain.' Where had those words come from? The Buddha? Tashiko?

My horse fought me with every step as we rode towards Lesser House. What would I find? Who would I find? Should I kill him – or would I forgive him? What if he had another girl there? I prayed: Please, Lord Buddha, guide me. With a deep sigh, I closed my eyes for a moment. My horse stopped.

I opened my eyes and faced the door. Such a small hut. I could not believe such misery had begun in such a charming place.

'Kozaishō,' Tokikazu interrupted my ramblings. 'The proprietor attempts to conceal himself here. My men are confiscating the goods he owes my lord.' He scrutinised me with clear eyes I could not read. 'Do you want to see the man?'

No, I thought again. I ached to kill him. I wanted to make him suffer.

'Yes, Captain.' Yes! I desired to see him tied down and under the hoofs of every horse on this *shōen*. Broken. Bleeding. Begging for his life. How could I do that with Tokikazu there?

'If that is your wish,' he continued, 'it would honour me to accompany you.'

'No . . . no, thank you, Captain. If I may be permitted, it is my . . . wish to see him alone.' I needed to see him alone. So I could slaughter him. Or forgive him? Again that thought. Where had it come from? How could I perform the Right Action when I did not know what it was? Forgive: the peaceful way. Kill: the right-minded revenge.

Tokikazu yanked his reins and rode off.

I was alone.

Descending from my horse, I wondered what would best honour my Tashiko. How could there be absolution for all the suffering this man had caused? How could I avenge Tashiko's honour – and maintain my family's?

Akio. Master Isamu. All their lessons. I recited the Noble Eight-fold Path. I repeated Right Thinking, Right Speech and Right Action several times. This usually calmed me.

The door of Lesser House. How often I had dreaded a new horror when that door opened. Now I would be the one to open it. This door to Hell. I checked myself: my two swords, helmet, chest, arm and hand plates, and the leg armour I wore over my *hitatare*. My riding shoes. All secure.

With one hand on my *tachi*, the other on the door, I slowly moved the screen, as I had so many times. Would I take blood, so close to my recent experience with the Amida Buddha? I prayed. I kept the scraping noise quiet.

Amida Buddha, allow me to take the Right Action!

I searched the small room, blinking in its yellow light. All appeared the same. He sat on a *futon*. His hair had thinned. His face, although bloated, was more wrinkled. The face of an ancient man. His eyes had shrunk to ink flecks. What was I doing here? How could I kill this old grandfather?

'Who are you?' Grunting like a sick animal, he took time to stand.

I took the readiness stance. 'Do you not know me? Do you not recognise me?'

'Should I?' His voice cracked. His body quivered like plum jelly.

Perhaps Tashiko's Buddha helped me. It would be easy to forgive this pathetic, frightened man. I removed my helmet. 'Yes. You should.' A step closer. 'I am Kozaishō.'

'Kozaishō . . . Kozaishō.' He squeezed his eyes as if to dredge my name from the recesses of his memory. His eyes widened. 'Oh – you.' His body stopped shuddering. He pulled his shoulders back. 'It is you. Of all the girls Goro brought me, I thought you would not be the one to return. With your omens. And training with the boys. You cost me a samurai. A good one at that.' The old man's voice was potent with anger. His words soared strongly; his tone slashed sarcasm. He smiled his old all-teeth-showing smile. A harmless old dog with no teeth.

I saw the arrogance and his pathetic attempt at superiority.

'Why have you come?' He spat.

'To say goodbye . . . and to cleanse you from my life.' With these words I knew why I was there. He no longer had a little girl who believed his lies, promises and stories. His stories.

His marvellous stories. This man had given me the stories that had taken me out of the Village.

'Is that all?'

'Yes.' The word seemed to come from Tashiko's spirit or, perhaps, from the Buddha Himself. 'I forgive you,' I said, in the voice for errant servants. I put on my helmet to leave.

He manoeuvred an arm behind himself, then brought it to the front. He held a dagger in the way he had once flaunted his whips.

'I have no need to fight with you, Proprietor Chiba no Tashiyori,' I said, in formal language. The words came forth with conviction. My hands no longer itched to put a sword into his lying, sadistic flesh. 'I forgive you. There is no need to protect yourself. I seek no revenge. Your *inago* in your next life will suffice for me.'

I turned to go. Sensed it first. Heard it next. Spun into a defensive stance. Sword readied. Do not give me a reason. It would provide sad satisfaction to spill your blood here in Lesser House, you wretched old man.

I waited. My chest drummed.

A faint motion of his blade.

The dagger fell to the floor. I heard him wail as I departed from Lesser House for the last time.

Leading my horse, I wandered through the *shōen*, to the ponds where Tashiko had taken me on my first day. The temple. Here I sprinkled salt around me, said my prayers and entered to light a candle for my beloved. Compared to Phoenix Hall, it was tiny and pitiable, as Chiba was now. I mounted my horse and named him Dragon Cloud, after the omen that had allowed my samurai training. We rode to the practice fields.

Around a circle, our samurai were shooting some animal, which howled, wailed and moaned. Drag marks in the grass attested to a huge dog or boar. I followed the ropes, which kept it within the circle of laughing warriors. Notching an arrow, I rode close. They parted for me, and I saw him. Chiba.

My childhood's demon transformed into a wretched animal, claiming my pity. I had to bring a quick death to the creature's suffering. Without another thought, I shot him through the chest.

When all those eyes turned to me, I realised what I had done. I lied, 'Kannon-sama must have possessed me. Please forgive me. I am sorry to have spoiled your sport.'

Tokikazu rode up and dismissed them. 'Yes,' he announced, to the soldiers. 'I do believe the Goddess of Mercy influenced you, Lady Kozaishō.'

I was so startled by his approval that I said nothing to him for the rest of the day, except the minimum required for politeness.

I had much to think about.

What manner of man was Tokikazu?

II. Portable Shrine

We travelled on the road north of Byōdōin, avoiding the city of Uji, and stopped. Tokikazu acted like the governor, sending spies through the countryside and waiting until they returned. While we waited by Ogura pond, I walked to the water, washed my face, rinsed my mouth and prayed. I called to the son of our Storm God, the Great Evil-doer, to appease him and ensure safety for the remainder of our travel to Heian-kyō.

That night, when we established shelter for the evening, Misuki, Emi and I were excited to be near the capital. We dressed in our costumes, sang and danced. Mokuhasa, the short, broad samurai with much hair on his body and one thick eyebrow on his face, played the *biwa*. Its sweet sounds filled the darkness, like a soothing breeze. His music was as gentle as his sword was savage. Joining him, I sang.

A memory of the marriage ceremony of my sister Second Daughter came to my mind. All my sisters and I were dressed in fine clothes and new straw shoes my father had made. Second Daughter and Fourth Daughter had taught me songs and dances, and I performed with my sisters. Father and Mother smiled more than I had thought was possible. Fourth Daughter was so content that she did not shout or lose her temper all day. I beamed at my memory and continued to dance.

In my mind I saw bodies falling, blood spouting, swords, arrows and the gaping mouths of men struggling to breathe, their open dead eyes.

The next morning, Tokikazu taught me a new stroke for my sword, Cutting the Sleeve, across the wrist.

The following day, as we rested near the foot of a modest hill, along the

Kamo river south-east of the city, we could see the capital: Heian-kyō. The rounded hills surrounding the city looked as if the Gods had folded it in their hands. Smoke from many small fires drifted above the tops of the trees. Beneath it, I saw buildings, houses so endless they were like flecks of dirt in a cave. Multi-coloured tiled and thatched roofs, the tiled roofs of temples and the red pillars of shrines showed through the smoke, like painted rocks exposed in a fog. I saw activity, too distant to be seen – ox-drawn carriages and carts from farms.

Sadakokai pointed out where each of the major shrines and temples stood. All of the samurai looked to the east, to Rokuhara, where Chancellor Kiyomori had established his city, one big house after another, each surrounded by gardens and numerous huts for its multitude of servants. This was where I was going. I did not journey through Heian-kyō.

Emi shrieked.

I turned to her. From a hill I saw *sōhei* carrying a portable shrine swathed in a dark grey cloud from its incense and candles. It was draped with deep purple brocade. When they heard Emi, the twenty or so monks moved back up the hill, surrounding the God within in its shrine. Thoughout my travels, religious gates, *tori-i*, had always marked a shrine, so this one was an oddity. Gauze-swathed men, faces hidden so they were indistinguishable from each other, guarded it, and each bore a heavy wooden staff. The *sōhei* assumed fighting positions. Taira foot soldiers encircled us. Tokikazu stood in front, closest to the *sōhei*. Mokuhasa and Sadakokai were behind, to the left and right of him. I stood directly behind Tokikazu and made the fighting square.

We stood far enough away from each other so that our blades would not touch. I unsheathed my sword, and saw that their weapons were already out and in position. Tokikazu's sinewy body was taut, like an over-tightened string on a *koto*. Mokuhasa was ahead to my left. His thick body dwarfed his sword. Sadakokai hummed sutras.

With shrill cries, the monks attacked, brandishing their staffs, which made sucking noises in the thick air. Their long white robes did not seem to move as they rushed at us. Suddenly in my mind, I stood on the practice field, but now with a real opponent swaddled in white gauze over black armour, face almost hidden. A lapse could mean death or dishonour.

Our samurai engaged the monks. One *sōhei* was much taller, which I knew could be an advantage. I kept my eyes focused on his, surrounded by the white gauze. They had black all around them so the whites gleamed like rats' eyes in stored grain. I gripped my sword tighter. He was strong, perhaps over-confident in dealing with a woman, and young but, from his strikes, seasoned. I was not. I concentrated on this monk and shut out the strikes and grunts coming from around me. I had to trust my fellows.

His eyes flickered; he sliced at me. I deflected and countered with my sword edge, rolled backwards. I had power from his stroke. I righted myself and thrust up. I heard him lose his breath. My sword pierced under his armour. Another stroke. I sliced from neck to belly. He fell backwards.

Holding my sword, I watched him before I turned away. His hand shook, holding something. I charged over and sliced it off, using Cutting the Sleeve, as Mokuhasa had taught me. The monk's hand concealed a *shuriken*, similar to other spiked stars I had seen. I watched again, but he was still. Tokikazu's advice had saved my life. If I had walked away, that would have been my death.

Scanning the scene, I saw the rest of the monks taking the shrine and running away, up the hill. Tokikazu, Mokuhasa and Sadakokai were unharmed. After scrutinising the area, we bowed as if we had finished a training session on the practice field.

I revisited the body of the monk I had killed, and wrested the *shuriken* from between his fingers. It was different from the ones I had used in practice: more points. I put it with my other weapons as a keepsake. Then we cleaned our swords and purified ourselves, scattered salt, rinsed our mouths and washed our hands.

'Thank you for your advice at Uji.' I bowed to Tokikazu.

'It was my duty. I swore to Governor Michimori to protect you from harm and deliver you to his home.'

Overwhelmed, I lowered my head. 'I do not have words,' I said, holding my emotions low in my throat.

Tokikazu smiled, his small eyebrows raised in delight. 'Commander Taira no Michimori will be pleased when I tell him of your courage with so large an opponent.'

'Please, Tokikazu,' I implored, 'do not allow knowledge of this incident to reach my lord's ears.'

III. A Secret

Tokikazu's eyebrows lowered to his shining eyes. 'Why do you not want Governor Michimori to know of your bold deeds?'

'Please tell him of the monks. The information may be vital.' I bowed again. 'We are at war, but I am unsure who the enemies are. My life has been simple. Now it is complicated. I do not wish the governor to know of this scuffle because he has sufficient problems. Also, I took the loyalty pledge, so I am honour-bound. My duty is to make his life pleasurable.' I could not tell Tokikazu that, while grateful to the governor, this was the first time, without assistance, I had executed a real fight all on my own. Such a potent experience: all my muscles and every limb tingled with exhilaration.

'And yet I must inform him.'

'Tell him about the *sōhei*, but do not add to his burdens with these . . . trifling details.' I looked past Tokikazu's high forehead. I extended my hand towards the field in which we stood. 'Compared to the battle at Uji, this was but a single flower in a meadow, was it not?'

Tokikazu growled in agreement, although scepticism and something else wrinkled his eyes and mouth.

'Perhaps if I tell you a story which demonstrates that if one focuses on essential details one can vanquish foes.'

'Only if you allow the others to hear it as well.'

I nodded and waited while he signalled to the others, who gathered as they finished cleaning their weapons and garments. When all was ready, I began 'The Monkey and the Baby'.

251

'A mother placed her baby near a tree while she worked in the field. Suddenly, a monkey picked it up and carried it high into the tree. The frantic mother yelled in terror and prayed to the Buddha. An eagle flew down to attack. Still in the tree, the monkey made a bow out of the swaying branches and shot the eagle. It fell dead to the ground. Seeing the violence, the mother continued to pray loudly to the Buddha. She was deeply afraid the monkey would harm her child, but the monkey delivered its precious armful to the frantic mother. The mother had looked only at the monkey's actions, not its motives.

'The mother's suffering could have been avoided. Attention to vital details is as important as deeds.' I studied the warriors' expressions to see what impact the story had made.

'Yes,' Tokikazu admitted. 'I direct all of us.' He looked at each samurai, 'Speak only of the *sōhei* as if we had seen them but not fought with them.' After the samurai separated from us, he moved closer to me. 'Well done. I understand why Commander Michimori entrusted us with your care. You are a worthy companion.'

'It is only my role. Who are these *sōhei*?'

'Warrior monks who come from Mount Hiei.' He pointed to the mountains north-east of the city. His voice dropped to a low growl. 'They come to plunder and ravage the capital.'

'I see.' His distress was clear.

'By decree, coins are forbidden in the capital. The monks come to acquire coinage. These *sōhei* have done this before, bringing their portable shrine to the city where no one dares to remove it.'

'Because otherwise the shrine's God will inflict vengeance?'

'So the shrine stays in the streets until the emperor pays their ransom.' His eyes showed the contempt of a hawk. 'Then they come back, take the shrine and their ransom and leave – until the next time.'

'Perhaps it is also payment for Chancellor Kiyomori's arrow long ago.' Sadakokai said.

I asked for the story.

Sadakokai narrated, stuttering less as he spoke:

'L-l-long ago, when Ch-Ch-Chancellor Kiyomori was a young man, he and his companions attended the G-G-Gion Festival in the city at G-G-Gion Sh-Sh-Shrine. One of his comrades had a little clash with one of the Gion priests.'

'Not s-s-such a s-s-small one,' he snarled.

'Chancellor Kiyomori felt his name had been d-d-dishonoured. He took his men, rode out and attacked the priests of Gion. Now, they carried a portable shrine at the time, not like the one we saw but a bigger one, with a bell in f-f-f-front. The capital always has the f-f-finest of everything.'

Here he spread his arms and hands wide.

'Chancellor Kiyomori shot an arrow straight into the bell, which rang loudly. The Enryakuji *sōhei*.' He stared at my confused expression. 'That is the name of the temple on Mount Hiei. The Enryakuji *sōhei* considered this an insult. Seven thousand of them rushed into the capital demanding justice. Because of his high rank, Chancellor Kiyomori's punishment was a small fine.'

'The monks seem always to be going into the city with more demands. I wonder what it is this time,' Mokuhasa commented.
'The city is no longer the Peace and Tranquillity Capital,' Tokikazu whispered in my ear, as if not to invoke some angry ghost.
The journey to my new home continued in uncomfortable silence.

IV. Temporary Home

We stopped at the gate of a vast village of estates and mansions, its walls three times as high as those that surrounded Chiba's *shōen*. The many guards scrutinised everything from our horses to our helmets. After we had passed through the gate, Sadakokai spread an arm wide. 'There are more than f-f-five thousand f-f-families and homes here.'

Most of the houses looked more magnificent than Big House at Chiba's – imposing. Less land, surrounded them, but each had more complicated buildings: the roofs over the *watadono* were substantial and ornate with carvings and statuary similar to those at Byōdōin. Hordes of servants scurried from the huts surrounding each mansion, back and forth, and herds of hooded priests pushed along the roads. I was reminded of Uji, and wondered which one could be Goro. I shivered, recalling his eyes.

Mokuhasa rode close to me. 'We live differently here. When we Taira in Rokuhara marry, the wife lives with the husband's family.'

'Where does a man's other wives live?'

Mokuhasa chuckled.

Sadakokai had pulled up on the other side of me. 'Oh, w-we just b-b-build another wing on to the house. For those with many w-wives, it can be – interesting, but that is why there is extra l-l-land with every estate.' He laughed. 'P-p-probably why I have n-no w-w-wives.'

'Nor does Michimori, but he still has a large estate.' Mokuhasa slapped his thigh and snorted.

'T-T-Tokikazu has enough w-w-wings on his house, I am surprised it does not f-f-fly!' Sadakokai laughed even more.

Mokuhasa chuckled. 'At Tokikazu's rate of additions, he may have to find yet another house outside Rokuhara.'

I did not find this amusing, but smiled, regardless. I pondered how many wives Tokikazu might have and what shape his home could take.

Tokikazu made a gestural bow. 'Lady Kozaishō, we have arrived at Taira quarters, Rokuhara. My lady, inside Main Gate you will see the home of the governer's father. We call it "Gateside", because it sits directly by Main Gate. The governor wishes me to escort you and your servants to your quarters.'

I studied the magnificent structure, the mansion of Michimori's father. I returned to my horse next to the ox cart where Misuki and Emi sat. Before I mounted to enter Main Gate, I bowed to Tokikazu. 'You greatly honour me with the governor's consideration.' I hoped to see more of Tokikazu, an odd but interesting man.

I had only a little understanding of Governor Michimori, but I thought he had shown a true face to me. He might wish to remove this vulnerability, me, from his sight. Yet there was the poem he had sent me. Misuki and I had read it. Could I believe what Tokikazu had told me? 'Commander Michimori ordered me and others to protect you in battle. He has never done this before.' I recalled that Tokikazu placed his open hand over his chest as he said this. I could hardly think of that possibility. Perhaps I was for the Echizen governor's samurai, or some courtiers, or perhaps to teach songs and dances to his wives and concubines. What if he wanted me for himself?

I had no answers to these questions, only excitement and fear. I was excited because this situation would be different from the old one. I was afraid: political leaders exerted their power over life and death as often as they feigned smiles.

'You may gather your belongings,' Tokikazu said, his face brightening. I longed to ask permission to arrange them so that I could check on my secret papers, but I knew that would bring suspicion.

'Thank you, honourable Captain Tokikazu.' Surreptitiously, I scrutin-ised my bundles, my multi-coloured *furoshiki*. Secret paper scraps (all logs of my customers, their habits and businesses) were sewn into the middle parts of my kimonos, hidden inside.

Tokikazu said, 'I will assign several men to carry them to your residence.'

My head felt like the inside of a temple bell. My residence! My entire wardrobe, makeup, livelihood and secrets, lay in front of the palanquin, like silk-wrapped gifts for giants. The caravan of our *furoshiki* marched by: red with peacocks, grey, blue, brown ships fighting dark blue waves, blue and green birds squawking on brocade, gold and brown tigers, and one small black dog playing among green bushes.

Misuki, Emi and I stood in front of Tokikazu. I informed him we were ready to go to our new quarters. At his request, we followed him, others carrying our bundles in a procession. I was careful not to smile, but the thought of the serious foot soldiers officially carrying our rainbow *furoshiki* was amusing.

To maintain my composure, I drank in each tiny detail of our new surroundings. Abruptly I saw my life as a tiny island – so remote – an implicit imprisonment. I noticed everything: samurai guarding the passageways, bemused expressions in their eyes, their shoes, the soldiers' uniforms with the governor's crest – the closed-wing butterfly. I had seen it on his sword earlier.

We bowed to the samurai in front and behind. Misuki, I know, imitated my lead and Emi followed her, as usual. We ambled through long corridors hung with banners and lined with identically dressed samurai.

The corridors had screens and doors along them. At first the screens were plain, translucent or opaque. As we walked, the frames of the doors were made of more decorative woods. Carved birds, trees and animals, such as cats, embellished them. While I kept watch on one side, I motioned with my eyes to Misuki to concentrate on the other. We halted at one door.

Its frame was thickly carved with gods, demons and leaves. Tokikazu bowed, his eyes slightly downwards.

'If you please, my honourable lord Taira no Michimori has ordered your Purification: Exorcism, Cleansing and Abstention. In several days I may take you to your permanent quarters, such as other wives and concubines have.' I stared at him with growing realisation, then adopted my usual neutral expression. I was most eager to establish myself in my new home. Wives! Concubines! I was not for the samurai, after all. Inwardly, I smiled to myself.

256

'I regret this, but I have my orders from Governor Taira no Michimori.' Tokikazu's eyes appeared curiously sad. 'I have been told the priest is old-fashioned. You are to undergo Purification in this place.' He meant Misuki and me. Since Emi had worked only as an assistant, there was no need for her to be Purified. Although Misuki and I were the focus of attention, it was refreshing to revisit the familiar customs. I bowed again and shared a short poem with him as an expression of gratitude:

> After snows and winds
> Bush warblers in plum blossoms
> Above icy waters
> The kind songs of a friend
> Changing the cold into spring

Tokikazu nodded, and his eyes blazed. Next he instructed the samurai to carry our belongings into a set of rooms. 'Forgive the small size. Your permanent home will be much larger.'

'Thank you, honourable Captain Tokikazu. Might I ask where Akio and his family are?'

His entire face was suddenly immobilised. 'He and his family are well provided for.'

His words sounded rigid as stone. What had he against Akio? More importantly, what did Akio hold against Tokikazu?

I turned my attention to the plain wooden floor, which shone, and the walls, which bore no tapestries or scrolls. Instead, the Gods' and the Buddha's names, with other writing, adorned them in bright blue, pine green and lustrous black. A simple *futon* hunched in a corner. A table rested next to the fireplace, and a stack of fuel was tied in a heavy cloth *furoshiki*. Books lay on the table, piquing my curiosity. The writing, I recognised, included parts of the Lotus Sutra.

A single opaque three-part folding screen stood beside the opening for other rooms. Again, the names of gods were written, but only in black. These plain rooms had the same names written on the walls and smaller tables. Smaller *futon*s leaned into the furthest corners. I seemed to have exchanged one hut for another.

No fire was needed because of the heat and closeness of the rooms. I bowed, and Tokikazu's eyes flickered over me appreciatively. His men stayed with us briefly, then returned to their stations. A novice priest, freshly shorn head, blackened teeth, and a little goatee below his lower lip, presented himself to inform us we had been assigned to the Chief Priest. In the next hour he would conduct our Exorcism and Cleansing.

Our Abstention, the third part of Purification, was to take place in these rooms. Tokikazu whispered that he had posted guards on our permanent rooms and our belongings so that no harm could come to them. His generosity touched me again – I had realised the danger to us if someone read our papers. With fear nearly leaking out of my eyes, I bowed as low as I dared without touching the floor. Tokikazu left us, and I heard him ordering food for us.

Preparing to go to the Chief Priest, we ate sparingly, and dressed modestly: no hair or shoe ornaments, only three over-kimonos and none bright, all with small patterns, such as trees, rivers, clouds and small animals, especially birds. Two more priests arrived, one missing part of his right earlobe, the other with extraordinarily large front teeth. They escorted us down a corridor to the ceremony and stood at either side of the opening to the altar room.

Before we went inside, I smiled reassuringly at Misuki because her hands were quivering. Perhaps she did not have, as I had, such marvellous memories of shrines. I had cleaned and guarded the Family Deity with my mother. Everyone had swept the Abode of Deity and the Stone Enclosure. My mother had hummed as we worked, and my heart had filled with the sound of her songs. Parading around the Dwelling House, we carried and tied the Demarcation Rope to keep evil away from us. The joy came back as I recalled how well we had worked together, Mother smiling and hugging me. Mother had named the water and rice gods and made me name them to her. It was the game my elder siblings had played on the long journey from the shrine to our home. At this memory I smiled inwardly and brushed Misuki's sleeve. The doors of the altar room screeched as they opened.

V. Misuki's Exorcism

The heavy doors opened to reveal the altar room, lit with flickering candles. In my sleeve I rubbed the coin Tokikazu had given to Misuki and me to pay the priest to cleanse us of our Women-for-Play and warrior states. Smoke from incense and candles filled the air. As I waited, it stung my eyes. In the dim light, the six-part folding screens' carvings reshaped to tangled shadows. My fingers identified the vines and faces of gods or demons.

I saw no *nusa*, the Purification wand with white cloth strips. Beautiful music and singing evoked a childhood memory of the Festival of the First Fruits. That day had been special. My mother, my sisters and I had cleaned the shrine. My mother and two older sisters, Second and Fourth Daughters, invoked the Divine Father and Divine Mother as we entered. We children had the luxury of a sleep at midday because the ceremonies began in the middle of the night.

We offered our rice, vegetables, fish, and placed them before the Chief Priest. Silence, everything dark. No one told me the names of the Gods or even let me ask questions. I could only hear the dancers. With no lights, I could barely see them, their steps, their gestures. My parents had carried their *nusa*, flapping, in the dark.

Misuki and I knelt on deep red cushions in front of the altar, and I glimpsed the back of the priest, who was dressed in red, gold and black. He lifted the cowl from his head, and I saw that his hair was wrapped in a stiff knot and held high with sticks sharpened at the ends. He strutted in an odd but familiar way. He dropped behind the altar and returned, face forward. When my eyes grew accustomed to the darkness, I recognised him.

Goro.

He carried an elongated package, wrapped in paper with gods' names written on it in the same colours as his robes. A singer and *biwa* player hid behind screens with curved black edging and sculpted beasts of prey. Since I could not see the singer or musician, I presumed they could not see me. Other than them, there were only the three of us.

Goro stepped from behind the altar, unwrapping a massive brush with thick, stiff boars' bristles (almost three forearms long). He circled it around his head as he invoked the Gods in a low chant. He intoned in a rigid monotone, contrasting with the melodic notes and mellifluous voice that had come from behind the screen.

I glanced at Misuki. Should we leave, scream or cry out for help? Had my new master fed me to this monster? Yet Tokikazu had been so sure that this was what Michimori wanted for me. Could Goro have deceived Michimori? Or perhaps my honourable lord did not know it was Goro. Perhaps he had decided on a different priest, but Goro had sought me out.

I heard Goro had obtained a Black Hat. He was cunning and influential.

I could run away. But where would I go? I could fight Goro – I had before when I was smaller and less proficient. But there could be no honour in either course of action.

I had pledged loyalty. Tokikazu had been confident that this ceremony was what Michimori wanted for me. He had shown me the order with Michimori's seal. If that was what my new lord wished, I knew where my duty, my honour, lay: in this room, without my weapons, without a struggle, I would submit. I prepared myself as if I were going to Hitomi's Hell Hut. But afterwards, I promised, I would find Three Eyes, named after an ogre in a story, and take revenge for Tashiko and perhaps for me.

When I think of this later, I feel it all again. My fingers tremble.

Goro turns to Misuki first, dishonouring me by performing Exorcism on my servant first. He recites her crimes of impurity. He gestures, as if to brush the offences away from her, over her face, arms, torso and legs.

'The coin.'

Misuki produces hers from her kimono.

He points silently, and she places it in a little bowl in front of the altar. She bows and he dismisses her with a sign. As she leaves, Misuki glances at me, fear creeping into her eyes, like a flooding river.

I am alone with him.

Goro moves to me slowly with the unnatural smile I recognise from my time with Chiba and Hitomi.

Trapped by my family's honour and my oath to Michimori, I breathe in and out slowly so that I do not appear panicked. My heart beats faster than the music. I bow, glancing furtively for instruments of torture or death. I fear my life will end as had my beloved Tashiko's.

He approaches. Passivity is safer, but I want to scream, to call for my serving girls, as I did at Hitomi's. If I run out, no one will understand. My unclean, unknown story against his priestly one. I am ensnared like a rabbit.

Silently I call to my childhood gods as I remember the injuries I received from other such men. He approaches me, chanting praises. His voice is strong and loud. His eyes glint with gold from the candlelight.

'May the Goddess Seori-tsu-hime, who lives in the white waters of swift-flowing rivers purify you and grant you swift-flowing forgiveness.'

He sings, quite loudly. His knuckles punch the rhythm on my shoulders and back and crush my skin.

'May the Goddess Seori-tsu-hime, who lives in the white waters of swift-flowing rivers, send you white-water Cleansing with pure liquid forgiveness.'

I do not flinch – that always encourages them.

He strikes my shoulders as he would a drum. His voice is louder, bolder, drowning the battering. 'May the Goddess Haya-akitsu-hime, residing where ocean tides meet the sea paths, show forgiveness.'

With both hands he clenches the front of my kimonos and wrenches them off my shoulders . . .

'May the Goddess Haya-akitsu-hime have pity on you in your filth.'

. . . and down to my waist, exposing me to the smoky air. Even with the incense and candles, my moist skin is chilled.

'May the Goddess Haya-akitsu-hime remove your impurities and wickedness.'

I hold my breath. In the cold my shoulder twitches, a slight shudder, which I know will enrage him.

261

It does.

His voice thunders and hisses. The blows come faster, more deliberately, aimed . . .

Terror blazes in my chest. I glance up. His face is that of a demon guarding Hell, but with a smile.

'May the Goddess Haya-akitsu-hime have pity on your wretched life.'

Now with each syllable his brush strikes my shoulders, my neck . . .

'May the Goddess Haya-akitsu-hime take back your impurities!'

. . . my back and my breasts . . .

'May the Goddess Haya-akitsu-hime hear your pleas for forgiveness . . .'

Each word is accentuated with the sound of bristles thrust heavily through the air . . . and the crack when it collides . . .

'. . . and grant you cool cleansing of all impurities.'

The warm blood cools on my skin . . . I can no longer control the shaking . . .

'May the God Ibukido Nushi, Master of the Surging Place, send your impurities to the nether world.'

He pushes on my chest with the brush's wooden handle and forces me on to my back.

'May the God Ibukido Nushi, Ruler of the Spouting-out Point, send your foulness to the furthest bottom area.'

I fall backwards, my legs splayed open over the deep red cushions . . .

'May the God Ibukido Nushi, Overlord of the Spurting Site, dispatch your filth to the lowest territory.'

He wrests aside my skirts . . .

'May the Goddess Hayasasura-hime, who dwells in the nether world, dissolve your impurities.'

. . . and the wooden handle stabs with each syllable . . . His other hand clenches himself, then pushes on my naked stomach, keeping me down. I submit, I do not move . . .

'May the Goddess Hayasasura-hime, who lives in the furthest bottom area, decompose your foulness.'

With sharp wet sounds his brush slashes my skin . . .

'May the Goddess Hayasasura-hime, who rules lowest territory, destroy your filth.'

. . . and pierces me below . . .

'May the Goddess Hayasasura-hime, who is lord in the lower sector, dissolve your impurities.'

The brush stabs with each phrase, slashing, tearing . . .

'May the Goddess Hayasasura-hime, who endures in the bottom land, grant you forgiveness.'

I think he will stop. No. He intones my list of impure crimes, and the bristles pierce my skin and Golden Gate.

Drops of blood fly and glint against the lights. Do not scream. I hold the Goddess of Mercy in my mind . . .

He stops. Breathes hard. 'The coin. My payment.' He takes it slowly from me, caressing my palm. 'The priests taught me in the monastery. I grew to enjoy, relish, yearn for this. You crave it as well, I can see.'

I stifle the vomit surging sour and hot in my mouth.

'I insist on you, my own Creator Goddess, my own Izanami. Next time I will be Izanagi, and we will make the world.' He strokes his genitals, motions for me to dress and turns away, with more Purification chants.

With his back to me, my heart liquefies to molten metal, where my vengeance will be forged at my leisure.

BOOK 11

I. Abstention

Misuki waited outside the altar room and bowed, acknowledging me. Shooting a wide-eyed belligerent glare to the guard, the one with the missing earlobe, her eyes softened when she looked at me. She took a cloth to wipe the blood from my face and neck. Cleansing baths were next.

Abstention required silence. On the way I memorised each guard's face. They had all shared in this conspiracy: they were strangers. Where were the samurai who had guarded me in battle and to Rokuhara? Perhaps Michimori had not ordered this torment. Yet I had seen the order, myself, surrendering me to such a man as Goro. The samurai, especially Tokikazu, knew I was to undergo Purification. And I was, after all, the property of the Echizen governor.

I faltered in the corridor because of the stinging gashes between my legs. The baths seem to move further and further away until my legs felt as if I had shuffled four *chō*.

Entering the room for Cleansing, I saw yet another priest. He wore Goro's threatening smile, the tips of his ugly white teeth gleaming and his clouded left eye reflecting the candles and the water. This priest scattered salt at the bath's corners. Perhaps not like Goro, I thought, and fear began to release its death grip on my chest.

I breathed more easily. I had only to be cleansed by immersion in water. I turned to Misuki, whose eyes had widened with dread. The priest was pouring heaped bowls of salt into the tiny bath. In the Village a pinch of salt at a bath's corners had sufficed. There were no friendly faces. I could not avoid stepping into this new scourge.

'All is ready for you.' The priest motioned to me, grinning with his thick lips.

I did not speak. I did not make eye contact with this new *oni*. I straightened, memorising his features.

The gashes dripped blood down my legs, and the bruises already showed. Seeing this, Misuki went into the water first, holding out her hand. I clutched it as if it were my *tachi*, but tighter.

She moved her lips, but made no sound. I recognised the spell for protection from the Lotus Sutra: '*Iti me, iti me, iti me, iti me, iti me; ni me, ni me, ni me, ni me, ni me; ruhe, ruhe, ruhe, ruhe, ruhe; stuhe, stuhe, stuhe, stuhe, stuhe svaha.*'

I did not make a sound in Misuki's steadfast presence. This torment thwarted Goro's purpose, although it intensified my agony. The saltwater closed my wounds and helped me heal without scars.

Several priests led us back to our temporary quarters. During those long, silent days, we wore white silk and plain straw shoes, and ate only rice gruel. I saw only the faces of those who had persecuted me, especially that of Daigoro no Goro, or Three Eyes, named for the *oni* in one of my stories: I remembered each priest – blackened teeth and little goatee, right earlobe missing, large front teeth, thick lips and clouded eye, and the lost three teeth. Those faces bred my plan for reprisal. It burned brightly, like dry leaves for kindling, unlike my vengeance for Tashiko, which had simmered like a pot on a dying fire.

I needed to take my revenge as thoroughly as I had been tortured. I did not think my heart could heal until I saw the head of Three Eyes on a stake. My desire for his death surprised me. I heard Tashiko's voice and remembered her gentleness, yet my craving for revenge was that of a raging boar.

> Tashiko's agony!
> All my stories for nothing
> Cruelty again
> An armoured fist within my heart
> Must strike this demon, and soon!

During my days of Abstention, fan-shaped papers folded into little books distracted my thoughts from vengeance. On every page, drawings danced below the text, which was highlighted with gold and silver.

After three days an unknown priest stood at my door to inform me my Abstention was complete. Tokikazu, Sadakokai and Mokuhasa accompanied me through the corridors to my new home. The new, heavy kimonos pressed against my wounds yet even Tokikazu, handsome and dressed in beautiful clothes, did not seem to notice any difference in my gait. Three Eyes, as sly as he was cruel, had not injured my face, neck or hands.

I was relieved to see the honourable faces of the samurai, and they had brought Emi with them. She cried when she saw me, so great had been her loneliness. I held her and wept too.

We arrived at a nearby mansion. Tokikazu announced, 'This is an entrance for wives and concubines.' Sadakokai tapped the little bronze bell attached to a carved demon. The sound trickled through the dark corridor. I heard footsteps.

My heart shuddered. More torture?

In the formal way, Tokikazu stated, 'You are to be cared for by the women who will come. The honourable Aged-One-Who-Waits-On-Women will answer all your needs. It has been an honour, my lady Kozaishō.'

They all bowed to me, to Misuki and even to Emi. I was being treated as a wife or concubine. Could I believe Michimori's poem? Anxiety tightened my throat. It was not my place to say anything but to thank Tokikazu and bow, which I did. He and the others moved back to the end of the corridor. Then we waited until the door opened.

II. Obāsan

An old woman stood at the door, looking like the perfect grandmother. She had the whitest hair and, with her flying white eyebrows and creased skin, her face glowed golden. Her warm black eyes moved quickly in welcome, for which I was grateful. We greeted each other properly. She said, in a cracking but strong voice, that the honour was hers and pointed her claw hand towards my rooms. I followed her to another new and unknown destiny and thought of a poem from the Lotus Sutra:

> Between the oceans
> Of the living and the dead
> I profoundly wish
> For the Heavenly Way World
> Unharmed by these churning seas

The robes of the honourable Aged-One-Who-Waits-On-Women were shades of blue within the same fabric, like the colours of the sea, an unfamiliar yet elaborate brocade. Her tiny body appeared as if it would snap like a dry branch in midwinter. She walked at such a pace that I had difficulty keeping up, with my injuries. I had barely a moment to examine the rich woods framing each of the *shōji*.

Even with her speed, the old woman's braid did not swing. When she stopped, she said, 'These are your rooms, mistress. The Lady-in-Charge-of-Rooms and two serving girls are coming. A bath is being prepared now, and then there will be food.'

I nodded as she paused for breath.

'If there is anything else you require, you need only ask the Lady-in-Charge-of-Rooms.' She did not smile with her lips but with her eyes.

Lowering mine in modesty, I nodded, bending my head.

'Governor Michimori is thoughtful,' she said. She pointed to an opened box on the table that contained extra strings for my instruments. 'Especially for a man with no wives.'

I bent down, for she was much shorter than I, and kissed her wrinkled cheek, calling her Obāsan, 'grandmother'. Her cheeks changed colour at the informal word. As our eyes met, we giggled. Fast friends from that moment, we helped each other through the next months.

Before Obāsan returned, I was briefly alone with Misuki and Emi. Misuki and I needed a code, so I declared, 'From this time until such a person as Diagoro no Goro will no longer exist, he is to be called "Three Eyes".'

'Why, Lady Kozaishō?' Emi tugged at my sleeve as she had when she asked about the dances at Chiba's.

'He is Three Eyes because he is named after the *oni* in a story. Remember, Three Eyes marries a daughter while he is in human form. He takes her to a house, which has a hundred and one rooms. When she looks into the one forbidden room, she realises he is an *oni* who wants to eat her.'

'While escaping she meets the prince!' Emi recalled.

'Yes,' Misuki said, 'and the prince sets a trap.'

Emi squealed. 'I remember! A lion and a tiger eat the *oni*!'

I promised myself that some day I would see Three Eyes' head on a stake. Later, since Misuki was the only one who knew what had happened, I demanded that she tell no one.

'My lady, I do not understand why such evil, such injustice, is rewarded with our silence. Our new lord would certainly punish Three Eyes,' Misuki argued.

'No.' I responded, sighing. 'We must not tell him for many reasons. Three Eyes may be using me as a pawn to injure our lord. We must not take risks in a game when we do not know who are the opponents. Also, I do not wish to begin my service to Governor Michimori by complaining. See? My injuries are already healing. If such violence is done without cause, the evil-doer, in time, will be punished.'

'Like the story of the Handless Maiden,' Misuki said.

'Yes. The parent who cut off her hands was punished with a horrible death. If this priest is what Tokikazu calls the People-Above-the-Clouds, I wish we were under the earth. Yet I believe that justice will be done.'

III. New Home

Since it was summer, the large brazier in the centre of each new room was empty. The first room included an alcove, *tokonoma*, in which a painting of men and women in elaborate clothes hung. A writing table offered cushions partly hidden by its legs, which were carved with leaves. On this table, next to the *biwa* and *koto* strings, sat a lacquered writing box with inlaid mother-of-pearl trees – so beautiful. It was a shame my writing was poor.

Next to a *go* board there were two lidded containers for the pieces. Each lid displayed the Taira butterfly in a circle. The board and its feet shone, while its gourd-like legs were thick and round, with carved swirls.

My quarters extended to three more rooms, each sumptuous, but not quite as elegant as the first. A bathing room directly adjoined the largest room. On the outside of the building was a veranda, a *watadono* with long eaves. Further a *hisoshi* – a type of curtain – separated each room along this watadono. Privacy had, at least, its appearance. The eaves' shadows cooled our quarters during the midday heat. Beyond the veranda lay a serene garden and a pond, an invitation to a private paradise.

Why was I here, like a respected woman of rank? I dared not think this was true, for fear it would burst like a bubble in boiling soup. The men I had known had often defaulted on their promises, no matter how sincerely they had been made.

At our first meeting Michimori had shown a sense of humour. After our time together, he had carefully plucked every piece of straw from my hair, then chuckled. 'I had to pay handsomely to play with you in a make-believe barn . . . with real straw.'

I had thought it funny at the time and giggled. However, nothing gave me an indication he was capable of playing such a cruel hoax. To place me, a Woman-for-Play, with the women of his household, was out of character with the Michimori I had met.

I thought of another fleeting dream I had had – but this was not a dream! – that someone like Michimori, with power and money, favoured me, cared for me, perhaps as a concubine. It had brought a small inward smile, and sadness at its absurdity.

Three women came into the room and interrupted my reverie. The eldest was the tallest, handsomely plump, and her short hair glistened. She must be the Woman-in-Charge-of-Rooms, as Obāsan had mentioned. The two behind her were shorter, their *kosodes* plain, short-sleeved and ordinary, like their faces. One was also slightly plump, but the other was extremely thin, with a bad complexion. Their names were Number One Serving Girl and Number Two Serving Girl. Number One's eyes smiled, and Number Two merely bowed, her face indecipherable.

I made a little bow to the Woman-in-Charge-of-Rooms, who bowed deeply and asked permission to speak. 'We are here to serve you. These two are to stay in your rooms. What do you wish? Honourable lady, please tell us what you would like to eat, and we will arrange it for you.'

I looked at Misuki and Emi. We had never been offered a choice of food. The memory of childhood hunger passed over, like a storm's first stirring in a stifling Hour of the Monkey. I took a deep breath to hold on to the difference between then and now: eating boiled leaves that my sisters had picked in the fields, and now to choose whatever I liked.

Misuki and I conferred on our decision: fried eel, roasted sea bream, vegetables and noodles. One of my wealthier customers had spoken of sea bream as his favourite fish. While I trusted his judgement on other matters, this was my first opportunity to test his culinary recommendation.

'But,' I added, attempting to sound indifferent, 'add whatever looks pleasing.' Staring straight ahead, I dared not make eye contact with Misuki for fear of the monstrous tittering that might overtake us.

'And melon,' Emi whispered, in a bold tone. 'Could we please have some melon? And you could tell us the story of "No Melon to Spare".'

274

'It is bad luck to eat fried eel and melon at the same meal,' Misuki said.

'No eel, then,' I said, in my ordering voice.

The serving girls brought bath water, but I waited until they had left before I undressed: I did not want them to see my injuries. It was a relief to be alone and let Misuki wash carefully around the bruises and cuts. Then I soaked, and although Misuki did not mention it, I know I fell asleep. I awoke refreshed, but my fingers had wrinkled and the water had cooled.

Number One Serving Girl brought new clothes, but Misuki dried and dressed me, heedful of my wounds. The under kimono was of cream silk. It felt cool and smooth next to my body. The outermost kimono was spectacular – a blue heavy-stitched stiffened silk with designs of trees and birds. The red lining matched the birds. New clothes delighted me, but even those light summer kimonos scraped my raw skin.

Misuki called for the serving girls to return as she applied my makeup. They dressed my hair, which took considerable time because of its thickness and length – it fell to the floor. The ornament that Number One placed in my hair matched my lip rouge. My sandals were the same brocade as my outermost kimono. Number Two brought a mirror. I did look beautiful.

Dressed and ready, I retold the story of 'No Melon to Spare'. The serving girls listened.

A greedy farmer, taking his early melons to sell, stopped along the hot road. There he ate a small part of his expensive harvest. An old traveller asked, 'Honourable driver, would you spare a grandfather one slice of melon?' But the driver gruffly refused.

The old man said, 'Well, I will grow my own.' He gathered fallen seeds, planted them, and spat on each seed with an accuracy that no mere human could have achieved. The driver and several travellers watched as the plants grew and transformed into full-sized melons.

The grandfather took a knife and began to eat. Nearby travellers asked if they could have a slice. With the face of the Goddess of Mercy, he told them to share all they wished. Each traveller took plenty. The driver was unable to sell his crop, because so many had

had the grandfather's delicious melons. An itinerant priest commented, 'One who begrudges a single slice will lose all.'

After bathing, we waited for our dinner and our fate. The former was delicious, the latter delicious and dangerous.

IV. Service

Before the meal, I sent Misuki with the serving girls to supervise the unpacking of our clothing and costumes, makeup and toiletries. Later we sent them on prolonged errands and searched out my concealed logs and other papers. The thin walls and well-kept furniture provided few places to hide them so we created the required spaces by using old combs to squash them into cracks and between or behind *shōji* frames.

Misuki agreed to keep the larger papers in her socks and other clothing because I might be called upon to remove mine. The future was unknown and I wanted to keep my precious intelligence safe.

Our first real dinner in Rokuhara arrived in a procession with four servants, each dressed in rich fabrics made into plain kimono, *kosode* or trousers with jackets. The Woman-in-Charge-of-Rooms led them.

All of this far exceeded my dream on the day I was sold to Chiba. I sat in a polished wooden room while servants brought food in lacquered bowls on trays inlaid with gold and silver. The chopsticks were not merely glossy black but decorated with such detail I hesitated to touch them.

The lacquered bowls aroused memories of my first meals with Chiba. When I saw the trays I recalled those meals, and the many I had shared with Tashiko. Tears trickled from my eyes as rain overflows a pond.

After the servants had left, we discovered that the food was delectable. Misuki, Emi and I ate, chattered and compared the food, the chopsticks and each bowl. The sea bream, as the former client had boasted, was indeed an excellent and fragrant fish. The food was arranged artfully and we cooed like swallows before feasting on each dish. Sometimes Emi laughed and clapped at vegetables cut like flowers, or colours that rivalled my new robes. The enchanting meal caused me to put aside my fears momentarily.

Obāsan came into our quarters. 'In court,' she explained, 'everyone is required to leave their bowl empty.' She amused us with stories of high-ranking nobles wrapping fish bones and sneaking them into their sleeves. I understood this gentle lesson, but we laughed at the thought of not being able to empty our bowls.

The next day Tokikazu sent for me early, at the Hour of the Dragon. Misuki dressed me carefully to avoid hurting me, but the weight of my armour was immense. The messenger took me through the corridors' labyrinth and then to a northern field.

I practised stationary archery first. That morning Tokikazu and I were first on the Arrow Way. I looked for Akio, but did not see him, nervous to be with Tokikazu alone. Why was I tense to be alone with him? At the end of the long, narrow field were targets of bamboo hats tied to stakes. To make it more difficult, the early-morning breeze buffeted the hats.

'No, little peony,' Tokikazu admonished me, soon after I had begun. 'You have forgotten to look away from the target. Your form is not your best.'

I sighed. I agreed with his criticism and wished I could share the cause of my distractions.

'We shall do this together,' he whispered, as he wrapped his arms around me from behind and placed his hands on my wrists. 'Like this and this.' He touched my shoulders, not realising this caused stabs of pain. Breathing softly but audibly, he touched my back, whispering about breath. He moved my head with his hand to remind me of the draw, meet and release.

My eyes could hardly focus, but the Goddess of Mercy allowed me to remain silent, afraid my voice would give away my distress – my physical pain and that I experienced at his closeness. Was I attracted to two different men?

'Kozaishō, you are a good student. You have made much progress in a short time.' His hands remained wrapped around me. His entire body quaked, although his voice was steady.

He was leaning against my back, his fingers touching my hands, wrists and neck. I endured his body's restrained tremors. His movements and words commanded propriety. His honourable allegiance to Michimori shone like the sun through autumn maple leaves.

'Thank you for your kind words, but you exaggerate my skill.' I controlled my tone as carefully as I used to with a new client, hiding my physical suffering and unease at his arousal. He acknowledged my words with a wave. Perhaps he was unable to speak.

> Samurai teacher
> Holder of my lord's honour
> You show me honour
> From your patient discipline to
> Your denial of desire

V. Practising and Politics

Almost a month later, Michimori returned, but he did not send for me immediately. By then I had healed, and could now enjoy my favourite archery game, with the triangle targets set at intervals. The horses' hoofs' drumming rhythm rocked me as if I were in a lover's arms and I shot at one target after another.

My horse's gait was smooth, so I shot fast and with accuracy. My speed and precision had improved after much work with Tokikazu, Sadakokai and Akio. Those early weeks were difficult, but I loved practising and becoming competent, working on a path towards an honourable life, although a peach stone nipped my stomach when I thought of Michimori.

Part of each day included sword on horse and throwing daggers or *shurikens*. After the Initial Movements sword techniques Tokikazu had taught me, I completed formal exercises and practised with *bokken* in earnest. Parry and double cut with body leverage. Back counterattack with double turn. Evasive turn and double cut. Double cut with evasive turn on knee. Tokikazu's eyes smiled, even when he was locked in combat with me. Mine did too. His beauty captivated me.

After practice at Chiba's I had had to bathe, since he preferred me to do so. At Hitomi's I was allowed to practise only before any customers arrived. At Rokuhara, after a long session, servants brought perfumed cloths to remove the sweat. More servants approached to re-dress my hair and replace torn or soiled clothing. Then more servants brought fragrant foods in lacquered dishes and drinks in porcelain cups.

Besides practice, there was much else at Rokuhara and Heian-kyō. With guards, Tokikazu, Mokuhasa, and sometimes Akio, took me to *sumō* wrestling. The escort defended me from beggars, but particularly from the pervasive groups of young priests who might perform mischief or worse. All of us sought the priest with the broken nose. I watched the Great Champion throw his opponent out of the Holy Circle while wearing his Sumptuous Loincloth.

Mokuhasa enjoyed the court dances and knew I did too. Court dances encompassed subtle, yet meaningful and eloquent movements. Special court music played with the full court orchestra. During these performances I sat behind the screens with other high-ranking wives and concubines. Hardly anyone spoke, but their eyes assessed each thread of my clothes and measured the suitability my *irome no kasane*, colour combinations, for the season. Obāsan and the court ritualist deliberated for hours on my clothing. It had to be perfect for a palace enclosure appearance. After I returned home, the music and dances soothed sleep for many nights.

Throughout these excursions, Tokikazu, Mokuhasa and Sadakokai discussed politics. Akio and I listened. Only the provinces in the north-west consistently supported the Taira Clan. Minamoto forces were gathering in the east.

Returning from a *sumō* match one evening, Sadakokai spoke of how Chancellor Kiyomori had infringed Retired Emperor Go-Shirakawa's authority. Kiyomori was endeavouring to earn the emperor's favour again, but was not confident of doing so.

'Emperor Go-Sh-Sh-Shirakawa has fingers as long as spider's webs,' Sadakokai said, and gave me a knowing look, 'in the capital and in each p-p-province. If Chancellor Kiyomori can do this, it will be a g-g-good thing for us.'

'We are in need of allies now, but we must isolate the emperors from our rivals. There are many, not just the Minamoto.' Mokuhasa spoke softly.

'I wish Chancellor Kiyomori well in negotiating this political maze.' Tokikazu tapped Mokuhasa on the back.

'Yes, I heard the *sōhei* armies of Mount Hiei and Nara might unite.'

Sadakokai shook his head. 'I heard a rumour too. About Chancellor K-Kiyomori. They say he might have to take the emperors away from our enemies near here. Maybe Fukuhara. To p-protect our p-power and his grandson.'

Mokuhasa gestured to Tokikazu. 'With no offence intended against your judgement and leadership, Captain Tokikazu, I wish Governor Michimori was one of those making the decisions, with the Minamoto and *sōhei* from the north and the south.'

'We would all be fools not to agree.' Tokikazu's eyes turned a bitter brown.

I wondered if these problems would make my plans for revenge easier or more difficult.

VI. Journey with the Emperor

With Obāsan, her nephew, Ryo, Tokikazu and our samurai, I created a small network of messengers, as Michimori had. I used my serving girls, although I did not trust them yet. Gathering information was like collecting grains of millet, many seeds to make a mouthful. Three Eyes, the fiend and demon, seemed to have evaporated.

That first month at Rokuhara, however, I gained other information. Stories abounded about the burning of Miidera. There had been a siege. The Taira leaders, with Michimori as second-in-command, had burned some buildings and several priests had died. While I was sad about this, the monks had committed treason against the emperor and Chancellor Kiyomori. Nevertheless, I did not think well of burning temples.

Obāsan agreed with me. 'Punishment, yes,' she sighed, and put one hand on top of the other, 'but not destruction.' I placed my hands around hers, remembering a priest unworthy of death.

The next day, Rokuhara was transformed into a summer beehive, servants, samurai, priests, hatted and non-hatted aristocrats all chattering together. No one walked. Everyone ran through the corridors. It was rumoured that the entire capital was moving to Fukuhara.

The next evening Obāsan rushed in, her plait streaming behind her like a groomed horse's tail. 'It is true!'

'What?'

'The capital is moving to Fukuhara – on the third of next month.'

'So soon? Is that possible?'

Obāsan raised her eyebrows and said informally, 'When Taira no Kiyomori decides on an action, it is done.'

In fact Obāsan was mistaken. We left earlier, on the second, not the third, of the sixth month. She said it was a good month to travel since it was rainless. Not that we had any choice.

We were not to leave until the Hour of the Snake, so we watched the procession assemble until Tokikazu came for us. Thousands of mounted samurai and foot soldiers edged along each side of the road. From a distance the cavalcade resembled a long column of ants – well-dressed, colourful ants. Some ants rode horses, some rode in ox carts, and servant-ants carried the higher-ranking ones on tiny leaves. We would ride: the samurai on horses, Misuki, Emi and the serving girls in an ox cart, I in a palanquin, and Obāsan, later, in the ox carts with the others overseeing serving women.

Obāsan indicated the higher rankings, like Chancellor Kiyomori's. He was of the first rank, the highest to which a commoner could aspire.

'I did not know it was possible for a commoner to have rank.' Emi put her hands together, and her eyes brightened.

'He is the first warrior to have this honour,' Obāsan continued. 'Senior nobles are the first, second and third ranks. Those ranks are reserved for chief ministers in the Council of State.'

'But Lord Michimori is third rank?' Emi asked.

'Yes. Fourth and fifth ranks are key posts. Below fifth rank, a person cannot freely enter the imperial walls. They are mere officials.' Here Obāsan made a false pose of dignity.

We were too far away from the procession to detect the different combinations of scents. Each person formulated their own incense. Yet what colours! I studied the courtly women's sleeves, which draped out of their palanquins and ox carts like butterfly wings. Naturally nothing else showed.

Obāsan said, 'Courtly women entertain behind a curtain at home and never show their faces, just their sleeves.'

'I suppose that is why kimono colour combinations are so important,' Misuki said to herself. Obāsan smiled and placed a hand on Emi's shoulder. 'Yes, dear one.'

After the imperial guard, the reigning emperor came in his formal dress, and next the two retired emperors, Go-Shirawaka leading, also gloriously attired. Emi shaded her eyes against the glitter.

Chancellor Kiyomori led in an exquisite palanquin, lacquered with gold and silver *makie*, followed by his women's equally elaborate palanquins. Next came carts and the imperial carriages with their escorts. Obāsan named each one she knew.

The Fujiwara regent was next, followed by Munemori, a son of Kiyomori, Michimori's cousin. More of the highest-ranking officials, their women and escorts passed.

We joined the procession, with Tokikazu, Akio, Mokuhasa and Sadakokai as our escorts, among the third-rank people. Michimori rode ahead with his father and uncle, so I was deprived of his company. Akio shadowed Tokikazu, but, thank the Gods, he kept close to me and conversed whenever he could. He and I discussed the changing political situation. The Fukuhara monasteries would not make trouble, although the *sōhei* on Mount Hiei and Nara had gathered against the emperors. After the burning of temples, it was logical to assume the monks bore antipathy towards the Taira, and perhaps the emperors as well.

To peep through the curtains of my palanquin, watch samurai on horseback, the countryside and the imperial guards trotting back and forth furnished me with nearly as much pleasure as watching courtly dances. For me the trip lasted but a breath.

As we approached the new city, scenes from Hitomi's domain streaked through my memory. How long ago it was that the Village of Outcasts had loomed ahead, so immense to me. Through the horrible sixth month's heat, an endless file of the People-Above-the-Clouds from Rokuhara and Heian-kyō, their samurai and soldiers, their servants, cooks, and seam-stresses, travelled to the shore. From a distance Fukuhara looked like a primitive toy compared with Heian-kyō, but it enlarged to a detailed miniature the closer we approached.

At Fukuhara servants ran back and forth. I avoided the clusters of hooded priests who roamed the corridors like scavenger birds on a beach. Could one be the priest I was seeking? I scanned for a crooked nose below empty eyes.

Our serving girls settled Misuki, Emi and me into rooms from which we could view the sea, a sight new to us. Our quarters were more rustic than they had been at Rokuhara, but compared to the Village of Outcasts, they were luxurious. My possessions, especially my writing box, had arrived safely. Misuki had ensured the security of my logs and other papers, procuring every paper out of the hiding places. All were undisturbed.

With some leisure while the servants scurried about, I studied my belongings. Inside my writing box, four or five brushes lay on a small tray, also inlaid with mother-of-pearl and yellow stones. Each brush was a singular beauty, with a painted design on one, inlaid woods on another. Each represented a miniature world to me. My determination grew stronger to improve my writing with these beautiful new tools. Here, where the *kuge*, the People-Above-the-Clouds, revered beautiful calligraphy, it was crucial I do so.

I also needed tools to continue working out a plan of revenge. Writing was only one of them. I needed more trusted contacts. Tokikazu was helpful, as were Obāsan and Ryo, her nephew who was now a part of my circle of spies. How was I to make sufficient connections to obtain information about my powerful enemy?

With all I had learned so far, I knew little about Three Eyes.

What would happen when Michimori arrived? Might there be another Three Eyes in Fukuhara?

As the *kuge* say when kept waiting too long, 'The calendar was almost unrolled.'

BOOK 12

I. Sea Bass

Most *kuge* rejoiced at the cooler coastal temperatures at Fukuhara. I imagined the sun rising from the white-tipped sea in the early pink sky. I wished to smell salty breezes during winter. Hardy since childhood, I had always relished brisk weather.

Obāsan had many talks with me during those early days in Fukuhara. She began by saying, 'You need to know about Governor Michimori.'

Settling in for a story, I made myself comfortable in front of the writing table where I spent time after my field practice.

'Are you aware he is now second-in-command of all the Taira armies?'

'N-n-no,' I stuttered, my eyes wide, without regard for decorum, because we were alone.

Obāsan asked if she could arrange for her favourite court ritualist to visit me regularly.

'Yes,' I agreed, but not before I asked timidly, 'May Misuki sit with us?'

'Yes, my lady, but to what end?'

My response came easily: 'She is a trusted friend as well as a servant. I rely on her as much as I do upon you.'

Obāsan's fingertips stroked the back of my hand. 'All right.'

I had studied much, but knew little. I promised myself I would listen closely to both Obāsan and the court ritualist. Every shred of information was useful to me: it might reveal the head of Three Eyes and set it on a spike. Misuki joined us and Obāsan began, 'The Taira Clan traces its ancestry from Emperor Kammu, whose grandson first bestowed the name. Generations later, Chancellor Kiyomori has risen to the highest status possible for a commoner. Kiyomori's second youngest brother, Norimori, is Michimori's father. Did you know Michimori is Norimori's firstborn?'

Misuki stopped sewing, lifted her head and nodded. We both knew that much, but neither of us said anything.

Obāsan continued, 'Kiyomori became great through gifts from the Gods. He rescued the emperor during the Hōgen Disturbance and became deputy of the Imperial Office for all of Kyūshū. Finally the emperor gave him the rank of Chancellor of the Realm, Junior of the First Rank.'

'Kiyomori's grandson is . . .' she paused and lifted her arms up to the heavens '. . . Emperor Antoku.' Obāsan bowed slightly to me. 'Governor Taira no Michimori is from a long line of gifted warriors.'

'Imagine!' I murmured, as I returned Obāsan's bow. My thoughts reeled from the recitation of the ranks and power into which I had been thrust. What was I doing among these people? How could I survive here, especially without Michimori, whom I had not even glimpsed since my arrival?

'Let me share a story with you,' Obāsan leaned back on a pillow, enjoying herself with an eager audience.

'Chancellor Kiyomori went on a pilgrimage to the Ise Shrine with his escorts, a favourite wife, her ladies and some notable Buddhist priests. I mean the Tendai priests from Enryakuji, the ones from Mount Hiei, not the Shingon priests who were out of favour.'

As she mentioned the word 'priest', my eyes must have shown emotion. She touched the tips of my fingers. I wondered if she knew. Our eyes met.

'You know?' The words scarcely left my throat. Misuki looked at me, and subsequently at Obāsan.

'We are not to speak of such things,' Obāsan whispered. Her eyes darted to the rooms where the serving girls were and back to me. I motioned with my eyes to show understanding. So did Misuki. Obāsan cleared her throat with a mock-cough and continued in a louder voice.

'While servants were playing Kiyomori's favourite song, turbulence near the boat caused them to stop. The escorts looked over the side of the boat and drew their arrows in readiness. Others remained on the other side, so all was secure. The noise became louder. With greater commotion and spray, a vast sea bass leaped out of the water and threw itself into the boat.

The priests proclaimed it to be a sign from the Buddha. "We must eat it today," they interpreted, "for it is an omen of immediacy."'

'They ate on a fast day?' Misuki asked quietly, leaning towards Obāsan.

'They feasted on the delicious fish. Kiyomori became the great leader he is now.' Obāsan turned her palms upwards. 'Michimori is following in Chancellor Kiyomori's path.'

'You speak with such respect and devotion.' I left my question unasked.

'When my husband died in the Hōgen Disturbance twenty-four years ago, Kiyomori attended the funeral and recited a poem to honour him.

'My sons, the ones who are alive, are with Governor Michimori. My two eldest sons died in the Heiji Insurrection. Chancellor Kiyomori and Governor Michimori attended their funerals. Kiyomori dressed in elaborate brocade to honour my children. Michimori, even then, as a young man, embodied the Majestic Calm of a great leader.' She added, with a soft smile, her eyes far away, 'His essence is Pure Tranquillity. You can depend on Michimori, as I have, for the clean action from a pure spirit without emotion.'

I had much to think about, some hope, and went to the practice field that day in silence.

II. Summoned

Tokikazu and Akio trained with me in the fields and target areas each day, unless Divergent Directions forbade it. I disliked those days away from Tokikazu. His conversations and stories amused everyone, except Akio.

The varieties of cutting with my *tachi* grew familiar, and I improved slowly with *kisagake*, moving the blade in a quick whip-like action with each type of cut. Since Cutting-the-Sleeve was the first stroke I had learned, it was my best. Others improved. Some I had learned from travelling samurai at the Village of Outcasts. The samurai in Rokuhara, most subscribed to the Sanjo branch of the Yamashiro School. Relearning took time, since the differences were subtle yet important.

Every practice session included bow and horse, as well as short swords, daggers, knives and *shuriken*. I wondered about the *shuriken* but Tokikazu, my doting friend, often said, with a shake of his head, 'You need to know everything.'

Obāsan brought me anything I wanted. Through her, I learned to read better. With writing, though, I still struggled, like a kitten in deep mud.

As for locating Three Eyes, my trusted people asked discreet questions of those we knew could keep secrets. For now, that was only a few. Tokikazu led me to others who were also safe harbours in what I found was an agitated sea.

Information arrived, often in morsels, too small and scattered to make a recognisable pattern. Even worse, it was often false. During practice, Sadakokai heard that Michimori was coming to Fukuhara. I did not believe this because Sadakokai had foretold it many times before. On this occasion I learned that the source of information was unlikely to be accurate, and that was important.

One particular morning practice was difficult because I was tired. *Kōshin* had been the night before, and everyone had remained awake all night. The court ritualist explained that Kōshin came every sixty days and that everyone kept vigil all night. Otherwise, worms in our bodies would travel up to the Heavenly God and report our misdeeds. The Heavenly God could decide to shorten our lives or end them. I did not believe in these worms, but the *kuge* did, and I had no wish to take chances.

Obāsan interjected, sweeping three fingers in the air, 'If we slept, three different types of worm might attack us and cause illness, perhaps even death.'

Misuki thought it strange that neither of us had heard of it before, but she had remained awake.

I completed my practice, and Akio reminded me, 'Samurai feel no weariness and no hunger.' I felt sad because I certainly felt both.

A few days later, Obāsan raced in while I was having my bath, her plait flapping against her back, like a hooked fish struggling for water. 'He is here!'

'Who?' I thought of Goro.

'Commander-in-Chief Michimori!'

'Now?'

'You were the first person I came to see!'

'W-who, h-how . . .' I had not expected Michimori so soon, probably because of Sadakokai's mistaken warnings.

'My nephew Ryo knows one of the guards,' she breathed. 'We have much to do. Ryo overheard Governor Michimori say he was going to send for you.'

'I thought he had forgotten me,' I murmured.

Obāsan touched my shoulder, tugged at my hair gently and left. After a brief meal, the serving girls, Misuki and Emi arranged my hair and makeup, then readied my clothes. I found myself humming as I decided on which story to tell.

I settled on a simple tale of enchantment. A young lady, entranced by a prince's love potion, becomes uninhibited. This story did not require costumes or props. I could manage with what I had already planned to wear.

When Obāsan came back to escort me, she had transformed herself into a regal bird. She wore heavy silk, thick with textured patterns, and the colours matched, from the blue-ribbon bird in her hair to the threads in her outer kimono and her shoes. The blue was a deep sky-without-a-cloud blue and made her white hair more startling and beautiful by contrast. Her eyes glistened more than they had when we first met. She touched my cheek with a finger.

'I am an old woman, so I will not compliment you on how you look.' She gave a small smile, and added in her most grandmotherly tone, 'Remember, the Empress Aiko thought learning more important than clothes or a flirtatious manner.'

With that, she held out a new incense burner and put a scent on my hair and clothes. I admired the lotus-shaped burner. Each leaf was a different bright colour. I had never seen its like.

The dream I had cherished on the day I was sold to Chiba had come true. I was in a palace, wearing many-coloured robes, while servants set dishes of gold and silver before me. How could it be true that only the dreams of priests, high-ranking nobles and royalty came true? Even after Purification, I was a Person-Without-Rank, a Woman-for-Play – from a Village of Outcasts, summoned by the great Governor of Echizen, Third Rank, nephew to Chancellor Kiyomori. To what was I summoned?

I glided down corridors banked with tall screens and carved wood, the ceilings decorated with shining gold. Apprehension slowed my feet. My heart seemed to batter against my teeth. I had been sold three times already. I hoped Michimori would not sell me again.

Even if I were given to the guards or worse . . . I tried to banish those images, recalling that I had brought honour to those I loved most. 'Look!' I argued with myself. 'I am with the emperors, in Fukuhara, dressed in Michimori's clothes and cared for by his servants. He thought me deserving enough to purchase me.'

The poem he had sent me! I had put it in my sleeve to give me courage. I remembered my place in the procession to this city. How could this not have a favourable outcome?

'Perhaps,' I made a small prayer to the Goddess of Mercy, 'I am spared for a different fate.' I thanked the Goddess for allowing me to bring honour to my family, whatever was to happen now.

III. Meeting Again

The ever-present Tokikazu and Obāsan escorted me through more corridors to the Great Room. The door displayed startling wealth and power, with the faces of demons and gods carved into the shining brown and black woods. There was gold everywhere. I heard the agreeable music of several *koto*.

Guards opened the door to a room large enough to contain all the houses and huts at Hitomi's. Soldiers stood everywhere, all in the same uniform. The ceiling was made of solid gold, and silk banners with the Taira butterfly crest hung from the walls.

Michimori sat on a raised platform several *shaku* above the floor. He was less handsome than I remembered, in bright elegant robes of gold, deep blue and purple, the light hue of the highest ranks, not the royal shade forbidden to all but the imperial family.

Samurai surrounded him, but were far enough away that he appeared to sit alone, though protected. Behind him, against bare walls, there were several three-part folding screens, painted with bamboo, birds and flowers. In front of the screens three *koto* players sat with their thirteen-stringed instruments. The music was soft and pleasant, as was the incense.

Obāsan left me inside the door with whispered directions: approach halfway to the raised platform, bow to the floor and wait. Tokikazu reminded me at the last moment about the Buddha's five-part bow, while his hand skimmed my back. I prayed my shudders would be attributed to meeting Michimori, not to Tokikazu's touch.

I performed the five-part bow, while my pulse pummelled me from stomach to eyes. I remained head down, lying flat in front of Michimori, for an unending time My limbs became tired and stiff, but I did not move, as I knew I must not.

Someone, he or another, shifted position. I heard the rustle of heavy clothing gliding over more cloth. A throat clicked, a sound I remembered as Michimori's. Each man had his own.

The clicking first, and next, my honourable lord's voice: 'You have found favour. You have completed Purification. You and your ladies-in-waiting are ready to enter my household. Have you been shown your quarters?'

'Yes, my honourable lord, Echizen Governor Taira no Michimori,' I say, not daring to look up, rubbing my nose on the shining wood floor. He calls my name. I raise my nose high enough to peep over my hands to the source of the voice.

A faint chuckle fills my ears, like soft duck down, and he utters a single command, 'Approach.'

I am unable to move.

He calls again: 'Kozaishō, arise and sit here beside me.'

Surely he will not chastise me while I am seated next to him. I glance at him. His eyes are smiling. Glowing.

His hand encourages me to stand. I do so, my head slightly bowed and my eyes lowered. I approach, bow to the floor again and squat where his hand has gestured, directly before him. My fears vanish, like rain into dry ground. The same hand waves several times to the samurai, who rearrange themselves in two concentric circles along the far perimeters.

He smiles with his eyes, as he did when he thanked me after our time together at Hitomi's.

'Are you willing to work for me? Work diligently?'

What an odd question. I answer, as I know the courtly ladies respond, with a poem:

> All creatures travail
> Starlings sitting joyfully at dawn
> Tiger moths eat their fill
> Butterflies pollinate flowers
> Does the bee not earn its honey?

In his face I discern candour and look hard at him to convince myself he has no knowledge of my torture by Three Eyes. Goro had undoubtedly commanded some of the guards during my Purification. But, no, Tokikazu had *specifically* said it was Michimori's request. He had explicitly requested in writing that I did this. Tokikazu had waved the note at me, and I had glimpsed Michimori's seal.

I had pledged to please this man. Just as I had pledged the death of Three Eyes.

'Do you know why you are here?'

Michimori's words bring me to the moment. The unknown again. This is my fate! I reply with nightmares scratching my throat, burning it. My heart bounces against my chest.

'No, my honourable lord, Echizen Governor Taira no Michimori.'

'Because you enchanted me, though I know you are not a fox, or a witch, or a sorcerer. You are a sharp-witted woman and I want you near me.' I look up in astonishment. His eyes beam as he says:

> Willow warbler trills
> Sunrise appears with starlings
> Sounds more exquisite
> Closer to hearth and home
> More beautiful near my eyes

'I have made a Judgement-of-Quality of what makes a perfect consort. I want a real partner in these times, and . . . I want you.'

My lips and eyes open wide.

'I have brought you here to marry you. You have a gift for strategy, for putting information together and, most of all, for survival, Madam Hitomi told me about you. You are an excellent judge of men. I need that quality in people around me. And,' he adds in hushed tones, 'of greater importance, you are my soul-keeper. You are the Northern Wife, the first wife, in my heart.' He pauses. 'What is in your heart now?'

I have never heard anything so poignant. I reply to the elegance of his words:

> The forgotten bird

Is now delighted to sing
Preened for a good life
Basking in the new sunlight
Out of past seasons' shadows

I bow to the floor, concerned at my boldness: I am not a Person-Above-the-Clouds – perhaps it will be taken as an insult or that I am pretending to be *kuge*. I glance furtively at him, but his brown eyes are as bright as the noon sun. When I see this gleam, several of my fears are set to rest. I put my sleeve over my face as if to smile. Can he truly care for me? How can I marry him?

Tears of relief trickle, but I do not wipe them away. I do not wish the samurai to know I weep. That is of far more concern than damage to my new finery.

IV. Three Cups of *Sake*

Michimori says, 'Come, let me tell you a story.'

What does he really know about me? I have no illusions, no matter what he says. He sent me into battle well protected, but he also threw me weaponless into the jaws of Goro. Now he is gentle and seems kind. Death, no matter how dishonourable, must be in this tale. More rape and abuse? Perhaps to be used for his personal samurai – or thrown to all the samurai. My stomach lurches at the thought. Michimori promises much, yet happiness is fleeting and marriage to a *kuge*, Third Rank, is hard to trust.

'My captain, Tokikazu, visited you. He reported that you were fierce in combat, had the voice of a warbler and were beautiful beyond cherry blossoms. I decided to see for myself.'

My body startles at the mention of Tokikazu.

'Next, his lieutenant, Ichirou, spoke of you. He mentioned your special talent for matching each man with a story. He sent one of his men, a man hungry for power over weaker men and women. This man became gentle and content.'

He tilts his head to the side. 'He still carries a white flower with one red petal for "Grave of the Chopstick". Did you know?'

I shake my head.

'Ichirou suspected you were the reason. Later, Tokikazu sent Ichirou to you. He had lost his ability for combat because he had grown so large, much to the shame of all. Ichirou reduced to a proper size. Another changed man.'

Why is he recounting my successes with his men? Ah, I remember. He spoke of this when we first met. As he enumerates another success, the strap around my chest releases, smoothing my breathing. Yet why? Is he setting me up to ambush me?

He turns his muscular chest towards me. The distance between our bodies decreases. 'I believe your wisdom and competency in changing men should be close to me. So, Kozaishō, what are your thoughts?'

He motions with the fingers of one hand, which gives me permission to speak.

My mind writhes: my stories, my vengeance for Tashiko, my new owner, who may have allowed Goro to assault me, now confers praise. Can a hideous demon hide in this man, after all the good I have heard of him? His ways and all the talk about him make him a Bodhisattva. Only Tashiko was worthy of that honour. Confusion swirls, and I try to concentrate. My master has commanded. I must speak.

I gaze at the floor and see his deep-set dark eyes above broad cheekbones reflected on the polished floor. In my most formal speech: 'This is too much honour, my lord, for I am only a woman, a mere Person-Without-Rank, who likes to tell stories.'

'You are no longer a Person-Without-Rank.' On the floor I see he turns his head to me, and his eyes glow.

He lowers his voice so that the guards stationed along the perimeter of this cavernous room cannot hear. 'We cried together. Our tears have remained within me.

> 'My complete spirit
> Has been stoken from me
> Snatched and soaked into
> Every single stitch and thread
> Of the kimono you wear.'

I recall his painstaking tenderness at Hitomi's as he repeats the poem he sent me, but I dare not trust this fleeting fragment. What manner of two-faced demon is he?

Michimori gives me another poem, written in silver ink on the finest paper I have ever touched. The perfume of his incense, strong with sandalwood, drifts towards me.

I read:

> Dew huddled on leaves
> Flowers drinking the dew
> Each helps the other
> Left hand benefits right hand
> Horse, bow, samurai – all one

A magnificent poem. Exquisite calligraphy. My thoughts reverberate: a sensitive poet, admired by Obāsan; a commander who ordered me into battle, yet protected me with his personal guards; last, a beast who secured my honour with a loyalty pledge, then submitted me to Goro's tortures and rape.

'Eh?' he asks. 'We speak alone.'

I survey the room. I see my dream of the night before I was sold to Chiba: dressed in many robes, sitting on the shining floor, surrounded by wealth. I stammer the usual proprieties: 'I am overwhelmed by the unforeseen honour you bestow upon me. I know I am unworthy, but I shall . . . do all my unworthy soul can do . . . to please you.'

He waves away my words. More sandalwood. 'Are your feelings the same as mine? I wish you to marry me. Tell me,' he leans forward as he voices each word, 'what – is – in – your – heart?' He raises his bristly eyebrows, expecting an answer.

I risk my life. I take two breaths, an old habit from the *shōen* of Chiba. I know he has the power of death, yet his face is so benevolent, so serene. I state what is faithful to my feelings, hands over abdomen, the place whence this truth is coming, and perform the five point bow: 'In my heart, admiration for one who has risen to greatness, respect for one who knows his people so well as to hear of such as I, gratitude for one who has such compassion for the lowest, rescuing and raising me to a place of honour. Also fear, to serve one who holds life and death. My fear is that I might displease my honourable lord and be sent back in disgrace to the hell from which I have been saved. I shall willingly undergo whatever further punishments and injuries my honourable lord chooses, but I entreat him not to include my servants in any harm.'

Silence. I wait for the shuffle of shoes towards me. No samurai comes to take my head.

'Kozaishō,' he says, grim and reverential. He touches my face, and lifts my chin with a finger. I hear the voice and the humming, then the sound I remember, Michimori's sound. My eyes focus upwards to its source. His brown eyes gleam like fresh snow in moonlight.

One side of his face twitches up. 'You are to be my wife. As your lord and husband, I give you my word that I will never send you back to a place like the Village. No more punishment.'

I swallow and take a ragged breath. No more torture? First he directs Goro to beat and rape me, and now he wants to marry me? The word 'wife' encourages me.

'I do not understand, my lord. Why did you require me to undergo such torment? And at the hands of someone who detests me and whom I abhor?'

The tenderness in his face evaporates.

His back stiffens to the hardness of a *naginata*'s edge, ready to slice away the life from anyone within reach.

'You think I would hurt you? Or make you suffer? How can you imagine that?'

'Because of the Purification ceremony. Daigoro no Goro performed it for my servant and me with . . . with brutality. He . . . and Captain Tokikazu . . . said it was your wish.' I bite my tongue, my arms rigid. Will this information harm Tokikazu? Yet I must speak the truth.

Michimori's eyes widen. His neck muscles are more rigid than a wooden saddle. 'Who is this Daigoro no Goro?'

A weaponless blow strikes me. My hands form into rigid fists. 'The priest, Daigoro no Goro, the Tendai Taira priest.' My breath comes faster. 'You do not know him?'

Michimori's mouth compresses to the thin straight line of an arrow.

He waves a crooked finger. Tokikazu rushes from a far corner of the chamber, clattering swords, and sprawls directly in front of Michimori.

'My honourable lord Taira no Michimori—'

'What do you know of Daigoro no Goro?' The muscles of Michimori's jaw bulge and recede.

Tokikazu blanches. His body flattens to the floor.

'Tell what this abomination has done to my bride.' Michimori's torso swells to twice its girth.

'While we were returning to Rokuhara, he bribed one of the lower-level guards and murdered three, substituting his own. He was alone with Kozaishō and her servant during their Purification . . . and the Cleansing water was . . .' he sighed '. . . heavily salted. We found blood in it. We have taken the bribed guard's head, found the bodies of the murdered guards, and those we think were Daigoro no Goro's own guards.'

'Think! And?' Michimori's voice a deep crescendo.

'Daigoro no Goro escaped.'

Michimori's eyes turn blackish-brown. His voice is as sharp as a *naginata* tip when he asks, 'Did you tell Kozaishō the Purification was my order?'

Tokikazu's legs quiver. His left hand reaches inside the right breast of his *hoeki no hō*, pulls out a piece of paper and prods it along the floor to Michimori.

Michimori studies it. His features remain unaltered, although his skin reddens, mainly his thick neck. He sits, breathing unevenly.

Clearing his throat, he says, 'Not my hand. A close appearance. Not my seal, but also close.'

My jaws clamp tight and my hands squeeze into fists. Not his orders.

Tokikazu's limbs loosen on to the floor.

'Look at this false seal.'

Tokikazu crawls over and peers at it.

Michimori opens his writing box, takes his seal and shows them both together.

The two men, head to head, scrutinise the red squares.

'See, here and here . . . and there,' Michimori indicates the differences with his fingers.

'I will teach all the personal guards, my lord, before—'

'No.' Michimori bends forward over Tokikazu. 'No *seppuku*. I forbid it. This is not a matter of *your* honour. This concerns our clan and a formidable infiltration. Find him!'

Tokikazu disappears from the room.

Michimori's eyes flash storms. 'How could you think I would hurt you?' His words are honed and pointed.

'How could I?' My voice mirrors his tone. 'Tokikazu told me you requested it. Goro told me it was your particular preference. I submitted only to demonstrate my fidelity. I undertook the loyalty pledge with my soul's blood. And my honour. Otherwise Goro would be dead. I regret my offerings are not appreciated. But worse – not necessary.'

His shoulders slope downwards. 'Did I give you any – any indication I might be such a devil as to desire the gift of your pain?'

'No. You did not. What else was I to think? I arrived at your estate, having known you only briefly, and Tokikazu—'

'I agree. Tokikazu will pay with—'

'Daigoro no Goro, should suffer, not Tokikazu, my honourable lord.' I want to protect Tokikazu from the monster who attacked me.

Michimori's eyes widen at my daring to interrupt, but he listens. He bends to my face, and I lower my voice. Not even his personal guards, who are nearer than the others, can hear. I provide him with a concise history of Three Eyes. Only his left eye twitches at the recitation of Goro's abuses and his broken nose. My fingers, red and white, are cramped: my fists have been clenched.

He presses his fingertips against the raised platform and says to himself, 'In outward aspect a Bodhisattva; at innermost heart, a demon. I have met such priests before. Some apprentice monks have weaker spirits than others.' He sits back, his eyes soft again. 'Kozaishō, I humbly ask you to forgive me for not protecting you, for not holding you near me.'

'If you can forgive me, my honourable lord, for trusting Daigoro no Goro and accepting your desire for punishment rather than my own experiences of your Right Mindedness. Obāsan has extolled your virtuous heart.'

'No. It is I who beg your forgiveness. I promise Daigoro no Goro's head to you – and more, if it can be arranged.'

I see the waters of repentance in his eyes. After a time, he rubs the back of my hand with a finger. 'Guards. My personal guards, shall be with you always.'

I gulp, clear my throat and make another decision. 'I humbly request that Akio, the samurai who has been my teacher for many years, now be one of my personal guards as well. As my honourable lord said, Akio is here and he can attest to my *bokken*'s work on Goro's face.'

Michimori pulls his paper and brush from his writing box, writes, and calls, 'Messenger.' A guard rushes to the platform, lies on the floor with one palm up. Michimori folds the paper like a flower, gives the messenger directions and drops the note into an open palm. The messenger scuttles away.

He turns to me. 'You have already asked me about him. I keep my word. Akio is with my troops. His family has a comfortable place to live. Consider it done.' He rearranges himself on his cushions so he is closer to me. 'Now you have heard what is truly in my heart, and I have heard what is in yours. I say again, I wish you to be my wife. Will you consent?'

Concubine, a possibility. Wife? Marriage? He is nephew to the emperor's father. He is truly the noble, the *kuge*.

'Why, my lord?'

What does he want from me? What kind of pawn am I – and in what kind of game? A wife has more responsibilities. As a concubine, I would be freer to search for Goro. 'My lord, I have no need of marriage. Why should you?'

'I need to marry you.'

'Surely not.' A small smile wipes my lips. 'You may have me as often as you desire. Whenever you wish.' What more does he want? 'Surely you know my oath binds me in fidelity. Have not my sacrifices proven my trustworthiness?'

'I have been enamoured of you since I heard Tokikazu describe you. I love you more now because you have proved more honourable with your sacrifice. Still, I *must* marry you.'

'I do not understand why it is necessary.'

His hand brushes across mine.

The easy touch brings quivering to my spine.

'To protect you. To give you deference and rank. Above all other reasons, to have others give you the high respect and esteem that I already accord you. This is not without precedent. Minamoto no Yoshitomo has a mistress. Her name is Ōi, I think. A *chōja* at Aohaka Inn in Mino Province, if my messengers are correct. They usually are.' His smile is broad, and his arms stretch out to each side with a slight lift in the shoulders.

'My uncle, Kiyomori, had problems with Hotoke, another Woman-for-Play, I believe. Know that I am not my uncle, neither do I waver in my feelings as he does. I am not married and never have been. I will be faithful to you, my beautiful sparrow.'

My eyes fill with the long-sought goal achieved. My breath shortens and my arms tremble.

Deference and rank? My father had required me to be mindful of our family's honour. How much more honour can there be in third rank? Third rank visits the emperor, his palaces, his festivals. How much more respect can there be in becoming the wife of the nephew of the emperor's grandfather? He is offering an honourable life, one my ancestors and my family will cherish.

I nod, indicating agreement, because I fear my words will tangle. I dare not think of Tokikazu, our friendship and – understanding.

The warm brown eyes crinkle, and he makes an odd motion with his hand. A servant brings a lacquered tray, holding three red cups and a *sake* jug. Another servant pours *sake* into all three cups, each larger than the next, and finally removes the jug. The servants leave.

'Is *sansankudo* known to you?'

'N-No, my lord.' My limbs are still shaking, but I am glad to have spoken these few words.

He tilts the smallest cup and allows a few drops to spill into his mouth. '*Sansankudo*, three sets of three means nine. Three – the perfect number, because it is indivisible. We drink three times from each cup,' he says quietly.

He hands me the smallest cup, and I swallow as he has. I return the cup to him and he drinks. 'For your safety, and to provide you with my rank and recognition, we are joining in this public place.'

I sip, suddenly aware of all the samurai's eyes focusing on us. He drinks. We alternate, until we have each sipped three times from each cup. He maintains his focus on me. When I return his stare, his intensity shoots through me, as if already piercing my womb, and I drop my eyes often, to the cup or the floor.

All three cups are empty. We are married. In public. With witnesses.

I resolve to be an honourable wife, devote my life to him and sacrifice myself for him if he asks it.

Michimori motions to his personal guards.

Words rumble like thunder in my head. 'Marry.' 'Wife.' The room revolves like silk spinning. Now married, now third rank, now of the nobility. Tashiko and I could never have imagined such a possibility.

Tears flow from the persistent grief of my lost love, from being forced into a position I do not know how to occupy, with duties I do not know how to perform, and into a rank that holds such honour that even my distant ancestors must sing with joy. I hide my face in my sleeves to conceal my feelings, not knowing how low to bow to a husband. I force myself to make only the deepest bow without the full five-point one.

Personal guards, Akio but not Tokikazu, thank the Goddess of Mercy, conduct me through the corridors to my lord's chambers. I hear a musician playing in another room. All of the servants are absent, except Obāsan, who lights a delicate incense. I recognise the scent from my first meeting with Michimori. The brazier glows. The room becomes a garden of tender scents. The *futons* and cleaning cloths are arrayed. Refreshments sit in covered bowls on a table, gold accents shimmering like early dawn. The table's shape resembles the one Chiba used in Lesser House, worlds away.

I sit and close my eyes. Opening them, I see Obāsan standing behind my honourable lord. He walks to me and puts his fingers through my hair, like a comb. In a low growl, without turning, he commands Obāsan to be gone, and she is.

He takes my hand to help me stand. 'No stories,' he murmurs into my neck. 'My wife,' he says, skimming his face over mine. 'My love,' he says, spreads my robes wide and surveys my body with his hands as carefully as he had his maps for battles and traces Goro's few remaining visible injuries with a fingertip.

I release his robes, but he holds my wrists. 'No, my beautiful samurai woman.' His face lights up. 'I have dreamed of you, of this. Let me give you happiness. For my delight. My wife.'

I see tears drip. I catch one on the bent knuckle of a finger. The top of my head floats at the word 'wife'.

'Never doubt me again.' His voice is strong and stern.

'This is beyond my dreams.' I remove another tear from his sun-darkened cheek, his face thinner than I remember. 'You have brought me back from Hell, yet I remember the demons.'

He massages my neck and shoulders. 'How frightened you must have been that morning at the Village after I left. I did not have time to explain. I rarely do.'

He stops, shrugs and smiles, a sweeping smile I have never seen.

He clutches me to him. His heat pushes through his heavy *hitatare*. 'I will never allow us to be apart again,' he says, and picks me up as if I were an empty quiver.

Michimori sets me on the *futon* and kneels beside me. His hands caress my face and neck. 'We will never be separated again. Perhaps that will help to silence your devils, Kozaishō.'

He places his head on my stomach, his arms clasping me, and weeps. I put one hand on his head and the other on his shoulder. So much passion. Is he crying for joy? Or sadness?

I loosen his clothing, rubbing his thick black hair, trying to soothe him. His sobs subside, and his hands seek my Gate. His fingers press against my skin, tender as gosling down, and I spread my robes. Desire bounds forth at these mild touches, his smooth strokes, and the bold, meticulous kneading. I cannot keep my hands from embracing him through the brocade with a long slow rhythm.

My honourable lord pulls my arms away, chuckling now. 'It is my right to delight you, my beautiful strong wife. Allow me.'

With that admonition, I lie on the *futon*, burning and shaking with craving. Is this the way with husbands and wives? He permits me to touch only his chest, neck and face. Nothing else. Impatience controls my limbs, and my hands brush his chest, many times, keeping cadence with his. My breathing frays. My legs unfetter – open in the excitement.

He groans and enters. He rises on his arms and knees and rocks us together to give me bliss. Satisfaction plucks at my body again. Again. I clutch his shoulders. We dance for hours.

'I hope never to spend another night without you, my brave Kozaishō.'

I lie beside him, aware of the growing knot of fear in my stomach. With such an influential husband, perhaps I have acquired new, fiercer and more dangerous enemies.

When his breathing becomes more regular, I fall asleep.

V. A Hunter's Dog

This was the beginning of the best, the most difficult and the most perilous time.

I had never thought of marriage, yet the samurai treated me as his bride. They bowed to me as to any of the other wives, although Tokikazu often included a knowing nod or wink. At first these honours were uncomfortable to accept.

Michimori's family's other wives and concubines signalled the same hostility as to any other new wife, I supposed, but they showed outward courtesy. I worked hard to earn my place among them. With appropriate protestations that I was undeserving, I gave them most of the gifts my husband heaped on me. But I did not give anything to my new servants, for I had learned how to manage servants at Hitomi's.

In the first of our night-time talks, Michimori charged me, 'As my wife it is not your work to perform dances, songs or even play the *biwa* or *koto*. Only play if it is your own desire.'

My own desire. I did not know what that would be, besides the practice field and to see Three Eyes' head on a spike.

'Nevertheless, bush warbler. I expect you to sit behind the screens in a room similar in function to the ones you saw in Rokuhara. You are to look through the hinges, observe and listen when men visit. Later, we can discuss our findings.'

He taught me the political language and implications, and I taught him to hear with another ear and see with another eye. A captain who boasts of conquests and wealth, yet comes to the palace with uniforms of second-rate silk, is a liar. The way the head is held or the rapidity of darting eyes can yield much information about the truthfulness of the speaker. Michimori and I talked and compared notes, trying to outguess each other with our hypotheses.

He also showed me how he folded his notes so I would not mistake forgeries for his. I designed my own distinct folds and practised them. For the writing I waited for Misuki, because hers was acceptable and mine was not.

When I had grasped how Michimori wanted me to serve him, I said I would be his Hunter's Dog, recounting this story:

Long, long ago in Mimasuka Province, humans were often sacrificed at the Shinto Shrine of the Monkey. One month a thirteen-year-old, an only child of elderly parents, was chosen. They were sad and shared their wailing with all who would listen.

Inuyama, a hunter, heard their distress. He asked the unfortunate parents if they would allow him to take the place of their daughter. The parents protested at first, but Inuyama insisted. The parents finally consented, with more tears.

The day before the sacrifice, Inuyama secretly put two of his dogs into a large chest and carried it to the shrine. He himself was to stay all night in the shrine and be sacrificed to the monkeys. He waited in the dark for a time, but as a hunter he was patient and skilled. When he heard the scratching of the monkeys' paws, he opened the chest. Inuyama and his dogs fought the monkeys and won.

The monkeys begged Inuyama to call off his dogs, saying, 'Please, no more! Let there be no more human sacrifice!'

Inuyama considered this, and in that moment the shrine's priest also cried out, 'I am the Deity of the Shrine! No more! Let there be no more human sacrifices!'

The villagers, brought by the parents, heard this and stopped Inuyama killing the monkeys. Later, with joyous feasting, the daughter married Inuyama, who had saved her life.

When I related what had happened to Misuki, she said, 'Be careful. As they say, you are a kite breeding with a hawk.'

VI. Another Road

Practice, drill, sitting behind the screens, being with and talking with Michimori filled my days and nights. Despite these activities, Misuki and I slowly sought out others who could help us find Three Eyes. There were only a few we could trust. Misuki and I tested them with a little game. I shared some inconsequential gossip with a potential contact. During the next few days Misuki spoke with their servants and tried to extract from them the information I had imparted to their master. If she succeeded, we found another possible enemy or, at least, someone unreliable. If not, we tried again until we felt secure. Misuki was excellent at wresting hearsay from others, and we counted a few allies.

We sent out for information, but all led nowhere. Three Eyes, the other priests and the guards who had stood by, had seemingly vanished. No one we asked had any information. Or perhaps they would not tell us.

'Friends one day, enemies the next,' Misuki reminded me.

Visions of that priest's head stuck on a spike lingered in my morning prayers.

Between Akio, who accompanied me almost everywhere, Tokikazu, Sadakokai, Mokuhasa and all our new trusted contacts, we were closing in, not on Goro, unfortunately, but at least on the priests who had betrayed me. We planned when the five or six of us were alone on the practice field. I made sure to check the direction of the wind so that our voices would not carry.

Winter arrived. Most of the other women complained of the cold and our poor surroundings. Listening to them, I thought of my hut at Hitomi's and pretended sympathy.

In the tenth month, with the cold worsening, we heard that Minamoto no Yoritomo had gathered a force and advanced to the east in Suruga Province. Along the Fujikawa river's banks, Taira forces attacked and strategically retreated. In Fukuhara, the decision was taken, and within weeks Kiyomori ordered all to return to the capital city.

Because of rampant illness, the return procession proved less elegant than the journey out had been. The sounds of coughing surrounded us, with thoughts of the bad omens it brought. Otherwise we travelled mostly in silence. Perhaps the cold kept people quiet.

One day in my palanquin I heard horses close by. Peeping out through my curtains, I saw Tokikazu, Michimori, Akio, Mokuhasa and Sadakokai riding towards me. They had left the procession, bringing an extra horse. Directed to mount, I did so and followed them – we had agreed I would wear my riding clothes that day. Misuki had also dressed me with my collar and helmet.

We rode swiftly away from the procession. As I galloped over the hills, I saw them. Several of Michimori's samurai were standing guard in a circle, facing outwards. In the centre there were nine poles. On each one I saw a head.

Michimori said, in his usual understated way, 'My samurai suggested these fiends might enjoy the countryside. I agreed.' He motioned to the nine stakes.

'Thank you, my lord,' I whispered.

'One decided to help us with target practice. Please join us.' Anger spouted from Michimori's eyes, but the rest of his face was like dull wood.

With a grim expression Sadakokai handed me my bow and quiver, saying, 'W-We have s-s-started without you, but we thought you m-might . . . wish to p-p-partake.'

I looked to where Sadakokai had gestured. On the other side of another hill, below the circle, the Cleansing priest was tied to a large archery target, his arms and legs spread out. Several arrows stuck out from his body. His top knot was intact, but his eyes were twisted. His face was heavily sprayed with blackened blood, as if someone had lacquered his skin. A cloth was stuffed into his mouth, but he produced muffled screeches.

His eyes – as hard in dying as they had been in life – bulged in terror and fury.

I gazed at Michimori and the samurai. We all held our bows. Michimori nodded to tell me I was to go first. I did so, followed by each of the others. We repeated this process until there were few sounds or movements from the target.

Michimori rode over to me. 'Mokuhasa tells me you are good at learning new sword strokes. You may practise if you wish.'

I curved my fingers around my sword's hilt. I remembered the Lotus Sutra, in which the Buddha says that anyone who curses the Law near the Buddha will be forgiven. But one who does injury or harm to anyone who espouses the Law will suffer greatly.

I thought of Emi's smiling face as she recited her prayers with me. I thought of Misuki, such a faithful and steadfast companion, and my beloved Tashiko, lying dead with her neck encircled by that ring of rope-torn flesh. I stared at this priest's eyes, not wide with pain and anger as they were now, but filled with glee as he filled the bath with salt.

'Yes,' I replied, in formal language. 'Thank you. I will.' I did. First the Small Priest's Robe Stroke, cutting deep into one arm. I used the Priest's Robe Stroke, slicing across his neck and other arm. I said the name of each stroke, breathing carefully, taking my time, performing each stroke meticulously.

Afterwards, Michimori cut the priest's topknot from his head. 'Your messengers proved as useful as mine. I need you to make sure that all the filth is here.' His hand swept across to the poles.

'I will, my honourable lord.' At Michimori's signal, the samurai gave way for me, and I rode down the hill to the circle. Tokikazu rode beside me, although there was no need. I directed my horse around each head, examining each face against the list I had made during my Abstention. Some were difficult to identify, distorted in death. The missing right ear lobe and the little goatee were easy to spot. I used my dagger to lift lips, checking for large front teeth, lost teeth, and to open closed eyes to find the clouded one. Each was a match, and my list complete. But for one.

'They are all there, my honourable lord. Except one. Daigoro no Goro.'

Michimori's eyes darkened. Nevertheless he spoke softly. 'There is much you do not know. It is more dangerous than I realised. This priest who arranged for your – your . . . I deeply regret your suffering. My intention was and is to shield you from danger.'

'I know, my lord. Please do not blame Captain Tokikazu. He has been attentive and cautious. He has taught me much, on and off the fields. Three Eyes is ambitious and cunning.'

'You represent a new threat to Three Eyes. It concerns the sects of priests, the Minamoto, and our emperors, especially Retired Emperor Go-Shirakawa. You are unaware of most of these matters.'

I nodded.

'There will be tutors for you once we return to Rokuhara. There, you will not be as exposed, for my own guard watches are strict and will be stricter.'

Michimori answered the unasked question: 'There will be no punishment, but more guards will be kept closer to your quarters.'

'Thank you, honourable Michimori.'

'Let us return to the procession, Northern Wife.'

We completed our journey to Rokuhara, where more lessons awaited me.

BOOK 13

I. New Work

The beginning of another month, and I had just finished the usual monthly defilement, which now happened for Misuki, Emi and me at the same time. The heavy rain, like herds of running horses on a roof, made it difficult to read, but my apartment offered comforts. Misuki and I played *go*, while Emi sewed.

Obāsan glided in. 'Captain Tokikazu slipped me a note from Governor Michimori. He wants you in Grand Room again,' she announced, handing me the sea-green paper with his special folds. The handwriting was his own. The courtly elegance of his brush shone on the textured paper like black stones arranged on white sand.

Michimori rarely sent for me at that time of day, but Obāsan usually knew in enough time to bathe, dress and prepare me without rushing. I went over to her. 'Thank you, Grandmother.' Our foreheads touched briefly, as insects drinking from flowers.

There was little time for bathing, but Misuki and Emi had taught the serving girls the rhythm of preparations. Emi would comb and dress my hair, which was no small task, with its flowing length and bulk. Number One Serving Girl readied my kimonos, while Number Two matched my shoes. Misuki prepared makeup and would write an answering note, if one was required, Emi was left to do my flowers. All had begun their tasks when Obāsan made her announcement.

'What do you know about this meeting?' I probed Obāsan.

'Nothing,' Obāsan said. 'Even the captain did not know more.'

I went as prepared as I could with my *biwa*, a ruse.

When Tokikazu came, he explained the orders. He did not stare as if he were a starving man and I the first course at a banquet. Whatever was to take place was unusual and important, despite what Obāsan had said or did not say.

As my forehead touched the floor in the Grand Room, Michimori commanded me to approach. He motioned to his guards, who retreated to the perimeter where they could see, but not hear. The only ones who remained near were Akio and Tokikazu, as usual.

Michimori moved towards me. There was no smile in his eyes, and the lines around his eyes and on his cheeks were deep. 'I need your opinion of someone and their actions. I consulted with advisers, but I would like your view.'

'My lord.'

In a lower tone he added, 'Nitta no Shibasaki from Shinanō Province has come to pay his taxes but gives little. I expected far more, for that is a well-cultivated area.'

Nitta no Shibasaki's name sounded like an almost-forgotten verse of an old childhood song. 'May I ask questions, my lord?'

He motioned with a finger.

'First, how well are neighbouring areas faring?' I asked. 'Is there a reason why some people prosper while others do not? Perhaps certain types of weather, pestilence, infestation or other conditions.'

His finger indicated that I should continue.

'Next, what does he look like? How large a man is he? What clothes does he wear, to the tiniest detail? What clothes did he wear to travel? Check the type and number of his servants, his conveyances and the provisions he brought for the journey. Their quality and quantity will yield more reliable information about his wealth than anyone else can provide. If they are lacking, I could trust small payments, regardless of climatic conditions, but if his provisions are luxurious, or his servants are fat, I would suspect deviousness.'

'Take two discreet men,' he ordered Tokikazu and Akio. 'He is a relative of Go-Shirakawa.'

Tokikazu and I bowed and listened as Michimori described our mission.

318

II. Secret Papers

Michimori spoke to Tokikazu first. 'Go to Nitta no Shibasaki's carriage. Lady Kozaishō will accompany you. If anyone asks about your activities, advise them that Lady Kozaishō, eh . . . has never seen anything so grand and wishes to inspect it closely.'

As if to seek agreement, Michimori's enquiring eyebrows became bent as trees before a storm, and I motioned my approval.

'If Lady Kozaishō does not find what she needs, escort her to Shibasaki's residence in the guest quarters. Say you heard of the loss of his *koto*. Knowing how much he loves music, at my request, you are to assist him in finding it. Say you are honoured to be of service, and do not make eye contact. Search thoroughly, Tokikazu.'

Tokikazu narrowed his eyes and pursed his lips, his unripe persimmons look. 'Akio will have a *koto* in his robes.' We bowed, hiding smiles, and left.

Escorted by Tokikazu and Akio, I walked back through the corridors of Rokuhara. First I insisted on going to my apartments where I collected sewing implements. While the samurai waited outside, I sent the serving girls and Emi out on a spurious errand. Now Misuki and I could search my hidden papers without fearing discovery. We found the log I remembered. His name was there! Nitta no Shibasaki! I knew him. I hid several papers deep in the folds of my sleeve.

We went to the stables where the carriages and palanquins were stored. Shibasaki's carriage appeared modest, but when I felt the curtains and cushions, they were made of rich fabrics. I found objects stuffed in secret places. With the samurai standing near, I used a needle and opened seams. There were coins, not only in the fabrics but deep in the stuffing. When I had finished, I carefully closed all I had opened.

Later I laid a few of the coins in Michimori's hand. I said, 'This was planned, my lord.' Relieved to avoid a direct confrontation with Nitta no Shibasaki, Michimori leaned back on his cushions.

Looking at his countenance, I thought:

> Crisp white mountain peaks
> So close to heaven when viewed
> From low in the grasses
> All the birds sing his praises
> Commendable is his face

I pulled the papers from my sleeve and shared their contents with him: Shibasaki's bragging about his many wives, their lands and his evasion of tax payments. There was also information about Shibasaki's peculiar physical desires. These I did not share.

Michimori sent his questions with only a look, and I explained about the logs I had brought from Hitomi's.

'You have confirmed my suspicions. I was unable to do this directly, as you understand. His alliances are with the Minamoto and Go-Shirakawa.'

I murmured objection to the compliment, and observed his eyes.

> The house swallow's thanks:
> For a true friend's citadel
> For sanctuary
> For the wind on which she rides
> For the rain that nourishes

'How may I show you my gratitude, house swallow?' His fingertip greeted my cheek.

I studied the warm brown eyes and blurted my secret longings. 'I am a peasant girl, who desires to speak and behave like other women here. I have no lineage and no property. The only way I can be worthy . . . is to serve and to learn.'

My mouth dried, making it hard for me to speak. 'I wish to know what the courtiers know: Chinese, poetry, classics, mathematics, rhetoric, politics, law, strategy, divination, music and medicine. I wish to learn all.'

I kept my eyes down, for this was an audacious request. Perhaps he had expected me to ask for a new kimono or trinket, but I had petitioned for larger favours. I risked his wrath and beyond.

I did not venture to look at his face. He made no sound. No command to commit *seppuku*. In the silence I let out a breath, although my eyes remained closed. I smelt the sandalwood incense of his hair. He had bent his head to me.

'If it is your wish,' Governor Michimori whispered, 'I will arrange for more tutors.' He tilted my head up with his fingers. 'However, Obāsan has already shared your love of ink and paper with me.'

'Thank you, my lord.'

'Yes.' His voice was suddenly filled with grit. Had it been there before? 'You need tutors. First, in calligraphy.'

'My lord, I did not request a calligraphy tutor, but if you wish—' I winced, attempting to keep the agitation from my face. My failures at the brush haunted me, especially in this place, where all were judged by their brush, their choice of words, even the colour and character of the paper.

'Wish? I demand it.'

I flushed at his words, which were harder than before. I was reminded of Chiba's voice, before he had hit me the first time. Inwardly, pincers gripped. The old scars on my back ached. 'I will obey.' I tasted spleen, but swallowed. 'Is there a problem?'

'Dishonesty *is* a problem.'

'My honourable lord Taira no Michimori, I do not know to what you refer.' I reverted to formal language. The air between us was frigid.

'Do you not?' He selected a few notes from the large number always piled next to him, scooped them into his hands and tossed them across to me. 'Are these yours?'

He knew! Drums resounded in my chest, cheeks scorched, high summer heat poured on my head, rivulets of sweat rolled down my back. How could he have found out? Obāsan would never have given me away. 'Yes.'

'Is this your hand?'

The room revolved, my vision in whirlpools. I stammered, 'No, my lord. It is another's.'

He pushed a brush, paper and ink to me. In his commander's voice he ordered, 'Write down one of your lovely poems.'

The brush burned like ice. I could not keep my face blank. I grunted, grimaced and wrote, trying to hear Tashiko's voice as she had taught me.

Michimori watched. My hand shook. The bird scratches I made were worse than gruesome. Every groan he emitted decreased the legibility of my characters.

When I finished, he snatched the paper. He moved his head from side to side and furrowed his brow over darkened eyes. 'The worst. My lowest rank of soldier could do better.'

Tears of disgrace cascaded. I could not keep a wobble from my chin. 'Yes, my lord.'

'This must change.' He knelt beside me, the grit gone from his voice. 'I know you will work hard with this calligraphy tutor. I cannot abide a wife whose brush is like a peasant's.'

III. Players

Back in Rokuhara we occupied the same rooms we had previously. The impermanence of life – 'the floating world', as courtiers call it – changed with the tutors and my studies. I learned to talk without using the peasant speech of my parents. The most difficult task was to eliminate the last syllable of each of my country words. Obāsan and Misuki reminded me daily, hourly, almost continuously. Over the months I heard, through Misuki, that ridicule of my language by other wives and concubines had diminished.

Misuki and I found ourselves in training every day with Tokikazu. I loved her gentleness, but on the practice field Misuki became quickly fatigued. She did not enjoy military studies.

As demanding as warrior training was for her, calligraphy proved even more perplexing to me. My handwriting was of the primitive I had been born, and mortified me. Although my speech improved my writing was abysmal.

Beautiful writing was the most important attribute of a courtier. It delineated the classes, separated the refined from the common. Misuki's brush was better than mine. Misuki had written for me, although I had not permitted the serving girls or Emi to see. Now my calligraphy tutor's pointer often met my knuckles.

My literature tutor was a polite and distant relative of Michimori. His broad, reddish nose turned upwards and wrinkled, like an old cherry, when he concentrated. He was familiar with every character ever put on paper. He puffed his cheeks and shook his jowls. 'There is so much of which you are unaware.'

I read more.

During those long months of study, he shook his head, then grunted, shook his head, then told me 'The Tale of the Genji.' Misuki and I shared titbits of it when we were exhausted from other readings. We appreciated To no Chijo's classification of women. Teasingly, after reading 'The Tale of the Genji', Misuki referred to Sadakokai as 'Fragrant Captain', but never to his face.

Some of what I learned was significant and some was, as Obāsan said, 'as useless as wet feathers'. The Gods were good to me, and I remembered most of what I read. I stuffed Chinese poetry into my sleeves to read.

Our serving girls shared my poems with other serving girls. After a time I found the courage to show a few to my poetry tutor, who intoned nasally, 'You may have a trifling talent,' and sniffed.

Although unusual for a woman, I was privileged to have a tutor in Chinese. He was delighted by his elevated status, due to Michimori's high rank, and kind to me. He wore his hair long and hanging down his back, as Obāsan wore hers. When he corrected me, especially my many writing errors, he did so as though he were saddened by my mistakes in his wonderful language. With long fingers and longer fingernails, he pointed to all the mistakes in each character and sighed. 'Write that again . . . and again.'

In his favour, he was not affiliated to either the Taira or the Minamoto, so his rebukes remained between the two of us. With the literature tutor, my mistakes travelled to others with derision. After the first month he was unable to find many.

I remained alert. Because of the looming risks of Three Eyes or his agents, I carried my sword, always. Misuki, too, carried a weapon but concealed it. She practised with me rather than with the samurai, who grew bored working at a beginner's level. Tokikazu remained with me at each session, and I relished his presence, although our camaraderie had held a different flavour since my marriage.

I agreed with Shōtoku Taishi, whom I had studied. He was the Crown Prince, the Philosopher of Righteousness who lived before the capital was in Nara, almost eight hundred years ago, and who brought Buddhism to Japan. He said, 'All men are influenced by partisanship, and few have wide vision.' Perhaps Michimori was one of the few.

IV. Number Two Serving Girl

Servants prepared special meals when the beginning of a new day and a new month or year arrived together. Steamed and pounded rice cakes had to be eaten to ensure long life and health. In addition, we ate abundant sweets: jellies, toasted acorns, pastes of beans and of seaweed, plums, even tinted and sugared rice cakes.

Misuki said, 'Eat several persimmons, for fruitfulness and happiness!' She watched me eat them, then scattered parched soybeans in our rooms to dispel *oni*.

One came anyway.

It happened while I was resting. Our last meal had been rice and red beans so I was not hungry. I gave Misuki and Emi permission to eat in their room.

Misuki returned almost immediately. 'Lady Kozaishō, the food tastes odd.'

'Eh?' I asked, imitating Michimori's style and smiling to myself.

Then I saw that Misuki's eyes shone with as much fear as they had when the *sōhei* had attacked us near their portable shrine.

'The spices overwhelmed Emi,' she said, 'and she could not eat any of the food at all. She had stopped after having eaten only a little and called the two serving girls to scold them saying, "You have made a poor selection. Or, worse, you've allowed the food to be bad."'

Misuki related all: 'I talked to each serving girl. Number One's eyes stared down in shame, failing in such an important duty. Number Two's eyes twitched. Her mouth contorted. "What is wrong with this food?" I demanded. "What has happened?" Number Two hung her head. I picked up her chin until her face was directly in front of mine. Her eyes went empty, and her spirit disappeared. I was not sure what to do. I pointed to the floor. I told them, "Stay here. Do not move or there will be severe punishments." They prostrated themselves. I said, "Take no action. Remain here. Do nothing until my return, no matter how long." Then I came to find you, my honourable Lady Kozaishō.' Misuki nodded after speaking.

'Poison,' I whispered. I called for Emi to bring boiled water while I selected the special herbs. After steeping, Misuki drank, and I helped her to vomit.

'Thank you and the Goddess of Mercy for your sensitive palate,' I said, as I wiped Misuki's face. 'Poison is probably why the food was highly spiced,' I reasoned, just loud enough for her to hear.

'We must kill the snakes among the geese before all the eggs are gone,' Misuki murmured.

We discussed a plan. I did not confide in Emi, but sent her on an errand. I did not confide in Michimori either, because his fury might have spoiled my plan. Misuki scurried to tell Tokikazu, almost always on guard near me.

When Emi returned, she held Number Two Serving Girl's brown and white cat. The two serving girls had remained prone. Misuki and I stood in front of them. Next to Misuki was the tray with the beautiful lacquered dishes holding the poisoned food. I gave the cat to Misuki and sent Emi away again.

'Thank you, Misuki,' I said, controlling my anger at seeing the serving girls on the floor. 'Now we can begin our festivities in earnest.' I motioned for the girls to rise.

Misuki held and stroked Number Two's cat. Number One cried now, the front of her tunic speckled. Number Two's face looked as though someone had pulled the skin back tightly over her skull so that her eyeballs popped out like a frog's.

I was careful to speak the opposite of my feelings, softly and slowly.

'We see no reason to blame the food on either of you. All you did was bring it. There are merely too many flavours for us to eat,' I lied. 'We wish to know who spiced it to an unacceptable level. Who was the cook? Who gave this food to you?'

I stared directly at each serving girl, and Number One suddenly blurted out all: which guard, which cook. She even reported which priest was in the cooking areas to check the special foods for the ceremonies.

Looking into Number Two's eyes I said, 'Now we understand. Misuki, give the cat to Number One Serving Girl.' Next I directed Number One, 'Hold this cat. Do not let it go.'

With the cat held down, it was Misuki who ordered Number Two Serving Girl: 'Feed the food to your cat.'

For a few moments, Number Two's eyes flashed hatred. She plucked her cat from Number One's arms and ran. I knew she would not stand for harm to come to her beloved animal. Neither had I any wish to harm an innocent cat. We merely wanted her to confess, which she did by running. Tokikazu captured her as she left. I hoped her torture would lead to information that validated Number One Serving Girl's.

After sending for Obāsan and the Woman-in-Charge-of-Rooms, I asked Number One to play the *biwa* for us while we dressed. At least I would know where and what she was doing. She played, not well. I said nothing about the unusually poor music.

When Obāsan arrived, I took her aside. 'If Number Two Serving Girl confesses . . . and . . .' I whispered the name of the priest and the cook in her ear. 'Perhaps you know someone who could attend to those two. I would be particularly interested to know with whom they have conversed.'

Obāsan pressed her wrinkled lips together tightly. Then she said, 'Ryo, my nephew. He works with that cook. Perhaps I shall visit him today.'

'Number One Serving Girl must remain closely supervised. She must never be alone. She must be with you, me or Misuki on every task until we can be rid of her.'

'My lady Kozaishō, I will search and find the best replacements for both girls. It may take a little time, but in the meantime I shall send you mine.'

'Yours?'

'My personal servants. It is better to be rid of Number One Serving Girl immediately. I will see to all.'

'Yes . . . good. Thank you, Grandmother.' As we were alone, I kissed her crinkled face.

After making further arrangements with Obāsan, Misuki and I had to leave for the General Confession Ceremonies. They took place in the palace enclosures and lasted for three consecutive nights. Emi, Misuki and I travelled in an ox cart. As usual, Obāsan's wisdom had impressed me, and I shared it with Misuki.

'I know we cannot trust the priests,' Misuki confided quietly. I told her Obāsan was hunting for new serving girls.

'I do not wish to see Number One's head on a spike,' I admitted. 'This was not a wrongdoing on her own. However, I have requested that Number Two Serving Girl is not allowed to share her failed mission with others.'

Misuki put her hand on mine. 'You are trying to remember "No Melon". "One who begrudges a single slice, will lose all!"'

'Number Two Serving Girl could not have been acting on her own.'

'She might have allowed the poisoning of her cat. She did not. Perhaps there is some kindness in her heart despite her terrible deed.' Her mouth quivered with terror. 'Kozaishō, Rokuhara contains worse people than the *sōhei* you met coming here.'

'Yes, for then we could see the enemy. Here they are invisible or identical or both. I have not yet found Three Eyes.'

I told Misuki of my intention to locate and take vengeance on the poisoner, and she agreed to assist me.

Misuki's eyes filled with a combination of the worries and distress I felt myself.

'It is more dangerous than at Hitomi's. We must remain alert always, as with an unknown first-time client,' I said.

Misuki squeezed my arm in agreement. 'Should we speak to Lord Michimori about this?'

'No. I need to seek my revenge in my own way. Michimori is too busy to be bothered with such trifles.'

'Trifles?' Her brows and mouth formed her deepest frown.

'I shall consult with Tokikazu and Akio. I rely on their wisdom.'

'Lord Michimori will not think this such a small thing. You risk his wrath.'

'I will risk it.'

The ceremonies or their holiday screens did not hold my concentration. I do not know if Misuki enjoyed them. Although Emi delighted in the festivities, she whimpered at the Horrors of Hell painted on the screens.

I did my best to think of wrongs I had done during this last year. Happily, killing an innocent cat and a not-so-innocent girl were not among them. The next two nights of General Confession were easier, but not for Emi, who had nightmares. This was an inauspicious way in which to begin the new year.

I resolved to fight my own battles and find the true poisoner myself.

V. Samurai Training

Ironically, the safest place was field training, because it was open and because many different factions were represented there. No serious mischief could be done because there were witnesses. I felt more secure there than I did in my own quarters.

There was no break from study with my warrior training. Sun Tsu's *Art of War* particularly interested Michimori. From 'The Army and Defence' in the Taihō Codes we memorised how many mounted men and foot soldiers there were in a division, how many in a regiment and in a battalion. While we both thought the Taihō Code was astoundingly dull, Sun Tsu was more difficult, since it was in Chinese. Misuki found it dreary; I thought it useful.

The practice exercises became complicated. Misuki did well in hand-to-hand techniques, but she found archery hard. Her tutor continued to remind her to 'catch the wind with her hands', but she never grasped this. When I had been a young girl it had proved difficult for me as well. The *naginata* remained unwieldy, due to my height, although I attempted it as often as I could tolerate the sniggers of those watching.

One day Akio came to the field with an odd-looking weapon. 'It is a *shobuzukuri naginata*. Tokikazu suggested it because of the shorter handle and longer blades. See,' he demonstrated, 'it makes the slashing strokes smoother.'

I took time to become familiar with it, and then practised on straw men. The quick stroke upwards towards an unprotected groin would disable anyone.

'Monks on horseback stand in the stirrups and whirl *naginata* around them,' Tokikazu told me later.

'Even with the *shobuzukuri naginata*, that would be a wide span.' I eyed the distance between me and him. 'The defence?'

He guffawed. 'Stay far away and shoot him or his horse.'

On horseback, I hit the square-shaped targets and the grass hats swinging on posts. Dogs were also used as targets but I took care not to hit their faces with special padded arrows. I hit the strips of paper hanging from a stick as often as anyone, except Tokikazu, Akio, Sadakokai and Mokuhasa. They were the best, after Michimori.

Misuki did not care for horses. She worked elsewhere. Sadakokai named her 'Lumbering Badger', which stuck. Misuki disliked his gentle mockery, but her love for me compelled her to continue.

We both revelled in the stories Tokikazu narrated as we performed these exercises. I loved to hear his voice while I watched his muscles tighten. Once he told of how the Taira and Minamoto had become bitter enemies:

Taira no Masakado, Governor of Kuanto Province, was studying in Heian-kyō. He was offended by someone in court and started a revolt, but others of the Taira Clan stopped it. Problems between the clans began when Masakado was pardoned, not punished. The Minamoto never agreed to the pardon, and from that time the two clans were bitter enemies.

In other stories he told us of the great heroes of the Hōgen and Heiji Disturbances, primarily daring deeds of Michimori's uncle, Kiyomori, who had put severed heads on spikes. I enjoyed imagining that.

Michimori often used *The Art of War* when we discussed strategies at night. Mokuhasa and Sadakokai spoke of the refinement of Michimori's swordlessness. A samurai with swordlessness proved his prowess by fighting so rapidly and soundlessly, it was as if he wielded no sword at all.

BOOK 14

I. Temples

A few Taira commanders returned to Rokuhara, boasting of their latest victory over the Minamoto. Unfortunately the Minamoto had not retreated. Instead they scattered, like pheasants, making ensuing battles impossible.

In the corridors, on the *watadono*, in the gardens and on the practice field, arguments flew about whether or not there would be war. Misuki said she had discovered knowledge of the probable war. She had returned from one of her long rides with Sadakokai. 'I saw them!'

'Saw whom?'

'The birds. Swarms of bramblings, *atori*. Sadakokai saw them too.'

'Swarms?'

'Yes. Hundreds and hundreds. They attacked each other among the branches for twigs to make nests. You know what they say?'

She did not wait for my answer.

'When swarms of brambling begin their life-and-death struggle for twigs to roost, the noise, the competition and the ferocity are so great that to witness such an event presages war.'

'Truly?' Misuki nodded her head with great solemnity. 'So it is recorded through history.'

I could hardly keep the corners of my mouth from lifting. Then I recalled her premonitions before Michimori rescued me from Hitomi.

'Oh Kozaishō, much more than war. It is *mappō*. Our world is so defiled, there is almost no redemption. The bramblings prove it. We must concentrate on the thirty-two physical signs of Buddhahood. Invoke the name of Amida Buddha and meditate on his deathbed scene. Do this tonight and every morning. Promise!'

Despite this talk, I had my own war, and I swore to follow through on the promise to myself – to find and remove the poisoner.

He or she would point to Goro, my ultimate goal. I discussed my plans with Misuki and Obāsan.

'When I confronted former Number Two Serving Girl, she named a cook and a priest as conspirators.'

'My nephew, Ryo, works with the cook. If he visited the priest, he could discover the person for whom they both work.'

'Yes,' Misuki added. 'Such a person must indeed be the evil-doer.'

Three days later, Obāsan whispered to me, 'I arranged for Ryo to meet you on the field where you can be private. He suggested he disguise himself as a servant. He will be the one today to bring refreshments.'

'How will I know him from the many true servants?'

Obāsan's grin moved up to her eyes. 'White hair, like me.'

Beyond his white hair, he bore no resemblance to Obāsan. He murmured the names of the cook and the priest to identify himself to me. 'To whom do they answer?' I asked, with a cup in front of my lips.

'Norahito,' he said, with his head still down. He had done his part, and I returned to the practice field. Michimori had included that name in the list of possible traitors.

I decided to create a unique set of robes. I left the selection of fabrics to Sadakokai and Tokikazu, since the former had access to the splendid fabrics used by *sumō* wrestlers, and I appreciated the latter's efforts to assist me. Following the selection of fabrics, I would arrange for the robes to be sewn. I required a craftsman whose reputation and, most importantly, loyalty were flawless. Obāsan knew of the right seamstress. Fabric selected and a robe constructed then sent to our poisoner as a gift by a neutral but important figure: that was how I would trap the guilty one.

The political games of the emperor seemed to be beyond the Taira Clan, like a child grasping for fruit on a tall tree. The emperor's regent sent to the city of Nara a messenger, who was subjected to grave insults, including the cutting off of his top knot. Monks painted a face and wrote 'Kiyomori's head' on a wooden *kemari* ball. They kicked and beat it around a field. This was Lord Kiyomori! The grandfather of the emperor! How hideously disrespectful, especially for monks.

Rumours circulated that Kiyomori was ill, which made the chatter of bad fortune worse, if that were possible. Michimori and I visited his uncle on his sickbed. Kiyomori's estate demonstrated perfection in every corner: the lily-covered pond, with its curved bridge, invited strolling; manicured trees and bushes reflected how Heaven might look; abundant flowers drew butterflies. When Michimori met me outside his uncle's mansion, he told me that the Chief Constable of the Yamato Province would mediate. This situation with the monks demanded delicacy, and this constable had earned a reputation for diplomacy.

'Yes,' Michimori muttered the next night. 'There can be no violence. My uncle shows admirable restraint, although the monks kicked the ball painted with his face.'

'I have faith in your wisdom, but I wonder if you would exercise such restraint if it were *your* head.'

At this Michimori laughed for the first time since his uncle had become ill.

Later Michimori related the Yamato chief's tale to me in a high voice, imitating the chief. ' "I and my five hundred men arrived at South Gate of Kōfuku Temple. I received the usual greeting. The gate opened and a monk showed a small party of us to the gallery courtyard. With no warning, the monks attacked us from all sides." '

'How treacherous,' I said to Michimori, trying not to laugh at his falsetto.

'No. It was stupid.' Michimori had returned to his normal voice. 'The chief should not have trusted the monks.'

'What happened?'

'The monks captured sixty of the chief's men and decapitated them.'

I gasped at the grave insult. 'What action will your uncle take?'

'He ordered thousands of soldiers to Nara. My cousin Shigehira is now Commander-in-Chief, and I . . . am deputy Commander.'

'I am fearful for your new honour.'

'Will you come?'

'Yes, but please honour me by saying *sutra*s to protect yourself.'

My plans for the special robes were postponed. As we travelled to Nara and Kōfukuji, I shared a short story of monks' contentiousness in the hope of decreasing some tension and anger.

Not so long ago, two priests disagreed on everything. One believed in one scripture, while the other believed in another. Their great rivalry culminated in a contest. Each priest was given one *chō* of land to plant rice.

The first priest planted, irrigated and said prayers. The second seemingly did nothing. So while the one *chō* of the first priest's grew rapidly, only weeds grew in the second priest's land. Nothing grew except a gourd tree, which completely covered the entire *chō*. When the first priest harvested his *chō* of rice, everyone noticed the second priest's tree, heavy with large gourds. Before the first priest finished harvesting, someone cut down one of the second priest's gourds. It contained more than five *tō* of rice. Indeed, each gourd contained at least five *tō* of rice. The second priest boasted of the strength of his scriptures.

With this reminder of their staunch rivalry, our troops journeyed south to the Nara temples. At Kōfuku Temple, Commander-in-Chief Shigehira divided the soldiers into two columns, led by himself and Michimori. We began at the Hour of the Hare, not quite dawn. The fighting commenced with whistling gourd arrows shot from both sides.

A pitiful experience. The Taira were mostly mounted with our bows ready. The *sōhei* were all on foot. It was almost as easy as it was on the practice field, although there were more of them. Tokikazu and Akio stayed close to me, but there was no need: I fought well enough.

As taught, I waited to fight until someone announced his name to me, and then I declared my name. My long hair sailing in the crisp wind startled many monks, and they became easy opponents. I hoped to hear the traitors' names, but I did not. In my mind, their names were all 'Goro' or 'Norahito'.

The combat persisted for most of the day. Towards evening Shigehira ordered a fire to be lit near one of the temple's gates. A monk with a crooked nose slunk near it at this time, but he disappeared into the throng before I could shoot. The hostilities had ceased, fortunately, because my concentration had shrunk to a fierce pounding fist between my eyes, commanding that I locate Goro.

The soldier who lit the fire near the gate also set fire to one of the small shelters. The morning's stiff breeze hurled furious evening gusts, spreading the fire to the temple itself. The east and west chapels, as well as the pagodas, transformed into evil beauties, horrible red claws grasping for stars in the blackness. The night came awake, with the shrieks and screams of the confined monks and hundreds of assistants, apprentices, little boys. Their high-pitched wailing lacerated the stillness, like knives piercing flesh.

There was no opportunity to put out the fires because of the winds. By morning almost everyone and everything lay scorched in malodorous mounds, blackened stacks or shrivelled bundles. We marched in silence back to Rokuhara.

Because of the death of the previous emperor and national mourning, only meagre celebrations were planned for the approaching new year. In his apartments Michimori whispered, 'This is an ominous way to end the year. What will the Gods have for us?'

The bramblings and now this.

II. Secret Door

Late one night after sunset, Tokikazu rushed past the guard into my gardens. In my ear, as soft as the purr of a kitten, he said, 'Please forgive my intrusion, but Michimori requests your presence early tomorrow morning.'

I examined the tiny buds that had appeared on a branch, and remained silent, saying, 'Yes,' with only the flicker of an eye. His hand lingered on my shoulder, but then he departed.

Michimori required little sleep and rose early. Long before dawn Tokikazu safeguarded me through the corridors. 'There is a tailor who has what you seek.' He referred to the fabric for my plan.

'Where and when?'

'At the emperor's next art contest?'

'Too public. My garden. The Hour of the Monkey.' At that time of night I could leave Michimori and return before he awakened.

'As you wish, Kozaishō. But have you considered informing Michimori of this? He and others may be able to help.'

'Please, dear Tokikazu, do not share our plans with others. The more people who know, the more danger for us.'

'Us? For *you*.'

'I wish to do this myself, for my own honour. How much honour is there if I allow someone else to fight my battle?'

'I understand, Kozaishō.'

'I know you do. Thank you.' As I left, he combed his fingers through my hair, so alike to Michimori's touch, that it chilled me.

Three six-part folding screens, each made of split bamboo and set end to end, stretched the entire width of Grand Room. From there, I could view what happened without being seen. Michimori would be able to say truthfully that he had not seen me enter, since I had entered earlier. How clever he was, thinking around corners.

The morning gathered my full attention, like a courtly dance with costumes and singing. Many people waited for audience. Reports of rice and taxes, and phrases of 'noble loyalists', 'rebels' and 'locals' filled the air. I was my husband's second pair of eyes and ears.

Circumstances often compelled our inner circle to speak of business in public, particularly during the Imperial Tournaments. Sadakokai presented an idea: a code, natural names for the Taira Clan. Akio suggested the Minamoto be named after the hours.

I gave Sadakokai the name Paulownia, after the beautiful and useful tree; Mokuhasa, Sea Turtle for his broad back; Emi, Lotus; Tokikazu, Genji, because they were both philanderers; Akio, Oyster, for his reserve; and Misuki, Lumbering Badger, as before. Everyone refused to tell me my sobriquet, even when I probed.

III. A Game of *Go*

Tokikazu assumed more of my archery tutoring and Akio surrendered it graciously. He allowed his eyebrows to move down whenever Tokikazu was not looking, though.

The Bowmen's Wager on the Eighteenth day of the First Month concluded the new year celebrations. I joined the festival, despite my ongoing search for the poisoner. The emperor and his officers of the Inner and Middle Palace Guards attended in a great procession with many palanquins. I rode out into the country with the aristocracy, Tokikazu always at my elbow. Each ranked man wore bright courtly clothing. The flashing scarlets and crimsons, lapis lazulis and hydrangeas, peaches and oranges, all winter silks, paraded in a cacophony of brilliance across the archery fields.

When I said to Misuki, 'The male birds' feathers are exhibited with great flamboyance,' she giggled – softly, thank the Gods.

The tiny *mato*, placed long distances away, provided the entertainment. Two teams competed against each other, wagers abounding. Michimori and I placed a small one with each other, a story against a kimono. Michimori proved implacable and wagered that his own team would lose, despite my teasing and calling him disloyal. He merely shrugged, with a grin as usual, palms open.

I refused to wager against Tokikazu or Akio. I did not worry about the winner. Misuki and I played for *geta*. Emi wagered her handmade flowers against ices mixed with liana syrup, her new favourite, even in the brisk weather. Misuki and Sadakokai wagered also, but I chose to ignore them.

The crisp sound of arrows arcing through the bitter air was exhilarating, but made my fingers itch to shoot. Everyone's shouts and urgings competed with the arrows' flight and the *thunks* of their impact on the *mato*.

Losers were forced to drink a huge 'cup of defeat'. The winners received their prizes: imperial *shurikens*, with the chrysanthemum emblem, silks, lacquerware and arrows. Then all proceeded to the banquet for which I was glad; the cold had given me an appetite. Beautiful men and women performed courtly dances while we feasted on *mochi* cakes, nuts and fish, pheasant and quail, sweet potatoes, aubergines, carrots and onions and *sake*, much *sake*. Michimori drank a great quantity, and his eyes wavered, but his feet did not. Neither did his hands, and alone later, he feasted on me.

The untimely death of Emperor Takakura at the end of the first month was followed by Chancellor Kiyomori's death in the third. A mourning bell rang through his family's hearts – ear-splitting, public and painful. Michimori grieved, and I could not assuage his sorrow, although I surrounded him with song, dance, poetry and pleasuring.

Prayers to say, places to visit and processions to watch interrupted my studies. Thank the Gods, Obāsan and the court ritualist told me what to wear, what to say, with whom to speak, and which colours I could and could not use in my robes. Black was now the colour for funerals. Although it was tedious, I learned.

The restrained Third Month Third Day celebration compared poorly with what I remembered at Chiba's *shōen*. No monks attended the celebration at Michimori's. I remained alert, although I was not to be one of the dolls. My memories of Tashiko as a doll were easier to contemplate now, but I knew her spirit could not rest until I had completed my vengeance for her death. My chest tightened at this failure. Out of habit, out of desire to honour my beloved, I searched the crowds for the crooked nose, monk or not.

The *kuge* watched paper dolls floating along garden streams. Later I received some as gifts and gave one to Misuki, Emi, and each of my new serving girls. Cooks created treats, *hishi-mochi*, diamond-shaped cakes coloured red, white, and green. I recalled how Tashiko explained, 'Red chases evil spirits away, white for purity, green for health.' Cooks also prepared *sakura-mochi*, bean paste-filled rice cakes with cherry leaves, which had been a favourite with Emi.

The Buddhist monasteries blew wet snow on to this mountain of intrigue with their disfavour. Rumours spread that the Taira had angered the Gods with Kiyomori's illness and death as proof.

During the nights Michimori and I reviewed these affairs and strategic players over and over again. One: our strengths included the regent, the son-in-law of Michimori's uncle, although he was young for such a post. Two: our followers were loyal. Three: our samurai had trained well, and previous battles had hardened them. Four: Michimori sent messengers to the monasteries to repair the damage to relationships. Five and Six: the Taira had defeated the Minamoto before. Twice.

Tracing my face with his fingers, Michimori explained with a glint, 'As in a game of Go, one should always have pieces that can move in numerous directions.'

I remembered Tashiko teaching me the same. I no longer felt the deep bite of longing for her memory. I cared now for Michimori, observed his strengths and ignored his difficulties. I remembered what Obāsan shared: 'Michimori has the Majestic Calm of a great leader and his essence is Pure Tranquillity. Depend on him for the clean action from a pure spirit without emotion.' I did.

The Taira Council met just days after the death of Michimori's uncle, and I attended behind the screens. Munemori, named Purple Grass, because his decisions proved equivocal, claimed to be Kiyomori's successor.

Purple Grass shared Kiyomori's last words: 'Taira no Kiyomori was happy to have served the Imperial House.'

Murmurings of agreement filled the room of the Taira Council.

'Kiyomori spoke of his honour in attaining the highest rank a commoner could attain.'

Mutterings again filled the room with nods now almost blowing a breeze. Some of the men displayed themselves like the mating crested ibis. I stifled a laugh, remembering Misuki's giggles at the Bowman's Wager and Michimori mocking his uncles and cousins. How dense the atmosphere had grown.

'Did he have any requests?' Shigehira, now called Oak, said.

'Yes,' Purple Grass said. 'He wished for the head of Minamoto no

Yoritomo. His final wish was to have Yoritomo's head hung on his tomb.'

This stopped all. The silence was as thick as a wild bamboo grove.

Oak looked at all present. He sighed for everyone to hear. 'It is clear we must prepare for war again.'

So the Clan did.

After the meeting I trudged to my honourable lord's apartments, not matching his brisk stride as I usually did. He left a trail of anger and bitterness, with his usual sandalwood scent. The fragrance and thoughts of war slowed my feet.

Upon our arrival in the apartments, a servant removed Michimori's outer formal garments. Although his favourite censer had been lit, he went out to the gardens. I trailed behind him. He paced along each path to the ponds and bridges. I did not attempt to keep up, but I did listen.

Pounding one fist into another, Michimori ranted, 'The Minamoto – especially Yoritomo! He is cunning. We should have named him Fox, not Go-Shirakawa.'

He stormed back into his apartments. I followed again, at a safe distance. He reached into his *hoeki no hō*, jerked out a map and slammed it on to the table.

'Look!' He jabbed a finger at the map, prodding each specific point. 'He is no longer here . . . or here . . . or there!'

Unfamiliar with the terrain, I followed until he pointed to a place I recognised. The markings on this map created a flat picture for me. I grasped the topography. 'Michimori,' I said, almost under my breath.

He raised his face from the map, and our eyes met.

'Remember I am your Hunter's Dog. I will be the samurai to sit behind any screen wherever and whenever you need me. I will be the samurai to fight beside you until your uncle's last wish is fulfilled.'

He unclenched his fists. Tears streamed in rivulets over those dark cheeks, and he lifted me to his face and sobbed into my neck. 'I fear we are doomed without my uncle.'

I wept also. The same dread had rung in me.

Gion's bell tolls
The procession of

345

Crested ibis
Strut and parade by
Driving us into downfall

The air had warmed by the Fifth day of the Fifth Month. There had been no festivals recently because the nation remained in mourning, but now the Tango Festival had returned. I received many flowers, even from Emi, probably after prompting. With the beautiful irises, despite the impending conflict, I thought myself most fortunate. Some stalks were white, like fresh snow, some golden, like sunshine; the rest were as purple as the angry sea before an autumn storm.

'We must cover the roofs,' Misuki insisted. She obscured them with iris leaves and mugwort branches. She pushed irises and mugwort into my hair, attached them to my pillows, wrapped them around my scabbard and stuck them on Dragon Cloud's saddle and throughout my palanquin.

'You do not have time to become ill,' Misuki chided. She clicked her tongue, reminding me of Mother, which stopped any arguments. I followed her instructions.

All wives, concubines and ladies-in-waiting attended a shortened Flower-viewing Ceremony. Our sweet Emi did not remember the Tango Festival from last year or understand what the imperial tournaments were, yet she clapped and laughed and bobbed her head at the music, dancing and painting from Chinese models. She tired easily. Accordingly, we sent her back to our quarters with an appropriate escort.

Most conversations in the fields concerned swordplay or poetry. Tokikazu wanted Minamoto no Yoshinaka to be called 'Rat'.

'N-N-No,' Sadakokai disagreed. 'I think he should be called "Hare" because he ran away when he approached our troops, just like that timid creature.'

Akio and Michimori laughed.

Then Michimori said, 'Let us keep that.'

Tokikazu's lips merged into a flat line, and his precision was less than perfect on his next shot.

III. Pretence and Counsel

Encouraged and supported by my companions, I lunged forward in my plans. Emi, Misuki and I could have died terrible deaths from the poisoned food. Those thoughts kicked my stomach like a heavy *kemari* ball.

Late one day Tokikazu escorted me out of Grand Room, and gestured with our predetermined signal, meaning that the clothing was ready. I drank the infusion of herbs that would keep me awake. In the middle of that night I left Michimori and crept into the designated corridor. Akio and Sadakokai were mountains against the faint light. We held up lamps to see the magnificent cloth, examining it thoroughly to remember each detail. The thick damask lay across our hands, heavy with embroidered trees and cranes. Its blues would fit perfectly into nearly any layering of robes.

I dared not make a sound, but I searched the eyes of Akio and Sadakokai, then bowed with gratitude. A robe of this cloth, given to Norahito as a gift by one of our own neutral priests, would bait my trap. I returned to Michimori's side before he had stirred.

On the practice field the next day, Tokikazu nodded approvingly. He said, in the formal way, 'My lady, it is my sincere wish that you enjoy your trip to the Kitano Shrine.'

The cue.

Misuki and I shared an ox cart, without Emi or the serving girls, for the short excursion to Kitano Shrine and its red- and white-blossomed plum trees. I prayed to Tenjin, spirit of the scholar and poet Sugawara no Michizane, the God of Calligraphy. I required His help with my poor brush. On our return from the shrine, Sadakokai rode casually past.

Behind the ox cart's curtains I took off my robes and gave them to Misuki to wear. My armour had been easily concealed underneath my layered robes. I dropped away from the procession where Sadakokai waited with a horse. We rode out of range of others and hobbled our mounts behind a tight copse of trees near a stream and shadowed our prey, an ox cart with several men.

Would this fight avenge us? Would Goro be there? Would I be able to kill him? I worked to calm my thrashing heart. Akio came up beside me and placed a hand on the back of my saddle. 'My lady Kozaishō, you have allies here if you want or need them.'

My eyes met his with thanks. 'This is an act I need to perform alone. That is why I have not informed my lord Michimori.'

Akio nodded, as did Sadakokai. I hoped they would not interfere. Where was Tokikazu? I did not risk asking Akio.

The ox cart travelled up the stream bank away from the mud. Two men climbed out, perhaps for a drink of water, perhaps to stretch their legs, more likely to plot and scheme against the Taira Clan. I saw only their backs. One was a man I had never before set eyes on, but I had held his offence in my mind for a long time. The brocade of his robe was embroidered with trees and cranes. This was the poisoner, the traitor.

Walking towards Norahito I called out my name, as I had in battles. He twisted towards me and placed his feet in the mud. He heaved his sword out of its scabbard – knuckles pale from gripping too tightly – eyes wide and dark. I had surprised him.

I took a defensive stance. The second man ran away with a shriek. Norahito bellowed and attacked. My Priest's Robe Stroke cut deeply through the traitor's flesh from his neck to his belly. His sword dropped into the mud. Blood seeped through the gorgeous cloth across his chest, paying for his attempt on three women's lives. Upright, he wavered, his eyes grew larger, gazing at me with malice.

'Why poison me? Who was behind this?'

His eyes glared. Swollen red. 'Had many collaborators.' Then he fell into the mire, face down.

Remembering Tokikazu's advice, I stood near, my sword ready to strike, my eyes focused for any movement. None. Yet I had wanted to question him, gain the information that would lead me to Three Eyes. Now this lead was gone, with a new cast of demons.

When Sadakokai and Akio returned, they were calm. The blood spatter on their robes informed me that they had dispatched the other men.

'Do we kill his servants to keep them quiet or can they be paid?'

'We can p-p-pay them, my lady,' Sadakokai said, and motioned to a bag of coins hanging at his waist.

'Do I need to send my sword to the polisher?' I wondered, as we rinsed our face and hands in the stream.

'Yes, my lady,' Akio said, 'when we return to Rokuhara.'

I had not realised I had spoken aloud. 'Shall I?'

'I know a polisher who will not talk.'

'Will anyone be waiting for us along our route home?'

'There were only f-f-four, now gone.'

'Thank you, honourable Akio, honourable Sadakokai.' I bowed deeply to both men before mounting my horse.

After I had stolen into my ox cart, we returned to Rokuhara. Later Akio rode beside the cart, and his eyes said I had taken the Right Action. I appreciated Akio and Sadakokai, but yearned for Tokikazu's companionship.

I pretended to have undergone the monthly defilement and a priest with the same reputation for silence as the polisher and the tailor cleansed me of the blood. Satisfied that I had protected those around me from at least this one traitor, I said special prayers for Tashiko, whom I had not safeguarded. I gave thanks and lit candles to the Buddha for my courage and His blessings, still wondering why Norahito had attempted to kill me and, besides Three Eyes, who else had been behind his action.

Most days Michimori requested my presence in Grand Room. Afterwards we returned to his quarters, where we whispered about the issues, the strategies and the people. Sometimes we giggled like girls over the antics we had witnessed.

'Tomorrow I hear the case of a wife who ran away and married another man. What do you say?'

'If the woman had at least one year to respect this man, and did not, the second husband should keep her. Married more than five years, the

349

marriage should be dissolved with no penalty. Less than five years, the new husband should compensate the first.'

How wondrous to be asked my thoughts, to be cared for and considered. The Gods had truly listened to me on the day I had run from Three Eyes' black horse. I never experienced hunger now or ate boiled-earth soup, although my tongue still remembered the taste. Thanks to you, Earth Gods! And now I had Michimori, a husband, protector and mentor. I studied his handsome face.

Tokikazu continued my martial-arts training with Akio. A priest, skin wrinkled like last year's peaches, continued my religious education. My lessons frequently included the music of his snoring.

Michimori shared more of his burdens with me as he grew confident of my abilities and knowledge, and I became secure in his respect and trust, taking refreshment in his private rooms. One night he grabbed a paper and shook it in the air towards the west, in the direction of the palace. An unusual display of temper.

'This is a new edict by the regent!'

I waited until the emotion had left his face. In private, Michimori did not often agree with the decisions his uncles and cousins made.

He glared at the edict, eyebrows down. 'Now everyone is gathering, like geese to eat.'

'Does this mean that Retired Emperor Go-Shirakawa, Fox, is renegotiating the Taira lands?' I touched the back of his clenched hand with my index finger. This was an attack on our Clan. Yes, Taira had become my clan due to my great sympathy for my husband.

He said, 'There is much honour but little sword among us. It had better change, and soon.'

IV. Birth Anniversary and The Coin

Michimori and I formed a single skilled archer with our synchronicity. He educated me in the partisan histories, language and innuendoes. I taught him that someone who bragged of conquests and wealth, yet wore low-quality silk was a liar. The way a head was held, the darting of eyes, the rapidity of blinks yielded information about a speaker's honesty. Michimori and I conversed and compared notes, our postulations and theories. We blended into better friends than Tashiko and I had been.

I became aware that my feelings for him had changed, and I wrote to him in my much-practised and not-much-improved brush:

> Winter chills dissolved
> Brown tree limbs against blue sky
> Now spring has thawed all
> Green growing all around me
> Spring's sun is your countenance

I planned an elaborate celebration for his birth anniversary with food and fine *sake*. It coincided with the Second Day of the Bird, the Kamo Festival, in the Fourth Month. Musicians, dancers, jugglers and players participated, since the massive and country-wide forty-nine-day Funeral Rites for Michimori's uncle had finished. Multi-coloured hollyhocks

351

bedecked everything: clothes, buildings, houses, carriages and palanquins, while most people's heads and necks were garlanded.

In the morning we travelled to the palace where the exquisite *bagaku*, the courtly dances, were performed.

'This is the left style of *bagaku*,' Tokikazu said, near me as usual.

'What is the difference between the left and right styles?' I asked, and Akio leaned forward to listen.

'The left style is favoured by the emperor, because it originates from China and Dai Viet rather than Koryō and north-east China.'

This meant nothing to me.

At the Hour of the Horse, with the sun directly above us, a great parade twined to the Lower Kamo Shrine. I scoured the packs of priests, all in headscarves or cowls, for the deformed nose that was seared into my mind. The dust bothered Misuki, but not me. Thousands of people and rows upon rows of carriages waited. My hand was wrapped around the handle of my sword, ready to strike.

The string of imperial envoys in elaborate clothing carried the emperor's gifts to the Gods for Purification and prayer. Tokikazu remained close and conversed with me, studiedly casual. He was in or near my carriage all the time. Which of those veiled monks was Goro? My fingers tightened around an imaginary bow.

After the several days of festivity, I went to Michimori's chambers as usual. He said, mostly to himself, 'The imperial envoys brought superior gifts from the emperor this year to Taka-Okami, the Dragon-God-Residing-on-the-Mountain, the God of Rain and Snow. Our western provinces are in drought.'

'Is that why I see so many farmers in the city?'

'Yes, we need rain. Badly. My provinces produce little rice.'

Sitting next to him, I wished him a joyous birth anniversary. 'I have something to say. I have wanted to tell you for some time, but decided to wait for a propitious day.'

He sat up and gazed directly at me. 'Yes?' he whispered, in formal language, which honoured me.

'When I first saw you in Fukuhara, you asked me to tell you what was in my heart. I said that there were admiration, respect, gratitude and . . . fear. That has changed, my honourable lord,' I answered, also in formal language.

He leaned over and placed my hand across his broad palm. His gaze penetrated my skin. 'Yes?' he whispered again. His voice swept me into him.

'Now there are admiration, respect and gratitude, but no fear. And, further, I . . . There is . . . I have . . . sympathy for you.'

I waited in silence, believing this would please him and because I did not know how he would react. He stood up. Silent.

Had I displeased him with this reminder of my previous feelings? Would he be angry, annoyed or satisfied?

He thrust his large hands around me and lifted me off the floor. Thundering, guffawing, he threw me into the air repeatedly, catching me each time as if I were a pillow. Placing me on the *futon*, he moved closer and loosened my clothing. Holding me, he stroked my face and body, and I did the same for him.

He placed his face against my neck; his tears wet my skin. We looked into each other's spirits. We pledged devotion, as I had with Tashiko but had long ago given up hope of experiencing again. When we quieted for the night, I presented him with a poem I had written for him with my new brush, which I had practised over and over until it was almost acceptable. With Obāsan's connections, I had located some beautiful blue paper without him knowing and also enclosed a crane's feather:

An empty nest waits
The cranes return for each spring
Two fly side by side, Wing edges almost touching
Each knowing the way home

He read it several times, touching my hair with one hand and holding the poem with the other. As he began stroking me, he said quietly, 'We finally feel the same. When trouble comes to you – and I know it will – allow me to be a full partner in your plans, not simply in the background. My loyal samurai were disguised as servants to Norahito. My fighting iris, you might have been hurt, or worse. My soul could not live, if you were not with me.'

Tears trickled, but I managed to say, 'Nor I you, my lord.'

Soon my head swirled as his sturdy hands fondled my breasts and hips. We satisfied each other meticulously, both weeping for rapture.

Every day I recited a *sutra* from the Lotus Sutra to protect Michimori: *atte natte nunatte anado nadi kunadi.*

While I no longer feared him, my new feelings increased my fears for him.

Summer carried harsher droughts throughout the west, with famine and plague. Nonetheless I continued learning from my tutors and in martial arts. I attempted to focus on these activities, not on the horrors of the city.

Crickets shrilled and shrieked on the practice field from midday to evening. Summer was gone. Tokikazu and the other samurai, including Akio, were pleased with my new skills, my bow and sword and sometimes my writing.

Tokikazu approached, almost touching. 'You are evolving. Near swordlessness with your sword, Kozaishō. What the Chronicles call "the wondrous power to vanish suddenly".'

Akio stepped closer and scowled at him. Tokikazu strolled away.

The returning wild geese created a dark grey cloud covering the sky when we stopped to take refreshment one day in autumn. Tokikazu and I, at his request, walked far away from the others, although Akio, ever vigilant, monitored us from a distance. With his back to Akio, Tokikazu reached into his quiver. 'This is for you to keep.'

'What is it?' I asked, of the closed fist he held in front of me.

'It is a rice ball with a Chinese coin in it.' He lowered his voice, which I thought odd since we were at a distance from others. 'The Taikan *tsuho* is a coin with a square centre.'

'Thank you,' I answered, not understanding the gift, but aware of his feelings for me. I hoped it was not to buy my favours.

He kept enough space between us to satisfy Akio. 'This is for you to keep. If you ever need me to come to you, send this coin to me, so I will know it is you and not a spy. It will be a signal between us. See? It is marked here on the edge so I will know it and that it is from you only.'

He told me this story:

Two samurai friends betrothed their newborn children. In good faith, the son's father gave a golden pin to the girl's father.

Mysteriously the son's entire family soon disappeared without a word.

Seventeen years later the betrothed daughter, still faithful, died from sorrow. The golden pin was buried with her. Two months later, the son returned, telling of his family's move, their poverty and the deaths of his parents.

The samurai allowed the boy to live in the house near their garden. However, the older daughter had already died. When the samurai family returned from a pilgrimage, their younger daughter dropped something. The boy picked it up, not knowing it was the golden pin.

That night the younger daughter came to the garden house and threatened the boy with dishonour if he did not make love with her. After many nights, the boy found he loved this daughter.

Realising he could not marry because of his betrothal to her older sister, they fled, but after a year, the younger daughter feared for her parents and they returned. The young man approached the samurai to apologise for his sins. The samurai, surprised, explained that the younger daughter was still in their home, deathly ill. She had been sick for year. The young man checked, and the younger daughter was not outside.

Suddenly the younger daughter appeared, in good health, holding the golden pin. She explained that the older sister's spirit had lived in her for the year to appease her grief. If the boy married the younger sister, the older one would leave and go to her a final rest.

Unbelievable as it was, the golden pin was evidence.

'So we may meet in the next life. This coin will be our golden hairpin.' He reached to touch me, then lowered his hand.

'Thank you,' I answered, letting the meaning of his words reach my heart. 'You give much honour. My heart spills with your generosity.' No one needed to know that a significant event had just taken place.

I returned to Michimori and the others, working with the spear in a far-off corner of the fields. 'As you may be aware, my dear Kozaishō, Michimori was not allowed to go to Echigo Province, where he would certainly have been of much help.' Tokikazu continued the conversation in which we were supposed to have been engaged.

'Yes. He was upset, so frustrated. I thought he would thrash the walls.'

'That will be why he attacked the straw men for so long. He covered a whole field with straw before he had finished.'

I looked at Tokikazu in discomfort. We both cared for Michimori deeply. We did not speak of the new Taira leader, Purple Grass, who lacked subtlety and knowledge of strategy. I doubted he had ever read *The Art of War*.

'Our staunch ally, Jō no Sukenaga, was killed in battle with the Minamoto Rat.'

'It is difficult to believe Rat and his army have not only been in many provinces but as far north as Echigo.'

'That is why I gave you the coin.'

Rokuhara was like an ancient animal shelter, every corner filled with spiders and flies. When I returned to my rooms, I did not know if I was the spider or the fly. I did not know if a bell remained where it was left, or whether everything had become a web, ready to catch any of us if we lapsed into the slightest inattention.

VI. Gifts

Late in the day or in the early morning, depending on Michimori's audiences and other court duties, Tokikazu, Akio and I worked on the practice field. As my ease with Michimori increased, so it did with these samurai. More accepted now, I remembered that only recently I had held no rank.

The Festival of the Weaver, the Seventh day of the Seventh Month, approached. Everyone watched the skies where the two stars, the lovers, the Weaver and the Herdsman, met. Like the emperor, Michimori spread leaves in the gardens and prepared for a sky-watching party, including special entertainment and food. Music was to be played all night, and the Magpie Dance, which I had never seen, would be performed. Misuki was praying for sewing and weaving activities. I planned to pray for music and poetry; my poor brush was better, but still not suitable.

Tokikazu managed to sneak me away without Akio and led me on a tour of the sword foundry. I had been careful not to be alone with him – his reputation as a libertine fuelled Misuki's gossip. However, his behaviour of late had been entirely correct.

Observing the prayers and rituals before forging a sword was like being a little girl again, in a shrine with my birth family. The rituals and chanting comforted me, yet memories of my family saddened me. The assistants rested until the master folded the hot metal. The rhythm of their mallets pounding relaxed me. The fire recalled the strength of Amaterasu, the Sun Goddess, early days at Chiba's *shōen* – and my plans for Goro. If fire could mould plain metal into the soul of a samurai, perhaps my plans for

Norahito's associates and Goro's destruction could be fashioned to protect me.

The next day Akio took me aside. 'After archery practice you should go to the shed across from the pavilion. We have a guest with a crooked nose you might be interested in visiting. Do not worry. The gift is well wrapped . . . and guarded.' He smirked.

Crooked nose! Goro – here? I shivered, suddenly cold. 'Why can I not go now?'

'We want to maintain as much secrecy as possible, little one.' He used his old name for me. 'Keep to your normal routine and be mindful. You do not have "bad days" with the bow any more.'

Practice consumed every arrow ever created for the entire city. I demonstrated no 'bad day', thanks to Akio's admonishments and my determination. Goro's face as the target assisted my aim. When would everyone else leave?

Hours later, after the field had emptied, Michimori and I walked past the pavilion to the shed. Tokikazu and Sadakokai stood, daggers and swords at the ready, attending a fettered and muffled man in priests' clothing. They barely took their gaze from their prisoner as we came in.

'Yes, honourable Lord Taira no Michimori.' Tokikazu addressed my husband formally.

'How is our "friend" doing?' Michimori sneered.

'He refuses to confess. He maintains his innocence.'

'Pull down that gauze. Let my lady look upon that face.'

The muscles of my legs and arms tightened and I was unsure that I could walk. I was to avenge Tashiko, Emi and myself. My honour would be restored.

I feasted my eyes on the face of the priest with the broken nose.

Every tight muscle relaxed. He bore a remarkable resemblance to Goro. I understood why Tokikazu had mistaken him for Goro. 'This is not he.'

Heads turned to Michimori for direction.

'Untie him, have him swear an oath of silence, then send him with a small escort to the monastery near Ise. That will be enough distance.'

Because of the formality of the situation, I did not cry but I wanted to scream. Not him! Where was he? I needed his head on a spear before my spirit could rest, before Tashiko's spirit could rest, before my honour could be restored.

Misuki explained to me that it was customary to offer gifts on the day after the Festival of the Weaver. I managed to find her a new robe and a writing box, complete with ink stone, brushes and a fine selection of papers.

Michimori presented me with a new set of armour in the *shikime zane* style. 'Here,' he said, his head bobbing with satisfaction. 'See? The scales are assembled, twice overlapping. Triple thickness, extra protection for you, my samurai woman.' His eyes shone with joy, and I reflected my delight back to him. The *shikime zane* style was rare, a magnanimous gift. I shared a poem of gratitude with him.

My happiness was transient. My throat closed when I saw that Akio and Tokikazu each held a *furoshiki*.

'Because you have finally mastered both the Thunder Stroke and Scarf Sweep Stroke, you have earned this,' Tokikazu announced.

Ceremoniously he gave me a sword, including a golden rabbit ornament in the handle. The *tsuba* showed the closed-wing butterfly of the Taira Clan. The belt cord of thickened peacock-blue silk was wrapped around a scabbard with a *makie* design of gold and silver trees, as radiant as the Sun Goddess.

Michimori glanced at Tokikazu in a way I did not recognise, grunted, then turned and strolled away.

My throat pinched, and tears leaped. I held the sword on my outstretched hands. I extended them further from my body so that I did not wet the blade or its scabbard. When my elation overcame my confusion, I found my voice. 'I am honoured more than I have words to express.'

I slipped the slightly convex cutting edge out of its scabbard. I held it for all to see, then replaced it in its scabbard. Next, I anchored it at my waist as I had done so many times with my *bokken*. Tokikazu smiled. His eyes gleamed. I shared this poem:

> Shining in the sun
> My *tachi*, a friend's gift,
> Smiles in the green field.
> A gift earned with so much toil,
> A gift of loving protection.

Tokikazu grinned openly, and Akio's face brightened, still ruddy from practice.

His massive shoulders tightened. 'I, too, have brought you a Weaver Star Festival present,' Akio said, in a low growl.

I tried not to show surprise at his anger, which was rare in him, except when he was near Tokikazu. The bulky package revealed a quiver, with rabbits running through trees in carved wood and mother-of-pearl. He had remembered.

Tears blurred my eyes. I thanked him for his graciousness and recited another poem.

Akio turned and towered over Tokikazu. '*What* are you doing?'

'I do not understand. We are merely giving Weaver Festival gifts to the Lady Kozaishō.' Tokikazu's body tensed like thick bamboo.

'I do not like what is happening here. It is not honourable. Desist.' Akio's growl had changed to a torrential waterfall.

'Akio, I have no idea what you mean.'

Akio put his hands on his hips. 'I will be direct with you because I want – and Kozaishō needs – this to stop.'

'This? What is "this"?' Tokikazu's feet took a defensive stance.

' "This" is your encouraging the honourable Lord Taira no Michimori's wife. Even he saw it tonight with that sword. You must stop. You,' Akio turned to me, 'and Kozaishō are in danger. Nearly dishonour and disloyalty.' Akio eyed Tokikazu from his superior height. 'He prevented your *seppuku* once, Tokikazu, when Kozaishō and he were married. Yes, I heard. That does not mean you are immune to his wrath. Stop this.'

I did not realise Tokikazu's attachment to me was so evident, but the sword and scabbard had announced it. Such a gift belonged only to a husband or lover. Akio, once again, had lit the Path of Right Action for me. Although I admired the sword and scabbard, and Tokikazu, I had not shown an attraction to him.

'Should I return the sword and scabbard?' I asked Akio later.

'Perhaps that would be best. Or you may wish to ask your *husband*.'

My husband said nothing about the sword or the quiver. I made sure to wear the armour for him, praising its every detail and his solicitude that evening, and ordered Misuki's brush for a suitable poem in silver ink on indigo paper. He did not speak all night and sent me early to my apartments.

Tokikazu's gift had upset him. What was I to do? I valued Tokikazu's friendship, but Akio's admonishments indicated that I should change my behaviour.

Many days later, Tokikazu sat beside me, but not as close as he had before, and motioned a servant away. 'The great Tenjin came to me in a dream,' he confided.

Tenjin, the calligraphy deity, rode not a horse but a bull. His crest was the beautiful plum tree. My pilgrimage to Kitano, Tenjin's shrine, had not improved my brush. I had grasped a plum branch in one hand while attempting to write, but it had not helped.

'Tenjin wore many robes in alternating black and white. In one arm he carried a huge ink stone, with papers under it. In the other hand he carried a *tachi* – your sword! I recognised the scabbard with its tree design.

'In my dream I asked, "Why do you carry Kozaishō's sword?" He placed the ink stone on a small table, and put papers next to it. He unsheathed the sword, lifted it and, with the Torso Severer Stroke, broke the ink stone.

'Then Tenjin said, "Teach the characters with sword movements, and she will learn." He turned, left everything on the table, including the sword and its scabbard, and disappeared into a mist.'

'I do not understand. Please explain what this means,' Misuki begged.

'I will teach Kozaishō characters as if it were swordplay, something at which she excels.' He took my *tachi* and fought some invisible demon in the air in front of him.

I was puzzled.

He said, 'Observe, and do as I do. Pretend I am teaching you a new stroke.' I watched again as he fought an imaginary foe. I imitated with my sword, which was not difficult.

'There! Do you not see? You have written "Taira" against the sky!' He was delighted. 'Try it again by yourself.'

I did as I had been told. Several times, often with minor corrections, I rendered the sword strokes in the air. After many tries with Tokikazu, he signalled to a servant, standing nearby, who handed me the prepared brush.

He thrust a piece of paper on to the bare ground and demanded I perform the same sword strokes on the paper. Reluctantly I did so.

Barbara Lazar

Although I had little hope of a fair result, I did not hesitate, because he seemed so enthusiastic.

'But, first, close your eyes. Pretend you are doing it in the air.'

I did so – and we gazed, astounded, at the work on the paper.

Tokikazu was jubilant.

After sufficient repetitions in the air, I composed several adequate characters. We worked on this every day. Over the next months I spent less and less time practising in the air before I could perfect the brush. From that first day, and every day, I gave thanks not only to Tenjin but also to Tokikazu who made my success possible.

That first evening Tokikazu brought a poem to celebrate my success:

> Below azure sky
> Sword strokes cut through the breezes
> With bull and with plum
> Kozaishō writes on air and earth
> And then finally on paper

Later, he gave me a little fan-shaped book with an extract from the Lotus Sutra. It was like those I had seen when I had first come to Rokuhara, lacquered over flakes of gold and silver, with drawings above the text.

The poem and the book remained in a secret place where Michimori would never see them. Akio's threats of dishonour and disloyalty persisted in my thoughts. My friendship and attraction to Tokikazu could not be mistaken for the great sympathy I held for Michimori. Lighting candles and incense, I resolved to be wary of sharing this attraction with Tokikazu, lest I lose my husband. Having seen *seppuku* at Byōdōin, I did not delight in the thought of it, especially mine.

BOOK 15

I. Festivals and Famine

More than a year of drought, famine and melancholy unfolded. By the Third Month of the new year, even our serving girls were grateful for the Festival of Iwashimizu – a change from the previous year's mourning and solemn ceremonies for the deaths of Emperor Takakura and Chancellor Kiyomori, the unrelenting scrutiny of other wives and the rest of the court. Misuki's ear for gossip about colours helped me avoid being the target of such chatter.

To Emi, I explained, 'We are going on a trip. There is to be a great procession. There will be dancers and singers at the shrine.' I enjoyed her enthusiasm on such occasions. She lightened our spirits.

The travel was not arduous. The Iwashimizu no Hachiman Shrine was west of Uji and a little south of where two rivers merged to form the Yodo river. As I stole glances from my curtained palanquin, Tokikazu approached its door repeatedly. 'Is your dagger at the ready? A samurai is ever alert.'

Akio's eyebrows danced whenever Tokikazu drew close.

I viewed evergreens, browning after a dry winter, dying large-leafed cypresses and pasania oaks. Emi loved to see ducks on the river. Geese were Misuki's favourite. She said their flight was so graceful. I was enthralled by the cranes: their bodies, especially their necks, held such a splendid shape against the sky.

The music and dancing at the shrine delighted me, despite my necessary wariness. Before returning, I asked Tokikazu and Akio for permission to follow the dancers and singers through Heian-kyō to Rokuhara to see more performances. Tokikazu agreed. He loved the music too, especially *gagaku*, formal courtly music. I preferred *bagaku*, with dancing and music.

Tokikazu led us through the two-storeyed Main South Gate. Beside it beggars sat on the ground, hollow-cheeked men and women with their large-eyed, big-bellied children, huddled in tatters. Most of the babies lay motionless, not crying or babbling, only staring out to some event of which no one else was aware. Through the streets ubiquitous clusters of priests passed my palanquin. Each time, my pulse quickened and my hands closed on my dagger. My eyes focused on one face after another, searching for a broken nose. Akio's eyes flicked this way and that. The priests without hoods appeared full-cheeked, and they all ignored the beggars.

Inside the gate, next to the temples, more beggars amassed with street prostitutes. They presented an uncomfortable contrast to the temple's red pillars and white walls. They wore tattered clothes and bore lesions on their bodies. Their hair had become thickened dirt mats. Emi wept at such sights. Misuki comforted her, but I was silent. I had never seen such desperation.

Tokikazu guided us by way of a main street. Dogs and people collected there, more than I had seen together except in battle. Sick, shrunken women and children gazed out of spiritless eyes, their bones barely held together with mottled skin. I gave thanks to the Gods for my good *karma*. What could I do to assist? There were thousands, and we were so few. I wondered what these people had done in their past lives to deserve such wretchedness.

> Famine in the land
> Sickened peasants crowd the streets
> Like poisoned rats dying
> Flies hover above bodies
> Infants suckle dead mothers

That night heavy winds, and cats mating, disrupted my sleep. I stepped over servants and wandered into my garden, lit by a three-quarters Spring Moon. I took respite from the day's intense surveillance in Grand Room.

The scent of peach and pear blossoms mixed with that of wisteria. Frogs provided an inharmonious drumming from their pond.

Even under my umbrella, the draught carried a recognisable incense that aroused me. The combination of cinnamon, musk and sweet pine arrived on the breeze, but not from my garden. My hand fingered my dagger. I paced back to the azaleas, nearer to my apartments and protection.

'Kozaishō.'

The voice was as sweet as the scent. Tokikazu. I had heard it in my memory, like this wind – ever present and lingering on my armour's leather. I had bathed in his incense, behind, beside and around me as I had travelled from the Uji Bridge to Rokuhara and on the training field, day after day after day since that time.

'How did you evade the guards?'

'I found a way.' A form moved out of the shadows. Tokikazu's face glowed in the moonlight.

'Have you found Goro?' I was ready. My hand clenched my sword, and my mind went to blood.

'No. This is not about vengeance. This is about – I come to you because – because I could not remain away another . . . night.' His voice lightened to the weight of a dried leaf. 'I have tenderness for you, Kozaishō.'

His words and presence moistened my Jade Gate, despite the lusty winds and the night. He said words I had not dared send into the air. Shivers crawled along my limbs and between my legs. My head buzzed with contradictory passions, my new, deeper sympathy for Michimori, my tenderness for Tokikazu and my struggles to uphold my honour, my honourable status, as wife of Commander Taira no Michimori, Governor of Echizen Province, Third Rank. I repeated my husband's full name to myself. I tried to see his face, but all I could see was Tokikazu's, right in front of me.

'You are quiet. What do you say?' He moved nearer and slipped under my umbrella, his musk and sweet pine crowding our windless space.

My body heated. My knees released. Yet somehow I was able to say, 'What can I honourably say? I am married. I am samurai. You are also samurai and married. Twice.'

'No one is here.' He placed my hand across his palm and lifted it to his cheek, stroking it along the side of his face. 'We could, at least, have tonight.'

I wanted to embrace the warmth and fragrance emanating from his vigorous body. The body I had touched and that had touched mine often, only in practice.

'N-no.' The word tumbled from my lips as if I were possessed. That was not my thought, not my hunger, not what I craved.

He pushed his body closer, still holding my hand to his face. 'You know I have great affection for you. I think you have the same for me.'

Yes! I heard myself say. Yes! Yet again I murmured, 'N-no.'

'Your words disagree with your eyes.' Tokikazu clicked his tongue.

The sound reminded me of my mother. It jolted me into remembering my commitment to uphold my family's honour. 'I pledged my loyalty to Taira no Michimori, as you have. We are both married. Akio has taught me the Noble Eight-fold Path. If you care for me, and I know you do, will you not assist me to take the Right Action?'

Tokikazu released my hand and clenched his into fists.

'My adored one, if the Four Noble Truths of the Buddha are indeed true, then although we may ache with longing, our attraction is not real or permanent.' I stepped away. 'What is permanent? Honour, loyalty and obedience. When we obtain our release from this life, perhaps we may be together in the next.'

'Kozaishō, with your eloquent speech, I am set again on the Noble Eight-fold Path, however reluctantly.' He bent his neck and withdrew from my umbrella. 'I pledge to you, on my honour and love for you and Michimori, I will not deviate again.'

The winds had dispersed his tears, but not the stifled fervour in his voice.

I was allowed but a moment. Voices and footsteps echoed behind us, quieting the frogs. Sadakokai and Misuki strolled into the garden. I lowered my umbrella to cover my streaked face. Tokikazu made a gestural bow and left.

'Why are you out here in these winds so late? I thought you were asleep,' Misuki said.

She had forgotten herself.

'How did Tokikazu enter this garden without m-m-my guards alerting me?' Sadakokai said.

'To what purpose are you here?' I said.

'You gave me permission, my Lady Kozaishō.' Misuki used formal language, and her words forced icicles between us.

'Even T-T-Tokikazu does not have authority to enter your garden, my lady, without the knowledge of the One-in-Charge-for-the-Hours, as I am t-t-tonight.'

Trapped like a rabbit. The frogs started their tiny drums again. I returned to my apartments, but I wondered if others had overheard.

II. Spiders

Sunlight, a breeze, and the *hototogisu*'s songs, the Fifth Month, summer: the day of another Tango Festival had arrived. Horse-racing and archery contests were to take place later. Misuki sought these events after she had filled every room with iris and mugwort to push away evil spirits. She had also ordered servants to bring Great Luck Rice Cakes – *mochi* and mugwort stuffed with sweet *azuki* paste. They were ugly and green, and I did not want to eat them.

Misuki grew stern. 'Everyone must eat at least *one* of these. With no rain and little rice, we need all the luck we can attract.'

Misuki was right and relentless.

I ate one.

On that particular day, as most days, my routine began with a walk through my garden before I met Tokikazu and Akio, who followed me, for drills on the fields or to Grand Room.

At mid-morning, the Hour of the Sheep, after an arduous session with the *bokken*, I returned to my apartments to wash myself and dress. I was required to be behind the screens before Michimori presided over Grand Room. In the midst of these ministrations, Number Two Serving Girl came into the room, interrupting, and said Akio demanded an audience.

'Did he say about what?'

'No, my Lady Kozaishō.'

I checked with Misuki, who nodded. She dressed me, and we went behind my curtain in the front room while I talked with Akio, as was correct. At first this curtain, *kichō*, had seemed extremely odd to me: when

I was inside the house, I was allowed to see men, other than my family, even those I knew well, only behind this curtain on its little platform.

'Please forgive the intrusion, but I must speak with you alone,' Akio said to the curtain.

Misuki stepped out from behind it, made a perfunctory bow, and left.

'Please whisper, Akio. There are flowers and birds around us,' I reminded him of our code, as I slipped on one robe after another until all ten were arranged.

'Kozaishō, I come to save you.'

'From what? From whom?' Was this Goro? Or someone else? My fingers tensed, but I had not yet replaced my weapons. I glanced to see if Misuki had brought them. She had not.

'I remind you of Fifth Daughter.'

I did not move.

'The one sold for land,' he continued.

My throat tightened, and I took a step away, dropping to my knees. Then I pushed back my shoulders. I had not thought of her in a great while. 'I am no longer Fifth Daughter.'

'I fear you have forgotten the honour of the family and the duty she owes her emperor, her clan, her husband and herself.'

'After all I have done? You dare to question me?'

'Please lower your voice. It was I who first put a bow into your hand. It was I who told you about honourable Hiroshi. It was I who followed you to the Village of Outcasts. Who more than I to remind you of honour and duty?'

'Yes, Akio. I remember a little girl torn from her family. She wears the scars from Chiba's floggings. She wears the scars from vicious men at the Village.'

'Kozaishō, I will tell you again. True happiness comes from the Noble Eight-fold Path.' He spat out the list.

I thought of my submission to Goro and was blinded by tears. 'I do. I have. I *am* samurai. The Buddha has led me to this Right Livelihood. To what else could you refer?'

He lowered his voice to the loudness of a cat's lick. 'Tokikazu. He is samurai, also. Why did you meet him alone in your garden?'

'Did Misuki tell you?'

371

'Sadakokai. Only in concern for your and his master's honour.'

'So he was the one.'

'I want to talk about *you*. If you do not desist, I promise to follow you, stay close to you. I will confront Tokikazu if you do not stop.'

Panic flashed through me. 'You would not dare! I am loyal to Michimori.'

A voice came from the back room. 'Yes, Akio. She is. She has been honourable.'

'Misuki?' Akio and I said at the same time.

'Yes, it is I.' Misuki's voice contained little of the humility she used when caught in the middle of suspicious or meddling actions.

'You were dismissed. Why are you here?' My tone was more severe than I had intended.

'Because of my faithfulness to you. I could not allow Akio to falsely indict you. Akio, it is untrue! I was there!'

'Sadakokai said you were, Misuki. I know.'

'Then why are you condemning Kozaishō?' Misuki's voice was quiet and meek now.

'Because to say "no" once in a garden is not enough. Because I know Tokikazu. Because I have seen you two training on the practice field when Lord Michimori is not present.'

'There has been only Right Action on my part.' I did not know if the trembling in my body or voice could be seen or heard.

Misuki stood between Akio and my curtain. In her sternest manner she said, 'That is true, Akio. I would know.'

I parted the curtain and stared directly at Akio. 'I deeply regret your suspicion of me. You have been father to me. I tell you the truth and am content with that.'

'Well, please be assured, all I spoke out of respect and profound concern for you. But I will communicate with Tokikazu again, if necessary.' Akio made a small bow and strode away.

Misuki pulled at me. 'Come. We must hurry.'

'Do not address me with such familiarity.'

'It is I, Misuki. I do not understand what I have done to displease you. I defended you, vouched for you and supported you. Why are you so angry?'

'Why were you and Sadakokai spying on me in my garden?'

'Oh. You are angry again. Why? Michimori loves you. He married you, gave you rank, made you one of the "fancies", as someone we loved used to say.'

Tashiko's words returned me to myself as Fifth-Daughter once more. I resolved to force myself to ignore my body's reactions when I was near Tokikazu. I *did* have sympathy for Michimori, my husband, my protector, my family, and I was, as he said to me, his life. 'You are correct, my dear friend.' I hugged her. 'Let us not quarrel. I ask only for your assistance in maintaining a distance between me and . . .' I could not say his name.

'Kozaishō, I will even train more with you, if that is what is required.'

We embraced again as I wondered if our voices had carried into ears that would repay us with evil.

That day Tokikazu waited to escort me in his blue brocade *noshi*, a braided sash around his slender waist, and matching *hakama*. His swords' scabbards enthralled my eyes, but their handles, heavy purple silk braided over dyed-red stingray skin with multiple gold dragon ornaments, made me gasp. In his formal dress shoes with the gold edging, my pulse increased. We greeted each other with our eyes. I forced mine blank, I thought of Fourth Son, my brother, the youngest one, closest to my age. He had always defended me when my older brothers teased me about my dreams. He had been my favourite. I imagined him toiling happily in my birth family's new field, the one purchased with my life. Dare I ask Michimori if I might visit them?

I reconsidered.

My birth family would not know me, with my teeth blackened, face white with rice flour and eyebrows plucked, wearing ten robes or my armour. I was now *kuge*, and they were peasants, scarcely above the *eta* in the Village of Outcasts. Would I recognise them? I could no longer recall their faces, just brief flashes, like lightning against a spring storm's darkened sky, that pierced my chest like a spear.

Akio always lingered close to me, but remained silent. However, Tokikazu and I whispered on the way to Grand Room, but never about finding Goro and other enemies of Taira except in their code names. I listened to Tokikazu talk about his wives and consorts. I admired him, especially for the phenomenon he had wrought with my calligraphy. I owed him for my new brush, which had brought my acceptance among the *kuge* and particularly my husband's delight. Perhaps we could be friends, like Fourth Son and I had been. My life, and my head, were contingent upon it.

III. Shoes

Later that day in Grand Room, I was fatigued by the Hour of the Cock, the sun almost gone. An old man had spoken for a long time, saying many words with little information. From a small province, he complained of pirates. Many vessels sailed along an important river in his province, and this route to the capital was necessary for tributes to important shrines. The old man wanted our protection. I heard his threat to block the river and its precious cargoes if no troops came. He was a snake who still had its fangs.

I examined what he was doing. One of his hands was fingering the edge of his robe. The other clenched in a fist when he told lies. He would make good his warning if he was denied action, and I wrote this down. He droned on. I placed my brush next to my writing box, since he said nothing else of value. To keep my attention fresh while listening to his monotone, I focused on the rest of Grand Room.

I studied the samurai. I recognised all but two. Queasiness roiled in my stomach. I was familiar with Michimori's guards, but not these men. They stood straight across from Michimori, furthest away yet were nearest the doors. Oddly, they were in positions where no other samurai could look directly at them. I scrutinised them, cautious to make no noise or any sudden movement to upset the screens.

Their pose was as all the other samurai. Their faces displayed little expression. I scanned each of them meticulously for any clue to their identities. The same sashes tied the same way as the others, the same lacing patterns in their armour. The shoes were the same colour, but the trim, yes, the gold trim did not go around one side.

I rapidly checked other samurai in Grand Room. The others' gold trim went right around their shoes. Surely the two unknown samurai brought harm – could they be assassins?

Moving like a cat in front of an unaware mouse, I crept up from my cushions. I wrapped my kimonos around my waist so that I made not the tiniest swish behind the man's solo song. I grasped my shoes and hems, each step on my toes. I avoided the squeaky planks. Holding my breath, I opened the hidden door slowly. Perspiration dripped between my breasts. Every moment could mean death for my husband.

An endless time to open, go through and, finally, close the door. I ran as a bird hopping from one safe spot to another until I was in a main corridor. All this time I asked, 'Who? Who? from whom can I obtain aid? Who is available at this time of day? Who will believe me?' I ran to Tokikazu's quarters. He was not there. To the women's apartments. Obāsan.

'Help!' I blurted, grabbed her arm and pushed her to run to Grand Room. 'Michimori is in deadly danger! Come!'

Obāsan kept pace as I told her of the peril. It risked severe punishment to enter without permission. She said she knew what to do.

I stood by Grand Room's great door, putting on my shoes. Obāsan went to the guards in front of it. Fortunately, one was Mokuhasa. We pulled him to one side and explained.

Obāsan rapidly instructed him, 'Push me into Grand Room. I will be hysterical!' He grabbed her. He marched in, dragging her. Next he shoved her forward. Mokuhasa loudly begged a thousand pardons for the interruptions. Obāsan screamed, *'Yah-eeeeee! Yah-eeeeee!'*

Mokuhasa said, 'There is this hysterical old lady who . . .' He made the special signal to our samurai.

The door to Grand Room shut. I repeated prayers of protection.

In our quarters that night, Obāsan related what had happened: 'At the signal, all but the two strange samurai shifted to the alert position, changed their posture, hands on swords. By then Mokuhasa and I had placed ourselves between my lord Michimori and the impostors. Captain Tokikazu rushed in front of him, too. Warned, Michimori stood, hand on sword, ready to protect himself with his samurai.

'The samurai surrounded the pair. The assassins fought, but were overwhelmed and prevented from committing *seppuku*.

'I continued begging for forgiveness – at the intrusion – so that men from the provinces would not know what was transpiring.' She cackled at her own cleverness.

At this Misuki smiled.

'Mokuhasa and the samurai who helped us will be rewarded.' Obāsan patted my hand. 'Governor Michimori said land or rank, maybe both.'

'Why would Governor Michimori do that when Kozaishō was the one who really gave warning?' Misuki's lips formed a pout.

I patted Misuki's arm. 'Mokuhasa and Obāsan truly saved him. Besides, since my presence was secret, I have no desire to be honoured.' Grimacing at Misuki and Obāsan, I added, 'If it had been either of you, you would have noticed such a blatant mistake sooner.' They protested. I had been fortunate to recognise the difference when I did. It had been merely my *karma* to save his life, as he had saved mine. I was truly grateful to have done so.

IV. Fly In Web

That evening Michimori provided a celebration feast. People of rank, along with Obāsan, Akio and their families, assembled in Grand Room. Akio's daughters had much changed. The oldest, Fumiko, was betrothed to one of Michimori's personal samurai. Obāsan had few relatives, but her nephew, Ryo, attended and sat next to her.

Servants brought each person a tall tray made of lacquered wood, which stood above the floor. Next they carried a lacquered plate and chopsticks to each person. In the centre of each plate lay a mound of polished rice. Small dishes encircled the rice, and in each dish there was a little treasure: early spring or pickled vegetables; pickled and baked sea bream and shellfish; seaweed.

Jokes and stories regarding defeated foes flew around the room. It was the Day of the Monkey, again, so I remained awake all night and away from our living quarters. Michimori took me to the required neutral place, where we walked in one of his many gardens.

He could thrill at a single new leaf or bud and thanked those around him in such magnanimous ways, all of which enchanted me, but that night he was silent. I reflected on why: he had almost been assassinated: enemies had penetrated his home. His captain had bestowed an indecorous sword and scabbard upon his wife, an indication of intimate attentions. I hoped he did not believe they were reciprocated.

Escorted, I returned to my quarters the next morning, bringing ices for Emi. I needed to refresh myself and go behind the screens. I entered my apartments.

A monsoon had knocked down scrolls, scattered pillows, slashed quilts, upset futons, torn clothing and stuck the pieces into the corners. It looked as if some child, in a tantrum, had been at work.

Spiteful, yes. Child, no.

I checked, and no one was in the apartments. My next thoughts went to my notes, stitched into hems. Those garments had not been touched. For what could they have been probing? I went out to my little garden. The fishpond and the flowers would help me work on my new predicament.

When I opened the *shoji*, I saw Obāsan and Misuki holding each other, their eyes swollen, their sleeves blotched damp. Behind them, a pond-soaked heap of robes. Protruding from it I saw small colourless feet. At the other side, thick hair spread like seaweed across two limp arms stretched out as if reaching for a cat.

Emi.

She was face down. I wondered if her face looked like Tashiko's after she had been murdered. I could not make myself turn it to see. I did not want to see. The pain of losing such a dear one, so hideously, again, seared me as if I had fallen into a fire pit. I stood, my body scalded, yet frozen inside.

I joined Obāsan and Misuki in a circle of sorrow for our lost one, the simple good one who had done her best. The hugs and tears could not stop my mind.

'What happened? How did she drown?' I screamed.

Obāsan's voice cracked: 'Behold her neck. The bruises on her shoulders.'

Misuki straightened the drenched robes. There it was, the same broken neck, the same twisted flesh, the same blank eyes. A lost friend, a lost companion. My eyes burned. Could it have been the work of the same man? Probably. Three Eyes.

The same as my beloved Tashiko. Obāsan held and comforted me. Much later she tried to coax me to eat, but I could not. My sweet Emi. My beautiful Tashiko. Obāsan stayed the night with me on my *futon*. Misuki wanted to stay, too, but she had touched the body and was defiled. I cried for the old and new losses. New horrors added to the old ones. Fear heaped on fear.

Oh, the senselessness!
A simple joyful woman
Long-time companion
Now a strangled, sopping heap
Rampage against this wasted death!

A message. Someone wanted Michimori dead, and I had interfered. Goro must have been behind this or Minamoto spies, perhaps even double spies. Goro had murdered my Tashiko and Michimori's guards. He had counterfeited the seal, and now perhaps strangled this innocent.

Since I had not touched Emi, there was no need for Purification. A proper priest, code-named Plover, officiated at the ceremonies. He had earned his name because he, like the bird, had no neck and stood quietly for long periods. The completed ceremonies reassured me a little.

We cried and prayed for Emi's soul to be reborn quickly into a happy life.

After the funeral, I took out my outrage and grief on a straw man with the *shobuzukuri naginata*. Tokikazu, Akio, my husband and I remained outside the pavilion to ensure that no one listened to us. Early morning proved best, because the birds would alert us with their silence or flight.

'This is unusual.' Tokikazu's lips disappeared into each other. 'They rarely leave a body for someone to find. This is a direct warning to you to stop.' With a demand and a question at the same time, he gazed directly into my eyes without regard for Michimori and Akio's presence.

I returned the stare. 'I cannot stop.' Turning to Michimori, I said, 'Will you help me to live safely?' I could not speak about my work behind the screens.

'It will be done.' Michimori paced closer to me. 'Tokikazu, Akio, you will assist Lady Kozaishō.'

Tokikazu gestured, which I knew for him was as good as a solemn oath and referred me to Plover, saying, 'We need to expand our network. You can trust this priest.' Plover was not of other factions and visited almost each day. He and I spoke of Tashiko and Emi, but mostly we talked stratagems.

Misuki found another clue. After Plover had left, she brought some threads. Obāsan and I recognised them: they matched the brocade Goro had worn at my Purification, purple and white.

Tokikazu brought Plover to my apartments.

'Yes, yes, these are his,' Plover agreed. 'There is more. We suspect he has Minamoto leanings. He disappears at odd times. He volunteers facts he should not know.'

I needed more information and contacts from everyone I trusted. Plover drew the lineage of families, reciting their histories beside the pond where poor Emi had died. Tokikazu and Obāsan listed people who had disappeared as well as a long list of enemies, which began with the name of Goro. Tokikazu had a personal stake in finding him because Goro had bested him and caused him to lose honour. Michimori doubled his mansion's guards and placed an arc of samurai around my garden's perimeter.

In the few days after Emi had died, Plover purified Misuki, at her request, and she returned to practising her archery with me. I was to go again to Grand Room.

'I humbly beg you,' Misuki requested breathlessly, as she came back into my apartments, 'do you know where your writing box and papers are?'

Cold pierced my chest and turned my stomach to a striking anvil. 'Yes.' I shuddered. 'I left them behind the screens in my haste to find Obāsan.' Our eyes met, and the harsh taste of panic permeated my mouth. 'Go to Obāsan immediately and tell her to find Tokikazu and Akio. We are in great jeopardy if those papers are found.'

While Misuki was gone, I prepared another writing box and gathered other papers to bring with me.

An aeon of panic and waiting.

I forced myself to sit still.

A note arrived from Michimori, with his paper's special twists: 'The flowers are safe.'

I took a deep breath before I reread his note. The icy anvil in my chest warmed.

Within a short time, he gave me a beautiful new document box, lacquered in gold and silver, inlaid with mother-of-pearl cranes flying through a sky with clouds of *makie* gold and silver. It was in this box that I kept my journal.

Akio guarded me through the passages to the screens. From that day I always carried at least both my swords.

The terror that gripped my throat became the friend who secured my safety.

V. Weaving Webs

With the extra daylight of spring, Michimori and I worked on the practice field after Grand Room. My fingers on arrows welcomed the warmth as much as the butterflies and horseflies, although they came in fewer numbers due to the lack of rain. I saw only the usual guards, but neither Tokikazu nor Akio was present. Michimori had a plan.

That afternoon we focused on stationary targets. Standing close, I waited on my husband. He used Akio's tactic of spacing the arrows in his quiver so that they were easier to reach and shoot. He hit the centre of the target three times, then circled to me. 'You see much of Akio.'

'Did we not agree that he would stay close?'

'Yes, but . . .'

I looked up at him. He was upset. Angry. 'Is there a problem with Akio?'

He shrugged his shoulders. Discomfort edged into one side of his mouth.

'What action would you have me take?' I had no desire to say his words for him.

'The two of you spend much time together.'

'How else can he protect me? Or teach me?' Did he begrudge Akio's time? Was this jealousy?

'The two of you spend much time together – alone.'

A light spring breeze caressed the air, yet it felt like the heat of high summer. He was accusing me!

'Akio has been my teacher and adviser since I was eight years old.'

'I understand.' He returned to the targets and employed Tokikazu's technique of holding two arrows at the same time. He shot one, notched the second. 'You see much of Captain Tokikazu.'

A statement. Not a question. Perhaps this was it. Was he suspicious? 'Yes, my honourable lord.' I used the formal address.

'To what purpose?'

I also used the technique of holding two arrows at the same time. I shot one, notched the second and released it immediately, as Tokikazu had taught me. I stared Michimori in the face, bold as the edge of a blade. 'To *that* end.' I stormed away to the pavilion to try to cool myself with some water. How dare he suspect me? After all I had said to Tokikazu that night in the garden! After I had pledged myself to Right Action!

'Come here!'

I halted. Breathed twice. Old habit. Then I strolled back to the targets. I focused my eyes away from him.

'Kozaishō, I am ill at ease. Tokikazu is as indispensable to me as ...' He raised and shook his bow in his right hand. 'He has two wives and several concubines.'

'I am aware of this.'

'I invest great trust in Tokikazu as my captain.'

His eyes could have pierced my new armour. 'I am aware of this too.' He knew Tokikazu had trifled with me. How? Perhaps he knew more. Could anyone know the heat between my legs when I saw him?

'In other matters I can trust Tokikazu to have liaisons with beautiful women.'

I held my gaze with difficulty and in silence.

He waved his hand to the other mansions, then placed his palm against his chest. 'And you are the most beautiful woman here.'

That was why he was distant. Take my head? Poison me? Divorce me? He had those rights.

Michimori shifted behind me, his arms over mine, and pretended to show me the fingering for two arrows at the same time. 'You spend almost as much time with Tokikazu as you do with me. You say you have sympathy for me.' His words transformed to the roughness of rocks. 'If you have sympathy for Tokikazu, be punctilious. I *cannot* and *will not* forgive disloyalty.'

Threats. He accused me. I had said no to Tokikazu! I had taken the Right Action. Flames hurtled through me until I dripped inside my new armour. My jaw clamped, and I wriggled to be free of Michimori's hold.

He compressed his forearms across my breasts until I could barely breathe.

'Stop, please,' I gasped.

He loosened his grip, but did not remove his arms. I remembered who and what he was. All of what he could do.

The quiet belied the reserve between us.

Bush warblers swept over the targets. Perhaps my father's spirit reminded me of my duty and honour. At that moment, seeing those birds, I pictured my father, and my thoughts clarified.

'My honourable lord,' I said formally, 'may I explain in your quarters?'

With a nod to the key guards at the perimeter of the target area, he strode home. I had to run to keep up.

We stood, face to face, alone, in his apartments. His features stiffened to those of a statue. 'Speak.' The word thrown at me like a *shuriken*.

'Before we were married,' I made my voice agreeable against the invisible hand choking me, 'you asked what was in my heart. You know that sympathy has replaced my fear. Akio has taught me since I was a small girl. He is like – no, he *is* the father I lost. That is all.'

I took time to prepare what I would say of Tokikazu. I could not lie, yet I did not wish to speak of the strong attraction between Tokikazu and myself.

'You are aware that Tokikazu resembles Genji, one woman after another. I have known this, also.' I grasped his forearms with my hands. 'There has been *no* disloyalty, nor will there be. Did I not prove my loyalty beyond question at my Purification? I allowed Goro to – to –' I bit my lower lip at these thoughts. 'Because I believed *you* had ordered it. How much more to prove my loyalty, my devotion to my duty and to your honour?' My shame at my attraction for Tokikazu both marked my face crimson and aroused my ire with myself.

I lifted my head, so he could better see my eyes. 'My honourable lord, my husband to whom I have pledged my life and loyalty, I *have* maintained both my duty and honour.'

His voice softened to chrysanthemum petals. 'I would die for yours.'

These few words sank into me, like a sword into my belly. Had he accepted the truth? 'I did not like how you forced me on the target line,' I grumbled, with tears flowing across my face.

He compressed his arms around my chest again. 'Like this?'

'Yes,' I growled, weeping still for the delicate and durable insistence of his arms against my body.

'You do not like this?' He lifted me off the ground, kicked open the *futon*, and laid me across it. He murmured against my ear, 'You are too beautiful not to have.'

I bent my knees and put my feet against him, still fuming. His thick chest pressed my legs apart. We wrestled briefly.

Then we ceased wrestling.

I was behind the six-part folding screens at the Hour of the Dog, nibbling a rice ball and working to stay awake. The rice ball was to allay my concern that my stomach noises, after all day without food, might betray my presence. I listened carefully to the new group, almost all of the provincial governors.

The drought, its poverty and pestilence, had caused a pause in the hostilities. Michimori and the other governors' tasks included the requisition of troops and supplies from the provinces. War loomed. Indeed, it had arrived inside the Rokuhara gate. The samurai in some provincial *shōen* resented the Taira Clan.

'No wonder they hate us!' Michimori had groused the night before.

'You have been vigilant and considerate of your responsibilities in Echizen. How can they hate *you*?' I wanted to touch him, but knew better than to do so when he was irked.

'My uncle and cousins have foolishly reduced land rights to the proprietors, which reduced their samurai's income as well.'

'You mean your relatives have alienated the people you need to fight in this war?'

He grunted in the affirmative, lay down, put his arm around me and, later, went to sleep.

By now I recognised each of the governors' voices: first, the one we had named 'Wisteria'. 'His father,' Michimori had whispered one evening when we were alone, 'was probably the son of an umbrella vendor. He made Wisteria an errand boy at a merchant's stall and has not been a true Taira nephew since he fled from the water birds.' He referred to an encounter in which, when the enemy suddenly released water birds, Wisteria's waiting soldiers had retreated prematurely.

Drake, another of Michimori's uncles, attended this meeting – a great singer and poet who fought with brush and *koto*. Nothing else.

Another governor sat close to Michimori. He had dense eyebrows and was thick of body and legs. He spoke gentleness with a voice like rocks grinding together. Akio had named him Large Cicada, for that timbre.

Last of all was Kingfisher, shorter than the others, an uncle with a booming voice. He leaped to display his arrows with their special feathers, as a kingfisher dives to catch fish. His reputation for accuracy and courage was rumoured by Sadakokai to be almost equal to Michimori's.

The group studied their plan to attack, making sure the conscription lists were adequate, the horses ready.

'Honourable nephew,' Michimori began respectfully, 'I beg a few questions of you.'

'Yes, Michimori, my uncle,' Wisteria responded graciously.

'I am not convinced we are ready for such a march. While we may have enough men, our supplies are not laid out properly or adequately.'

'We must move swiftly,' Kingfisher interjected. 'My sources say Yoritomo is travelling to his uncle, who is in Shinano Province. Even if we leave now, we may not reach them.'

'If the two Minamoto leaders reconcile, they will have a larger force against us,' Michimori concluded. 'It might be perilous for us if they reach agreement—'

'So it is settled. We will leave in no more than two days,' Wisteria interrupted, half asking and half commanding in his pusillanimous style.

'Since we do not have enough men, according to Michimori, perhaps we should recruit female warriors,' Large Cicada suggested, his eyebrows moving like caterpillars.

'If we did, I would put my coins on Lady Kozaishō – her spirit is great even though her warrior's wardrobe is not as dazzling as that of some.' Michimori referred to a Minamoto consort, Lady Tomoe, and her renowned armour.

The Taira Clan leaders left one by one, making small-talk. After some time, I returned to my quarters to be summoned. I was gratified by the confidence Michimori placed in my battle schemes, although unsure of our ability to triumph and uneasy that my husband still harboured misgivings about me.

VI. Journeying

Tenth day of the Fifth Month

After I receive invitations to the Imperial Palace for *bagaku*, banquets and archery contests, Akio brings the orders to me in my apartments. Only a select few deliver them to me, and Tokikazu only rarely. Another precaution. Michimori's hand or Akio's?

The order is to prepare for travel.

I am to accompany Michimori. This is not the hurried travel of before because there are thousands of people to be directed, fed and sheltered. I say silent prayers that the weather might remain cool. The new commander-in-chief, Michimori, rides as I have seen him before, runners coming and going, whispering into his ears, always the hub of a great wheel.

After conferring with his captains, Michimori gestures to me and I stride to Thunderbolt, his well-known mount. How imposing he is – his full armour, with its gold, black and red silk threads, and his helmet with its crescent moon shining like a brazier in a moonless night. My stomach squeezes in delight looking at him.

I will be riding beside him on Dragon Cloud. Much has changed since I was the little girl Proprietor Chiba had flogged and who had seen the dragon-like cloud and the white pheasant, which allowed me to be samurai. I allow my eyes to flicker a smile at my husband. I wear my new armour with the new helmet and face guard he has had made. My helmet is like his, but without the crescent moon.

Michimori's brows are set low. 'The runner believes Hare is joining his nephew, Rat,' he reports, 'and combining their troops. I am going to

Mount Hiei to seek the monks' support there for the Go-Shi – Fox, but especially for us.'

His eyebrows lift.

'Yes, I will go with you.' Our souls seem to touch, although this is no pleasure jaunt.

'Look over there.' Michimori points to a man sitting on a hill near our troops, besieged by servants. 'Drake has decided to take the day for meditation and music while we face pressure to ride north.' He glowers at the hill, then canters to make arrangements with his captains.

Twelfth day of the Fifth Month
At Mount Hiei, Michimori emphasises to the abbot and the head monks our alignment with the emperor. He tells the story again:

'When the righteous emperor had been seized by the Minamoto, Kiyomori freed him by dressing him in ladies' kimonos, pretending to be a lady-in-waiting, thus saving his life.'

'I am not hopeful, my lord.' I say afterwards. 'The abbot with whom you spoke, his eyes were as unpolished mirrors.'

Sixteenth day of the Fifth Month
The weather is colder at this higher elevation. I am pleased to have brought all the clothing I did. Thank the Gods, I am not frail like Emi but hardy, more like Michimori.

We intercept the rest of our troops near Kuchiki Castle in Wakasa and deliver the small number of *sōhei* from Mount Hiei. The white scarves over their heads and their black gauze robes over skirts add different shapes and colours to our multitude. Most of our troops wear their usual square *do-maru* armour. When they first arrived, I examined each one's nose with one hand on my dagger, the other on my sword. My heart drummed up to my throat.

Twentieth day of the Fifth Month
Michimori allows me to accompany him while he recruits in Echizen. He and Tokikazu tell tales of Tiger's Four Heavenly Kings. Each story is more

unbelievable than the last, but I enjoy them: they distract me from my empty and uneasy stomach.

We see no one. The villagers have fled, probably to higher ground where our full army cannot go. We find only a little rice – drought and famine are here in the west. I am grateful for the small portions. Recently recruited men complain but those close to Michimori do not mention it, particularly when they see we are as hollow in the cheeks as themselves.

Twenty-fifth day of the Fifth Month
I finally see Michimori's beautiful Echizen Province. The evergreens have survived the drought and cover the slopes in varied greens.

Tokikazu says, 'Unlike other governors, Michimori did not stay in the capital. He had frequent outings here.' He winks at me. 'When his underlings least expected it, he or his messengers appeared to ensure all was performed according to his wishes. He knows the *shōen* proprietors, the Chief Priests and abbots at most major shrines and temples.'

'Michimori will find more recruits?' My body heats: I have not seen Tokikazu for a time, but I keep my voice neutral. I force my eyes away from his striking face and think of others.

'Yes, hopefully.'

Michimori's knowledge, I pray, will be useful.

Third day of the Sixth Month
We ride northwards to Hiuchi, another mountain castle. According to the men scuttling back and forth to Michimori, it holds a strong Minamoto force. It is an ominous fortress, with huge hills in front and behind. Two rivers and a lake block its only entrance. The water glistens in the summer light, but is impassable without boats, of which we have none.

Sixth day of the Sixth Month
The commanders spend several days considering their options for crossing the lake, including poetry and other gratuitous activities from Drake and others. Misuki calls them 'as useful as the feathers of a goose'. At night Michimori and I rest briefly with our heads together. I am frustrated as to how we can proceed, but his fingers soothe my face.

'You will see, my valiant warrior, how the seeds I sowed while governor will bear fruit.'

I gaze at him in the darkness with sadness and hope.

'I have friends who have pledged loyalty throughout this province, not only warriors but priests. I trust the Gods and the Buddha to protect and guide us, just as I was guided to you.' He begins to touch me and our tent becomes warmer. He brings delight to me, and then I drift into sleep.

A short time later, Misuki and Mokuhasa awaken us. They bring a message from Michimori's friend, Abbot Master Saimei.

The abbot master's letter reveals all. The lake is no lake! The Minamoto dammed a mountain stream to create it. Abbot Master Saimei suggests logs be broken or cut. Then the water will subside.

> A secret friend comes
> Buddha's mercy gives us aid
> The lake disappears
> Blessed Goddess of Mercy!
> Swiftly we will vanquish foes

In the middle of the night Tokikazu, Akio and I lead a party of fifteen selected archers to protect the men who will swim to remove the logs. No birds, no frogs or crickets, probably because the lake is so new. The thick silence makes our footsteps echo. I hear my heart and practise breathing to quiet its din.

With a stern look at Tokikazu, Akio places himself between us. I am protected and, in the armour my husband gave me, I do my part. The Taira leaders forbade Michimori to go on this mission. He is too valuable to lose. I agree, but the scent of Tokikazu's incense kneads my underbelly.

The eighteen of us hold together in the darkness, shoulder to shoulder, arrows pointing from the arc we form, listening, waiting, discerning between splashing of our swimmers and any noise from the enemy.

The quiet hours trickle sluggishly past under the moonlight. I suggest we change places, around our arc. Each of us will better maintain our attention. Tokikazu whispers, 'Yes.' Akio places himself between us at each exchange.

Finally, the surge of flowing water. Success.
Tomorrow, battle.

Tenth day of the Sixth Month
Michimori and the other commanders are victorious at Hiuchi. My fights
are successful, without difficulty, almost without effort. Not even a scratch
on my boot. The entire castle and the Minamoto who remain surrender
today. The enemies who did not retreat are secured.

'Too easy,' Michimori says that night. 'Much too easy.'

I agree, and gloom descends. I do not sleep well.

We march north again to Kaga Province where the enemy is.

VII. The Trap

Over meagre rations and a small fire the commanders meet after our victory at Ataka.

Drake says, 'Now that we have two solid victories, no men are leaving the ranks.'

'They did well for themselves,' adds Large Cicada.

Kingfisher glances around. 'We have them on the run.' He makes a fist in the air and nods at the others. 'We should follow them north to where we can subdue them.'

I see his huge head bobbing even from my vantage-point behind a makeshift *kichō*.

Michimori rises from the circle. 'The Minamoto are not so straight-forward. Did not anyone think the retreat a little abrupt? Too soon?' Michimori's darkened eyes glare against the fire.

'That is because we so cleverly mastered their strategy at Hiuchi,' Large Cicada retorts.

Others utter mild curses in agreement.

'I am not so sure,' Michimori says. 'My scouts report that many of their force did not engage us at all. When I spoke with my men, they saw foot soldiers rushing back to Ataka but wearing samurai clothing.'

A few mumble in agreement, but do not agree to travel home.

'This is important!' Michimori pursues the issue with fingers splayed taut on his thigh. 'If you will not consider returning, at least divide our

393

forces to march to Kurikara. It is too dangerous a place with what the Minamoto know of us.'

Kingfisher speaks again: 'Regardless of their information, the division of our troops is a prudent idea.'

I hear grunts of assent.

So it is decided. Michimori, since he is more familiar with the land, will go with Kingfisher to the north with a third of our soldiers.

Twentieth day of the Sixth Month

Michimori cannot sleep, which is unusual for him. I attempt to soothe him with music, but it brings him no comfort. Finally, early in the morning or late at night, I cannot say, he speaks to me.

'My sense of foreboding does not go away,' he murmurs. His fists grab the quilts.

I have no reply. I say little to him when he is like this.

He sits and continues talking while stroking my hair. 'We have been travelling too long. We lack the element of surprise. The enemy knows where we are. With the battles we have won, the last one too quickly, they must know our full strength.'

He gazes up and is silent again, so I venture a reply, 'Perhaps with this plan to divide, we may have some measure of surprise. What else can we do?'

'Right! What else is to be done?' His muscles tighten like those of a cat ready to spring. 'The others will not listen. I say go back, or seem to go back, then turn and attack suddenly. They are sure of their plan, and I am duty-bound to it, not mine.' He runs his hands through his hair and grunts. He speaks mostly to himself, not to me.

I know of no story strong enough to match his agitation. Therefore I lie down beside him and give some physical comfort. I stroke his neck and back. Finally he sleeps a little.

My husband says less and less to me now that is not essential. I know he carries the burdens of war and the growing distance between us saddens me. I have not told him about the child.

I called Misuki to me before I retired with Michimori. Now we squat near a flowing runnel from one of the many rivers so that our voices cannot carry.

394

'I want to talk to you about this.' I pat my middle.

Misuki wears a grin.

'I need your help. I am always watched, and time is short. I ask you to obtain herbs, like the ones we drank at the Village, but those used for the aftermath, rather than for prevention.'

Her grin vanishes.

'You understand what I am asking?'

'Yes.' She places her hand on mine and rubs it. 'You have not talked with the father?'

'No. We are at war, Michimori insists on my presence, and I shall need to travel.' I rest my hand on my belly. 'If this interferes with my husband's requirements then it is an honourable course of action to avoid it. You know it is only a month. Therefore, I am considering taking the herbs.'

'Not decided, then?'

'No, my sweet. Not decided yet.' I embrace her. 'But please find them for me.'

'I will, my lady . . . my friend.'

We put our heads together and ponder the stream's coursing.

Twenty-second day of the Sixth Month

The smaller force takes to the north through Noto, crosses to the central part of the Kurikara Pass and arrives at the eastern side of Mount Tonami. Through the mists the white flags of Rat fly on a hill below. Kingfisher agrees to rest with the advantage of elevation, especially since the Minamoto force appears to be considerable.

The samurai water and tend their horses, then rest, or most do.

Michimori maintains his qualms, and even Tokikazu cannot mollify him.

I stay away from them and rest next to Akio, who recites *sutra*s to me, probably content that I am at a distance from Tokikazu.

Twenty-third day of the Sixth Month

Today, at last, the enemy engages in a formal, civilised battle.

First the whistling-gourd arrows, followed by an exchange of sharp-pointed arrows.

Individual combats in small groups follow, and next our larger samurai, but not, thank the Goddess of Mercy, our commanders or Tokikazu. Mokuhasa and Sadakokai do well for themselves. Misuki may have permanently imprinted her fingers on my upper arms, watching. The last of the preliminaries include a selected one hundred men to engage in individual combat, from which the Taira, again, emerge triumphant.

In the mountains there is no space between day and night. Night comes soon. Therefore both sides retire.

Twenty-fourth day of the Sixth Month
The feet of an enormous *oni* throb beneath me. Earthquake?

I glimpse Michimori. His eyes are open. He leaps up. Heavy drums flog the earth – the final fury of the great God of War, flailing the ground, jarring us.

I hear before I see it. The air is thick. The mountain shrieks from a long way, but comes closer – and closer. Louder. Coming nearer. What is it? Danger! I gather my weapons and find my horse.

I smell it before I see it. Cattle. The odours of animals, the smell of a herd. The stench of panic – with the bittersweet smell of fire. Fire! Where is it? Men's screeches and shouts.

In the smoke, the dark, I can barely see them. Moving fire. Firesticks! On fire! The oxen are on fire! Flames and smoke coming from their horns! Hundreds of moving flames coming down the pass – towards me!

BOOK 16

I. Return

We grabbed the horses and clambered on to them. Wails and animals' shrieks plummeted over the black edges of the earth. Death cries boomed against the mountains, like sword strokes on stone. The smells of blood and torn flesh smothered the air. Horses' hoofs trampled bodies and sucked at the mud made with their pulp.

The darkness, screams and echoes lasted an aeon.

That morning, when the sun emerged, few were left, a ravaged crop after a ferocious storm.

The march home began.

In retreat we travelled south into Kaga Province near Shinohara where, as Michimori's stream of beleaguered and breathless messengers foretold, we met the Minamoto again. Another battle on the Second day of the Seventh Month. My stomach filled with ice and slaughter, my brush too hefty and bitter to write any more of battles.

The Minamoto trailed and stalked us, like the animals they were, until we verged on the capital. Hare moved his troops towards Yamato, south-east of Heian-kyō, and Rat moved his directly towards the city.

When the Taira Council met again in Rokuhara, a saddened Purple Grass received a consensus from others to beg help again from Mount Hiei. We needed their *sōhei* army, our allies from before.

The messenger returned with bad news. Not only had our request been denied, but Mount Hiei was ready to receive Rat. Michimori had predicted this.

No one met anyone else's eyes. No matter how many torches were lit, the corridors subdued my disposition into a winter night with snow squalls.

Despite Michimori's vigorous protests, the other commanders opted to take a pilgrimage. Perhaps this one time Michimori was mistaken. The situation demanded prayers of intercession. The itinerary comprised three nearby shrines, none near Mount Hiei, because the *sōhei* there would make us vulnerable. Therefore they chose temples within a short distance of Rokuhara.

I needed prayers. With all my learning and pursuit, I seemed no closer to locating Three Eyes, let alone the poisoner's collaborators. No one could find the correct priest with a crooked nose and deformed soul. I prayed to the Goddess of Mercy to support me in the honourable retribution required. I prayed also for Tashiko's spirit, so it would not haunt me or become a *yurei*.

The servants made the preparations, and we departed. The end of spring, with the cooler mornings, improved many tempers. With the luxury of servants, this journey would demand less of us than our march north with the troops – but, surrounded by priests with their faces covered, I would be ill at ease.

First day of Pilgrimage
Plover, the priest I trusted, led us east to Yasaka-jinja Temple. I wore my armour to ride next to Michimori and the ever-faithful Tokikazu under Akio's scrutiny. Our pace was not rushed, a snail at evening. Michimori and I knew the commanders would take time to establish any course of action. At every small shrine along the road, I paused, rinsed my mouth and washed my hands, praying for guidance. I had to locate Goro. Soon.

We arrived at the temple for the evening meal. That night everyone prayed together in one group. A priest's euphonious voice added to the pious atmosphere. During the recitation of *sutra*s, they burned so much incense that my eyes throbbed. Misuki was surprised that the trees around our tent did not catch fire.

Tokikazu probably overheard, because he tittered softly. Akio stifled a snort.

Second day of Pilgrimage

Last night the Gods spoke of the poisoner's primary cohort – his face appeared in another of my vivid dreams. I wished to verify his identity, before I took my retribution.

Akio and Misuki believed me. They had experienced my dreams.

'Dreams cannot give you such information.' Tokikazu's cheeks sank with his grimace.

Akio told his story, and Misuki added hers. She was so superstitious, though, that Tokikazu had told me he did not consider her credible.

'Tashiko.' My lips tangled over her name. 'Tashiko was one of the most reasoned and reasonable people I know. She believed in my dreams. So strongly did she believe that she told me this story.

'An honest fisherman named Chōkichi dreamed that if he walked along the river and stopped at the first large bridge, something good would happen. While waiting at the bridge, a *tōfu* maker came up and asked him what he was doing. He mocked Chōkichi's reply, "I never take dreams seriously. I dreamed that gold was buried beneath the paulownia tree where this road crosses the next! Anyone who follows dreams is foolish!" The *tōfu*-maker walked on. Chōkichi went to the paulownia tree, found the gold and became wealthy.'

Misuki and I would confirm the identity of the poisoner's accomplice. That second day, and for the remainder of the pilgrimage, Misuki was to socialise with servants and gather information. I would no longer ride exclusively with Michimori but pass among the wives and concubines. My eyes craved to see the man who had strangled my sweet friend, and I had to know what he planned to do next. Tokikazu and Akio would protect me.

Next we travelled to Kiyomizu-dera near Mount Ōtowa. Tokikazu, who continued to tell tales, shared this one:

'Almost three hundred years ago, this temple was named by Enchin, a priest. He came to the Ōtowa waterfall nearby and met a hermit. This hermit had been waiting for Enchin so that he could abandon his hut and leave for the east. Enchin took the hermit's place and set a statue of the Goddess of Mercy inside the hermit's hut.'

Hearing this, Akio said, 'There is more to that story.' We pulled our horses together to hear, because Akio's voice could be soft.

'Years later a courtly man came to this area to hunt. He wished to kill a deer, since deerskin would be a good-luck charm for his wife, near childbirth. However, after he killed the deer, he met Enchin, who reminded him of the evil in killing animals. So Tamuramaro, for that was his name, buried the deer. His wife gave birth safely. Much later when Tamuramaro became a general and conquered the north-east, he gave thanks to the Goddess of Mercy of Kiyomizu.'

'I will show you Tamuramaro's burial mound at the temple,' Tokikazu offered, eyeing Akio.

Akio whispered, 'The grave groans whenever Heian-kyō is in danger.'

After this we remained silent until we arrived at Kiyomizu-dera.

There, near the burial mound, Misuki's eyes enlarged until they filled her whole face. Her lips trembled; her body quivered. She chanted prayers for protection, moving her lips without sound, over and over. Her sensitive nature had absorbed the story. I required her to be alert, not rigid with dread, so I swept one arm around her waist and grasped her hand.

Kiyomizu-dera comprised more than twelve buildings of varying sizes. The buildings were on several levels, of which each was constructed with stone walls and steps. Large groves of trees formed a perimeter close to them. With only budding leaves, they resembled spiders' webs in a forgotten corner. Could this be another trap? Goro could be anywhere here.

Misuki calmed at the temple, and I shared some intelligence. Hoichi, Mokuhasa's cousin, had verified enemy sympathisers among us. He and Mokuhasa would flush them out.

Late into the night we developed a plan with Plover.

Michimori, his élite samurai and I met individually with the priests. Alone with one, I checked his nose. Straight. I relaxed a little.

'There are certain *sutra*s you must say now to keep a new life strong.' He smiled at me.

Afterwards, I pulled Misuki into a garden. We strolled to the middle and squatted face to face. 'I have made a decision. There is no need to gather those herbs.'

'Yes, Kozaishō.' Misuki grinned and placed a hand on her own stomach. 'I understand.'

We embraced as only two dear friends can, weeping for new life and for death.

Away from the city, the trees around Kiyomizu-dera were coming into leaf. With the new growth and superabundance of green, I thought of all that was growing and wrote this poem:

> Blossom time arrives
> Rain beating against the roof
> Green leaves burgeoning
> Tiny pale buds on bushes
> Who will the spring produce?

Third day of Pilgrimage
Everyone travelled to Hōshō Temple, the third one. Misuki snuggled next to my body as we moved on in the cool morning. I nestled back.

At a more appropriate time, I promised myself, I would share my secret with Michimori. His reticence and taciturnity of late rendered me hesitant. I did not wish to add to his burdens of authority. I chose to wait until a more propitious time. When would that be? Who could I ask? Misuki said Akio, but I believed Tokikazu had Michimori's ear.

After we reached the gates, Tokikazu said, 'More than a century ago, Hōshōji was built in the place where one of the old palaces stood.' His eyes related his sentiments, without words, without touch, but I owed loyalty and love to Michimori.

'The first building is the pagoda, which has eight sides, nine storeys, and is eighty-four *jō* high, like a painted mountain, rising tall out of the earth,' Tokikazu finished his story. Akio trailed us, scowling at one of us, then the other.

I settled into the tent just outside the temple. The Chief Priest and his ranking priests made elaborate greetings. As with those at previous temples, they remained in their heavily hooded robes. They assured us of private meetings with a priest. I was reassured, but decided I would have no meetings with any priest unless my dagger was with me.

Before the meeting with the First Ranking Priest, another priest showed me, Misuki, and my serving girls their Amida statue and added:

More than a hundred and fifty years ago, this is the statue to which Fujiwara no Michinaga tied his string. He died holding that string attached to the beloved Buddha to ease his entrance to Heaven.

I remained at the Buddha's feet for a time. My eyes dripped with the chance of revenge for Tashiko and Emi. In the moment's perfection I also remembered Byōdōin and its colossal shining Amida Buddha.

Fourth day of Pilgrimage
Today I and other samurai arranged the snare's jaw. Hoichi had discovered the names of two more men, besides the one in my dream. The Chief Priest and the two ranking priests agreed to have Plover disguise himself as a priest of Hōshōji. He could pray and behave like a Temple priest with his wide hood and cowl. He would meet with each person suspected of traitorous thoughts, actions and murder. I prayed Goro would be found and captured, too.

Plover confirmed the names of the three men who did not speak with loyalty that night. Michimori, Tokikazu, Akio, the other samurai and I planned the rest. Plover would meet the men again and make his proposal for their attack.

Here Misuki and I said and wrote the formula for protection:

adande dandapati dandavarte dandakushale dandasudhare
sudhare sudharapati buddhapashyane sarvadharanai-avartani
sarvabhasyavartani su-avartani samghaparikshani
samghanirghatani asamge samgapagate tri-adhvasamgatulya-arate-prapte
sarvasamgasamatikrante sarvadharmasuparikshite
sarvasattvarutakaushalyanugate simhavikridite

Fifth day of Pilgrimage

Misuki borrowed armour from Mokuhasa, since he was closest to her size. I wore mine under my clothes. Many guards, as well as Akio, Mokuhasa and Sadakokai, hid in our tent, away from the lamps.

Michimori forbade Tokikazu to join us. 'He is too valuable to lose.'

Some small part of me was relieved that I would not be forced to lie next to Tokikazu.

Yet Michimori had said this harshly, unlike his other directives. Was his true reasoning that he did not trust me, again? Or that he did not trust Tokikazu *and* me? Could the target of this distress lie somewhere else? Yet I was outraged at the implied distrust of Tokikazu with me, and desolate at the lost faith of my husband in my honour. My honour, which I most valued and for which I had fought over and over again. Where was I to find it except in blood?

We pretended to sleep. Sadakokai feigned snores, and Misuki worked to stop herself from giggling. Fortunately, she had had much practice in this.

We waited in the dark, listening to the night birds and the trees' soughing, inhaling the different perfumes of the samurai.

Then we heard it. The crunching of armour against armour. I squeezed Misuki's hand. Fortunately she did not move or cry out. Waiting. The delicate soundlessness of a sword out of its scabbard.

Someone jumped up and yelled. A sword glinted against the lamps. Akio came from behind. I heard the clash of sword against armour and the grunt as someone fell. Akio's grunt. Was he hurt? Dead?

Sadakokai, who lay beside Misuki, leaned over, dagger drawn, and attacked with a throaty sound. I aimed my dagger and threw it into the third traitor. A dull thud and a shout as it gained its mark.

Two betrayers in custody, two conspirators seriously wounded, and one dying, five in all. Soldiers sequestered them. One of the seriously wounded bore the face I had seen in my dream from the Second Day of this pilgrimage.

Michimori granted Plover the rank of Chief Priest at one of our temples. Such munificence. I hoped all the traitors were found – our goal to remove the mice from the storehouse. Emi had been avenged, and I was pleased, for the moment.

Servants had cleared the wreckage of my tent and readied it for sleep. Later that night, I heard groaning. Tamuramaro's burial mound. Did this mean peril for Rokuhara? The capital? Both?

The Chief Priest presented me with part of a *sutra* written on blue paper in thick silver and gold lettering, like the sun and the moon together. I placed it with the piece Chiba had given Tashiko in my crane document box from Michimori.

At this time, it was right that old and new were together.

I thanked Kannon-sama, the Goddess of Mercy, for my close ones' and my safety.

II. Enemies

My sleep had been disrupted since Emi's murder. I approached the priests' practice field early, before most servants, in the Hour of the Tiger. Tokikazu and Akio were due in a short time, and I made my way to the pavilion to see if the morning rice had been delivered.

I heard two men arrive and talk while I ate. I recognised the voices.

'One last time, I warn you, Tokikazu.' The anger in Akio's voice sliced through the thick haze outside the pavilion.

'Stop, Akio. My sentiments are not like cherry blossoms. They are trees. Pines. They will not change, regardless of the danger she is in.'

'I spoke to her about her duty. And her honour.'

'You truly thought you needed to?'

I remained motionless, the better to listen.

'This is not one of your lovers' games. I have known her since she was a little girl.'

'Akio, she is a grown woman now.'

At this I said yes to myself.

'Have you seen what Chiba did to her back? No? I have. When she was only nine or ten. A sight I have not forgotten.'

'No.' The resentment leached out of Tokikazu's voice.

'Imagine what Chiba did to those girls because he was forbidden to use them as he wanted.'

'No. Akio.'

'Do you know what Goro likes to do to girls of my daughters' ages?'

407

I did not stir, frozen in memories. Copper pheasants cooed in their nests.

'*I* know, Tokikazu. *I* know.' Akio's voice crackled as he snapped out the words. 'That is why I went to the Village of Outcasts willingly. Joyfully. I needed to protect my girls. It would have been only a short while before he discovered them.'

'He?'

'Goro. Daigoro no Goro. You remember him?'

Tokikazu grunted several times and spat. Goro had cost him dear.

'We must not let this *oni* in priest's clothes near her again. Goro killed her lover, a girl named Tashiko, in the same way that he murdered Emi!'

'Her lover? Kozaishō had a female lover?' Tokikazu's voice was suddenly as faint as a wispy cloud.

'The only difference between Tashiko's and Emi's deaths is, hopefully, that Goro did not have time to torture *and* rape Emi before he strangled her.'

A snarl of revulsion pierced the pavilion, a spear into a *mochi*.

'Yes, Tokikazu. That is what he likes to do. Torture. Rape. Then strangle.'

'Loathsome! What evil!'

'If you dishonour Kozaishō, she *will* be punished. Do *not* do that. Please. Know also I *will* come for you.'

'I assure you my feelings for Kozaishō are honourable.'

'I must have your word.'

'Akio, I give it to you. I will not dishonour Kozaishō. I will not.'

'She is another daughter to me.' His words floated like an autumn leaf on a pond. 'Let us protect her, then.'

'Agreed.'

'But remember, I shall continue to watch you.'

'If you must, Akio. Now let us find our recalcitrant student and put her through her paces.'

'Yes. She will need her skills.'

'I fear so.'

That night Plover met me. I saw his white-streaked hair glistening under the new moon near the plum trees.

'I could not tell all earlier, my lady.'

'All of what?'

'All of the men we questioned not only admitted Minamoto ties, but direct orders.'

'From whom?'

'Daigoro no Goro.'

The sound of that name sent a shiver of anger up my back to my neck. 'I am not surprised. Is there more, valued Plover?'

'He told us where to find Goro.'

My body flushed hotly. 'Where? You know why I need to find him.'

'Yes, my lady.'

I looked him in the eyes. 'You know what I wish to do. And you know what he has done.'

'Yes, my lady.'

He gave me the information.

'I will arrange a false assignation by the river. Can I rely on your discretion?'

'By that you mean silence?'

'Yes. At least until my meeting is over.'

'For you. Also for our honourable Commander-in-Chief Lord Taira no Michimori.'

I heard a sigh. I waited and stared into his eyes.

'Yes, my lady.'

III. Honour and Blood

He sat near the side of a stream, his back to a small wood fire, wearing a black *kanmuri*. How silly that hat looked on his ugly face. I stood silent and waited. My mouth tasted of sand. He blinked as he noticed my sword and my thumb resting on its *tsuba*. I had devised this scheme since he had tortured and raped me, more than three years ago.

I had envisaged a fight, but he held only a dagger. An honourable way would have been to give him an equal weapon. I had no intention of treating him honourably. He had lost the right to such from the moment he had misused his power.

'You!' He recognised me.

'Yes. Kozaishō, wife of the commander-in-chief, the honourable Lord Echizen Governor Taira no Michimori.'

'It is said Michimori is never without his Woman-for-Play. Perhaps he is here to protect you,' he sneered, and glanced to each side, standing. 'Where is he?' He gave a short laugh, but looked around with fear in his black eyes.

'I stand here alone.' I stared at him, then set my face guard and helmet. He would either run or fight. I hoped he would fight.

'Alone?' His face contorted into a true mask of wickedness, from the face of an egret to that of a hawk.

My sword could do the deed. My arrows could bring him down if he ran.

His foot made a small shift backwards. He was going to run. I pulled two arrows together out of my quiver and then set my bow.

His eyes darted to his right. Two arrows notched.

His eyes flashed left.

I raised my bow.

His eyes looked upwards. He shifted back again, slightly. This was sweet, seeing him try to control his fright. He had harmed me for so long; he had earned it.

Another step backwards.

Another.

I smiled and directed my thoughts. A pull on my bow.

His left heel pivoted.

I breathed with an arrow.

He turned.

Zap.

Readied my second arrow.

Zap.

Both targets struck.

There he lay, face down, legs askew, an arrow piercing each thigh.

With caution I strolled to stand at his head. It moved to one side and up a little. His eyes burned red with what I hoped was fear, possibly pain or hate.

'That was for Misuki. My servant and friend. For her anguish. You let her know of your "Purification" trap for me, but she was powerless to prevent it.'

His lips pinched together. He took loud breaths, while his eyes flitted back and forth. He righted himself. He wrested at the arrows.

One wound bled profusely. I could not allow the bleeding to kill him. I grabbed a long piece of wood from the fire and staunched it. He screeched as a demon from the deepest Hell. I threw away the wood and unsheathed my sword. He fell back into the sand, then wobbled to his feet, panting hard.

Staring at him, but far enough away that he could not kick me, I said, 'I want to relish this as much as you amused yourself in harming me and mine.'

I stepped back to view all of him. I feigned moving my head down as if to look at his feet and cut off his broken nose. He howled, raised his hands to stop the gush of blood, and knelt in the sand.

'Now you will not have to live with that broken nose.' I forced my lips upwards. 'That is for the innocent life you took. My Emi's. She was the servant you strangled in my apartments. You used her as if she were a piece on a *go* board.' His moaning became a rhythmic drone.

'Even if you have a hundred tongues in your mouth and utter a thousand prayers, never speak ill of monks or violate women, or you will incur more penalties.'

My last stroke cut lightly into his belly. His intestines bulged across his forearms and thighs, and he dropped backwards into the sand. He scrutinised the viscera oozing from his belly. He knew an excruciating death was impending.

'That was for the poor girl named Tashiko at the Village of Outcasts near Uji. You murdered her for your pleasure. Then you shortened her funeral. You cut her life force. You dishonoured her . . . and me. Her soul has wandered for years because of you!

'And you made a sham of my Purification ceremony. You raped me! You used your power in perverted ways. You persecuted me and my servants. All those attempts to kill me and my husband!'

Then, as he howled with pain, I yelled at him: 'You vicious, debased, perverted, evil man! I hope you are reborn as a slug in springtime when the bramblings fight and mate. I hope you are reborn as a mosquito larva in a long drought and die. I hope you are reborn as a snake, with no teeth or fangs, and crawl on your belly in the dirt until you die of starvation. I hope you are reborn – no, I hope you never have a chance to attain enlightenment. I hope you never know the Buddha.'

His hawk eyes spilled with tormented tears. His eyes swelled white and wide, gazing at me.

I could not continue to torture him. I had inflicted ample pain for honourable retribution. With one stroke I took off his head, then set it on a spear in the sand.

Retrieving the cleaning cloths from my horse, I removed all traces of his wickedness from my sword and replaced it in its sheath.

I had fulfilled an honourable revenge. I thought of Emi's smiling face as she recited her prayers with me. Of Misuki, such a devoted and dedicated companion. My beloved Tashiko, lying dead with her neck encircled by that ring of rope-torn flesh. I stared at Goro's eyes – not wide with pain and fear, but as they were the last time I had viewed them, glinting in candlelight, flickering with power, viciousness, lust and brutality. This had been the Right Action.

Tokikazu confessed later that day that he had positioned archers and samurai around the area. After my first arrow, he had ordered them away. Servants obliterated all footprints, except mine.

I would never have known if he had not told me. Surely he is a Bodhisattva working here on earth.

My delight in taking a life dampened the fires of my victory. What would my father have said? I had taken the honourable path and action without gratification or gladness.

Had Michimori helped Tokikazu protect me? Perhaps not.

That evening, after being ritually cleansed, the entrance to Michimori's mansion appeared the same; perhaps it was I who had changed.

Michimori sent for me and, with Tokikazu and Akio as escorts, I hurried to his apartments.

'How did you fare?' Michimori's flat voice denied his flashing brown eyes.

He knew. Tears sprang from my eyes before words could form. Alone with my husband, I grabbed his broad chest and breathed with heavy sobs. He combed my hair with his fingers and with his other hand massaged my back. When I stopped crying, he murmured into my hair, 'It is different. With someone you know. And *for* someone you know. Is it not?'

Pulling back slightly, I said, 'Yes. I cannot believe Three Eyes is truly gone.'

'He is dead, my, my—' Michimori stroked the tears off my face. He pulled me hard against him. 'Please be wary. Three Eyes was not the last of our enemies.'

'Oh, Michimori. I will.' I wanted to be with him as we were before, to be closer to this embodiment of a great leader's Majestic Calm, his essence, Pure Tranquillity.

He pushed me back and we stood apart. His eyes changed to a distant black, and his voice became dry and flat. 'I have ordered Captain Tokikazu not to commit *seppuku* after my death. Rather, I have ordered him to protect your life.'

'You honour me, but I—'

'Go, Kozaishō. Leave me now.' He turned away, back muscles twitching and tightening.

I wiped away the rest of my tears, put on a neutral face and left.

How bittersweet my vengeance. I had triumphed over an *oni*, only to perhaps distance my husband.

IV. Vision

Later, Tokikazu and I paused in our shooting practice. The heat penetrated the pavilion, but with the end curtains opened, a whisper of a breeze mitigated the oppressive warmth. The heat had persuaded most archers to return to the monastery's waterfalls and ponds. I waved the servants away.

After they had left, we were alone, and I observed Tokikazu. He wiped the dampness from his body. Last summer I had been aroused when I had watched him cleanse himself. Now this action had the same effect, but I required only his advice on how to protect my husband, so dear to me.

'What is it?' He smiled.

'I need your advice.' I looked outside the pavilion to see if anyone lurked. 'Tokikazu, I am with child.'

'Sit. What do you need?' He clutched my shoulders as if I might fall.

I placed a fingertip on his drawn-together eyebrows. 'I am well. There are plans to leave Rokuhara. You know more about that than I, more than anyone but Michimori and the other Commanders. I have not yet informed him about the child.'

'Are you happy about it? You look serious. Are you considering . . . ?' He opened his arms.

'No, not that. Yes, I am . . . content to keep this child if I am able to.'

His arms and his voice dropped. 'Then what do you require of me?'

'I need to know if now is the time to tell him or if I should wait.'

'You protect Michimori. Again. Still.'

'As is my duty.'

'Only duty?'

'No – I have come to love him.'

'The Gods of Fortune smile on him at every turn.'

'Perhaps in another time or life . . .' I lifted my hand to his cheek. I cared for him also.

Tokikazu pulled away as his body stiffened. 'We both have our duties.'

Had I hurt him? I allowed my hand to fall to my side. 'Will you assist me?'

We heard a rustling. Tokikazu pulled on his dagger and rushed outside.

In a moment, he returned. 'Just birds. Kozaishō, you wish to know if now is a convenient or injurious time.'

'Yes. When can I tell him, "I am carrying your child"? Michimori relies on my observations and suggestions.'

'Yes, but your concern persists, rather than the jubilation I have seen in my wives.'

'Military and political matters demand my full attention. You know this.'

I waited and fanned myself. We sipped watered *sake* and ate rice balls. He gazed at the food, seeming flustered and dispirited. Ants trailed across the pavilion's grassy floor. Mosquitoes and flies hummed in and out of the open curtains. Moorhens and thrushes pecked at the ground, their dark backs shimmering in the heat.

'And, yes, Tokikazu, I am pleased. I want to say, "I am carrying your child."'

A sound behind the pavilion. Like the rustling of cloth. Footsteps.

Our heads turned to the east at the same time.

Tokikazu sped outside, dagger fully opened.

Within a short time, he came back, sweat dribbling. 'I could see no one.'

'Why did you not follow?'

'Fear for your life, Kozaishō. It may have been a trap.'

We exchanged wary looks.

'I say to you, now is *not* the time.'

'Thank you, Tokikazu.'

'Back to practice, then.'

I sipped the rest of my watered *sake* and went out into the sweltering sun.

Who had been outside, and what might he have overheard?

I was not yet aware that rumours were already rushing to Michimori.

The first morning after returning to Rokuhara, I walked on to the practice field and heard yelling. It was Michimori – with a savage ferocity I had only overheard in battle. His targets were what alarmed me most: fresh corpses.

That night, I awoke with another vivid dream. I shared it with Michimori.

'This one you must tell the Council yourself,' he said.

Never had I spoken directly to them. 'I cannot. *You* must present it.'

'This is yours to share. I have loved you for such a long time, yet . . . yet . . .' His fingers played with my hair as if with Koto Strings. 'You and your dreams are a great gift to me and the Taira Clan.' He stopped abruptly.

I knew he loved me, but he hesitated. He had restrained himself the previous night, and many before. He truly did not trust me. I had no knowledge of the rumours about me or who dispersed them.

He said, 'The message is extremely clear to me. But, let us see the Dream Diviner before we go to the Council.'

I agreed: addressing the Council would be a monumental step.

After the Dream Diviner, the Council assembled again in the middle of the night. A *kichō* was brought close for me to sit behind, as was the custom with court women.

'Kindly listen to Lady Kozaishō's dream,' Michimori requested.

After vehement arguments on each side, the Council agreed to allow me to speak.

I began, hoping my voice did not tremble too much with the honour. I had never spoken to the Council openly. My throat constricted. With difficulty, I articulated my words. I was not sure if they could hear me over the pounding of my chest. My ears surged, like an incoming tide.

I relaxed as I did before I loosened an arrow. I began:

'A red bird is in a grove of trees, each carefully trimmed. It sits on the topmost branch over the Sacred Mirror, singing a *sutra*, and wearing the Sacred Jewels, while holding the Sacred Sword in one claw. A white hawk swoops near the red bird. To save its life, the red bird flies away. It carries the Three Sacred Treasures and flies far west until it reaches a wooden nest near the sea. As the red bird settles on a branch, the hawk advances and the red bird flies away again. This time it flies north.

Most of the meaning was transparent, but the Dream Diviner spoke to the Council after I had finished. He stated that the red bird was the young emperor and the white hawk the retired emperor, Go-Shirakawa. The danger of the latter to the former was clear, but no one could decipher the second attack.

After the Dream Diviner had left, Oak coughed and declared, 'First we must see to the safety of our emperor. I believe we have sanctuary in the city of Dazaifu in Kyōshō. Let Purple Grass take the emperor and his family with a swift group to the Old Defence Headquarters in Dazaifu. He will be safe there.'

I heard grunts of assent and saw heads nodding in agreement. Purple Grass said, 'Yes, and a small group moving quickly will be best.'

'Let Purple Grass beware,' Michimori warned. 'Lady Kozaishō's dream suggests the Fox has long fingers. Do not settle comfortably in Dazaifu. Be ready to flee again.'

'We will keep runners available continuously between us.'

That evening, I said several *sutra*s for the safety of our emperor and for us.

Commander Purple Grass left within a day, taking the Emperor Antoku, the royal family, the Three Sacred Treasures, and all the provisions they could manage to safety. Exile. Would they ever return?

Perhaps it was truly the end of our world, *mappō*, as the *kuge*, and also Misuki with her bramblings, had feared. I had predicted it with my dream. What *karma* was that for me?

III. Burned

Misuki placed both hands around one of my ears and whispered, under the noise of the carriage and oxen, 'Kozaishō, my sweet, I bring unfortunate news.'

I was not worried: it probably related to her astrological formations, which were disparate to this world. I hoped it did not involve her hitting me with sticks again. Or drinking some horrible potion designed to keep me from harm. It was neither.

'Sadakokai told me he overheard Large Cicada speaking to Lord Michimori.'

My back straightened, and my muscles tensed.

'Large Cicada spoke about Tokikazu.'

I leaned my ear into her hands to hear more clearly every word.

'He overheard you say you were carrying Tokikazu's child. And that your husband had an obligation, if you were disloyal, to take your head or command you to commit *seppuku*.' She pulled her cupped hands away from my ear and turned directly to my face, shaking her head, her eyes distressed, her hands clasped, as if in prayer.

I took a deep breath to cool the rabid fires in my chest. 'You know I am not disloyal in any deed, do you not, Misuki?'

'Naturally. I defended you to Akio when he accused you. I will come to your defence again. I trust you, Kozaishō. Completely.'

I could not speak, only laid my head on her shoulder and loosed furious tears.

★ ★ ★

Another meeting was called in the night. More samurai guards were stationed outside Grand Room when I slipped behind its screens.

Lamps threw eerie shadows over faces worn from broken slumber and worry. A runner hastily advanced to the sombre group. Oak motioned with a hand and uttered his usual cough. The samurai guard bowed low, then raised his head and torso but remained on his knees, speaking so that I could not hear.

Oak nodded and addressed the group. 'Fox is preparing for a pilgrimage.'

'What?'

'Where?'

'Mount Hiei.' Oak waved the guard away who left in silence.

Incredible news! My stomach snapped tighter than the closing of a twenty-five-fold fan. I sat behind my *kichō*, but the commanders' throats strangled with alarm – or perhaps it was mine. With the silence I concentrated on my stomach pain and the repercussions of the Fox's latest strategy.

The Oak coughed again. 'We could prevent Fox going, but this does not portend well.'

'Without Fox, we have only the young emperor to assert our authority, and he, perhaps everything, is in grave danger,' Michimori stressed, beating one fist into the other hand. He was most handsome when he was fervent.

'How can you conclude that?' asked the Oak.

'Have you learned so little?' Michimori's voice deepened. 'The emperor does nothing unless it profits him. We know his piety is always convenient.' He spread his tree-like legs and placed a hand on each hip. 'Something is imminent. I do not like it.'

'Do you believe he would plot against us?' Large Cicada raised his Taira eyebrows into a broad black arch.

'Fox considers our protection to be captivity. He has plotted against us, and will again. Let us counter by saying the emperor is on a pilgrimage too. Let us maintain our power base with Emperor Antoku.'

Kingfisher glanced at Michimori and announced, 'More information. Boar is near, in Yamato Province.'

This was the province directly east of Heian-kyō, too close.

'I have a runner who says Rat is in Ōmi Province, also close to Mount Hiei. I trust no coincidence.' Michimori's resonant voice echoed while the

420

lamps seemed to flicker with each word. 'Ōmi is even closer to the city than Yamata.' He folded his branch-like arms across his wide chest and stood as if nothing could dislodge him from that spot.

'Is it possible that Rat and Fox are forming an alliance with Mount Hiei? What action must we take?' The Oak put questions to the others as if the priests were contemplating a national defilement. The world at war – against us. There was a long quiet, but for the popping of the brazier.

Michimori broke the silence by putting to them the plan he and I had discussed after I had told him of my dream. 'We are, by our most trusted runners, outnumbered with Hare in Yamato in the south-east and Rat directly east. Now Fox, Mount Hiei and their *sōhei*. We are only days away from our unconditional defeat unless we retreat . . . immediately.' He lifted his arms to plead his case.

The commanders argued about the brutal strategy Michimori and I had devised. Disputes arose – one point, then another, differences, disparities, new ideas, old ideas. Hands in the air. Fists on hips. Yelling. Gesturing. Pointing. Stomping.

Eventually Oak and Large Cicada assented to Michimori's and my plan. They convinced the others, but agreement came only in the early morning.

Destruction was the only feasible solution: Rokuhara must be burned and destroyed – the entirety of Rokuhara, all five thousand mansions, with the servants' homes, and especially with all the supplies and food we could not carry. The entire city must be razed. Nothing must be left for the enemy.

I ordered my servants, and they packed everything they could. Within a day everyone had departed.

'Misuki.' I checked her eyes, fringed with red. 'Have you bundled everything?'

She nodded.

With tears, everyone scuttled – like spring birds searching for nest materials – servants, guards, samurai, ladies, wives, concubines, grooms and serving girls. Several small groups of samurai, ordered to leave last, set torches to each estate and storehouse. They planned to set fires from north to south and from west to east.

Red flames and clouds of black smoke consumed the houses as the large column of people moved methodically towards Hōshōji Temple. The ships travelled the route along the northern shore of the Inland Sea. We were bees absconding from a burning hive.

A horse cantered up to me. Tokikazu. He stopped next to me, lifted his head and shook it. I looked at his face. He wiped off the sweat with the back of his hand then rode on.

The smoke rose into the sky, as if from a mountain of rotten incense. The heat of our lives scorched our hearts. It singed our faces, then our backs as we abandoned Rokuhara, riding through the black and grey air.

Michimori passed me on Thunderbolt. He slowed and grabbed my forearm. Tears poured down his sunburned face and his face guard steamed in the cool air, yet his broad features remained stoic. I placed my other hand on top of his. For a precious moment our horses marched in parallel, and then he went on.

> Dwellings of Rokuhara
> Burning resplendently
> Our homes bedazzle the sky
> We depart into dimness
> Wherever *inago* leads

V. Enemies of Enemies

Sailing along the coast, Taira ships loaded with supplies shadowed the troops to provide a quick escape if we were attacked. My husband's runners, samurai and assistants shuttled to and fro, usually at dusk, night or early morning, and became as commonplace as my storytelling. The commanders joked that they had been weaned on fighting pirates and therefore were happy with our naval strength. Michimori believed it would not be sufficient.

Yashima, a port city along the Inland Sea, afforded a modicum of comfort. Spy-prostitutes brought information about the Minamoto with little danger. I considered my life at Hitomi's, how different my existence had been there.

Michimori and other commanders needed to learn not only of Rat but also of his cousins, the three pugnacious siblings: Horse, Sheep and Tiger. There was trouble in the Minamoto family, and this might be to our advantage.

One evening Sadakokai brought me Michimori's order to dine with him. It had been such a long time since my husband had chosen to do that. Fortunately I was like my mother, who barely showed a pregnancy until the last month or so. Also, under my armour and layered robes, my growing belly had not been evident, and he had not seen beneath as we had not pleasured each other since returning to Rokuhara. He had spurned all my overtures.

★ ★ ★

'I like the Inland Sea. Here at Yashima, I can always hear the water,' I said to Michimori, inside the tent, as he applied incense to his helmet and armour, hoping he would talk to me about something other than tactics, strategies and the enemy, hoping we could return to the intimacy I had enjoyed with him, hoping he would forgive or forget what had estranged him from me.

'Yes, I, too, find the sound of the ocean pleasant.'

My face warmed at his words. 'My honourable lord, I am glad it pleases you.'

'I ordered a meal for tonight that may please both of us.'

Would he at last tell me what had caused him to be remote all this time? Why had he refused my offers to couple? Had I not convinced him before of my honourable behaviour?

He called for servants, who brought food and a small brazier already red with coals. They arranged dishes of rice, turnips and fish, then removed themselves. The light was strong for this time of day, down here in the south, the Hour of the Cock.

'The dragonflies, I understand, were abundant, earlier in the year. I regret we missed them.'

He spoke to me of dragonflies! 'I have seen a few blue and purple morning glories, and my servants have found some of the last chestnuts and berries.' I relaxed with the neutral topic. I allowed my eyes to smile at him. He returned an amicable look, but some of him held back. Large flocks of dunlins sang their *'jew-lit, jew-lit'* refrain against the green sandpipers and their *'chooy-lee, chooy-lee'*.

'With all those birds, the fishing must be good, Michimori.'

'I can trust the birds.'

I chuckled, but the bitterness and desolation radiating from his eyes made me stop. I stepped back and managed to say, 'Michimori, you can trust more than the birds.'

His posture straightened. 'The most important aspect of this life is honour and that means trust, loyalty and obedience.'

'I agree.' About whom was he speaking?

'You agree? You?'

His sarcasm penetrated like an arrow into my throat. He was talking about me. Had he believed Large Cicada? How could he after I gave him my word? The world pounded inside my body like a hammer. I struggled to concentrate and speak. After long moments, I was able to say. 'I do not comprehend your meaning.'

'I will explain.' He sat and motioned for me to do so as well.

The hand that gestured was stiff with tension.

He called for servants, who brought a bottle of *sake* and two cups.

His sandalwood incense mixed with the odd odour of the warming *sake*. Usually pleasant, they triggered my stomach to clench and push bitterness to my mouth. Lowering my head, away from the odours, I gulped not to retch. I was too advanced to be queasy. The steam from the *sake* evoked spring and wisteria, poison and death.

'Do you converse with others about honour?' Michimori said.

'My lord, this is a topic I often discuss with Akio, Sadakokai and Mokuhasa.'

'Not Tokikazu?' my husband asked, while pouring a cup of *sake*, his voice like the point of a dagger. He brushed his sword as he handed me the cup.

'Tokikazu and I have completed our discourse about honour.' I studied his hand, with my stomach like a ship's knot. Would he take my head? How could he still not trust me?

'I would think the topic of honour should always be of interest to you.' He poured himself a cup.

'I believe honour is made up of loyalty, truthfulness, obedience and trustworthiness.'

'You include obedience with honour?' Michimori said.

I took my cup, stifling another gag. 'Obedience is essential to honour.'

'Kozaishō, if you assert all four constituents – *all* are indispensable to honour . . .' He leaned over, as he had before he married me, when he had first asked what was in my heart. 'If this baby is mine then I command you to drink your *sake*.'

His words slashed like a *naginata*. I took a long glance at the dark brown eyes I cherished. I had failed in my wifely duties. Wretchedness passed through me. He did not know how much I cared for him – he did not know how far he could trust me. 'My honourable lord and husband, I *do* proclaim that all four elements of honour live within me. This baby is yours – as it could only be – and I drink to honour it.'

I raised the cup to my mouth, inhaled its toxic odour, and then, as my heart pounded the drumroll of death, tilted the cup to my lips.

Michimori batted it away with the back of his hand. *Sake* splashed over me, and shards littered the floor. As he swiped at his eyes, I saw that his hand was speckled with blood.

I awaited his instruction.

His torso and hands trembled. 'I believe you.'

I pointed to the *sake* he had poured for himself. *Sake* from the same bottle as mine. 'Why?' The question scratched from my throat.

'If you had refused to obey me or not convinced me of your honour, I would have drunk the *sake*.'

I diluted the spilt *sake* with my tears.

'Kozaishō, I could not live in a world with your disloyalty, and I would have ended my life. First by drinking the same poison, and then . . .' With one finger he tapped his sword.

The bottle of *sake* made its way to the ground outside the tent.

My husband directed the guards not to disturb us. We removed our swords and other impediments.

The rest of the night was as if we had met for the first time, united again. Our melding demonstrated the clean actions from Pure Spirits, of which Obāsan had spoken when I had first met her. At some time in the night, he awakened me with his insistent hands. When we completed, he said, 'I know.' He laid his hand on my swelling stomach and stroked it and the baby stirred on its own.

That morning he lifted me and swung me around, laughing. 'I am thirty years old. This is my first child!' He patted my stomach and looked at me with shiny brown eyes.

Much later, our army fought at Mizushima, but Taira troops did not walk through much enemy blood because Rat's troops soon surrendered.

A surprised Oak asked the Council, 'Why would they do that?'

Michimori concealed his frustration and irritation, and in the telling only straightened his fingers on his leg. 'I anticipated Rat might gather his remaining troops and retreat to Heian-kyō. He will not risk control of the capital.'

The commanders received this in silence while they lowered their

426

heads, their eyes hollow with the grasp of their thorough and final homelessness. Silent but for, as the *kuge* said, 'the weeping on silk sleeves'. I thought of our homes:

> Red sky behind us
> Rokuhara is burning
> Blazing on our eyes
> Our home's annihilation
> Smouldering crimson sunsets

In the next days Taira spies in Rat's camp found the sought-after information. Rat had captured the retired emperor, setting fire to one of the palaces. However, his kinsmen banded together and attacked him near Uji Bridge. Subsequently, scouts suspected that Tiger approached the capital to strike, rather than aid, his cousin Rat. Tiger moved towards the capital, and we defeated an enemy cousin, Boar, who turned against Rat. Rat and his brother-in-law died at Uji, where I had fought my first battle.

My sorrow and Misuki's tears flowed when we heard about the misery of Lady Tomoe, consort to Rat, after losing both husband and brother in a single battle.

'I lack her fortitude,' I whispered into Misuki's neck, as we held each other.

'She made her way to Echigo and became a nun to say prayers for her husband and brother.'

I pulled away. 'Again Lady Tomoe's courage shames me. I could not bear to be parted from Michimori. The impermanence of the world would vanquish my desire to be alive without my honourable lord.'

> Summers without sun?
> Springtime when no flowers grow?
> Snowless warm winters?
> No burnished leaves in autumn winds?
> Life with no loving lord? No!

While the Minamoto fought among themselves, the Taira leaders convened meetings and committed to a plan. Three bases along the Inland Sea needed strengthening.

'With Yashima, Hikoshima and Ichinotani,' Large Cicada argued the obvious, as he did time and again, 'we can maintain control of the eastern entrance to the Inland Sea.' All the commanders agreed, because it was the next logical step.

Logical steps in the past had not always been advantageous to the Taira.

BOOK 17

I. Settling

Tomorrow we shall reach Ichinotani. I wish to hear the sea chant again.

Michimori lay beside me, after delight, but his mind revisited the troubles. 'Fox is trifling with us, dividing us from his guardianship, not giving us his approval. Trying to separate us from the young emperor. After all their complaining,' he pointed in the direction of the meeting tent, 'they will discern this . . . eventually.'

He thought of them as a 'situation' that required strategies, just as when we played *go* or backgammon.

'So, it is time for us to move?'

He did not smile, although he stroked my shoulder. 'Yes. We should leave Yashima within a day.' We sat and examined the map next to our *futon*.

'Fukuhara?' I pointed on the map. 'We could go east by ship.'

He tapped my forehead with his little finger. 'Precisely. See here? That's Hiyodori Pass. A gap in those high hills behind the Ichi Valley. The valley goes from Hiyodori Pass to the coast.' He traced his finger along the map.

'How safe is the Hiyodori Pass?'

'The only creatures who can climb it are monkeys.' Now he emphasised each point by repeatedly stabbing his finger on the map: 'With the mountains behind us, the sea in front, Ichinotani to the west and Ikutanomori to the east, we should have a safe place while we build our defences. I hope Oak will agree.'

Michimori had recommended such strategies before, and his plans, when approved by the Council, had brought success.

A city, even a small one, could offer some respite and safety. Fukuhara provided comforts such as buildings, rather than tents, and streams of fresh water. Although a fortress and rather primitive, it proved more civilised than anywhere else along the five to ten *chō* of camps. Little was said of Rokuhara. Our lost home. I shared this poem:

> Snow-crusted branches,
> Like Harima rice, heaped silver
> While Rokuhara's fires
> Burn slowly in our hearts' eyes,
> Sunset on that last day

I was not aware of how severe the situations were until we received an Imperial Envoy from Fox. I moved to the *kichō* for formal meetings and recognised the imperial colour and chrysanthemum.

My chest tightened, and I gasped when I saw him. The Envoy was covered with mud, panting, like his horse, and appeared exhausted. He advanced with a stride that suggested he was a separate species of soldier, of man. He presented the document and retired to await our response.

The emperor commanded the Taira Clan to 'return the Emperor Antoku and the Sacred Treasures by the Seventh day of the Second Month'.

Faced with this demand, the commanders, except Michimori, were like cats running from dogs. They gestured, they postured, they talked, and then they paced back and forth.

Most commanders were afraid of Fox's strength, which now had the backing of Mount Hiei's *sōhei* as well as Tiger, Sheep *and* Horse. Their uncle, Boar, had joined them as well. They had united against Rat, and now against us.

The whole world was at war with the Taira Clan.

Last year Minamoto leaders had fought among themselves.

Now, together, we toiled to increase our numbers before marching. Misuki trekked frantically from one hill shrine to another, saying prayers and lighting candles and incense.

'Do not light anything else or I will suffocate you!' I said. She ceased.

At the next council meeting with the commanders, Michimori put forward his suggestions. Since Fox watched, most, but not all, of us would change our location. Further, we did not know where these Minamoto leaders were.

Purple Grass agreed with Michimori, knowing Oak did not trust his judgement but trusted Michimori's. We set off again.

After a relatively short journey by sea from Yashima, we landed in Settsu Province, between Fukuhara and Ichinotani. Misuki vomited throughout the voyage, but I was not ill. I enjoyed the rolling vessel, and its rocking kept the baby still.

> The Taira love the sea
> Its songs murmur in our ears
> The pulse of oceans
> Its ever-sounding *sutra*s
> Like *karma*'s overwhelming rhythm

As Michimori had anticipated, this area provided scope for us to build our defences. The young emperor and his entourage were secured on a ship at a distance from the shore. Only the commanders and their personal samurai knew the exact ship and the spot at which it waited.

Tokikazu and Mokuhasa reported to Michimori beside the early-morning fire as he and I ate. They walked with a jaunty step. It was good to see Tokikazu again. He brought promising news. 'There are fresh supporters,' he reported, after the customary greetings.

Michimori acknowledged the good words. I kept my eyes away from Tokikazu's.

They spoke of great defences, which we could hear being built not far away. They speculated that we might return to the capital.

> Sun curling behind clouds,
> Grinning, laughing at the ocean,
> The roar of sea waves
> Still dancing with the breakers
> A hundred aeons from now.

As I rode with Misuki and Tokikazu, I saw that Michimori had been right. The Ichinotani Fort had thick earthen walls with an outer layer of stone. Guards stood watch on top of wooden structures, which reached below sea level. Misuki stopped her incessant singing of *sutra*s when she saw the fortifications. Thank the Goddess of Mercy for some quiet!

Fukuhara, where the women and children were expected to stay, lay between Ichinotani and the Ikuta Woods. The mountains loomed to the north of us. Nothing but rabbits or monkeys could scramble up or descend. Our growing fortifications were to east and west, and the numerous ships held to the south, harboured off the narrow beach. Safe. For the moment.

People mended armour and *naginata*, and assembled arrows, while many slept from the fatigue of repeated marching. Spring hinted at its return. Large flocks of cawing black-headed gulls shed feathers to their summer plumage. On the beach wavy lines of siskins with their '*djwin, djwin*' created a rhythm of laughter.

Misuki and I spoke of singing and dancing for the commanders. Atsumori, a young samurai, practised his flute. Although it was no longer my duty, I elected to accompany him on the *biwa* until well after dark. The flute and the string were magical against the murmuring of the Inland Sea.

II. Banished

I write after riding from Ichinotani to Fukuhara, and back again.

The next morning, we heard that a small group of our troops had been overthrown by Tiger. Afraid that morale might deteriorate, the commanders attempted to silence this news. Plans like fireflies dotted the air. Thoughts of marching and retaking the capital floated above each fire.

Some talked. The optimism among the common soldiers drooped like new barley shoots in early-summer heat. The commanders remained alert. Extra guards were posted, not only in the west at Ichinotani where we expected an attack but also in the east.

Michimori took charge at Ichinotani and doubled the watches on the ships. He anticipated an attack that night or the next day, so he arranged small groups of guards with alternating short watches. That way, they remained fresh.

'I fear for the young emperor, the empress and their entourage. Men on ships and ashore are checking for any kind of attack, although we do not expect them by sea because of our naval power.' Michimori enfolded me in his arms as he spoke, 'They are cunning. They may catch us unawares. They have before. Several times.'

The flaming oxen on the mountain pass had surprised everyone, and thoughts of that night on the mountain brought unintentional shudders through me.

Most commanders were posturing and parading themselves again. They targeted Michimori. They mocked him in songs, singing that he and

I never travelled anywhere but together. We had not slept apart for a long time, except when duties demanded or when he had doubted my honour.

'It is said that Michimori holds a higher allegiance to you than he does to the clan,' Misuki told me.

'Let them laugh.' Michimori grimaced in jest when I questioned him about the sarcastic songs. 'You are my heart, and I need you.' He wrapped me against his chest. 'You are one of my great advisers. I do not wish to travel anywhere without such knowledge or attention.'

But the Council ordered that I be removed from Ichinotani and sent back to Fukuhara. We were to be separated immediately. It was too distracting for Michimori to have me with him.

Jealousy. None of them had a woman willing to go to battle and camp with the soldiers. Their wives lodged in neutral monasteries or the Fukuhara palaces, with servants and monks to attend them.

Michimori sent me this poem, marked with his tears:

> The waves clutch the shore
> Seeking a grounding refuge
> Grey waters beneath clouds
> One seagull floats restlessly
> Flying alone with the grey—

III. Tokikazu's Armour

Isolated but not alone, I record my friends' assistance.

Although Akio took me north to Fukuhara, my staunch Misuki had to stay at Ichinotani, probably to isolate me. Tokikazu had travelled with me previously, but he was ordered away and was to return to Fukuhara later that evening. In Fukuhara, Tokikazu could not be found, and the commanding officer placed me in a house with other wives. I retreated to a corner near the *shoji* to the outside and slept to assuage my frustration and misery.

There the Gods sent me one of my dreams, albeit brief, of two mated rabbits, one chasing the other. Before the second rabbit could catch the first, an eagle attacked, seizing the first. The second rabbit huddled alone, near a pond of shimmering brass. I awoke, wet and shuddering, in my under-robe, convinced I must bolt to Michimori or Tokikazu.

Guards had confiscated the beautiful armour Michimori had given me. I dressed as best as I could and withdrew from the building like a cat stalking a bird. I thought of Tokikazu as I sprinted towards the shore. Any movement in the direction of Ichinotani might alert the commanders' spies. Yet the Goddess of Mercy was good, and I found Hoichi, Mokuhasa's cousin, standing sentry on the shore, a favourable sign as obvious as when a fire starts at the first attempt in a fire-lighting ritual.

'Look at that ship. Who is on it?' I pointed first to this ship and next to that one, questioning loudly. Then, whispering, I asked, 'Will you take a message to Tokikazu tonight?'

'Yes. We know each other and are assigned to the same area.' In cunning and strength, he rivalled Mokuhasa: Hoichi neither turned his head nor showed surprise.

'Explain my situation and tell him I must meet him before dawn.' I elected not to inform Hoichi that I was going to Ichinotani. The less anyone knew, the better. I did tell him where I slept.

'My lady, it will be a great honour. My cousin embraces you in high esteem.'

'Thank you, Hoichi. He is dear to me.' I gave him a coin from my former life as a Woman-for-Play so that he would keep our conversation to himself. Even though he was Mokuhasa's cousin, I decided to take no risks.

I returned to the tent. I needed to sleep before my next activities.

I was awoken, seemingly moments later, by a scratching sound. Scratching back, I played the quiet cat and brought out the pieces of my old pink smock, always with me. Tokikazu and I embraced. We crossed to where his samurai lingered and we could speak without much danger.

'I received your message. What do you need? How can I help you?' He blurted his questions in rapid succession, in the same way that he discharged arrows.

'You must not have heard. They have banned me from Ichinotani and from Michimori. I am to stay here. They seized my armour.'

'I heard.'

'Can you . . . ?'

He waved to his attendant. 'Yes.' He turned to his servant. 'Go to my tent, assemble my practice armour and also find and bring the Lady's weapons. Bring them here, with two – no, three fresh horses.'

'Thank you. Tell me of Ichinotani and—'

'Michimori is well. They are reinforcing the east and west borders and the fort. Michimori says there will be an attack, some kind of unanticipated manoeuvre. The other commanders do not believe him. They speak of marching back into Heian-kyō.'

'The capital? So soon? What fool's tale have they heard?'

'I agree with Michimori. We are not ready. Tiger will make some manoeuvre. Who can forget what happened at Kamakura?'

I shivered to my bones at the memory of the oxen stampeding, the noise, the blood, the bodies and deaths. 'Will you escort me to Michimori tonight?'

'Yes.' He folded and twisted a paper. 'We will say I have a message . . . and a messenger.' He held up the 'note', waved it across my face and smiled sadly.

I put my arms around him. My tears of relief dampened his breastplate. We held each other, listening to the owls in the mountain trees that blended with the waters' resonances.

'Listen, my treasured Tokikazu, we have no idea what awaits us.' I laid my hand across my swollen midriff and looked into his eyes. 'If it arises, please teach this child the gentleness and strength, the tenderness and courage, the arrow and sword of . . . Michimori.'

'Kozaishō, you know I will. If there were an honourable path, I would have taken you from this war.' He motioned to the fortress, the ships and in the direction of Heian-kyō.

Tokikazu's attendant came back with horses and armour, and they helped me dress. The attendant had brought extra clothing for me to wear under the armour. That way it would not be dangerously loose.

With me as the 'messenger', we three returned to Ichinotani, where Tokikazu asked to see Michimori. As we neared his tent, the guards recognised me, probably by my height or my hair because the practice helmet and face guard covered most of my head and face, and Tokikazu's armour hung past my knees. Michimori knew me. Not for a moment did I surprise him.

Michimori gave the sign for dispersal. We sat alone, gazing at each other. He recited:

> 'The light is coming,
> Summer sunshine is here now,
> Dull dressed samurai,
> She smiles with red saffron lips,
> Making winter far away.'

'You are my light as well.' I smoothed my palm against his cheek, sunburned and golden. 'You have been for a long time. Please allow me to fight beside you.'

He shook his head with an unmistakable firmness. His eyes were both hard and desolate. I did not argue – dared not. I simply held him again and placed my head against his chest, inhaling his sweat and sandalwood.

He made rounds that night and returned at regular intervals to observe me. I slept lightly. The wind was high, and I awoke each time he entered our tent. I offered him refreshment, which he took several times. Michimori was my heart. I could not be parted from him for even one night.

IV. Mountain Surprise

Misuki is beside me in a tent. I will write what has happened.

I awaken to the sounds of crackling and a smell noxious enough to make me wince. It was not even dawn, but Michimori was no longer beside me.

Outside my tent I heard noise – shuffling, grunting.

'Minamoto on the beach!'

'The enemy!'

'To the ships!'

The sharp stench of bodies on fire.

I slip on the neck collar and helmet. A dagger down each leg guard. Where is Michimori? I finger the pink cloth inside the chest plate. Still there. I strap on my quiver, put my bow on my shoulder, grip my sword and charge outside.

All the Hells simultaneously. Men on horseback torch our tents and supplies. Fallen friends bleed. Groans. Missing limbs. Strange voices snap orders. Fumes – every breath is like sucking in hot coals. Birds shriek.

'There is one!' A voice to my left.

I slice across his stomach. He falls. A crimson puddle oozes under him. Enemies running in my direction, pointing at me.

'Take her alive!'

The Minamoto, on horseback, down the mountains. They ride through our bulwarks. Torches, haze, fire, arrows – everywhere. A squabble of seagulls clouds the shore. The air scorches my eyes. Dying men call, wail, howl.

The blood rises through the sand into my spirit.

On my right, Akio. 'They are taking wives of the ranked. From Fukuhara and monasteries.'

We mount the two saddled geldings on the ocean side of the tent. I will not be taken alive. They might kill my baby. Or, worse, take my baby – without me.

'Michimori? Tokikazu?' I scan the growing inferno. Our warriors sprint to the ships. Men on our ships urge them to escape. Michimori would not do that. Neither would I.

To the west, mounted samurai ignite our tents and fortifications, beheading foot soldiers as they run away. Barricades ablaze. I search for Michimori. A gust flashes hideous odours, searing my face. I force back bile.

Akio motions. We urge our mounts north and then west, to Michimori.

A brushfire eats our first barricade. My sword reflects the flames' colours. Sweat dribbles down my back. Smoky clouds spew high. I guide my horse. More screams. I push faster. Their troops stream from the west, ants out of their mound.

A horseman swings, grazes my shoulder. I wrench my dagger and gouge across his face. Squealing, he plunges to the ground. My hand and arm sting. I move on.

More around us.

Akio yells, 'Side to side!'

We close together – head to tail. Swords set. Advancing to my husband. Most hesitate when they see me, long hair, large with child.

Akio takes a head. I sever a leg. Cut the horse under the next. Another head. More blood surges. Another cry. Akio and I carve a swathe. By my count together we stop ten or fifteen. Good numbers. I need luck.

Approach the barrier. Going to Michimori. My gelding shies. Blaze too high. Heat too much. Cannot pass.

Around to the next barrier. Another fiery wall – cackling as if laughing. Far beyond, Michimori fights two, three.

Only a moment.

They bolt our way. 'Take that woman!'

'The road along the beach!' Akio gallops to the voice.

The beach: almost empty. A clear path to the west. Through the smoky haze, my husband and Tokikazu, beset.

To the west and up the mountain to Michimori. Akio joins me, and I race around piled bodies. Avoid knots of Minamoto.

I have to reach my husband. I will die with him rather than be taken prisoner.

Akio? One engages him. I race on.

Two sprint towards me. Swipe. A head. The other one, young, eyes wide, mouth open. A stroke. Surprised noise. Most think me an underling, not worth an arrow. Another. Behind me – beach, road east, west, mountains. No one. Except . . .

Where was Akio?

To my right. Fighting three. I shoot. Two. An arrow in an older face. One. An arm.

I hang my bow over my saddle. On the way to my beloved.

I ride above the mountain base and spot him. But Tokikazu is riding away on Thunderbolt! He is no coward! What is that?

My eyes follow Michimori. Bodies at Michimori's feet. More readying for him.

From the east – an archer. One arrow hits his back beneath his left shoulder. It bounces off.

I let out my breath. He keeps fighting. Now three more tumble down the swale. Now two. I advance closer. His sword gyrates on a volcano of bodies spewing blood, limbs, heads.

More archers arrive. A monsoon of arrows soars. Most miss. Some hit their own. Some stick in my husband's armour.

Too far away to shoot. I force my gelding, but he slips on the steep terrain and falters.

What can I do? Ahead, Michimori. To the east, Minamoto. No one on the beach. No Akio. No Tokikazu.

Glance back: no Tokikazu or Akio.

Glance forward: Michimori.

He roars with each stroke, over and over, his howls almost drowned by the thundering tide below. With each bellow more quivering bodies flop, topple.

Fresh ones close in. Two in front, three each beside and behind.

And archers, more and more archers shoot him in the neck.

I strike with my stirrups. My horse only snorts and tosses his head.
Michimori stiffens, taking the blow.
Another through his eye. His body sags. Collapses. Samurai slog up.
Then – the stroke. They take his head.
His blood erupts. Gone. Falling upon corpses slain by his own hand.
Too late. Too far away. My whole body tightens into a white-hot coal.
Unable to die beside him. Despair and rage consume me like a pyre.
His spirit is with his ancestors. Nothing more I can do. No small
comfort to give. Nothing, nothing to do for him.
They wrench off his helmet and seize his head. My stomach falls
to the bottom of the deepest water. They cheer and throw his head into
a box. A head box. They brought a head box. They planned to take his
head as a trophy. A trap. A dishonourable murder.
I flatten to the thinness of summer silk. I am emptied. Bloodied
and stunned, I ride back among the enemy, hearing the combat...
My vision blurs. I allow my mount to go wherever he will. All I see: my
husband's head. Dizzy. Pain jabs, punches and crushes, squeezes me.
Blackness.

Misuki sits beside me, a cup at my lips. 'Your water has broken, Kozaishō.
Drink. You will need your strength.'
At first I do not understand. I endeavour to stand. Contractions. Labour.
I need to protect my baby. His baby. Our baby. Tokikazu. Perhaps he
is alive, but how to find him? 'Any servants left?'
'Only three.'
'Foot soldiers?' I already know the answer.
Misuki remains silent.
Misuki has waited for me. Most have left on ships or been killed. The
beach and the sand are clear of our soldiers, except for corpses and body
pieces, enemies and blood. The ships are going back to Yashima.
I talk of the treachery. Words come from somewhere else, a story of an
oni far away, a long time ago. I tell her of that last stroke. I notice spots on
my armour. Tokikazu's practice armour. I wonder if it is raining. Misuki
removes the armour, piece by piece. The splotches still appear. She sits
and holds my hand while I tell her what I saw. Again.
Again . . . Misuki and I cry together. Then I write this poem:

Mighty fallen tree!
Struck down by cowardly hands
My lord lying there
The shade tree of my summers
Your icy broken body

It is night. Misuki feeds me. My throat swallows, yet I do not taste.

Now I can think what to do. I tell Misuki. She agrees to finish my story. History will record that I have honoured the great lord whom I have been privileged to follow, Governor of Echizen Province, Taira no Michimori, nephew of Taira no Kiyomori. I wish to record how my honourable lord was cut down. I will ask that a moral code, a code of honour and wielding power with integrity, which he followed, will be made known to every samurai and enforced by all. Never again should such a death befall so great a man.

V. The Coin

My Lady Kozaishō grieves profoundly, yet she orders me to write her final words.

'I have finished my story and my life, Misuki. It has been an honourable life. The Gods have blessed me many times – especially in my life's retrieval by my honourable lord's hand. I want to prove my respect, my honour, my love – by joining him.'

I write the rest of her story as she speaks. I swear on my parents' and grandparents' spirits to finish writing what has happened before I perform her other requests. I beg her to live for the best interests of her child, but she says, 'An honourable wife tends only one husband.'

We both know she would probably be taken as a concubine for the Minamoto, killed, tortured or worse. She expresses her desire to serve Commander-in-Chief Taira no Michimori in the afterlife.

'Now I must go to him. I must not be separated from him.' She dictates this poem:

> Thunder shakes the sky,
> Rain batters the calm terrain,
> Sorrowful eyes everywhere,
> Blind eyes chilled thoroughly through,
> I seek the sunlight no more

My name is Misuki. I have completed the birth and the death. May the Amida Buddha be praised and everlasting.

The shock of seeing Michimori murdered before her eyes causes Kozaishō to start her labour. I attend her. She shows herself to be a true samurai. She bleeds much but cries little. She asks me to search through our *furoshiki* to find Tokikazu's coin. With her permission, I send this to him with a serving girl. He arrives shortly after the birth in the early morning.

When my lady sees Tokikazu she screams, 'How could you leave him? How could you take his horse? You let him die!'

She almost falls to the ground.

Tokikazu dismounts from Thunderbolt and limps to her. On his knees in front of her, holding her hands, he moans, 'Kozaishō, Kozaishō, Kozaishō. I did not think I would see you again. It was Michimori who ordered me away. He ordered me not to die with him. He ordered me to live and protect you.'

Kozaishō lays her head on his arm. 'He told me he had given you that order.'

'The three of us could escape now.' Tokikazu strokes Kozaishō's hand. 'Come with me.'

'No, I cannot. But I need you to protect the child.'

'Michimori knew. That was the reason for his order and for sending me away.' His head motions to the mountain where Michimori died.

'No, Tokikazu. I cannot. I need to – need to follow my husband. I know you and I may be together in the next life. Yet for this one life now, I honour and love Michimori.'

'I promise to protect and raise the baby as if it were my own. How I wish this baby was mine!'

I hear his weeping.

My lady lifts a tired hand to touch the captain's face. 'My cherished Tokikazu, we both know such dishonour would have harmed the child.'

'We both loved Michimori too much. I will yearn for you in the rest of this life. I hope to be reborn with you. Soon.'

'And I with you, but I am resolved. You know there is only one Right Action. Sadly, it is not to go with you. However, I give you my most precious piece of straw.'

Tokikazu takes her hand in both of his and cradles it against his cheek. 'Your hand is like a white lotus leaf floating on this blackened and bloody world.' He weeps in soft sobs.

When they leave the tent, they come to me.

'My dear Misuki,' Kozaishō holds the child to her breast, 'Tokikazu has agreed to take the baby away.' She smiles and cries, gazing at Tokikazu. 'I do not know where. May the Amida Buddha and the Goddess of Mercy guide and protect them.'

Tokikazu says, 'Misuki, I will defend the baby with my life. I wish to stay and assist you, but I must go now or I will not be able to leave.'

I understand. I watch from a little distance as Kozaishō and Tokikazu say their farewells. I hear them recite the Lotus Sutra for protection. Silently I recite it with them.

He stuffs his arrows into the waist of his *hitatare*. He settles the swaddled child, positions the bundle inside his quiver and firmly attaches it to his waist. 'Not too late. You could come with us.' His eyebrows lift.

'A samurai wife has only one husband.' Her eyes fill and the tears topple on to her cheeks. She shakes her head. 'You do have my most precious piece of straw.'

Tokikazu says goodbye to me, mounts Thunderbolt and gallops away from the mountains and the Minamoto.

I write:

> The white-headed waves
> Batter the cold winter sand
> Their angry voices scream
> 'Run away, come away now
> Go away, run away, hide!'

I ask Kozaishō, 'What did you mean, piece of straw?'

'I thought I had told you all my stories. This is a story that reminds me of my life.

'Long ago a young man on his way to Heian-kyō prayed to Kannon-sama, the Goddess of Mercy, who appeared to him in a dream. She told him he could not receive mercy in this life because of past sins, but he would receive a gift. The next morning he was to pick up the first thing he found. The following morning he stumbled and a piece of straw stuck to his palm. Remembering the dream, he kept it.

On the road to Heian-kyō, rather than kill an annoying bee, the young man tied the bee to the piece of straw. Later, because the bee delighted a travelling mother's child, the young man exchanged it for three oranges. With compassion for thirsty travellers he met, he accepted their offer of silk for the oranges. Next, he traded the silk to despairing servants for their master's favourite, but now dead, horse. With prayers to Kannon-sama the dead horse revived. Last, the horse was bartered for land. The young, starving, yet pious man became, through his hard work and kindness, a wealthy and prosperous landowner.'

VI. Last Performance

It is a long day. I write Lady Kozaishō's last entry in her journal, her death poem:

> Near the bloody fields
> I dress in white kimono.
> The next adventure,
> After a life with honour –
> Life with my lord and Buddha.

I take great consideration in her dress. This is Lady Kozaishō's last act. She reads and reviews what I write.

I prepare seating mats. Not one of our samurai companions is alive. The Minamoto are at a distance. My lady knows her fate if she survives – death, forced marriage with a Minamoto, or worse.

In a loud voice, her cheeks bright with determination, she says, 'I must honour my great lord, but not as a woman. Instead I must die as any of his samurai . . . as Tokikazu would.'

So I strengthen myself to do what is necessary. Terrified, I ready the blade. The bright reflection of her in the *tachi* makes me squint. My hands are so cold that I cannot feel my fingers.

Kozaishō gives me her last instructions: take the papers to Tiger, Shogun Minamoto no Yoshitsune, the victor. I am to ask him to read this and remember to ask for the other kindnesses Kozaishō directs me. I tell her again that I understand and remember.

I thank my dear Kozaishō for all her tenderness. My eyes drip. She smiles with melancholy but ready eyes. We stroll arm in arm, holding on to each other, to the appointed place. She kneels on the mat. I arrange her kimonos. I light candles and incense and am amazed when the fire starts at the first attempt, a clear sign of favour.

I comb her hair. After all these years, I still marvel at its length and thickness. I assure her the top knot is perfect. I help her open the stomach of her kimono and reposition the folds to catch the blood.

She says her *sutras*, as I do. Her eyes are dry. 'I am going to join my honourable lord Michimori. The little warbler will be with her protector.' She thanks me and bends her neck. She takes her dagger and I hold the sword.

I nod.

I tighten my body and concentrate.

I look into her sweet eyes. She moves her hands over her dagger.

Kozaishō jabs the dagger far into her belly with a breathless sound. I strike at the side of her neck. Her head falls. It drops beside her spurting body, spewing torrents of blood. She dies a true samurai. I am, at least, a witness to that.

I lay out her legs and arms, wash them, and straighten the folds of her robes. I wipe my hands on the cloths we put aside. I take the papers, cover them in waterproof cloths, and place them in the document box, the one with the cranes. All is done as my lady wishes.

I clasp the document box and dagger in one hand. With no head box, I grasp the top knot of Lady Kozaishō's head carefully in the other. I walk to Shogun Minamoto no Yoshitsune. May the Gods be merciful to Lady Kozaishō's great spirit. I will ask what I have sworn to ask, or die myself.

BOOK 18

By order of Shogun Minamoto no Yoshitsune, after the battle of Ichinotani, Seventh day, Second month, Third year of the Juei Era, it is written:

At dusk a woman staggered through the sand, moving westward across the battlefield and through the smoke of burning tents and bodies. Clusters of crows scattered before her, swelling in a froth of feathers. Their stark cries screeched against the coming night. She stepped in silence among the dead and dying. The birds shifted behind her, cackling and feasting in clumps.

The woman's tears smeared the dried blood on her face in pink trails. Under her left arm she held a document box with a blade, a dagger, tied on top of it. In her right hand, dangling by its samurai topknot, she gripped a severed head.

Wandering across the blood-soaked sand, her clothes snagged on arrows, swords and fingers clutching the air for missing weapons. Each time she untangled herself, she lurched forward. Deaf to groans and pleas for water, blind to the thick knots of buzzard-hawks consuming corpses, she stared straight ahead, stumbling, oblivious to the brutal stench of entrails and the drone of flies.

Our great Lord Shogun Minamoto no Yoshitsune and his Four Heavenly Kings, the samurai who constantly protect him, observed this woman. Noticing the dagger, they formed a semicircle in front of the shogun, and their fingers crept closer to their swords. However, the shogun placed his fists on his hips and waited until she stood before him. The woman approached and dropped to her knees. She tilted to the left and placed the document box and dagger on the ground. The head wobbled. Crossing her left hand to her right side, she spread her robes on the ground. She lowered the head on to them with her right hand. She bent herself all the way to the earth.

Our lord Shogun Minamoto no Yoshitsune considered her. 'Speak.'

Her mouth opened and closed. Finally, her voice sputtered, and words spilled out like a waterfall. 'My name is Misuki, servant to Lady Kozaishō. I have completed serving her in ritual suicide. I swore an oath to tell her story.'

One of the Four Heavenly Kings cocked his sword guard with his thumb. 'I have no time to listen to a servant. I can cut off her head for this disruption.'

The second Heavenly King looked at the first. 'This may be the head of the infamous Lady Kozaishō.'

The fourth Heavenly King turned and addressed the shogun: 'Lord Yoshitsune, I, too, have heard of this Lady Kozaishō's accomplishments. Let us listen to this.'

All the Heavenly Kings shifted towards Shogun Yoshitsune to await orders.

Thus spoke the great Shogun Minamoto no Yoshitsune: 'If we do not attend to the request of this departed soul, I am certain her ghost will haunt us to the end of our days.' He lifted his hands to the sky and returned them to his hips. 'Let us honour our victory by hearing the words of her servant.'

'Thank you, honourable Shogun Minamoto no Yoshitsune,' the servant stammered, almost whispering, and prostrated herself again on the ground. She lifted her face a little and touched her tongue over her lips.

Shogun Yoshitsune snapped a command to his attendants, and they brought a jar of water. The woman held it in both hands and drank. The water spilled on her robes. Next, breathing as if she were still swallowing, she stared at the head.

Shogun Yoshitsune motioned for seats. When they arrived, he sat. 'Begin. I am ready to hear this story.'

She struggled with words. New tears cascaded streaks on to her robes. At last she took in a deep breath and said, 'My name is Misuki, servant to the Lady Kozaishō. She demanded I swear upon the souls of my ancestors that I perform three actions: listen and finish recording her story; assist her with *seppuku*; share her story with you, Minamoto no Yoshitsune.'

From her seated position the servant bowed towards Shogun Yoshitsune. 'I did swear. I gathered paper and brush with ink stone and brought the writing table outside the tent. I am grateful to you for allowing me to fulfil my sworn duty, so that I and my ancestors may rest.

'I assisted my lady in suicide, as she asked. I washed her body and head. No reason to scatter salt or wash my mouth and hands. I am in deep mourning and will remain with this defilement for the full forty-nine days . . . perhaps for the rest of my life.

'Following my lady's directions, I took the document box, the dagger and her head, and I came here.'

The servant Misuki placed the dagger and document box on her lap. She moved towards the head. After a long silence, she adjusted her mistress's hair with one hand, and with the other waved the dagger to brush away the early spring flies. Straightening, she set the blade on the ground. Opened the document box. Unwrapped and spread the papers. Cleared her throat.

She began to read . . .

GLOSSARY

Art of War, The	a Chinese book on warfare written by Sun Tsu
bagaku	ancient courtly dances
biwa	type of lute
Bodhisattva	A being aspiring and/or approaching Buddhahood, particularly through compassionate and altruistic acts, and often by postponing their individual entry into nirvana to aid others going towards enlightenment
bokken	wooden practice sword
chō	11,900 square metres or 108 metres (land and length measurement)
chōami	game with dice
chōya	the principal, leader, chief, or senior; successful
Cinnabar Cleft	vagina
Divergent Directions	As dictated by the Gods of Divergent Directions, required affected person(s) not to travel in prohibited directions. If violated, misfortune and/or illness might befall the person(s), or even an entire nation.
do-maru	square, torso-covering armour used by foot soldiers
Enryakaji	Temple on Mount Hiei of the Tendai Buddhist sect
eta	the caste of untouchables

furoshiki	square cloth tied at all corners to carry objects
futon	bedroll; mattress
Four Heavenly Kings	name given to four faithful samurai who were bodyguards to their feudal lord; they fought for and frequently died with him
gagaku	formal court music
geta	clogs, used in rainy weather
go	game of strategy, played with many little stones on a board similar to draughts or chess
gofu	globular vessels buried in mounds as protection from evil forces
Golden Gully	upper part of the vulva
harigata	dildo
Heian-kyō	former name of Kyōto, literally 'Peace and Tranquillity Capital'
higo zuiki	long plant fibres dried and soaked in warm water, often used to aid with impotence or to prolong erection. (Bornoff, Nicholas. *Pink Samurai: Love, Marriage & Sex in Contemporary Japan.* New York: Pocket Books, 1991, p. 157)
hishi-mochi	diamond-shaped cakes made for the Third day of the Third Month Festival or Doll Festival. They are coloured red (or pink), white and green. The red is for chasing evil spirits away, the white is for purity, and the green is for health.
hisoshi	curtain that separates a veranda from the interior of a building
hitatare	wide split pants
hogen	honorary title of rank
hoeki no hō	male's formal shirt-like garment
Hokekyō	a type of Buddhist scripture
hototogisu	one of several species of Japanese cuckoo. The *hototogisu*'s song traditionally signalled the arrival of summer.
hour of the:	Rat 11 p.m. to 1 a.m.
	Ox 1 a.m. to 3 a.m.

Tiger	3 a.m. to 5 a.m.
Hare	5 a.m. to 7 a.m.
Dragon	7 a.m. to 9 a.m.
Snake	9 a.m. to 11 a.m.
Horse	11 a.m. to 1 p.m.
Sheep	1 p.m. to 3 p.m.
Monkey	3 p.m. to 5 p.m.
Cock	5 p.m. to 7 p.m.
Dog	7 p.m. to 9 p.m.
Boar	9 p.m. to 11 p.m.

Jade Gate — vulva

Jewel Terrace — upper part of the vulva

Jade Stalk — penis

Jade Veins — upper part of the vulva

Juei — a named time period 1182–4

kaimyo — the posthumous name of the deceased, which differs from when that person was alive to help prevent the person returning every time his or her name is called.

kanmuri — a lacquered hat with a low cap at the front, a high bulge at the back

karma — metaphysical law that one's actions return to oneself, either in the current life or one's next life or lives

kemari — feudal game similar to soccer in which the ball must be kept in the air by using only the feet

kichō — a privacy screen about five feet tall mounted on a platform from which noble women had to entertain any male who was not their husband or family

Kinensai — Festival of the Spring Prayer

kisagake — fast whip-like movement of sword stroke

kiyoseho — a joined-wood technique in sculpture

Kōfuku — a temple name

Kōfukuji — the temple of Kōfuku

koi — Japanese carp

Kokinshū — a collection of poems

Konjin	one of the Gods of Direction, who moved in one of eight directions each day
Koshin	one of the Gods of Directions
kosode	simple peasant kimono with narrowed sleeves
koto	large stringed instrument
kuge	the nobility, aristocracy, the 'good' people
Kuyō	special funeral prayers to ensure that a soul will keep away from people on earth
Lute Strings	female pubic hairs
makiwara	a large straw target used for beginners at archery, usually placed close to the student
makie	a technique in which gold dust is mixed with lacquer and then applied
Man'yōshū	a collection of poems, ranging in date from the fifth century to AD 759
mato	the normal target for archers. The most common size is twelve suns, approximately 3.03 cm in diameter shot from a distance of twenty-eight metres
Monju-Bosatsu	God of Intelligence, associated with the lion
mochi	sweet rice cake, usually steamed or fried
Muko Bay	a bay near Ichinotani, now Kobe
naginata	halberd scythe-like blade-on-a-pole
Nihongi	Nihongi-Shoki, Chronicles of Japan, an official history of Japan compiled in 720
nusa	white cloth with virtues written on it, usually tied to a stick
obāsan	grandmother
ohaguro	blackening of teeth
oni	demon, ogre
Otofuku	folk-religion God of female sexual appetite
Positive Peak	penis
sabi	worn, used-up, sad
Saishōōgyō	type of Buddhist scripture
sake	rice wine
sakura-mochi	bean paste – filled rice cakes with cherry leaves

461

	served on the Third day of the Third Month for the Doll Festival
sansankudo	marriage ceremony in which bride and groom each alternate drinking *sake* from three different-sized bowls, starting with the smallest. *Sansankudo* literally means 'three sets of three equals nine'; three is a perfect number because it is indivisible.
seppuku	ritual suicide
setsubun	literally means separation of a season
shaku	29.7 cm, or 11.7 inches (linear measurement)
shikime zane	armour in which the leather or iron pieces are assembled twice overlapping to be extra thick
Shingon	sect of Buddhism
shōen	estate with lands, craftsmen and samurai
shōji	paper framed with wood used as walls and sliding doors
Shogun	commander-in-chief in charge of barbarians
sōhei	warrior monks
sumō	a type of wrestling
sutra	formal Buddhist prayer
tabi	socks with a single toe separation
tachi	long sword, usually worn when on a horse
Taikan Tsuho	Chinese coin with a square hole in the middle
takenaga	piece of cloth or ribbon with which courtesans in Heian Japan used to tie back their hair
Tale of Genji	novel written by Murasaki Shikibu, early eleventh century
Tendai	sect of Buddhism
tō	7.2 litres (capacity measurement)
Todai	a temple name
Todaiji	temple of Todai
tokonoma	alcove for displaying scroll, arranged flowers or precious artifact
tori-i	gateway or portal to entrance of Shinto shrines
Tosa Niki	a travel diary written by Ki no Tsurayuki
tsuba	the metal sword guard attached between the blade

	and the handle of the sword
tsuru	bowstring
waka	five-lined poetry
watadono	veranda, covered porch around a dwelling
yurei	a tormented ghost who stays with the living to take revenge or conclude unfinished business
Village of Outcasts	small town of prostitutes, tanneries and other such 'unclean' activities

Author's Notes

PILLOW BOOK

Noble women, and also peasants, who travelled on pilgrimages wrote a 'journal'. The women stored these journals near their pillows, hence the name. After a journal entry, a poem or two often followed. *The Pillow Book of the Flower Samurai* emulates this custom.

For more reading, the *Tale of The Lady Ochikubo*, *The Pillow Book of Sei Shōnagon*, and *As I Crossed a Bridge of Dreams* are some of the translated pillow books from the tenth and eleventh centuries, although, none of these women is a samurai, like Kozaishō.

MEASURING TIME

The Japanese adopted a sexagenary system, or Zodiac Calendar, linking the cycle of twelve months and twelve hours of the day (Rat, Ox, Tiger, Rabbit, Dragon, Snake, Horse, Sheep, Monkey, Rooster, Dog and Boar) with the five elements (Wood, Fire, Earth, Metal and Water). (Morris, Ivan, translator & editor. *The Pillow Book of Sei Shōnagon*. New York: Columbia University Press, 1991, page 380.)

Rather than Sunday through Monday, days continue cycling through the twelve divisions: Rat, Ox, Tiger, etc. Days are delineated as the Third Month, Second Day of the Rabbit, or Fourth Month, First Day of the Monkey, etc.

For people, the animal of the birth year, the elements (Wood, Fire, Earth, Metal and Water) and the alternating principles of yang (masculine/positive) and yin (feminine/negative) combined to create multifaceted personality configurations. Therefore each year included three different 'wheels' of features: animal, element and yang/yin. Please note that men are not inevitably yang, nor are women unavoidably yin. Yang and yin represents personality types, rather than gender.

I simplified to the element and yang/yin to avoid digressing into personality types and detracting from the story. Example: Kozaishō is a Fire and yang personality. She is a leader, promoter who is determined, zealous and always looking for something new. Misuki is Water and yin, a bubbly personality. She is also receptive, easy-going, philosophical, superficial and passionate. Hitomi is Metal and yang, a good motivator who can succeed in almost any profession. Akio and Tashiko are Earth, the former yang and the latter, yin. The Metal yang is ready to fight for truth and righteousness. The Metal yin is liked by others, strong yet compliant, gentle yet confident and tolerant.

RELIGION

The Japanese adopted Buddhism in the sixth century, while maintaining their Shinto beliefs. For centuries Buddhism was the religion of the aristocrats. Kozaishō, as the daughter of a cultivator, originally held Shinto beliefs. Part of this belief system included clapping to dispel evil spirits and a strong sense of ritual cleanliness, which Buddhism absorbed. Part of ritual cleanliness included, for example, ritual defilements such as menstruation and death. The washing of hands and rinsing the mouths before entering sacred areas is a Shinto concept.

Each temple and shrine associated itself with a particular sect of Buddhism or Shintoism and could be sponsored by political figures (head of a clan, emperor, Prince). Each maintained its own military force, sōhei, and was mostly tax exempt. The political, religious, social and military lines crisscrossed repeatedly, particularly in the latter Heian period, the time of *The Pillow Book of the Flower Samurai*.

MARRIAGE, VIRGINITY, MONOGAMY AND POLYGAMY

None of the Judaic-Christian-Islamic influences had entered Heian Japan. Virginity, at least among the aristocrats, was not a state to be desired in men or women. Moreover, adult virgins were considered suspicious and possibly corrupt or dangerous. Non-royal aristocratic marriages involved a man staying three nights in a row with his 'intended'. If he did not return after the first or second night, they were not married and each moved on. Children of such unions were simply acknowledged and accepted.

Polygamy functioned contrarily to what is commonly assumed in current times. When a man married, he moved in with his wife. Women generally inherited their parents' homes and property. (Court cases exist of widows suing for their property and winning.) Polygamous men travelled from household to household, i.e. wife to wife. However, Rokuhara reversed this by a wife (or wives) living in her (or their) husband's home.

Aristocratic women, and Kozaishō (after she married), customarily did not to show their faces to any men other than their husbands and families. The curtained platform used for this was the *kichō* (servants did not count.) Ironically among the aristocrats, according to diaries and *Tale of the Genji*, a man might sleep with someone he had never seen. While married women of the samurai were expected to be faithful, divorce was common, easy and frequently initiated by women and men alike.

POLICE

The Ministry of Justice existed in Heian Japan. Yet because of its impotence in protecting the populace early on in the Heian period, the offices of Ōryoshi and Tsuibushi were established. These positions were called 'Sheriffs' and 'Chief Constables'. (Samsom in *The History of Japan to 1334*.) I simplified this by using the term Constable.

ADDENDUM

I have endeavoured to write this account of a most dramatic and turbulent time in Japanese history with as much historical accuracy as I could. Those appreciated and named in the acknowledgements assisted me significantly.

But I must admit a major exception. The aristocrats in Heian-Kyō (present day Kyōtō) did not bathe much, if at all. They actually slept in their clothes, although it can be assumed they changed them at least once a season. I added the bathing to comfort modern readers who use and venerate running water.

Taira Clan Genealogy

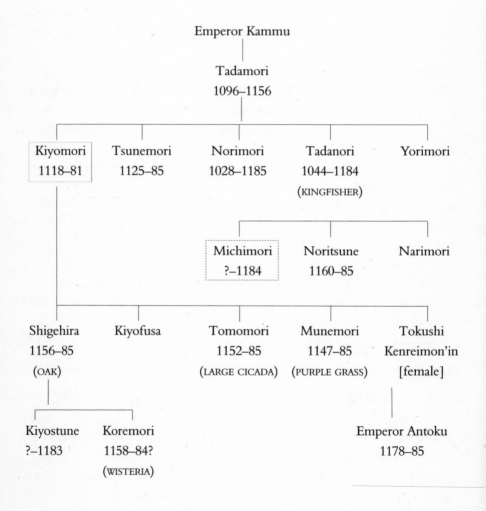

Emperor Kammu

Tadamori
1096–1156

Kiyomori
1118–81

Tsunemori
1125–85

Norimori
1028–1185

Tadanori
1044–1184
(KINGFISHER)

Yorimori

Michimori
?–1184

Noritsune
1160–85

Narimori

Shigehira
1156–85
(OAK)

Kiyofusa

Tomomori
1152–85
(LARGE CICADA)

Munemori
1147–85
(PURPLE GRASS)

Tokushi
Kenreimon'in
[female]

Kiyostune
?–1183

Koremori
1158–84?
(WISTERIA)

Emperor Antoku
1178–85

Minamoto Clan Genealogy

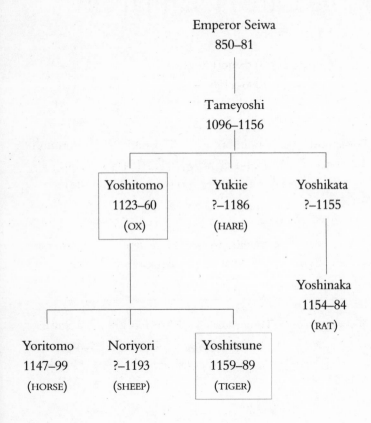

Emperor Seiwa
850–81

Tameyoshi
1096–1156

Yoshitomo
1123–60
(OX)

Yukiie
?–1186
(HARE)

Yoshikata
?–1155

Yoshinaka
1154–84
(RAT)

Yoritomo
1147–99
(HORSE)

Noriyori
?–1193
(SHEEP)

Yoshitsune
1159–89
(TIGER)

Genealogy of Emperors of the Late Heian Japan

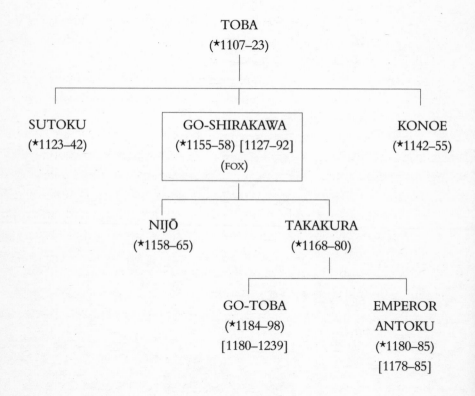

TOBA
(*1107–23)

SUTOKU
(*1123–42)

GO-SHIRAKAWA
(*1155–58) [1127–92]
(FOX)

KONOE
(*1142–55)

NIJŌ
(*1158–65)

TAKAKURA
(*1168–80)

GO-TOBA
(*1184–98)
[1180–1239]

EMPEROR
ANTOKU
(*1180–85)
[1178–85]

(* dates of reign)
[birth–death]